I0819896

FRANKENSTEIN
SOUL'S ECHO

Book 2 of 3

The Resurrection Trinity

PETE PLANISEK

Book and cover design by Pete Planisek
Photos by Scott Coons

Frankenstein Soul's Echo
(Book 2 of 3) The Resurrection Trinity/Pete Planisek

ISBN 978-0-9850982-4-7 (print)
ISBN 978-0-9850982-1-6 (ebook)

Book released in the United States of America
First hardcover edition, 2017

Published by Enceladus Literary LLC
Columbus, OH

10 9 8 7 6 5 4 3 2 1

www.enceladusliterary. com

For my family

CHARACTERS

*Ernest Frankenstein
Abrielle (Orfilia)
*The Creature
Tara Tierney Frankenstein
*Victor Frankenstein - deceased

Geneva
Christiansen

Salzburg
Jack Clerval
Costanza Clerval
The Duke
General de Corps d' A'rmee Oullet

The Wild Rose clan prisoners
Baseria Nalie
Etolie
Vochallet
Isyll
Sebbi

The Wild Rose clan
Jal Nalie
Espen Nalie
Nasi Nalie (Nagyanya) - deceased
Mayte Nalie – deceased
Patia Nalie – deceased
Judika – deceased
Kelv
Hytr

The Moon Shadow clan
Nicabar
Tasaria
Pias (Boier Amăgitor)

The Moon Shadow Fortress
The Old Ones
Pell
Ghul
Captain Ayt
Tyben

China
Xie Xue Maa
Ai Qui Maa
Wei Maa

France
Noel and Anne D'Aoust
Spies
Bellange
Chloe (Onella)
Berryer
Grenier

Bayonne
Paul (Cheval)
Sister Annette
Sister Michelle
Sister Josephine

Bordeaux
Amelie Sarah

*All characters from Mary Shelly's novel Frankenstein.

"I have seen tempests, when the scolding winds
Have riv'd the knotty oaks; and I have seen
Th' ambitious ocean swell and rage and foam;
To be exalted with the threat'ning clouds:
But never till to-night, never till now,
Did I go through a tempest dropping fire.
Either there is a civil strife in heaven,
Or else the world, too saucy with the gods,
Incenses them to send destruction."

– William Shakespeare
Julius Caesar (1.3.5-13)

Chapter 1
The Endless Dawn

Ernest shielded his eyes, and for a moment, the world was nothing but the pulsing blend created by shadow and light. He blinked fervently. He felt her knock into him and giggle as she raced by, down towards the meadow, which was awash in wildflowers and dazzling emerald grasses. The clean, cool air of the mountains refreshed him as he dodged among grass and stone in pursuit.

"Give it back."

Without turning around, she only shook her head, laughed, and tauntingly held up the object fueling his pursuit. Her dress and several glances backward slowed her escape, but escape was not the purpose of this game. Twice his hands snatched at her waist, but both times she deftly managed to elude his touch. Her eyes danced with mischief as she swatted blonde strands of hair away from them. God, he loved her smile. A shriek of mock panic escaped her as he tried to grab her a third time, the result of which sent them tumbling towards a mixed patch of strawberries and wildflowers. A swarm of tiny insects fled upwards, away from the disturbance of their world caused by the intrusion of the panting humans.

"Now … would you please … give me back my hat?"

Ailis rolled her body to prevent his hand from prizing the hat out from underneath her. The stalemate amused her.

"Perhaps … if you ask me nicely, Monsieur Frankenstein," she said haughtily. She seemed convinced he'd met his match, that is until he began to tickle her. Soon Ailis was berating him as she laughed and swatted at him with the hat.

"That wasn't fair," she admonished as she regained her composure and stuck his hat back upon his head at a ridiculous angle.

Ernest pushed it back on his forehead and grinned smugly, "I never said I play fair." His hand unconsciously caressed her hair, and she smiled softly as he leaned in to kiss her. But their lips did not meet. Instead there was only light. An empty, blinding light, which drove the dream from him mind and returned him to the lonely darkness of his life.

*

Upon awakening all he felt was pain and the sickening weight of unbearable grief. She was not here. His love, his friend, his soul was back in Ireland, resting beside her father, in a quiet cemetery. And he was here, adrift on the restless seas of the world.

As the ship rode the waves, a brilliant flash of sun briefly shot through the cabin window then vanished. Had they finally outrun the storm that had plagued them since leaving the Orkneys? How long had it truly been since he'd seen the sun? It hardly mattered.

The briefest of knocks was issued before the gypsy entered, pistol in hand.

"The Master orders you on deck," he spat contemptuously in French.

'The Master ...,' Ernest had barely spoken to Victor's hideous, self-proclaimed prodigy since they'd come onboard. Time had quickly lost all relevance, night and day blended obscurely as they roved through the tempest. The few respites the storm had allowed shrouded the vessel in fog and mist. Ernest had ceased winding his watch some time ago as it had stopped twice while he slept and was no longer a reliable gauge of reality. He'd been alone but for the thoughts recorded for him in his wife's journal. The journal! He'd been reading it when he'd fallen asleep. Ernest searched the bunk frantically but could not find it.

"Outside, now!" A second gypsy ordered as he joined the first in the doorway. He too was armed and bore an expression which left no quarter for arguing reason. Ernest relaxed. The journal probably was just buried in the blanket or had fallen and slid across the deck after he'd fallen asleep. Precious as it was he would just have to find it when he returned. Ernest could feel the cold air swirling through the door and took a moment to don his coat, then relented to the men's command.

The covered lanterns on either side of his cabin's doorway flickered angrily in the frigid winds. The sun had already been reclaimed by the sea, and the clouds and lightning again arched through the heavens. The heaving seas made walking extremely difficult, but Ernest's years spent on ships allowed his body to adjust his gait effectively. The two-masted schooner was handling these harsh conditions well, so far, but the longer they stayed in the storm, the more likely it became that ill fortune would find them.

More disquieting than the weather was the crew. The Moon Shadow gypsies, who seemed to comprise the bulk of men aboard, also seemed to highly resent his presence. As if they viewed him as some evil omen. But it was the others who truly worried him. He had seen only a handful of these cloaked figures since boarding, and though all appeared to be the size of ordinary men, even the gypsies gave them a wide berth. More strangely, these cloaked figures rarely showed any sign of movement. Even when waves washed upon the deck, threatening to drag a man back into the sea with them, the cloaked figures remained still. Their inexplicable behavior, coupled with their outward resemblance to the ship's 'Master,' disturbed him greatly. Did the same corruption of man exist beneath their robes or could they be something worse?

As he climbed the final steps to the deck, it was difficult for Ernest to imagine a sight more grotesque than the face he'd witnessed on the shores of North Ronaldsay Island. The face that the dark, brooding, shape now before him possessed. The devil's features faced astern into the most brutal of the winds. Ernest fervently hoped that the gale would not release the hood that now concealed the odious visage beneath. Perhaps sensing this, the cloaked man handed Ernest a spyglass, and without comment, pointed to a spot on the horizon. With the shifting seas, heaving waves, and swirling mist, it took Ernest sometime to ascertain what he was supposed to locate. Once it was clear that he had, the creature motioned him away from the stern and leaned in close.

"I'd hoped to lose them in the storm, Uncle. They have pursued us for sometime."

"Who are they?" Ernest yelled, as each word threatened to be taken by the winds.

"Avengers, from the nation we approach."

Ernest pondered this only a moment.

"This is their ship,"

"It is one."

Did that mean he had captured others?

"And what of her crew?"

The figure beside him was silent. Ernest turned away from him, but the nightmare followed and continued to speak.

"Unless the winds change, they will catch us within a day. Then there will be a battle."

"You can't outrun them?"

The figure nodded.

"They carry more sail and a more experienced crew."

Ernest thought quickly.

"Then surrender."

He caught a brief glimpse of those cruel black lips.

"There is too much at stake, for both of us."

Ernest felt a massive hand rest upon his shoulder and fought the urge to free himself.

"And what of their lives?" Ernest asked as he gestured towards the distant ship.

"I know of your battle experience at Trafalgar. Before you return to my presence, you must decide if you will help us defend this ship. The retrieval of your daughter, as well as your reunion with Jal's child, depends upon our success."

Ernest felt a gnawing cold in the pit of his stomach. How could this man know about his connection to Trafalgar? The unseen hand released him, and the immense creature returned to the stern. Ernest's head was swimming as he was escorted back to his cabin and locked within.

For a moment he stood and merely felt the deck shifting beneath him before finally collapsing onto a poorly constructed chair by the room's small desk. It groaned under the stress of its load, the back bowed as if ready to snap from the tension, but Ernest paid it no mind. His attention was now riveted to Ailis' journal, which was now set squarely in the middle of the desk. Wordlessly, he sought to reconcile himself with the object.

Was he losing his mind? Could it have been here the whole time? No, he'd been reading it before he fell asleep; he was certain of that. Then how had the journal come to be here, at a place almost entirely opposite of his bunk? He opened it and discovered that the pale green ribbon Ailis had always used as a bookmark now lay between pages different from those he last recalled reading. Could one of the gypsies have found it upon the floor and simply placed it here?

A new and most unwelcome thought suddenly burned within him. Could the devil above have come below and read his wife's journal while he slept? The thought of such a perverse intrusion enraged him. Anger and fear coursed through him. Though he longed to avenge this injustice, Ernest did not release his emotions. He could not afford to crumble under their weight. To display his true feelings would only further empower his captors and possibly aid their dark designs. No, he must devote his energies to reason. He must discover if the journal's condition was the result of an innocent accident or deliberate manipulation. If the latter, it meant no thought once written, no space provided onboard was safe. What could the true purpose of his presence here be? Would it make itself known to him only when it was too late?

Ernest decided he could no longer afford the tranquil peace offered by sleep. At least the beast above had been honest about one thing: there was too much at stake. He felt within his jacket and was relieved to find the decorative box, which Nasi had entrusted to him, was still present and sealed. Ernest's fingers caressed the box. Several times since his departure from Ireland he'd been tempted to open it. Nasi had specified this should only be done in a dark hour, as yet unknown to him. Ernest smiled bitterly at the thought. Had he spent an hour bereft of darkness since she'd issued the directive? His heart softened. Yes, Tara's birth, his final hours with Ailis had been blessings. Comforted, he released the box and withdrew his hand from his jacket.

Ernest gathered Ailis' journal and returned to the narrow bunk. The cabin was now all but dark as the storm reclaimed the ship into its lustful, vicious grasp. He closed his eyes for a moment and allowed his senses to open fully to the battle taking place all around him: urgent cries and orders from the men on deck, the strain of the wind and wave against the ship's timbers, the sudden shifts in gravity as the vessel challenged the storm. Could this cursed vessel actually make a safe port? And if so, what awaited him there? Perhaps they would sink. Then at least it would be over. Or maybe their pursuer would founder and no battle would occur. Slowly he opened his eyes. No, a battle was coming. He could feel it.

He tried not to think of death as lightning relentlessly stabbed the skies outside his window. Did he aid this crew in the destruction of another? If he failed to do so, would Tara and Baseria be forever lost to him as Ailis was now? Again his emotions surged in tune to the violent seas all around him. If he hadn't been so selfish she might still be alive. Tara would be home with them, and Baseria safe with her people. A sudden stinging pain jolted him from his reverie. He'd unconsciously begun to run his fingers through his hair, but failed to notice which hand he was using. The dim light permitted only a cursory examination of the angry, crimson tinged cut, deeply scored into his palm.

Despite the discomfort the wound afforded him, Ernest smiled. Abrielle bore an identical mark. The thought of his mysterious sister-in-law comforted him. The scar served as a constant reminder of their bond to each other, their oath to Ailis, and the promise of hope. The skin around the cut itched and throbbed. Where was she by now? Had she already found Jal and rescued Tara? Would they ever set eyes upon each other in this world again?

Ernest began to tear a small strip of linen from his sheets to rebind the wound. He needed to believe he would see her again. Before parting they'd each held numerous doubts about the other's ability to survive their respective ordeals, but they'd also recognized their only hope was their faith in each other. Actually if anyone possessed the skills to save Tara, a spy in service to Napoleon's Empire would seem to be a logical choice. Though more important than that was Abrielle's indisputable love for her niece and for Ailis. It was this love that would ultimately lead to either their shared salvation or destruction.

As he finished tying the bandage, Ernest found that his reflections about Abrielle provided him with a new inspiration. His sister-in-law would not passively sit and wait for others to decide her fate, of that Ernest was certain. The revelation that the schooner was a commandeered vessel, likely military, danced in his thoughts. If true then this cabin had probably belonged to an officer. Perhaps his enemies had finally made a mistake. Mariners, by nature, as well as necessity, tended to horde an assortment of items for various reasons. They might be curiosities that could be traded or sold, personal objects, or those useful in defense if a ship were unexpectedly boarded. Could there be a hidden cache left behind by the cabin's former occupant?

During his days aboard, Ernest had conducted a brief examination of his temporary home, but then he'd been concerned only with the superficial. At that time the most useful object he'd been able to locate was a corked bottle. He'd momentarily considered using it to convey a message requesting help until the futility of such an action had dawned on him. What could he say? He did not know his heading, destination, the name of the ship he sailed on, or what type of assistance would be most beneficial when the time to escape came. Besides, the endless storm only further elevated his doubts about tossing a letter into the sea. In such conditions, it might travel hundreds of miles before washing ashore or become trapped in the churning currents within the storm.

But now his eyes probed the cabin with a new energy and purpose. The darkness would hinder his progress, but lengthening the time the task would take might at least keep him awake. After taking a moment to decide where he should begin, Ernest set about his chore. He fervently hoped to locate a pistol, his own having been thrown overboard before they'd left the Orkney Islands. True, there were a few other objects in the room that could be used as makeshift weapons, but he doubted any of them would last long in close-quarter combat. If their pursuers caught them and came aboard, they would have no reason to treat him as anything other than a pirate. A pistol would at least give him a chance to defend himself. More importantly, it could also provide him with a means to wrest his fate back from his captors.

As he searched, Ernest tried to keep dark thoughts at bay. It was difficult. There were too many demons swirling within: past, present, and future. He was accustomed to uncertainty in life, but now that ambiguity was colored by a near crippling grief. The life he and Ailis had fought so hard to create was rent asunder. His loving partner in this world was gone, as was their cherished child. His soul felt shattered. It was poisoned by guilt and grief. Increasingly he felt lost. There would be no future, which left him alone with only the past and present. As in his life before, he was now to be forced, unwillingly, into participating in another pointless battle at sea. And as had happened so many times these past weeks memories, long buried, unbidden, tipped the senses, and there could be no refuge from their influence for Ailis was gone—the horrors of the past and present were free to assault his soul.

CHAPTER 2
TRAFALGAR

21 October 1805
HMS Mars

"… perform your duty, as a loyal subject and patriot to the Crown, then your fealty shall be rewarded, in this life and the next, if you stand with your brothers against tyranny and revolution and serve this moment with your fellows. Freedom through action, lads …"

Ernest and those now around him heard few of the words the stoic British officer spoke. This was partially due to the beat of drum and the call of fife, which beckoned men to station, however, they were not the only reasons.

Unlike this trained minion, he and the others were not committed to achieving glory and honor in the service of a distant and uncaring master and, therefore, had little interest in speeches regarding such matters. They were not officers of the line, nor enlisted volunteers. They were prisoners taken over two months earlier by these agents of the Crown to serve their own political purposes. Their lives meant nothing to those they 'served.' The only thing that truly mattered was that they did serve their self-appointed masters. Ernest was proud to be counted among those who resisted such undeserved allegiance. The price they paid was worked off by suffering through whippings, harsh words of beratement, and incarceration. But they had not broken under the manipulations of their captors and so this junior officer, desperate for their obedience, now stood before them and recited propaganda, most of which he undoubtedly believed.

Despite the circumstances, Ernest did pity the man. If he lost his life in the next hour or so would he truly understand why he so eagerly embraced death at such a young age? Did he simply exist in this world to serve as others saw fit? Had he ever questioned such things?

"That's sufficient for this lot, Lieutenant Easter. Secure those who will join willingly. Put the others at the bow and stern cannonade crew positions or back in the brig."

Easter proffered a crisp salute to Captain Duff who quickly vanished from view on the quarterdeck above.

"What should we do? Fight?"

Ernest did not turn to look at Ives Cross. The boy—he could be no older than fifteen—had, against Ernest's wishes, clung to him ever since he'd come aboard three weeks earlier. This was the second British vessel he'd been sent to since he and most of the men from the merchant ship he'd been serving on were captured in the Atlantic. Often men who had been seized by a press gang were separated at the earliest possible moment. The British feared their continued close proximity might lead to open insurrection. And so Ernest had arrived here and unwillingly inherited this would-be charge.

After nearly six years across the world, Ernest had been heading home, a shadow of the man he'd been when he'd left, life's barbarity having broken him. The trip was to have been a last effort to salvage the dim part of him that he could still recognize from his life before, in Europe. Rare had been the day that he thought of himself as the son of Alphonse and Caroline Frankenstein. For years, in fact, he'd lost that identity completely. Many now knew him simply as "the Swiss."

In late July, yet another engagement had taken place between vast naval fleets loyal to Britain and Napoleon. Men were lost and ships damaged, forcing the British Navy to employ forced conscription of any able-bodied men. They feared their homeland was prone to invasion if they failed to annihilate Napoleon's fleet, and this dread awakened a type of zealous fervor among the British sailors. They must succeed, regardless of the cost to themselves or others.

"Those of you who will stand with the Crown, step forward as men, now," Easter commanded. Though several shifted nervously, none of them moved.

"Your word first, sir," Ernest politely requested.

"What?"

"Your pardon, sir, but we'll not stir an inch without an officer of the line giving us his word that freedom shall be granted to those among us who serve you in this battle."

The inexperienced Lieutenant Easter looked somewhat ill. Clearly he had not foreseen this problem arising from these shackled creatures before him.

"Easter, sort out that rabble." The first officer leaned over the deck railing, looking irritated that the captain's order had yet to be fulfilled. Easter saluted smartly then returned his attention to the ten men assembled before him.

"I'd rather shoot you all myself," Easter finally declared.

"There's no time, Lieutenant," intoned one prisoner smugly.

Easter's nostrils flared, but he knew the grand moment was upon them. After months of sailing across the Atlantic in pursuit of the enemy, they all knew that the next hours would determine the course of European affairs for years to come. If he faltered in this simple duty now, all hope for honor or advancement might be lost. He lowered his voice.

"Very well, as an officer of the line, I give you my word," Easter muttered, a look of pure loathing upon his face.

Nine of the men saluted him then began to head either astern or towards the bow as soon as their shackles were released. Ives Cross followed Ernest, the lone dissenter, towards the bow. The young man was beaming with joy.

"I didn't think it would work, but ol' John Claggey was right. Did you see Easter's face … what's wrong?"

By now Ernest was used to Ives' naiveté when it came to such matters, but as the moment of battle drew near, he feared the boy would learn the harsh realities of the world too late. Should he tell him that Easter, as a junior officer, could not make such a bargain? That if the others believed they had outmaneuvered him they were fools? They'd gained only a moment of discomfort from the man and traded themselves for the illusion of power and the promise of freedom. In return, Easter now had them where the British wanted them—manning the most dangerous and vulnerable stations aboard. If it came to close range fighting, they would all be mowed down by shot, ball, and a generous amount of shrapnel. Of course, the same could have happened to them in their cell, which was probably why Easter decided to release Ernest despite his dissention. And dead men told no tales.

"Just stick close to me."

As they made their way forward, they passed a host of harsh, resentful faces. In fact several menacing midshipmen blocked their path or spat at their boots. Those they were to fight beside seemed just as willing to shoot them as any enemy sailor they would face today. It wasn't surprising. Most aboard viewed these prisoners as scum. Command inherently feared insubordination, so the crew had collectively been forced to work longer and harder due to the disobedience of these criminals. Ernest and Ives did their best to ignore the British sailor's open animosity.

"Swiss," a voice behind them barked. It belonged to the boatswain, who was followed closely by a Royal Marine. Ernest studied them a moment paying careful attention to the extra musket the Marine held.

"What's this?"

"Orders," the boatswain said somewhat apologetically.

During his weeks aboard, the boatswain had consistently struck Ernest as an honorable man. Under different circumstances they might even have been friends.

"Easter?"

The boatswain nodded as the Marine handed Ernest the musket and the heavy ammunition bag.

"Wants you up with the sharpshooters in the rigging, trimming the sails. Cross, keep goin' forward."

"But I can go up with …"

"No!" both Ernest and the boatswain roared simultaneously. Ives shrunk slightly before he began to walk away.

"Ives," Ernest called calmly to his retreating companion. The young man stopped and turned, a sour expression on his face. He didn't understand. How could he? Ernest was certain that Ives' story about stowing away on one of his uncle's merchant ships was only a half truth, at best. In fact, from the scant details Ives chose to reveal, Ernest often wondered if the boy had any family at all. He knew that Ives would tell him the truth one day, but for now how he'd truly come to be here remained a mystery. His lack of basic seamanship skills and overall awkwardness made it clear that this was most likely his first sea voyage, to say nothing of his initiation into combat at sea.

Working in the rigging, a dangerous prospect under normal circumstances was often a suicidal duty during battle. In close combat, the goal was to strip an enemy vessel of her masts and sails, and then render her easy prey for either a boarding or fire ships. Up among the masts, he would be targeted with canister and grapeshot from enemy sharpshooters along with mortar and cannon shot. Allowing Ives to accompany him on such a treacherous duty was unthinkable. Though highly dangerous, at least the deck would afford him some cover. But Ernest knew none of this really mattered to the boy.

At times Ives Cross' stubbornness and reverence for him reminded Ernest of his own departed younger brother, William. Perhaps that's why, in spite of himself, he had taken to watching out for the boy, who now was staring back at him with seething distaste.

Ernest considered his next words carefully.

"In battle, even brave men duck."

Ives appeared to consider this idea as he studied both Ernest and boatswain, who nodded slightly in support of the statement. Had the advice come from any other man aboard, Ives probably would have ignored it. He'd been fooled too many times, but he trusted Ernest.

"You remember that too," Ives finally counseled. He smiled, tightly, then continued onwards towards the bow cannonades.

The boatswain shook his head as Ernest affixed the ammo bag and musket over his shoulders, "Shame when young men fall in with the wrong crowd."

"He didn't ask to be in this war," Ernest observed.

"No, the Almighty chose him to be. Just like the rest of us."

The two men exchanged a brief, even look then shook hands.

"Watch out for him."

"Good luck, Swiss," the boatswain bade to Ernest as he began to ascend the port rigging.

His clothing whipped his body rhythmically in the wind, which was adequate for the sails but not strong. He hoped it wouldn't fail them. As he rose higher in the rigging, the battle began to reveal itself to him. The Mars appeared to be in the lead position of a long column of British ships, trailing aft. To the north he could see more sails stretching out in another battle column. Both were heading towards the sails of the Combined Fleet—an armada consisting of ships from both France and their Spanish allies. Their sails, which all but covered the swiftly approaching horizon, seemed to be rather loosely organized at present but the steadily growing clouds of smoke, emitted by gunfire, and ships already engaged in battle, made gathering a clear view of the enemy difficult. The British columns appeared to be driving into the heart of the Combined Fleet. If the winds held, the Mars would be under fire in less than ten minutes.

Far below him, the ship's decks buzzed with action and energy as men loaded weapons, shifted sails, and bellowed orders. The sound of cannon echoed over the waves, and flashes from the ignition of gunpowder peppered the obscuring smoke ahead. Despite all of this, Ernest took one last moment to savor the world around him.

The sea was the most fantastic reality he'd ever known. The complex blend of untamed energy, terrifying and awe-inspiring beauty, the raw natural wonder, and unpredictable forces for good or ill made it so. Even now, as they plowed the waves towards battle, on to death and terror, he could see dolphins playfully escorting the ship. The air was still fresh and alive with the unique scent of the ocean. Regardless of the near tranquility of the moment, an absurd question posed itself to him. It was a well-trodden thought but one that still plagued him—for in all his journeys, through the lonely, painful years he could never discover a real answer to it. What was he living for?

Those he loved or cared for had all preceded him in death. Was his presence here, now, as the boatswain maintained, by the design of a higher power? Did he believe in one? Were the events about to unfold meant to reunite him with those who had already discovered the mysteries that lay beyond the mortal veil? Was there a purpose to his life? Ernest closed his eyes and shut out the world. He saw so little good left within him. He couldn't fathom how Ives or any one else ever could.

A strange warmth from his hand and forearm rejoined him to the moment. The ship shook slightly, either from their own guns firing or from taking enemy fire. To Ernest's surprise, they were nearly on top of the masts of a French frigate. His thoughts stolen by time, he'd been oblivious to the enemy fire driving into the sails. He looked below and saw some men were already wounded or dying on the deck. Several bodies were already being thrown overboard. Ernest cursed his carelessness as he climbed further upward. He must have been grazed by shrapnel. He hoped Ives was doing a better job of adhering to his own advice about ducking.

Just then a section of mizzen mast, sail, and rigging exploded behind him, embedding razor sharp splinters into his exposed skin. Ernest's nerves danced with pain. This was to be only the beginning. The Mars' guns answered with a deafening salvo of their own moments later. The thin winds abated and smoke now hung thickly all about them, enshrouding countless enemy ships within the obscuring clouds. As fire continued to be exchanged through the suffocating haze, an ever increasing chorus of agony bellowed below him as the casualties mounted.

It seemed to come all at once. Just as Ernest gained his position manning the main topgallant, a new cry was heard. The shout was quickly drowned out by the dual sounds of cracking timber and a hail of long shot and cannon fire. The foremast, along with the sail, rigging, and crew crumbled. Small arms fire now raked the main mast, tearing sections of the canvas sails to ribbons. The ship heaved as she heeled, either to line up a shot or avoid some. The motion brought down more sail and rigging. The Mars was rapidly being reduced to an uncontrollable hulk and would soon be adrift upon the swells.

Again the keel shuddered under enemy fire, and this time, the main mast shifted. All about Ernest those still alive in the rigging began to gingerly, but rapidly, descend from their unstable perch. Some didn't make it. The shifting waves, crumbling mast, and continued fire of the enemy caused some to fall directly into the greedy sea. One Marine near Ernest was disemboweled by shot, his entrails falling onto the deck before his body followed.

Ernest himself fell the last few feet to the main deck, viciously wrenching his knee. Seconds after reaching the deck, the boards quaked beneath him as the starboard side gun crews, topside and below, broadsided a passing French ship. The resulting smoke obscured the deck and made his progress towards the bow difficult. He kept slipping on blood, being run into by others who were moving through the haze and stumbling over the dead who littered the deck. He came upon one poor gun crew whose powder had ignited. Their skin was all but melted beneath their silent, still forms. The grotesque sight only strengthened his resolve to reach the bow and Ives.

When he reached the forecastle, he discovered that the shattered mast, with its sails and rigging made further progress towards the bow all but impossible. Still he must reach it. Freeing himself of his jacket, he began to navigate the maze. Narrow pathways took him towards the starboard side, where he found a mound of debris that was impossible to surmount. If he wished to reach his goal, there was only one option available: he'd have to climb out on a section of mast, which hung over the water and expose himself directly to enemy fire.

"Ives!" He shouted over and over, but the din of battle made it unlikely any one on the opposite side of the wreckage could hear him. The sudden report from the bow cannonade and a puff of smoke made it clear that someone was still alive on the other side. Ernest peeked over the side and spotted the approaching enemy vessel. He'd have only a moment before they were in small arm's range. Without thinking further, he flung himself onto the projecting beam and worked to reposition himself to jump down on the other side of the debris pile. He began to swing his body, and just as he released the beam, several shots whizzed by his head. He'd made it by seconds.

"Where'd you come from?" an astonished sailor asked as Ernest thudded onto the deck. His injured knee screamed with pain, the echo of which now pulsed through his ankle.

"Where's Ives?"

"Who?"

"The kid they sent up here."

"You're daft. There's no kid up here," the man said waving to his companions as he completed firing another shot. The collapsed mast was actually providing them with more cover than they'd have under normal circumstances, and they were taking full advantage of that fact.

"What's the Swiss want?" an older man asked.

"Some kid," the younger sailor replied throwing up his hands.

"Ives Cross."

"Didn't the boatswain grab some kid just before we stared firing?" another sailor asked as he worked to reload the cannon.

"Yeah, took him aft," the man's companion nodded as he worked the ramrod.

Ernest waved thanks and began to head back towards the protruding mast. He was less optimistic about making the jump safely this time.

"Hey, Swiss," the older man pointed to a small gap in the debris pile, "tell 'em if they want to win this thing, I need more powder up here." Ernest thumped the man on the shoulder then began to crawl through the maze. His knee protested each time he moved, but this was still safer than the alternative. A cannonball smashed into the wreckage immediately behind him and collapsed the passageway through which he'd traveled. He heard screams followed by a hail of shrapnel that pierced some of the canvas then silence.

As he began to drag himself aft again, a new pain made its presence known to him. Something was apparently now buried beneath his left shoulder blade. It took many painful minutes to complete the passage back to the forecastle steps.

Though the Mars and her crew had been horrifically maimed, they were not out of the fight yet. By fate or chance, some men remained uninjured, and a host of them were working to try to steady the damaged main mast. If they could work the rigging to reset it, they might be able to get underway again. As these men worked, they were constantly harassed or killed by fire issued from passing enemy ships. Ernest staggered aft, dizzy with pain and blood loss. His progress was arrested by a hand grasping his arm. He was surprised to find it was Lieutenant Easter, who was wiping Ernest's blood off his hand.

"Get below to the surgeon, Swiss."

"Ives?"

"Get below, that's an order."

The conversation ended abruptly as the man who was working immediately next to them had his chest hollowed out by shot. Distracted, Easter didn't see Ernest continue aft.

The quarterdeck was pure chaos. The remnants of the mizzen mast were scattered about the deck along with the dead. Several officers were congregated around a headless corpse. One wept openly.

"Who's in command now?"

"Give us a minute," the weeping man begged the officer.

"We don't have time. The Captain did his duty. We must do ours."

"I think you are, sir," a junior officer decided. "Every other senior is injured or dead."

"Good God. Did anyone see where his head went?" the newly appointed captain asked in disdain as he beheld the headless corpse of his predecessor.

"I think it's overboard," a pale looking officer affirmed, "Captain Duff was leaning over the railing when it hit him."

"Conduct the body below."

"Sir, there's no room."

"There is for him. Swiss, lend us a hand, poor fellow. You need to go below anyway by the look of you."

Ernest knew the Commander was right; he was too weak to climb over the debris aft. He and another injured junior officer bore Captain

Duff's remains below.

Though he tried to prepare himself for the grim sights and sounds below, Ernest found both overwhelming. They left the Captain's body with those who had been fortunate enough to succumb to their wounds, piled near the hatchway, waiting to be disposed of. Crammed inside the next room were the wounded where Death stalked the deck. The condition of many within seemed hopeless: hands or feet shot cleanly off, disfigured burn victims who howled in pain, men who were bleeding profusely from an assortment of holes gouged into their flesh and organs. Beyond this mass lie those awaiting amputation. A pile of rotting limbs now bereft of their owners lie on the floor. The agonized screams of those being operated on shook the timbers of the ship as well as any shots now striking her sides. It was among those awaiting the saw that Ernest located the boatswain and Ives.

Ives appeared, mercifully, to be unconscious. His face was burned, his ears were gone. A pool of blood stained the deck beneath him, but he was still alive.

"I tried, Swiss. I tried," the boatswain coughed.

Ernest moved over him. The man's right leg was crushed and would obviously have to come off. He took a gulp of spirits then continued.

"Thought he'd be safer, aft with me. The mizzen, when it fell, crushed my leg. Kid was tryin' to pull me free when the stern took a direct hit…ignited the cannonade's powder. Then they opened up with the muskets and pistols. It was so thick, like iron rain passin' over my head. He's deaf now, bleedin' to death inside, I heard the surgeon say. They're gonna toss him over."

No sooner were these words uttered by the boatswain than men appeared with the surgeon who pointed to Ives. Ernest fought to stand.

"You can't do this. He's still alive."

Ernest knew firsthand what agony the boy would suffer drowning.

"He's done for and we need the room. Carry out my order," the surgeon commanded to the men. They bent down and as they lifted him Ives shrieked in pain. The startled men paused.

"Get him out of here!" the surgeon roared. "Bring that one in."

Other men hurried to scoop the boatswain up from the deck. He cried out in pain as they jarred the leg about to be amputated.

"Swiss!" The word was barely intelligible, but the motion he made was not. Unnoticed by those carrying him away, the boatswain pointed to the deck where his pistol lay. The directive was plain.

Tears of anguish and pain traced paths through the grime on Ernest's face as he moved to retrieve the pistol. It held one shot. The tortured screams the boatswain howled were the last sounds that Ernest registered. He was going into shock both from his wounds and from the knowledge of the task he must complete. Through the throngs of the dead and dying, he traveled back to the hatchway. Suddenly the ship rocked violently. The main mast had finally collapsed. Ernest was thrown into a wall; the force of the impact drove the shrapnel further into his back. He almost dropped the pistol as he fought to remain conscious.

Only the sufferings of those from his nightmares drove him on as he managed, finally, to crawl up and out of the hatchway. He could not allow Ives to suffer the terror of drowning. As he fought to stand, he saw them swinging Ives as they prepared to throw him overboard. Ives was still shrieking in pain. Ernest lined up the shot. William's dead face hovered before his eyes. He fired.

The shot tore through Ives' cheek and blew out the back of his head. As he watched the motion of Ives' head in death, Ernest relived the moment, eleven years earlier, when he'd witnessed Justine's head snap upward as her neck was shattered upon the gallows. The surprised men dropped Ives' body instantly, and it disappeared over the side. Ernest's quaking form slumped to the deck in shock.

CHAPTER 3
THE FINAL HOMECOMING

Geneva, Winter, 1810

Jack Clerval deeply inhaled one last puff off his cigar as he considered the entrance before him. He held the smoke in for a long time before releasing it. He was annoyed, and despite the cold, he was in no real hurry to go inside. Christiansen's letter gave no detail for the purpose of this errand, which had brought him hundreds of miles in the dead of winter from Salzburg. The roads had been intolerable, the hour was late, and he was down to two cigars. To top it all off, his decision to make this trip, once again reignited the feud between himself and his talented but volatile wife, Costanza.

**

"You say you love me, but how then can you do this?"

"Ah, Stanza, you know I love you but …"

"Then stay, my love." She climbed onto his lap. "This night means everything, Jack. Tonight I will sing for you, only for you," she leaned in close and nipped at his ear.

Jack sighed as he thumbed the letter from Christiansen, which could not have arrived at a worse time. It was Costanza's big night. A wealthy and highly influential member of Salzburg's elite had commissioned her to be the featured artist at an exclusive winter's ball ceremony to be held at his luxurious estate. The performance was her best chance to date of securing the attention and patronage of even more wealthy benefactors—whose support would make her the toast of not only the stages of Salzburg, but perhaps one day, all of Europe. Didn't he owe it to her to be there? They'd fought, divorced, remarried, loved, loathed, lied, and to a degree supported each other's vices. Both were selfish, vain, unapologetic, and overly passionate. They were everything to one another, including perfectly wrong.

There were only two people in the world who could entreat him to leave at a time like this. Sadly, one of them had, and Jack feared it could only be due to events involving the other. He pushed her back gently and prepared himself as best he could for the inevitable. Even before he spoke the words, the softness of her expression hardened to a look of incredulity.

"It's got to have somethin' to do with Ern. I can't just …."

She pushed herself away harshly and began to pace the room, her long flowing purple robe tracing her exasperated motions across the decorative floor.

"Oh please … I need you in Geneva now. Who would send such a ridiculous letter and be serious? And it says nothing of Frankenstein, who just abandoned you in Ingolstadt."

"He didn't leave me, somethin' musta happened," Jack snapped as he pulled a fresh cigar from his vest. He was too agitated now to even light it. Her arms flailed wildly at his statement as if she were swatting away nuisance insects.

"He did, Jack. He did leave you. You owe him nothing. He is not your master; do not run across the Alps like a dog back to Geneva merely because you are bidden do so."

Jack folded his arms and scowled.

"Oh, damn it all, I crushed my cigar."

"Write your Christiansen back. Tell him you'll leave in a few days, not this morning."

"I can't," Jack quietly said.

"Why?" Costanza demanded.

"Because you saw …," Jack caught himself, but the damage was done.

"I saw nothing that night. Nothing."

He couldn't blame her denial. The memory of the mummified hand grasping Ernest disturbed him as well. They hadn't spoken openly about it in months. In fact, the subject of Ernest Frankenstein had become almost a taboo between them. There were too many dark and disturbing mysteries surrounding the man. Seeing him again had awakened too many grim memories of Henry's death, and his wife knew that. In her mind nothing positive could come from more contact with Ernest. He was best relegated to the past so that she and Jack might embrace their future. But secretly, Jack knew it was a future that could never exist until he solved the truth behind his brother's murder. And Ernest's quest to discover Victor's past was the key. They'd been close, he knew it.

"I'll write you when I get there."

Costanza hurtled a vase into the wall beside Jack's head.

"Don't bother!" She left before he saw the tears in her eyes.

*

Jack rubbed his eyes. Christiansen better have something good here to drink or he was libel to curl up on the office floor and go to sleep as most decent folks had done hours ago. Of course if he were decent then guardians of the city, whom he'd bribed generously, would never have revealed to him the secret means to enter Geneva after the gates had been sealed for the night. He consulted his watch by the moonlight but decided it must be wrong. When had he wound it last? Jack hurled his still burning cigar carelessly over his shoulder and exhaled a last cloud of smoke before entering the building.

He hadn't actually expected anyone to be here at this late hour, but despite this, he could hear the low din of muted voices from inside Christiansen's office. Now that he was actually here, this visit seemed even more ill-advised than it had in Salzburg. At least there he'd had Costanza to argue about it with; now he only had himself to reason with. What would he find on the other side of that door? Logically it should be Ernest. Who else could keep Christiansen here at this atypical hour? But what if Stanza was right and Ernest had abandoned him deliberately in Ingolstadt? Did he hug him or punch him? What if he found Victor—the man he still blamed for Henry's murder—and not Ernest on the other side of the door? What if all of this had to do with some inane business transaction for his father's merchant fleet? In that case he'd have some very strong words for Christiansen indeed.

The door to the office proper was locked. Jack banged against it heedless of how it might startle the occupants of the room. Actually, as he knocked, the thought of their startled faces amused him even more.

"Who's there?" the slightly shaking voice of Christiansen asked.

Why not have some fun?

"Only a poor traveler in search of spirits, sir." Jack did his best impression of a drunk. Considering the practice he'd had over his lifetime, it was masterfully done.

"Then go and find a pub. This is a solicitor's office, not a tavern."

"Ah, please sir. I haven't got a coin on me, just lookin' for some help on a cold night, and then I'll leave you in peace."

Jack was having a hard time not spoiling the moment by laughing. He could hear Christiansen consulting his companion. After a moment of silence, the door slowly opened a crack. Jack grinned and stooped over slightly as he began through the door. He might as well carry the act out until the last second.

"Oh bless you kindly … ah CHRIST!!!"

As he crossed the threshold, his arm was seized, pulled sharply upward, and his elbow was driven into the back of his head. His momentum into the room was corrupted as his attacker used it to pivot him painfully into the wall beside the door, which was slammed shut simultaneously. The wind knocked out of his lungs, he wheezed dryly as he fought to force air back in.

"It's all right. Release him," he heard Christiansen say.

Instantly the pressure on his arm was gone, though his shoulder and neck muscles still burned terribly.

"Damn it, Ern, when'd you get so jumpy?" Jack asked to the figure behind him as he tried to stretch his wrenched shoulder muscles, which were threatening to become one great knot. There was no reply. He turned.

He'd never before set eyes upon the young woman who stood before him, but he would never forget the smoldering passion alive within the gaze from her delicate but intense brown eyes. They seemed to see everything. She was tall; her brown hair was partially braided and pulled back, the rest hung behind her slender shoulders. Her dress was conservative yet elegant at the same time. She backed away from Jack without comment and walked silently to a nearby window, turning her back on him.

"Jack, meet Abrielle, Ernest's sister-in-law," Christiansen said.

For a moment Jack looked blankly at her as his mind fumbled with this new information.

"Oh, that just figures," he muttered to himself finally as he continued to massage his strained sinews.

"Pleased to meet you I'm sure," Jack stated sarcastically as Christiansen handed him a drink. He nodded a silent thanks and waited for Abrielle to acknowledge him. She didn't.

"She always this friendly?" he finally asked Christiansen who shrugged slightly.

Still Abrielle did not move. Her attention was riveted to something on the street below. Jack and Christiansen exchanged a look then began to move to silently join her at the window. Before they could reach her, however, she turned abruptly, crossed the office, and began to resume her gloves, hat, and outer garments. She winced slightly as she worked to pull on her right glove.

"This was a mistake," she said simply by way of explanation to the men's puzzled faces before she began to head for the door.

"Please, what's wrong?" asked Christiansen. "I beg you, mademoiselle, you have traveled too far under such tragic circumstances ..."

She held up a hand to silence him. Her attention was fixed on Jack who was now staring down into the street.

"Jack, what's ...?"

"Ssshhh!" Abrielle hissed at the older man, "Do you see, do you see what you have done?"

The accusatory question was directed at Jack. The cold windowpane fogged a little as he breathed, but he himself remained still.

"That's impossible," Jack's brow furrowed, "they couldn't ... not through the secret entrance."

She hesitated only a moment.

"Monsieur, I thank you for your time," she inclined her head faintly towards Christiansen then purposely resumed her hurried steps towards the door.

"Jack, what is it?" Christiansen demanded, obviously torn between heading for the window and arresting Abrielle's flight through the nearby doorway.

"Three of those damn gypsies are down there," Jack replied quietly.

"His carelessness brought them. How can I trust him with so vital a mission if he's too inattentive to notice when he's being tailed?" Abrielle challenged, "No, it is safer if I handle this alone."

Christiansen put his hand on the doorknob a second before she reached it. With her back to Jack, her intense gaze fell solely upon Christiansen, but he did not waver.

"If you truly believed that mademoiselle, you would not have come here."

Her lips parted a measure, and her gaze grew momentarily distant. At least until Jack broke the silence.

"All right, if we're throwing out accusations, how do I know they didn't all follow you here?"

"Jack, you're not helping."

"Not trying to be helpful, Christiansen. You acted as if you knew someone would be down there. What time did she get here anyway?"

Christiansen hesitated and looked to Abrielle.

"I have been here four days. I sent him a letter announcing my arrival three days before that," Abrielle stated evenly.

Jack's jaw all but dropped.

"What in blazes is this?"

An unspoken message passed between Christiansen and Abrielle, who gave the older man a brief wry smile before she began to remove her outerwear.

"Come, monsieur. It is late, and you have traveled far to join us," she smiled at Jack.

"So what now we're all friends or somethin'?"

"Jack, come on. Sit down by the fire, please. Despite appearances, we are very happy that you are here," Christiansen affirmed.

"What about them?" Jack jerked his head towards the street.

"They will be dealt with but not now," Abrielle declared as she used the hook end of the fireplace poker to maneuver the log she'd just added into place. The room brightened a bit.

Christiansen held out his arms to take Jack's heavy travel cloak and hat, which he surrendered after taking a moment to retrieve his second to last cigar. He ignited it then thumped down unceremoniously into one of the ornate but comfortable chairs near the fire.

"Have you eaten tonight?" Christiansen inquired.

"Not really hungry just now," Jack rejoined as he watched Abrielle cross the room to retrieve something from her own winter travel wear. As she handed him a sealed envelope, he noticed an extremely painful looking cut encompassing nearly the entirety of her right palm. Abrielle sat down quietly in a nearby chair, waved away Christiansen's offer of tea, and closed her eyes.

Jack studied the undated letter, penned hurriedly in Ernest's hand:

Jack,

My dear friend, I can only hope after the host of sorrows I have suffered that this letter finds you well. My haste and the fear of eyes not meant to see these words preclude me from laying bare any great detail but I must call upon your stout heart again. I am sending you my sister-in-law as my agent. She is most capable and will inform you what must be done in order to save my daughter. I pray that one day I will look upon you both again.

Yours,
Ernest

Jack looked to Christiansen who was silently smoking a cigarette as he leaned on the mantelpiece, but he did not stir. Abrielle must have sensed that Jack was finished reading. She did not open her eyes before she began to speak.

"Ernest believed that I mailed his letters before we left Ireland. I was unwilling to trust our enemies, so I brought them here myself."

Jack eyed Christiansen who still seemed unwilling to meet his gaze.

"Where is he?" Jack demanded.

"He was heading towards the Orkney Islands, North Ronaldsay to be precise," Christiansen answered as he tossed the remnants of his cigarette into the fire. A tense, silent minute passed. Something made Jack fearful to ask the next question.

"What of his wife?"

"My sister is dead." Abrielle's eyes finally opened as she spoke these words in a hollow tone. She studied her wounded hand a moment then she stared, unseeing, into the fire, "and my niece has been abducted."

Jack sank into his chair as if a great weight had been thrust upon him. Christiansen rubbed a troubled hand over his balding head. Abrielle met their eyes.

"We're going to get her back," Abrielle vowed, her voice tinged with sadness, bitter resolve, and anger. She was fighting hard not to allow the grief she hid to overwhelm her.

Jack now burned with his own righteous sense of indignation.

"It's those bastards in the street, right?" Jack started up but Christiansen forced him back down into his seat. He shook his head.

"We have many enemies, Jack," Abrielle continued as if nothing had happened. "We must be ready before we confront them."

Christiansen hovered over Jack until the younger man waved him away, dropping ash all over his leg. They were right. He needed more information before he acted.

"Can you stay here, in Geneva for a while?" Christiansen asked.

"Whatever you need," Jack angrily declared. He pushed all thoughts of Costanza from his mind.

"Good. I need you to go to Hungary," the beautiful woman stated.

Jack faltered slightly.

"Hungary?"

"That's where Ernest was taken after his abduction in Ingolstadt. Apparently the same people are responsible for taking his daughter," Christiansen explained.

"Tara, her name is Tara," Abrielle spoke the name with soft reverence.

Christiansen briefly laid a reassuring hand on her shoulder, but he did not allow it to linger. It seemed as though he was apprehensive about doing so. From Jack's brief time around her, he could well understand the benefit of staying on Abrielle's good side, but Christiansen seemed genuinely intimidated by her.

"All right, what do you need me to do in Hungary?"

"Locate a group of gypsies known as the Wild Rose Clan. Their leader, Jal Nalie, took Tara."

The whole situation made Jack irate.

"Damn gypsies …"

"Your only task is to find them, Jack," Abrielle declared commandingly as she rose from her chair, "then you will return here and wait for me."

Jack was crestfallen and angry. What was the point of sending him hundreds of miles to find Ernest's daughter only to abandon her again? True, he didn't have much experience with children, but he could handle himself. Or did she doubt he could?

"Is this because of those …?"

"Hhumm," Christiansen cleared his throat before Jack could unleash a string of profanity.

"… gypsies down there who you say followed me?"

"Partially," her face was inscrutable.

Jack eyed his companions suspiciously.

"I'm afraid we all share some responsibility for their mutual presence," Christiansen began, "one has been watching me since Ernest left Geneva with you, Jack."

"I allowed another to follow me," Abrielle stated, "but the other did follow you through your secret entrance through Geneva's walls."

"How? It cost me half a cellar of vintage red wines every ten months as a bribe just to use that entrance. Dad will kill me if he finds out."

"When he finds out, Jack. And that entrance isn't the best kept secret these days," Christiansen eyed him suggestively.

Jack blinked.

"Wha … you know about it?"

"Must be all that fine vintage red wine the men are drinking during those long nights on duty, tends to loosen their tongues about certain secrets," Christiansen wryly observed.

"Ah." Jack hurled his cigar into the fire.

Abrielle suddenly hovered over him, the coldness in her demeanor highlighted by the dancing shadows.

"The point is that you cannot assume what our enemies will do. Relying on old habits could lead us all to ruin, and from now on, you must obey my orders."

"Orders, huh? My wife tries those. Normally don't work too well," Jack stated smugly. Seemingly out of nowhere, Abrielle produced a knife and held it under Jack's throat.

"I'm not your wife. And if you do anything that endangers Tara, I will use this. And you won't be pleased with the results, I promise. You will obey me."

He felt the slightest increase in pressure from the knife before it disappeared again. Jack was too stunned to protest. She loomed over him a moment longer then slowly walked away from his view. He leaned back in his seat and fumbled for his last cigar. So she was deadly and beautiful. Jack couldn't decide if he was absolutely terrified of this woman or if he was beginning to like her. Still she had rattled him. When was the last time he'd deliberately smoked the final cigar he had with him before replenishing his supply?

Christiansen was absentmindedly rubbing his own neck.

"Well, good, that's settled then," Christiansen diplomatically asserted.

"I will need to leave in three days, earlier if the weather changes. Do you think we'll have him ready?" Abrielle asked the older man.

"Ah, that depends. Jack, how are you at learning languages?" Christiansen inquired.

"Long as its useful to me and not some Ancient Greek nonsense or such, I'm pretty good, why?"

"I'm going to teach you Gaelic," Abrielle said flatly as she again studied the figures in the dark street below.

"What for?"

"Encoding messages; I've already taught the fundamentals to Christiansen in case I have to leave early."

"Where are you going?"

"France," Abrielle replied quietly.

"It's complicated," Christiansen sighed at Jack's incredulous expression.

"No kidding. That sounds familiar," Jack shook his head.

"We fight not one enemy, but three, each separate but connected," Abrielle stated as she returned her attentions to her companions.

"Great, more riddles and what sounds like the start of a long story. Well, Christiansen I've changed my mind about eating."

"Abrielle, I left some food on the second shelf on the cart in the back room. Would you mind …?"

She was out the door before Christiansen finished. For a moment neither man spoke for fear she'd return and overhear them.

"Jack, I really must apologize for your greeting tonight, but she insisted on seeing your reaction to the gypsies.

"Guess I passed, huh. Christiansen, seriously, what's her story?" Jack whispered.

Christiansen hesitated a moment before nervously shaking his head.

"Sorry, both Ernest and she were quite adamant that I not reveal her full story to you."

"Why?" Jack asked.

"To protect you, and us, in case you're captured or … worse."

"Huh. Yeah, hadn't really considered that possibility. Ernie sent you a letter too right?"

"Not now, I think she's coming back," Christiansen stiffened.

"She said there are three enemies?"

"Yes. This Jal's group, another rival gypsy clan in France, and the master they serve."

Abrielle appeared in the doorway with a large covered tray.

"Yeah, who's that?" Jack asked lazily.

Christiansen paused.

"Victor's son."

*

If only there was some other way. Abrielle tried to reflect upon all that brought her to this château on such a bitterly cold night. The iron hard sheets of snow shone in the bright moonlight. She'd known where he was for years, but it had never occurred to her that she would one day have to stand before him again, to plead for a favor. The last of which still haunted her to this day.

By now he must know she was here. It was incredible that a man like Bellange would willingly allow her to linger, unchallenged, this close to his home. Perhaps retirement had changed him, as some rumors purported. She would know soon.

Maybe it was the modesty of the place that surprised her. Abrielle was about to see the third most powerful man in the whole of Napoleon's Empire, but his home, though impressive, was plain. No honor guard attended, no gates impeded free passage; a few of the windows bore candlelight, but the house was far from aglow. All was tranquil. The only sound breaking the deep silence of the night was the hoot of a lone owl. No doubt it was all part of the illusion created by the spymaster for his visitors, the spider awaiting his unsuspecting prey. Hadn't one of his earliest teachings imparted to her been the idea that one should only be visible when it was advantageous to be? That notion now stood solidified in the stone edifice before her. It was a disguise, to be used then discarded as the demands of life dictated.

As she approached the door, it unexpectedly opened. Abrielle felt her reflexes begin to initiate their well-rehearsed movements, but she stifled them. Only a swirl in her tracks in the snow and dissipating vapor trails from a slight increase in her respiratory rate betrayed her momentary reaction.

A figure appeared in the doorway. The man was unarmed or so it appeared. His hair all matched the snow, he bore that subtle look of bemusement, so agitating yet so familiar to her. Abrielle's eyes darted around her, but nothing more happened. The owl repeated its ageless call to the night, then silence.

"Welcome to my home, Abrielle," Bellange's smile deepened. "I've been expecting you."

Chapter 4
Whispers of Deceit

The words of greeting dissipated into the thin air of the frost-charged night. None were returned as Abrielle's mind and senses furiously sought any insight into what this tactic might gain him. He'd expected her? Was it possible they'd known her true whereabouts all these months?

She searched his face for clues, but knew it would be a futile exercise. He wore so many false faces, a fact she'd often marveled at, for he assumed them with such ease. Even the name he bestowed upon himself was false. Had he ever possessed a true identity of his own? She banished these musings from her mind as again he spoke.

"Have you finished?"

"What?"

"Assessing your situation, wondering what the old man is plotting. I noticed you surveying potential escape routes as you approached."

Abrielle allowed herself to relax a degree.

"As you always taught me to do," she replied.

He chuckled softly.

"Well, if you're done and care to join me by the fire, I'd be most grateful. This cold air dulls the senses and will bid me to bed early if I remain out in it too long."

Abrielle hesitated a moment longer then sedately continued towards him. Her resolve was fixed; she must speak with him before she was apprehended. He was the only one she could think of who might possess both the knowledge and the will to help her. Bellange, the man who had shaped so much of her life yet remained such a mystery.

"Merci, monsieur, I am most grateful for your civility," she humbly stated as she allowed him to remove her coat once they were inside.

"Think nothing of it, mademoiselle. I am pleased to once again share in your company," he said, indirectly acknowledging the rift between them.

"I will be brief."

This time it was Bellange's turn to hesitate.

"Your time is yours," he nodded, "please leave your weapons here with your cloak. I promise no one will take them."

Without protest she produced several deadly possessions. It would be pointless to attempt to hide them from her former master. He allowed her to retain one small knife before they began down a long, dark hallway.

"You keep no servants, sir?"

"No, that's the problem with being a retired spy. You never seem to trust anyone again, though I do retain a rotating group of temporary help procured from the countryside."

He held out his hand to indicate the direction they were to head. Abrielle tried to hide her smile at the thought of Bellange as some type of country squire. Did any of the locals know who it was they were truly dealing with?

"I must apologize for calling upon you so late," Abrielle began as they sat down before an inviting fire in a room, which could only serve as the library, "but my need is great and my time short."

"Of course," he agreed.

Bellange studied her a moment then rang a small bell set upon the table beside him. How could the old servant who arrived with an equally ancient dog have heard such a soft, delicate chime? The dog immediately gravitated to the new stranger as his owner stated his needs.

"My guest is thirsty. Something warm, perhaps?"

Abrielle petted the dog who was already slumping against her chair in blissful abandonment.

"Yes, tea … or something stronger," she suggested.

Bellange's servant left and returned with the requested refreshments in short order, however, the dog remained and soon became a fixture curled up before the fire. Abrielle savored the warmth that coursed throughout her body as she drank. In another time and place she might actually be able to relax and enjoy herself. Her journey from Geneva had been long and lonely; still a part of her treasured it for it had also been peaceful. And peace was something she'd seen precious little of in her life.

"So you were expecting me?" she asked casually as she poured Bellange another cup of tea and handed it to him.

"It's not without precedent that a rogue Imperial agent should come to me," her former mentor stated.

"And why would you think I'd gone rogue? I thought you had retired." Abrielle blew wisps of steam away from her drink. He smiled.

"How I conduct my retirement is my business."

"Matters simply required my attention elsewhere," Abrielle said by way of explanation.

"A half truth," Bellange observed as his eyes drifted from her. His sharp features suddenly seemed to sink. He was no longer the master spy, but an old man.

"When they came to me, I knew they'd grown desperate. I truly hoped I'd never have to see your face again," Bellange admitted.

This statement was so astonishing that she nearly dropped her cup and saucer.

He held her gaze.

"I'd hoped you were free," he explained.

"Free? What would you know of the word?" she challenged harshly.

Bellange rose and calmly walked to a shelf of books.

"The great philosophies of the ages tower before us here," he observed as he regarded the shelf. "Man's essential nature scrutinized, destroyed, reshaped by great visionaries, the work of demi-gods of wisdom. But was Aristotle mad? Voltaire[1] a fool? Can freedom and power and wisdom exist as one divine force? Can one man hope to balance these into equality?"

The color in Abrielle's cheeks rose.

"And what would an Imperial demi-god care of my freedom?"

He turned remorseful eyes upon her.

"Power has not granted me freedom, only the ability to take it from others."

Abrielle fought against the emotions surging within her. This was Bellange. She tried to remain unmoved by the expression of self-loathing upon his face. In a sense this man was a demi-god, who molded his creations to fit his needs in the name of the Empire. If not for him she would have been executed. Her life had served his. But she now saw herself also trapped within his statement. Though she rarely admitted it to herself, for a long time now she'd needed power, but what had that need cost her and others? Her mind recoiled.

Unexpectedly Bellange resumed his seat and put his head into a

1 French writer and philosopher during the Enlightenment.

hand.

"Has something happened?"

His eyes again rose to meet hers, but he did not raise his head.

"It is a bitter thing to enter one's winter and realize that you have betrayed all you ever loved. I have willingly participated in corruption of the ideals of the Revolution and in so doing, I have killed my own sons. I had four once, now…."

Dimly, Abrielle heard a distant clock begin to toll the hour.

"… the youngest died two weeks ago on the Iberian Peninsula[2]. The war there is savagery beyond description," Bellange stated, a haunted look in his eyes.

"I remember," Abrielle replied somewhat coolly.

The Peninsula War as it had come to be known was a great embarrassment for Napoleon and a vicious, grinding bloodbath for his troops. Spain was to have been taken and forced to submit to his will, but instead, the Spanish and their English allies had not only stood their ground but begun to push back at great cost to both sides. Caught in the middle were thousands of Spanish civilians and guerrilla fighters, desperate for vengeance.

Abrielle hoped Bellange's son, if he existed, had not met too gruesome an end. Surely with his connections the spy master should have easily been able to keep his son from being sent to the Peninsula battlefields.

"What was his name?" she asked earnestly.

"He loved the mountains, you know. Crossing the Pyrenees[3] would have been a grand adventure for him," Bellange wistfully noted.

"What was his name?" Abrielle repeated more gravely.

Bellange looked at her as if trying to remember it. She knew the torments of grief all too well, but never would it take her so long to recall the name of one she'd loved.

"You had no sons, did you?" she charged, sensing his subtle manipulations.

"I am sick with grief," he plaintively stated. "Why did you come here tonight, Abrielle? So we could whisper as we once did, as I taught you to

---

2 geographic region of Western Europe containing Spain, Portugal, etc.

3 mountain chain between France and Spain.

do?"

"Yes, I need information."

Bellange closed his eyes.

"I'm retired."

"A half truth," she vehemently contended.

"A choice then," his eyes opened slowly and fixed coldly upon hers. "I will no longer be a slave to Napoleon's Empire. That was never the goal of our great rebellion."

Abrielle tried to interject but was cut off.

"I'm glad it's you they sent. Now, at the end."

His countenance grew pleading.

"Do not be deceived as I have allowed myself to be. The Emperor is a traitor, a lesser man who has corrupted the ideals of the Revolution, who will bring us all to ruin if he is not stopped."

Abrielle pulled away. She didn't want to hear anymore of Bellange's own traitorous talk.

"I will forget these words. You're mad with grief by your own admission."

She jumped when he clasped her hand firmly.

"Let us whisper then again, as we once did, as I taught you to do."

"Please, don't say anymore."

She turned from him, freeing herself from his grasp.

"You have come to hear my last words, I must speak," Bellange asserted.

"I told you, I came for information," Abrielle reiterated.

"In service to the Empire?" he demanded.

"No," Abrielle managed after a moment of indecision.

"Tell me, my child, what do you know of conspiracy?"

The questions were coming too fast. She needed to regain control.

"I will not turn you in," she promised.

He seized her hand violently.

"We both have loosed the bonds of servitude. Stop pretending that you're still bound. Tell me about conspiracy."

The emotion in his voice and countenance disturbed her. The Bellange she knew prided himself on shielding his emotions from others except when needed. Was this part of some grand manipulation?

"What would you have me say? I am no stranger to them. I've ended them before in the name of the Empire. So have you."

An abrupt noise carried down the length of the hall and shook the very stones that comprised the floor. Angry voices barked orders and doors thudded as they were roughly thrown open. Abrielle felt the man's grip loosen.

"You must stop them before it goes any further," Bellange commanded.

"Who?"

He staggered back from her and grabbed a book off the shelf. Abrielle sprung from her seat, desperate to stop him from drinking from the vial he withdrew from the book's pages. She needed him. He was of no use dead to her. Their struggle only ceased when the metallic sound of musket and pistol hammers being cocked intruded the library. A host of well-armed French regulars held weapons upon them. Bellange dropped the vial and held up his hands. Abrielle did likewise. A trooper bent and sniffed at the vial.

"Poison," he reported to a superior.

"I should never have sent you on that final mission," Bellange said as they affixed irons onto both him and Abrielle. "I am repaid for my cruelty. But for that, you might believe me now."

The apology caught her off guard, as she lunged at him but was forcibly pinned to a shelf of books by the military agents. Others began to lead Bellange out the door. How could he even attempt to apologize for the last mission he'd personally sent her on? The scars of which tainted her very soul.

"You've always used me! You lying bastard!"

He struggled against his guards to slow in the entrance and turn a degree.

"My youngest's name was Andre Gramont."

Their eyes engaged only a brief moment before the troops shoved him roughly out the door but not before a few last words reached her ears.

"… need … end the conspiracy."

A deep stillness descended upon those left in the room. Bellange was gone, and she'd never even asked him the question so vital to her own mission: Where was the clan of gypsies, who called themselves Moon Shadows, hiding in France?

*

Abrielle shivered against the cold stones which comprised her small cell. She tried to divorce her mind from her body's discomfort and to focus on that which she could control: her thoughts. She'd been left alone, except for the daily deposit of the meal tray, for at least eight days. During that time, she'd tried her best to decipher the real implications behind her enigmatic meeting with Bellange. Locked away with nothing but time the task should have been a relatively simple matter, however, truth remained an elusive oasis.

What had been real? She simply could not accept their exchange at face value. Not with Bellange involved. This was a man who'd trained countless, silent legions in deceit and trickery, all in the name of serving Napoleon and the ideals of the French Revolution. These whispers of an inscrutable conspiracy and the sudden existence of his here untold phantom family espoused Bellange's trademark tactics of deception. Confuse the subject, play upon their sympathies, then strike when their fears and clarity of judgment had been largely abated. He was laying a trap for her, wasn't he?

"'I should never have sent you on that final mission.'"

The statement burned within her. It coursed through her like the poison she'd kept the spymaster from imbibing. Had that been real? Could the troopers' timely arrival have been previously arranged? Had they been looking for her or had they actually been seeking Bellange regarding this conspiracy? Was his apparent grudge against Napoleon something he'd already acted upon? An assassination attempt perhaps? Bellange certainly possessed the means, and ostensibly, the motive for such a course of action.

She needed to get up. Her body was shaking itself apart in the chill, cold air of the cell. There was little room for her to wander, though. Rats and insects now held dominion over the corner where she'd taken to piling the remnants of her rotten meals. Her waste bucket, which had only been emptied once since her incarceration, sickened her to be near and rendered another portion of the small cell all but uninhabitable. That left her a very narrow area in upon which she could pace and retrace steps.

As she walked, she tried to stretch the kinks in her neck, but to little avail. The constant strain of her incarceration, the uncomfortable bedding, the nauseating scents, and incessant shivering made them permanent fixtures of additional discomfort. Though wholly unpleasant, these physical trials could be managed. But the mental and spiritual fatigue was beginning to take a toll.

Several times she awoke and thought she heard Tara crying; she'd fallen back asleep, whispering her name in the dark. The murky cell largely deprived her senses of any real means to measure time. She thought it had been eight days since her arrival, but that was based solely on the number of trays she'd received, and there was no real pattern as to when the trays arrived. Even though she'd know incarceration was a likely outcome of her return to France, each day she remained immobile was a day she was prevented from aiding her niece.

What had Jal done to her? Had Jack found her by now? What had become of Ernest? Had she already failed all of them?

Confronting Bellange for information had been a dangerous and desperate gamble. Ernest could only give her vague information about the location where the Moon Shadows had captured and abandoned him. And none of it proved that the mountainous area was their true home. It could have taken her weeks or months to locate them on her own. Of course, she could always have gone to Hungary and attempted to rescue Tara but then what?

It was impossible to believe that if she rescued Tara they would leave them in peace. She was dealing with groups of fanatics. Could another Moon Shadow member, aside from the one she'd dealt with outside of Geneva, have followed her across the Alps and reported her location to French authorities? She'd been under their observation now, off and on, for weeks. What did they already know about her? Maybe they'd decided to use the machinations of France to annihilate her.

Abrielle paused. She needed to believe that her efforts to confront the Moon Shadows here would help Ernest. Without securing Jal's daughter, all their great efforts might be wasted. Perhaps this Baseria was being held here in France. But it was still difficult for her to believe that France would ever knowingly tolerate gypsies within the very heart of the Empire; at least not without protection from higher authorities. Could they factor into Bellange's mysterious conspiracy? She leaned against the wall, tired of wading through endless possibilities. No, she never really had a choice about returning to France. The question now was would she ever leave it again?

The fact that no one, as of yet, had interrogated her did not bode well. The poor meals, harsh environment, the loss of time, the mutterings of her fears, and all her sufferings so far were a mere prologue for that yet to come. She'd avoided thinking about her eventual interrogation because she could really do nothing to prepare herself for it. The great mysteries swirling around her made it so. Would Bellange stride through the door to her cell and offer her freedom in exchange for a new pledge of service? Or had he been fairly arrested, entrapped at last in his own web of lies? But why was he so frantic about conspiracies?

Bellange seemed to think that she was running some sort of independent operation to quietly murder him. He'd been expecting an assassination attempt on his own life. Could any of his words or actions have been vaguely sincere? He also seemed to see her as a source of hope for a problem he couldn't handle. Could all of this merely have been to test her loyalty? Was she now to be hanged as a traitor? She renewed her steps, counted them as she swung feverishly about the narrow room.

"'I should never have sent you on that final mission.'"

Her eyes hunted for a means to escape this dungeon as she fought to subdue the image of Paul's face. She tried to banish the persistent phantom from her mind.

"'I should never have sent you on that final mission.'"

Ailis' accusing face briefly appeared in her mind's eye then vanished. Her sister had never known the monster Abrielle truly was. If she had she would never have asked her to raise Tara after her death. Her vision clouded as tears formed along the edge of her vision.

Abruptly she stopped and smacked the stone wall before her with her hand. No, she needed to find a means to escape, not continue to dwell on such dark matters. She must find some way to prepare for her interrogation.

Just as this thought entered her mind she heard the jingle of keys, followed by the sound of metal scraping inside of the lock. The door swung lazily inward and flickering lantern light caused her eyes to blink uncontrollably. The figure with the lantern stood aside and backlit the silhouette of someone else. Abrielle staggered backwards a step. It was not Bellange. Though she still couldn't see her clearly, the scent the figure wore left no doubt as to who stood in the doorway. Her heart sank.

"Bonsoir, Abrielle," Chloe said.

CHAPTER 5
IN THE EMBRACE OF REMEMBRANCE

Abrielle's breath caught in her throat as Chloe glided into the cell. The woman was clad in an expensive dress and wore jewelry that sparkled in the dancing flame of the lantern in the hall. Of all the people her captors could have chosen, Chloe was the only one she truly feared. Upon reaching Abrielle, the woman paused only a moment before pressing her lips gently to both of the younger woman's cheeks. She allowed her lips to hover over Abrielle's, whose heart was now racing. Then she smiled slightly and stepped back.

"Welcome home, Abrielle."

The words were gentle and sincere. Chloe's eyes seized upon Abrielle's wounded right hand. She delicately took it into her gloved one and studied the cut.

"My, we have been careless."

Abrielle fixed her eyes upon the guards in the hall, each with a drawn weapon in hand. She felt Chloe's fingers interlace into those upon her left hand.

"Come."

Much to her own surprise Abrielle began to follow where she was led. The light grew stronger as they approached the entryway. There was still time. Though she was unarmed, if she was quick she might be able to snap Chloe's neck before the guards shot. She felt a mild increase of pressure on her fingers. Chloe had probably surmised that Abrielle might be contemplating escape, but the motion was more of a reminder than a threat. Chloe was in control, and this simple reminder terrified Abrielle anew.

Chloe was capable of anything, but if Abrielle lashed out, she would fail Ailis, Tara, and Ernest. There was no escape. As Bellange had been led away to meet his fate, he'd remarked how he was repaid for his crimes. As she entered the bright hallway, Abrielle could not help but remember her own and wondered what the price would be.

***

Bayonne, France 1794

"I found you!"

"You cheated. You watched. There's no way you could have found me that fast," Paul challenged.

"No, it's your fault for wearing squeaky shoes. Besides, I always find you," Abrielle smiled.

Paul grabbed the apple she was reaching for and began to taunt her with it by holding it just beyond her grasp.

"Give it back!"

"Get taller."

Abrielle shoved him and Paul laughed.

"Give it back or I'll tell Sister Michelle," Abrielle threatened.

Paul studied her a moment, then wiped the apple on his sleeve and took a big bite. Abrielle's lips puffed out slightly as she pursed them. He'd called her bluff. Actually it was a foolish one to begin with. Both of them were ignoring their respective chores. She was supposed to be hanging clothes in the nearby laundry room and him scrubbing the hallway floors.

Chores were boring but she always found Paul, three years her elder, interesting. He was certainly more fun to be around than the sniping, whiney, tiresome girls in her wing of the orphanage. It was too bad that the only time she really got to see Paul was when they were both punished at the same time. Of course this meant that she took to getting into trouble on a regular basis just so she could be near him.

She lunged for her apple and slipped slightly on the wet stones he'd been scouring.

"Come on. You still owe me for my twelfth birthday."

"I stole that fabric you wanted," he reminded her, but this did nothing to abate her efforts. She would get her apple back. Suddenly Paul stood up straight and began to move his hands rapidly over the apple.

"No, Paul!"

"Too late," he grinned as he held up his empty palms.

"Where'd you hide it this time?"

She searched frantically for it but to no avail. Paul was a good thief, but he was even better at hiding the evidence of his crimes. He laughed hysterically at her fumbling attempts to locate her food.

"You're a dirty thief, Paul Cheval!" Abrielle fumed.

"No, your apple is dirty. But I cleaned it for you." He withdrew her half-eaten, hair encrusted apple from the filthy water of his scrub bucket.

Suddenly it wasn't funny anymore. She'd teach him this time. She grabbed a nearby lump of soap.

"Paul! Abrielle!"

Both children jumped at the sound and sight of Sister Josephine as she hovered like an angry storm cloud in the doorway. She was quick to punish, by paddle or labor, and certainly did not appreciate two children, already serving a punishment, who were fighting. The day ended with both having relatively sore behinds and mouths that were crusted with the residue of the soap they'd been forced to hold between their teeth for hours after lying to her. But it was not part of the day that would forever make it memorable to Abrielle.

Very late that night, she was roughly shaken awake. She swung at the air briefly, then tried to roll back over. Sometimes the older girls especially liked to tease the younger ones by shaking them awake. The torment could last half the night at best or months at its worst. The last time something like this had happened, Abrielle hit her attacker as she retreated back to her bed. The tactic had worked, and the black eye the next morning had revealed the guilty party. She'd had no further problems with this type of harassment until tonight. The hand came again, and this time, she shot up in bed. Her hair a tangled mess, she flopped it over her head and she sought her tormentor, but the room full of sleeping girls was relatively quiet.

Annoyed, but tired, she lay back down once more to try to go back to sleep. It was then that the object on the floor by her bed attracted her attention. She pulled back the sheet and uncovered a small basket full of twelve apples. Her heart leapt as she searched for Paul but found no trace of him. A small note was tucked inside the basket:

Happy Birthday. Hide these before they get stolen!

Abrielle reached down, retrieved one of the dozen apples, and beheld it as a sacred object. Her fingers massaged its cool, taut surface; she breathed in the fresh scent. She bit into it and almost immediately spat it out. The remnants of the soap bar did not make an appealing mix with the apple. She used the sheet covering the apples to try and wipe more of the foul taste from her mouth. The second bite was pure bliss.

The sweet juices played over her tongue and trickled down her chin. She giggled with happiness as she savored not only her presents but the fact that Paul cared enough to give them to her. She'd never made friends easily; the orphanage environment and her own personality made it difficult. She often wavered erratically between being shy or arrogant, and the rare moments of encouragement she received from the adults around her only re-enforced that to most she was nothing but an ordinary, easily forgettable girl.

Many of the other girls proved to be false allies, abusive, liars, or so desperate for any sort of affection that their clinging ways alienated her. Still she'd managed to make a few friends, but life and the nature of the orphanage often separated them far too soon. Several of her friends had died of diseases or been adopted—Belle even by her birth parents who'd been so beset by guilt they'd returned to reclaim her.

Abrielle's life experiences taught her that it was less painful to remain unconnected. A family tried to adopt her once, but she fought everyone until she'd been allowed to stay. She was determined that ultimately she would control her own destiny. Abrielle looked at the other sleeping girls and the dirty, cracked walls, as her mind relived the lifetime spent here. She hated this place, but maybe, one day, her real family would feel as guilty as Belle's had about leaving her here and come to rescue her. In spite of herself, Abrielle could not help but imagine such a moment.

The floor was too cold to want to get up and hide the other apples. She retrieved a third and nestled back down into the warm blankets with it. Abrielle closed her eyes and began to imagine again that oft dreamt of day when her family arrived. Her mother would hold her, press her tightly against her breast, and promise never to leave her again. Father would kiss her and tell her what a brave child she had been. They hadn't left her here on purpose, how could they? She didn't deserve that; no one did. What could she have ever done to make them leave her? The question troubled her and she quickly sent it adrift.

She would have three sisters: two older and one younger. Abrielle, of course, would be the prettiest much to their chagrin. Might as well have a brother or two also; the eldest would be a great disappointment to the family while the younger would be clever and nice. He would be her champion and ally, and they would write each other every day.

At her new home she would never be ignored or beaten by anyone, unlike here where she'd suffered injuries from some of the older girls. Her family would listen, she'd never go to sleep hungry, they would marvel at her cleverness, her kindness, and above all, they would love her.

Sadly these thoughts only nurtured bitterness. Buried beneath these fantasies was a pain she rarely acknowledged openly. Someone in this world had hated her enough to abandon her here. What would she do if she ever had the chance to confront them? When she awoke hours later, the remaining apples in the basket were gone, as was the one she'd cradled in her sleep.

*

It happened several weeks later. Morning service had just concluded, and they were all heading for the dining hall to break their fast when the shouting was heard. As the voices grew louder, the children collectively paused, some laughed as they speculated as to the cause of the raised voices. Several of the sisters began to head back down the hall towards the orphanage entryway when an echoing shot was heard. The large gates screamed open, then armed men and women came into view and began to storm down the hallway. Some in the mob forced the nuns against the wall; others began to grab children at random.

A symphony of terrified shrieks and cries blended with the thundering sound of running footsteps and angry shouts. Abrielle's eyes searched desperately for Paul as she was being swept up by the hustling crowd. A young girl directly beside her was snatched up and hauled away by one of the invaders. Abrielle wanted to help her but was too frightened. She ran. They all ran.

The corridor ahead split: a set of stairs led to the boys' dorms, other hallways led towards the girls' dorms and classrooms, and a gate granted access to the courtyard. Abrielle fled across the cobbled stones of the yard and ran up another staircase, which led to the sisters' quarters. It was the furthest, safest place she could think of to run to. What was going on? Who were these people?

She reached the top step, only to realize that the imposing door before her was locked. She beat on it until her hands were numb, but no one came. There was nowhere to go and one glance from below would expose her immediately. Reluctantly, she hurriedly descended back into the chaos below. By now the armed adults were roving the courtyard, sweeping up the children before them. She managed to evade them and began to run towards the classrooms.

"Abrielle," Paul whispered as he emerged from a hiding place they often used when playing games. Wordlessly she ran to him. He grabbed her hand and began to lead her back towards the church.

"I think almost all of them went inside."

"Who are they?" she asked breathlessly.

Without warning each of them was seized by a firm hand as they passed the entrance to the dining hall. Shock and fear held their cries of surprise and alarm at bay.

"Be silent, children," a familiar voice instructed, "come quickly!" Sister Michelle released them, and they followed her without protest. As they passed the main entryway to the orphanage, they saw a black clad body on the ground. Abrielle began to scream, but Paul covered her mouth instantly. Sister Michelle ushered them into the church where they hid behind the altar.

"Who's ...?" Paul began to ask but was unable to finish the question.

Sister Michelle looked away and crossed herself.

"Sister Josephine, poor soul. She refused to let those Jacobin[4] monsters in. They killed her for it."

"Jacobins?" Abrielle managed.

"Yes, it's the Terror[5]."

This explanation meant little to Abrielle, but Paul seemed to understand. The noise of a door opening caused them all to duck lower.

"Michelle, are you here," a voice whispered, "I found Marie'."

Sister Michelle closed her eyes in relief for a moment.

"Bring her up here, Sister Annette."

The three year old Marie' looked pale, her eyes distant. Annette handed her over to Abrielle. She wrapped her arms around the girl as the nuns held a succinct discussion. Annette looked down at the crouching

---

4 radical faction, led by Robespierre, that was active 1789-1794 and created the Reign of Terror during the French Revolution.

5 also called the Reign of Terror, lasted from 1793-1794 and decreed that any enemy of the Revolution be harshly executed.

children.

"Do we tell them they're dead? We could lead them to the common grave," Sister Annette suggested.

"This is a mob. I doubt they'll know how many we have or who they are. We must say nothing."

"That must be why they're grabbing the children at random, hoping to make one of us confess."

"The Lord's mercy upon us," Sister Michelle prayed.

"What of the records?"

"I told her to destroy them, but you know how she is."

"Was," Sister Annette grimly corrected.

Silence.

"Any trace of the other four? Claire, Louis …?"

Sister Annette shook her head.

"The children are scattered everywhere, and I have no idea how many members of that mob made it inside."

The distant sound of more shots ended the conversation abruptly. The women exchanged a look of mutual resignation then Sister Michelle leaned over her charges behind the altar.

"No matter what you hear do not leave this church. I will come back for you."

The promise held no comfort for Sister Michelle did not appear to believe her own words. Abrielle nodded dumbly. Paul's expression darkened, and Marie' continued to suck her thumb and twirl a strand of hair.

The nuns left, locking the children inside. Paul ran down the aisle and tested the locked doors immediately. Marie' began to cry, the wails echoing off the stones of the church walls. Abrielle tried to console the young girl as best she could. Paul raced past her testing the storage room windows.

"You have to silence her!" he barked as he grabbed a tray from the altar and began to head back to the window in the storage room. Abrielle followed him with Marie'.

"Paul, what were they talking about? What's the Terror? Does it have something to do with the revolution?"

He spoke as he went to work on a rusted lock.

"I've only heard a few things, down in the kitchens, you know, when I was being punished. A deliveryman was warning the nuns about the

Jacobins' hatred of the clergy. Told them to be careful or they'd end up meeting the guillotine."

Abrielle considered this new information. Hadn't their former king died by guillotine only last year?

"But why hurt us? We didn't do anything."

Unpleasant as life here could be, Abrielle did have to admit they were mostly sheltered safely away from the riots, mobs, the worst of the food shortages, and the general chaos that had infected her nation during its, as yet unresolved, revolution.

"I don't think they care. There!" Paul grinned in triumph as the lock gave. They could sneak out the window and not a moment too soon. His clamorous exertions had masked the sound of the church doors shaking under assault from outside. Marie' began to cry anew.

"Shut her up or she's staying behind."

The doors to the church crashed open, and they heard orders being issued. If they heard Marie' now, they were all done for. Without preamble Paul grabbed her and threw the terrified babe out the window, the young girl's cries were muffled for a moment. Abrielle stared at him in angry disbelief.

"How could you …?"

"Some more back there!" they heard a gruff voice say.

They'd been spotted. Paul shoved her towards the window, but it was too late; a member of the mob was scooping Marie' off the ground outside. She and Paul surrendered to the forces gathered within the church and were led back towards the courtyard.

By now many of the children had been located and brought to the familiar cobblestone square, along with the nuns. Abrielle and Paul were forced to stand with the other children, who were loosely assembled around the square. As she took her place among them, she noted the absence of several of the sisters. Could they be in hiding or were they also dead? A sharp toned voice brought her attention to focus. Sister Annette was being interrogated nearby.

"Very clever, Citizeness, but the fact that you've given each of the children new surnames changes nothing. We know you're harboring the offspring of émigrés at this orphanage. We'll have them or we'll have your head."

The sister challenged him.

"Who are you to speak in such a manner to one who serves God?"

Annette's courage folded as the man loomed over the diminutive nun.

"A loyal patriot of the Republic[6], a devoted servant of Robespierre, and one who will not be swayed by a member of a clergy who have always sided with the corruption and abuses so prevalent in the Old Regime[7]."

He leaned forward.

"Would you rather they all be killed, huh? Tell us what we want to know or you can watch them march to the guillotine in your place, one by one, until you identify who among them is of aristocratic lineage."

The man lurched away from the bereaved nun.

He grabbed a frightened young boy and hauled him out before those assembled. A club now hovered menacingly above the child's head.

"If you care," he bellowed, "if you truly care for any of these … children, you will give up those whose blood threatens to poison our new Republic."

"No. No, they're dead! Leave us in peace!" Annette cried out. The man crossed the yard and cruelly struck her. She crumbled. He eyed those before him forebodingly, waiting to see if anyone openly dared to challenge him.

"Monsieur," the clear, even voice of Sister Michelle cut through the silence.

"Citizen," the man ordered contemptuously.

"Monsieur," the nun repeated more gently, "there is no need for any of this. Yes, there are children here born of a certain heritage, but they have no knowledge of this fact. They never will. Sister Josephine, who you saw fit to slaughter at the gate, destroyed all records of this long ago. They are now as much Citizens of the Republic as you or I. Please, sir … they are innocents."

The man leered at her as he hobbled toward her.

"Citizens of the Republic? This from one who twice addresses me in the old manner? As a monsieur of the Old Regime, with a title fit for

---

6 the First French Republic was established in 1792 to govern France as a replacement for the monarchy.

7 refers to the political and social systems of power that ruled France prior to the 1789 French Revolution.

slaves. They may be Citizens at present, but once they are again secured behind these walls, hidden away from our sight, you will undoubtedly return to teaching them the old ways of injustice and inequality, and return them to us as sources of corruption."

She held his gaze.

"We are all equal in the eyes of the Lord," she steadfastly affirmed.

"Let's test that."

The man signaled to two of his compatriots who grabbed Sister Michelle's arms and began to haul her towards an unfamiliar device in the rear of the courtyard. Strange, that hadn't even been here when Abrielle fled through here earlier. It must be something they brought with them. The mob of Jacobins forced the children to follow Sister Michelle.

"You can't do this!" a bruised Sister Annette sobbed frantically. She could barely walk, and blood ran freely from her lip. By now Michelle's guards had removed her habit and were tying her hair up. Abrielle studied the woman's face. It was calm; she whispered something—probably prayer—ceaselessly. Abrielle had never seen Sister Michelle without her habit on. She was quietly beautiful, motherly even, Abrielle reflected.

The impassioned agitation from the assembled sisters began to upset the children, most of whom were ignorant of what was about to happen. Confused, they wailed and again sought escape, but only a few managed to scurry momentarily away. Whatever was about to happen, the Jacobins meant for them to see it.

Abrielle wanted to look away; Paul told her to. Her own mind screamed for her to do so, but instead she watched as Sister Michelle was strapped down onto a table of sorts. Her hands and feet were bound to it, and as they finished this process, Abrielle's eyes were drawn to the angled sheet of metal menacingly suspended above the brave sister's head.

"NO!" her mind screamed. She loved Sister Michelle. "NO!"

An unnatural silence, one tinged with anticipation and dread, suddenly descended upon the crowd. Then the sounds came. The God-forsaken sound of the rushing blade riding the rails, the hum of metal as it sliced through supple flesh and bone, and the dull thump which signaled the end.

The triumphant man reached down into a basket and held up Sister Michelle's decapitated head for all in the crowd to witness. Several of the children fainted or became violently ill. Her lips still moved slightly as her blood coursed down the man's arm. The Jacobins cheered; the rest wept.

"Let this serve as a warning to any disloyal Citizen who would see the ways of the Old Regime maintained. The old traditions are dead as are any claims from that cursed Regime. We will leave you now, but the doors of this orphanage must forever remain open to the Republic—lest another example is necessary."

**

Had she been screaming? Abrielle's eyes blinked furiously as she tried to banish the nightmare from her mind and regain her senses. She'd seen her again. Abrielle's breath came to her in uneven gasps as the memory of the dream played upon her sleep addled brain. Was she still dreaming? Her damp hair clung awkwardly to her forehead, and she ran trembling fingers against the strands. Her breath was slowing beginning to regulate itself as the familiar sights of her room came back into focus. She hadn't been visited by this nightmare in some months. What could have caused it? Abrielle coughed. She wished she'd kept the basin in the room filled. Her body was ripe with thirst.

The sun was just rising. Perhaps it would help keep the ghastly phantom at bay. But she doubted it. The image had stalked through her mind for over four years now. Every time it seemed to have faded back into obscurity, it rose again to make her relive that moment forever seared unwillingly upon her soul.

Sister Michelle returned in many forms, all of them upsetting; sometimes in Abrielle's dreams, the events played out as they had, other times, like tonight's ghost, were more disturbing. In this dream, Abrielle was in the orphanage church. Paul was there, dressed in fine clothes, and then all had gone dark. She'd been alone. No, not alone. A rasping sound had echoed through the sinister gloom of the chamber. Her name; it had hissed her name, and then from the shadows, the awful thing had come: Sister Michelle's body, devoid of its head, dripping with glistening streaks of blood. The clutching hands of that abhorrent corruption had sought her, but so had that rasping, disembodied voice, "Abrielle."

She clutched at the sheet for reassurance. It was a dream, only a dream. But Sister Michelle's death was not. That nightmare really happened, and she'd watched helplessly as the unfortunate woman was murdered before her. Death had been made real to her that day, and so was the certainty that she could not rely on the sanctity of the orphanage walls to protect her from the outside world. The lingering anger and guilt of that experience buried themselves deep within her, merging with all the unspoken sadness she repressed. The fact that for two years after Sister Michelle's death the gates remained open at all times only added to the children's collective anxiety.

The Republic had fallen, and the Thermidorean Reaction[8] and the Directory[9] had each respectfully arisen in its place. But uncertainty remained. France, both internally and externally, had been at war now for most of her life, the threat of invasion constant. Recently, though, military victories and economic reforms were easing the chronic food shortages. Reformers also worked to ensure that The Terror was never repeated, but the fear that it could would never leave those at the orphanage.

Paul had left three years earlier in an attempt to avoid conscription into the military. He wrote to her at first with regularity, but during the past year or so, she'd received no words of comfort from her friend. He hadn't even written her with birthday wishes this year. His last letter, which she'd all but memorized by now, informed her that he was going to try to find work in a city to the north called Bordeaux.

Abrielle sighed as she began to change. She'd seen so little of her own country, she wondered what life was truly like beyond the certainty of the world inside the orphanage walls. What did her future hold?

Soon she too would have to make her way in the world. To that end, she took to helping the nuns with a number of duties: tending the ill, teaching Latin or music lessons in the classroom, and translating letters and paperwork to name a few. She discovered a particular aptitude with languages and enjoyed working with them immensely. The words transported her beyond this mundane existence and allowed her to transform her identity as she wrote responses. She found this role playing quite appealing, but in many ways, it almost didn't matter what she did as long

8 1794 movement to end the Reign of Terror and punish its leaders.

9 French Revolutionary government from 1795-1799.

as her life remained her own and was not one led by another. Of course, nearly any job was preferable to the chore she'd been shipped off to aid with over the past few days.

There was a long standing tradition that in the fall the orphans were made available, for several weeks, to any local farmer who needed help harvesting crops. It was dirty, exhausting, thankless work with harsh hours spent in any type of deplorable weather conditions. Abrielle had been helping to harvest a wheat crop when she injured her ankle by stepping into an unseen gopher hole. An additional insult was garnered when she raked the offended ankle on a farming implement of some type, engendering a deep gash.

The injury was slowly healing, but at the moment, she still walked with a pronounced limp in the morning. Fortunately, it did seem to dissipate the longer she was up and moving, but the open wound had become extremely sensitive. Perhaps she would attempt bathing later today, though thc bath's condition often left one feeling less clean then when they entered. The farm work at least solidified a deep conviction in her that she would never embrace a life that forced her back into the fields.

She groaned slightly at the state of her hair. Normally it was rather straight, but either from the damp air in the countryside or sweat-inducing dreams, today, the wavy curl, which sometimes appeared, refused to be brushed out. Frustrated, she searched for a ribbon or tie but found none. Perhaps one of the girls would be willing to lend her one; besides, they were undoubtedly responsible for all of hers going missing. She'd been very glad when this single room became available, but sadly, the tiny lock did little to prevent the theft of even the most minor luxury.

After spending two hours helping to prepare for the midmorning meal, Abrielle attended service along with all the other members of the orphanage. She then spent several more hours in the laundry mending clothing and supervising some of the younger boys who volunteered to catch mice in the kitchens and storage rooms. Their zeal often surpassed their logic when they found one, and too often, items ended up being damaged if a close eye wasn't maintained. Still her fitful sleep and the physical demands she'd been under made her fatigued. She ended up dozing for a time beneath a tree, recently stripped naked of its leaves, outside the kitchen. She awoke to Sister Annette, who'd become the head of the orphanage, gently shaking her.

"My apologies," Abrielle said as she regained her senses. What had the boys broken while she'd slept? Surprisingly no chastisement came. In fact, Annette looked rather happy.

"Come with me please, Abrielle."

Confused, Abrielle stood up and began to follow her towards her office. Her limp returned after her nap, accompanied by a new burning sensation in her leg.

They entered Sister Annette's office to find two people seated within. The man, who now began to stand, was older but not yet old, of average height, and his face bore an expression she could not quite comprehend. The other occupant of the room, a pretty, young, blonde-haired girl, no older than ten, who gazed upon Abrielle with a mix of affection and wonder, remained seated. In the silence that reigned upon her entry, they regarded one another. Abrielle began to turn to ask Sister Annette what was going on when the man suddenly spoke. His voice trembled as he began, but it grew steadier as the words came forth. He addressed her in French.

"Bonjour, Abrielle. We've traveled a long way to see you … this is Ailis and I'm … I'm Quinn Tierney, your father."

Chapter 6
Becoming

Abrielle had never known that the heart and soul were capable of producing such wholly discordant feelings. In the seconds measured by the slave that is time, her world collapsed. How could this stranger come to her now, on the cusp of womanhood, and claim her as a child?

Yet, she wanted to be held, to be forgiven, to know acceptance, but this was wrong. Her father? And was this her sister? She'd been good enough for him to keep whereas Abrielle had not? Had the nuns kept all of this from her? The heat of betrayal turned her cheeks crimson.

Dreams were not meant to become real. But here was a vision of all she'd wanted twisted before her, mocking her. This man who hated her so much that he'd left her here. His own child; he'd left her! This brutal realization made her head dizzy. The grotesque demon from her nightmares materialized beside him like an angel of death. It was his fault. It was all his fault.

Suddenly all she'd endured in her life ignited into a white hot rage. The years of loneliness, fear, uncertainty, the confusion, the pain of one who has so shamelessly been cast aside consumed her heart. He didn't love her. He'd never loved her!

In three steps she reached this imposter, this monster, and slapped him as hard as she could. The bones in her hand vibrated with the impact, her heart sung with rage. Then she saw the expression of shock and horror etched upon the young girl's face. It mirrored Abrielle's own feelings of disbelief and confusion. The girl's soft face judged her without judging her, it calmed her; almost weakened her resolve, but she would endure no more betrayals. Her fate was her own, and she hated this man, hated the nuns, and refused to accept this false sister. It was all a cruel lie; she had no family.

Some primal force had been awakened. She felt no pain in her leg as she spun and fled from that horrible room. She needed to escape; this above all else mattered. Her steps came in rapid succession as she beat down steps, across cobblestones and over wood flooring. Her body felt light, nimble. Nothing around her seemed safe or familiar; Abrielle was motion without thought.

The few people she passed she ignored, her frenzied flight through the kitchen gained her a small knife, which she purloined before pounding down the rear stairwell to the storage loading area. A wagon, empty of all but a tarp and several barrels, was just pulling away. She leapt into the back unnoticed by the driver and quickly wormed her way beneath the heavy fabric. There hot tears erupted from her eyes, giving voice to the untold misery within. The emotional pain was blinding, and eventually, it led her into the dark embrace of sleep.

*

Abrielle awoke first in a state of utter bewilderment, which turned quickly to one of terror. Where was she? This was not home … the orphanage. By appearances she was in a cabin. Of more immediate concern, though, was the fact that she was tied to a bed. Should she cry out? No, that would most likely only bring the person who'd done this to her. What about the knife she'd stolen? As she tried to move her body, a sharp pain bit through her leg. The pain echoed and pulsed all the way to her temple. Her startled cry did bring someone.

"'Bout time," the woman snapped from the doorway before disappearing.

She returned almost instantly with a slightly inebriated-looking man who wore a blood-soaked bandage over one of his hands. Abrielle tried to control her fears but failed utterly, crying out urgently for help.

"Oh hush, girl. I won't hurt you again. But you didn't give me much choice the first time. We just want to talk to you. Besides, only the wolves will hear all that shrieking."

She ceased her shouting as the woman sat down a safe distance from Abrielle. The man seated himself beside her and continued to draw from the wine bottle in his good hand.

"Where am I? Are you going to hurt me again?"

"You hear that, Noel? No, ' course you didn't."

She stood slowly then bent over Abrielle and lightly touched a bruise on the girl's forehead. She studied her eyes a moment, then apparently satisfied returned to her chair.

"You don't remember me hitting you then?"

Her thoughts were a jumble. She shook her head curtly.

"Well, that's what happens when you stab a woman's husband."

She tapped Noel who waved the blood soaked hand at Abrielle and proffered her the bottle, which she immediately declined.

"I did that?"

"Yes, we know you came from the orphanage in Bayonne. What I want to know is why were you hidden in the back of our wagon with a knife?"

How could Abrielle hope to explain her actions?

"Place musta really gone down hill since I left, eh, Noel?" She shouted these words at the man who watched her closely then nodded at the joke.

"He's deaf?"

"Almost," the woman nudged him lovingly. "Never fall in love with a man who serves in an artillery battery. Sooner or later they all end up deaf as posts. 'Course if he hadn't, God knows if we ever would have met. Well?"

"I … I was running away," Abrielle stammered. Slowly memories were returning.

The first time she'd awoken was because of the unwelcome sensation of cold air rushing all over her body. She dimly recalled seeing Noel's surprised face over the side of wagon. That he was deaf helped to explain why her presence went undetected for so long. She'd taken no precautions in releasing her sorrows.

"Hitched a ride then because of that ankle?"

Abrielle nodded dumbly. The woman sat back in her chair.

"See Noel, you're lucky you married me and not that Gabrielle creature you were so taken with. It's these pretty ones who are always crazy."

Noel snorted, rolled his eyes, and shook his head as he took another deep draught.

"I'm not crazy," Abrielle said defensively.

"Hiding in strangers' wagons, stabbing people in the dark, trying to run anywhere on an ankle that swollen and infected, through the mountains no less; no, you're the portrait of sanity my dear," the other woman scoffed.

Abrielle looked away, tears threatening to fall again. Would this awful day ever end?

"Now, now, no need for that. You just gave us all a good scare and a rude greeting. Are you hungry?"

The shifts in the woman's mood were all happening so fast, but Abrielle did have to admit she was hungry.

"Noel, do something useful, ya great lug. Get us some bread, some of that stew, lots of water—we're soakin' that ankle—and wounded or not that's enough from the bottle for one night."

As the woman issued orders, Noel polished off the remainder of the bottle, but nodded in affirmation of her directives and headed somewhat listlessly out the door.

"Honestly," the woman shook her head, "like a child, any excuse, any excuse. Saints preserve me. What's your name then?"

"Abrielle."

"Anne D'Aoust." She threw back the blankets and studied Abrielle's ankle.

"How long have I been here?"

"A few hours, but the trip from Bayonne takes about four or so. Well, I don't know how long it's been like this, but you've got a nice infection thanks to that cut. But all's well. You happened to pick a former military nurse's husband to stab. I think we can have you mended up in a few days. Now, unless you intend to repeat that lunacy from earlier, I'll let you loose. But I'm locking this door tonight, understood."

"Yes, madame," Abrielle asserted.

*

The cat turned half-opened, questioning eyes upon Abrielle. Why had she stopped petting him? Abrielle hastily repositioned Edgar and began to stroke his fur again. Approval was offered by the resumption of the oscillating drones issued by the cat.

"Don't know why I tolerate that creature, never been partial to cats, but he does keep the bat population low in the barn, caught three last month alone. Strange creatures, bats. Sometimes fly right by your ear at dusk. At least you never had to worry about them at the orphanage, eh."

Anne prattled on as she raced through another round of sewing with Abrielle. Noel dozed by the fire.

"I swear that man goes through four pairs of work gloves per month:

ripping 'em, losing 'em, putting 'em in … never mind. You 'bout done there?"

Abrielle considered her attempt at mending a shirt, only to discover she'd somehow managed to attach it to the bed sheet. Both women laughed. Abrielle freed herself from the bedding, and on wobbly legs, crossed the room to retrieve the scissors Anne had deliberately left there. Her patient was doing much better, but the former nurse was determined to make her use the still-healing leg as often as possible.

"Didn't they teach you needlework at that place?"

"They tried. I usually was serving some type of penance during class, so I didn't learn much."

"You're too bright for that type of nonsense. Now look, spread the fabric here, pin it back if you need to, but keep the material loose. You don't want to cut it too fine in case you make a mistake. There, good, now run the needle through like I showed you. Okay, all right, but keep the stitches closer together."

Several times Abrielle suspended her task to keep Edgar's twitching tail out of the way, but this second effort was more successful. Her confidence boosted, she retrieved another item from Anne's basket to toil on.

For about an hour, neither spoke as they immersed themselves in their respective tasks.

"Don't take this wrong," Anne quietly began, "aside from the stabbing, I like having you here … beats talking to myself all the time, but Noel should be heading back to Bayonne in a week or so for some supplies."

Abrielle nodded but said nothing. For the past eleven days, she'd been spending a great deal of time pondering what was to come. She was actually quiet fond of Anne and Noel D'Aoust, eccentric as they were, tucked away here in the Pyrenees, but she knew she couldn't stay indefinitely.

The D'Aousts had already practically adopted her in the short time she'd been here. In some ways it was only natural, after all Anne herself having been raised in the very orphanage Abrielle had fled. She'd met Noel shortly before he'd been wounded and cared for him afterward. They fell in love and moved to the mountains hoping that war would never find them here. Their farm would never make them wealthy, but it kept them fed, and so they returned a portion of that bounty to the orphanage in Bayonne several times a year.

Strange that she should come to find a family after so soundly rejecting another. Numerous times now she'd draw breath to confide in Anne the sordid details which had brought them together, but always she allowed the words to die unsaid. It was better that they evaporated, forgotten.

Did Abrielle fear that Anne might talk her into returning to the orphanage? Perhaps that was it. Or did she worry that to confide in her, to allow her guard down, might serve to bring them closer and prevent her from leaving? She struggled to understand her own poor heart.

"Anne … have you ever been to Bordeaux?"

Abrielle kept her eyes fixed upon the dance her fingers were contriving between needle and thread.

"Oh, might have passed through now and again when I was around your age. I think some of Noel's old military friends might live up that way. Why? You have a friend there. Family?"

"Maybe," Abrielle said quietly.

*

The embrace altered again. It began as the unexpected, jubilant reunion of old friends who had been separated a long time. She opened her senses fully to him. His clothes smelled of sweat and tobacco smoke; his hair tickled her ear. As it continued, their grasp softened with the growing awareness of the proximity of their bodies. Unspoken thoughts and feelings caused their muscles to shift, but neither relinquished the other.

Now that Abrielle opened her eyes, she discovered that they were staring into those of the perturbed young woman who'd been seated on Paul's lap when she had first entered the backroom of the *Liberte' Jardin Salon*. Abrielle held the woman's gaze, but she must have unconsciously begun to break her embrace with Paul, who sensing the change, released her, but not before kissing her on both cheeks.

"I didn't think I'd see you again. How did you find me?"

Abrielle held the other woman's gaze a moment longer before returning her attention fully to Paul.

"Are you kidding? I always find you," she proudly reminded him.

He grinned at her and waved someone over to place a request for food and drink. The woman shot Abrielle one last look of warning before moving off and to work on tuning her harp. Paul pulled out a seat at a nearby table for Abrielle then seated himself, running fingers through his hair repeatedly as if he was just waking up.

"So you're a performer now, a musician?"she asked as her eyes played about the room.

He nodded smugly.

"Play here, eat here, sleep in my own room upstairs. I love this place."

Abrielle smiled. This was about as happy as she'd ever seen him. Perhaps bringing her problems to him was the wrong idea.

"So what brings you here? Seriously, did they kick you out or something?"

She hesitated.

"I … it was time for me to leave and … I'm in trouble, Paul. I ran away. I have a little money, but you're the only one I could …"

He took her hand.

"No, no, of course," a slightly hesitant smile graced her lips as he continued. "They always need some sort of help around here. I know old Le Hir will be able to give you some type of work."

They argued for several minutes over who would pay for the food when it arrived and finally decided that each paying half made the most sense. In truth, Abrielle had not eaten this well in sometime. She'd separated from Noel in Bayonne when he went inside a shop to buy some wares. She'd left the D'Aousts a note thanking them for their kindness, promising that she would both write and repay their generosity in full.

By now winter's presence stalked the French countryside, and early on in her trip, Abrielle decided to travel along the coast. Anne had provided her with a map and hidden some money inside the traveling cloak she'd given to Abrielle and would undoubtedly be quite cross with her the next time they met for abandoning Noel in such a manner, but it was necessary. Now if he was pressed by anyone at the orphanage regarding her whereabouts, he could honestly say he did not know. That is if he said anything at all; in the month they'd spent together, she couldn't recall the giant man ever uttering a word.

As plates began to arrive, laden with generous portions of food, she thought of how so many of her recent meals had been obtained. Abrielle tore into the bread, devoured the ham, and savored the cheeses. She hadn't realized how hungry she truly was until she looked up and noted that Paul had only eaten a fraction of what she had. He said nothing but poured her some more wine. She was already feeling its soothing influence on her nerves. Her body relaxed, and for the first time in two weeks, she allowed her spirit the luxury of doing so.

Abrielle was a thief. She'd performed the occasional transgression at the orphanage, everybody had, but her solitary journey forced her to develop a new degree of skill. Wherever possible she'd slept in barns and stolen eggs. The coastline was richly inhabited with fishermen, and she took to watching them, waiting for when they headed out to sea and then breaking into their homes. Everything she needed she took: food, wine, clothing items, blankets to cover herself, and once even a valuable looking ring. She felt no real guilt; if they'd lived with her in the orphanage, they wouldn't have burdened their souls over the loss of such trivial things. People stole from one another, be it physically or emotionally, and that's the way it was. She'd only had one close call when she fell asleep in a cabin, and by chance or fate, managed to awaken and escape seconds before discovery. It was terrifying but thrilling at the same time.

But now she was warm, safe, well-fed, and full of questions for her friend.

"So what is this place? A tavern?"

"Oh, no it's more than that. These salons are intellectual meeting houses; they're a holdover from before the Revolution. 'Course with Napoleon's edicts, who knows where this country is heading now," he commented coolly.

Abrielle grinned at his seriousness. The Paul she'd known would never have concerned himself with such matters. She knew little about their new ruler, only that he seemed to promise hope for a more secure future. Anne and Noel had told her a little about him, but mutual lack of genuine knowledge about the man had made their conversations brief.

"Well, he's only been in power for a month or so," she said dismissively. He wasn't a Jacobin, and to Abrielle, that's all that mattered.

Paul appeared to be having second thoughts about the whole conversation as his eyes darted around the room. Abrielle presented him with a somewhat puzzled look, but he made no further comment on the subject of Napoleon Bonaparte; instead, he left to go speak to the salon's owner,

Le Hir, about her staying on.

"Hey, come here." At first Abrielle didn't realize she was being spoken to, let alone who the speaker might be. She was surprised when she turned to discover the young woman with the harp waving her over. Reluctantly, Abrielle rose and walked toward the young woman who absentmindedly plucked strings as her rival approached.

"Paul is talking to Le Hir," she stated, her head nodding in the direction of the men. "Are you planning to stay?"

"If possible, for now," Abrielle replied disdainfully.

The woman laughed softly as her fingers began to pluck the strings more purposefully.

"You have a talent then?"

"What?"

"A talent. Le Hir only keeps those around with talent, as does Paul," her fingers suddenly raced across the strings, eliciting a series of beautiful, lively notes. She abruptly ceased her playing, stopped the strings from vibrating, stood, and nodded for Abrielle to try. Abrielle primarily knew how to play the orphanage organ. But music was music; how hard could the harp be?

As she began to play, she quickly discovered that she could find some notes, but on the whole, found the instrument itself to be cumbersome. Her mind kept trying to turn the instrument into an organ, and so her hands played it as such. The result was an awkward and unwelcome noise. Pride kept her going until Paul came and touched her shoulder. Le Hir had not come with him.

"He said you can take cloaks at the door if you promise to never play that again."

*

For the first few months she worked at the *Liberte' Jardin Salon*, she saw very little of Paul. After spending days canvassing the town in search of him, this was more than a little disappointing. She worked in the front tavern of the salon, taking cloaks, serving drinks from the bar, placing food orders, helping in the kitchen, and occasionally showing some people into the backroom where Paul worked. He kept strange hours, and though they remained friendly towards one another, they also remained distant.

At first she shared a room with two other girls who also worked at the salon. Though they were pleasant enough to her, they too kept her at a distance and were often too involved in their own affairs to take much notice of her. Abrielle often felt as if no one really trusted her. Perhaps it was the environment they all worked in. While the front was often hot, loud, and crowded, the back was rather poorly lit, with a much smaller crowd, which often stopped talking the moment she entered. Paul and the other musicians, though, sometimes took part in these conversations; while other times, they seemed to play music to mask the discussions going on in the room.

She also noticed that Paul and the young harp player, Amelie, were very often together: touching and laughing. His aloof manner and insensitivity kept her up many nights brooding. How could he be so blind, so self-centered? Hadn't he felt something as well when they'd held each other after so many years apart?

Apparently he hadn't. She really was alone. Her sense of isolation and bitterness was only reinforced when she dwelled upon thoughts of the D'Aousts or the young blonde girl from the orphanage. For some reason, the child's mutual expressions of love and shock seemed to have permanently affixed themselves to her mind. Had she made a horrible mistake by rejecting their kindness so quickly?

During this lonely time, one of her roommates, Sarah, took pity on her and acceded to Abrielle's request that the girl teach her how to play the flute. Abrielle viewed this as a means to acquire a useful skill she could barter and as a rare chance to socialize. Sarah split her time between the backroom and the tavern, playing in one and serving in the other, though most of the time, all she really seemed to do was flirt with the clientele. Despite her efforts, Sarah, while offering her quality instruction, would remain primarily disinterested in getting to know her roommate.

The acquaintance was, however, to yield other benefits Abrielle could not have foreseen. When she left nearly three years after her arrival at the *Liberte' Jardin Salon*, she would be more or less proficient with at least six instruments and closer to Paul than she ever could have dreamed.

One afternoon Le Hir pulled her aside from her regular duties. Somewhat surprised, Abrielle followed him obediently into the backroom. It was devoid of any one but the compliment of players, all of whom bore mixed emotions of anger, apprehension, or fear.

"What's happening?" Abrielle inquired of Le Hir.

The man turned from her and picked up a flute.

"Can you play this?"

Abrielle hesitated, uncertain of what to say. Her last attempt to play an instrument impromptu had all but expelled her to the more menial duties of the salon.

"I …"

"Speak up, girl. I need a player tonight. Are you capable yes or no?"

Le Hir practically thrust the instrument into her hands. The players present waited apprehensively for her to make a decision. Amelie glowered at her. Abrielle looked to Paul, but his noncommittal expression left the choice up to her.

"I'll try," she nodded.

Relieved having some decision reached, the other players assumed their instruments as Abrielle sat down at an indicated chair and studied notes. Her fingers moved unconsciously over the holes of the instrument as she read. Paul began to count, and suddenly, the unanticipated audition commenced.

The music was airy and upbeat, and Abrielle was surprised when after barely playing more than a minute, they all stopped abruptly. Le Hir was waving his hand.

"She'll do. Get her ready for tonight."

His instructions concluded, the salon owner vanished quickly to attend to other matters. A few of the players murmured reserved congratulations before they too vanished. Paul remained, as did Amelie. He touched Abrielle's shoulder gently.

"That was fine, but we've got a lot of work to do before tonight."

Abrielle smiled at him momentarily before remembering the odd circumstances which had finally brought them together.

"Where's Sarah? I mean, she didn't sleep in the room last night but …"

Paul shook his head and began to walk back to his bass.

"That tramp won't be coming back."

"Amelie!" Paul warned.

She ignored him.

"She's pregnant, hid it from all of us for three months. Le Hir didn't even know."

"Sarah mentioned she's been instructing you," Paul interjected as he delivered a look of recrimination toward his harp player. She did not seem fazed by his chastisement as she began to reprimand Abrielle.

"You have to do a better job with your count; it's throwing the rest of us off our time…what are you smiling about?"

Abrielle tuned the unpleasant young woman out. This was her moment to savor. For the first time since leaving the orphanage, she felt truly needed.

"Come on, Amelie, go fetch the others. We've only got four hours," Paul observed, "to get the show ready."

"What show?" Abrielle innocently inquired.

*

Realization came to her in stages, and it was not until her seventh full performance that the epiphany was reached. The first three performances had her completely baffled as they made no sense, told no story, alternated wildly between music, conversation, and spontaneous dancing. Each was played out as if she were within an asylum show for lunatics.

When each performance was over, the select patrons, who'd been invited to attend, left using five separate entrances, and the players often packed up and left just as quickly. Being the newest member of the group, it was her inevitable task to pick up the room after all of the occupants had vacated. Paul seemed pleased with her musical talents, but offered no insights into these strange performances.

As she cleaned one of the tables alone after the third show, Abrielle made a surprise discovery. A piece of paper had been set alight using the candle at the table; however, it failed to burn completely. After casting about momentarily to make certain she would be unobserved, Abrielle picked up and studied the writing. It was a series of glyphs, numbers, and words taken from an assortment of languages.

Abrielle recognized it for what it was immediately; still it did not help to explain its presence. Were they being spied on or had someone in this room been spying on another? Could she hold some vital directive or damaging observation? If it were an encoded observation, made in jest between highly educated friends, could it merely be offering testimony that the show was a nonsensical disaster? She tried to picture who had sat at the table earlier and found herself unable to do so. Going against her natural inquisitiveness, she set the paper to the flickering flame, which enveloped it immediately.

The next show, she allowed herself the luxury of indulging her curiosity by carefully studying then committing to memory every face in the room; her efforts were to be rewarded the following show. She found it most interesting that all but three of the audience members that night had been present during the fourth performance. Even more intriguing was that while their performance was being carried out onstage, an entirely different play seemed to be being acted out among the audience. It was primarily nonverbal: hand motions, well-timed coughs, subtle nods, but all of these impacted the performance onstage. During the sixth show, she realized that patterns in these actions did play out. Her suspicions had been correct—the real show was being acted out by those surrounding the stage, but for what purpose?

One night she returned to her room only to discover that it had been vandalized. No, there was intent here, her mind told her as she studied the sliced mattress, rummaged clothing, and the dispersal of her other few possessions. Immediately she sought out Paul, who for once was separated from Amelie. He was drinking alone at the bar.

"Someone's torn my room apart," she shouted into his ear over the din.

He shrugged and nodded but made no further comment until she informed him that it had obviously been searched.

"Let's go for a walk," he suggested without waiting for her to agree. Paul grabbed her by the wrist and coaxed her quickly out the door.

It was summer, and the warm evening air revived her senses. When she began to talk, he walked faster, forcing her to keep up. He seemed to meander aimlessly, yet, purposefully away from the salon. They walked for sometime in relative silence before he shoved her roughly down an alley, which after a series of sharp turns, deposited them on the outskirts of Bordeaux. He looked about, and when satisfied that they were alone, confronted her.

"You didn't see anyone?"

"Paul, what's …?"

"Is it just your stuff or Sarah's too? Was anything missing?"

The questions and the situation in general were beginning to annoy her.

"I don't think anything's missing," she stated questioningly.

"You shouldn't have come to me with this. I don't want to be involved."

"I only came to you because I thought you cared," she said, backing away.

"Where are you going?"

"Back to clean up. You don't want to be involved, I'll handle it," Abrielle declared sharply.

"Abrielle … wait."

"I'm done waiting."

"What do you want from me?! I got you a job. You're not on the streets like I was," he reminded her.

"Who knows, I might have been better off than working with a bunch of spies!"

Paul froze for a moment, an unpleasant expression settling on his face. Abrielle shook her head and turned to run, but he grabbed her by her hair. He forced her against a wall, and she felt the cool metal of a blade against her back. She wanted to cry out.

"Did you kill her?"

"What? Who?" Her mind was racing.

"Sarah."

The young woman's image swam through her mind. Sarah was dead?

"Amelie said she was preg …"

The knife pressed harder.

"Did you? Did you figure it all out and tell your master, huh?"

"No," Abrielle sobbed, "no! Let me go, Paul, let me go. I don't know anything, I don't know …"

He released her and tried to kiss her forehead. She smacked him and sat down against the wall. Her nerves all seemed to be working out of sync. How could Paul have done this to her? She picked up a handful of gravel and hurled it at him. She was about to throw another handful when he grabbed her wrist, forcing her to drop them harmlessly to the ground.

He grinned at her as if they'd just finished one of their old childhood games.

"I had to be sure. I told the others, but I had to be sure it wasn't you. You're not that good of a liar."

"No, that's your specialty," she shot back accusingly as he reached down and offered her a hand.

"Fine. You're right. I ransacked your room. But I didn't lie about Sarah."

"She's dead?" Abrielle asked in disbelief.

"Yes."

Abrielle allowed him to help her up.

"When?"

"Several weeks ago. Throat slit. Le Hir found her behind the salon."

"Why would you think it was me?"

"Oh come on, Abrielle. You show up out of nowhere, try to have Sarah teach you music to get you into the backroom, and then she turns up dead all of the sudden."

"I didn't have her teach me the flute to get into the backroom, I did it because ...," she couldn't bring herself to admit her feelings, "because I couldn't live like I had to before." That wasn't completely true either.

"What, as a penniless girl working for nuns?" Paul studied her face.

"No, as a thief," she said as she met his probing gaze.

The last word echoed dully down the entrance to the alley. Paul's expression suddenly changed from serious and sarcastic to outright bemusement. He began to laugh uncontrollably. Did he consider her that inept a thief? Regardless, his amusement on her behalf enraged her. She began to stalk toward him to make her feelings known when he suddenly waved her off and regained control of himself.

"Oh … oh, Abrielle. You work in a den of thieves."

CHAPTER 7
THE SLEEPING FLOWER GIRL

Abrielle sighed deeply. She didn't want to get up, not yet, not with him so close beside her. She turned to draw herself closer to him only to find the warm depression in which he'd lain vacant. It was the small fire kindling in the fireplace beyond that warmed her, not Paul. She closed her eyes and recalled the days when he would have been here, kissing her awake, embracing her, telling Abrielle he loved her. Those days were not gone, but their relationship was changing. Too often as of late, she greeted the dawn alone.

Something was troubling him; she propped his pillow up behind her, drew her long legs up to her chin and rested her head upon her knees. Her fingers absently began to trace paths across her skin the way Paul often did as she sought to reassure herself. No, she didn't want to be awake and face the questions that always seemed to plague her on mornings such as this. She and Paul had been together now for over two years, but where were their lives going?

She looked out the window at the autumn sunlight, which was in its own test with time. It was on a day such as this that she'd fled the orphanage and those who would have claimed her as family. By now she'd all but banished the memory of the man from her mind, but the young blonde girl remained. Where was she now? Did she ever wonder what had become of Abrielle or was that unwritten chapter of her life closed? Initially, Abrielle felt only shock and bitterness towards her, a favored child, blessed with all Abrielle had been denied.

But the memory of that girl's look of shock and disappointment also remained. It connected them. Abrielle could see it clearly in her mind nearly every time she and Paul robbed someone, and slowly the guilt it caused was becoming more difficult to deny.

Still balled up, she rolled to one side and faced the fireplace. By now she and Paul's system of pickpocketing was fully perfected and they were becoming quite adept at burglarizing homes. Their target of choice simplified the matter. They robbed the summer residences of the social elite during the winter and their urban dwellings during the summer.

Napoleon's policies and the legacy of the Revolution put certain controls upon the wealthy and influential, but did not eradicate them as a social class. Therefore, the Revolution's fervent quest for equality and justice for all still had yet to be realized.

Paul did not like Napoleon. In point of fact, he quietly detested him. He and the rest of Le Hir's regulars in the back room of the salon spent endless hours railing against Bonaparte's policies, which they maintained threatened to destroy all of the progress gained through the Revolution. It was not a wholly unfounded argument. The First Consul seemed to issue new laws and philosophical views on everything: economics, religion, civil law, education, the press, and the rights of women, slavery, and war to name a few.

The French armies which once fought in defense of their homeland now marched across Europe and even Northern Africa on missions of conquest, purportedly meant to spread the freedoms of the Revolution. His most recent threat to invade England inspired a new level of paranoia in both his followers and enemies alike. Under his rule, France continued to rise in prominence and wealth as country after country submitted to his superior military tactics and adhered to his edicts.

As he rose in power, Napoleon began to limit access to it for others, while maintaining that any man who seized the mantle of enlightenment as he had was blessed with limitless opportunities. But those long-promised opportunities, first from the Revolution and now Napoleon, had yet to filter down through French society and be fully realized by all her citizens. Paul was constantly worried about potential spies, rumored to operate at every level of French society. Given the principle business interests of both her and Paul and the regular clientele at the *Liberte' Jardin Salon*, it was a legitimate concern.

The salon's chief business was to serve not only as a gathering place for political discussion, but also as a negotiating center for those trading goods and services on the black market. Since politics and illegal trade often went together, it was indeed a dangerous business to be in, especially as Napoleon's power grew. Their "shows" were actually an elaborate means of conveying information between clients for the negotiation or purchase of stolen goods. Additionally, they could also be used to mask the more direct discussions occasionally undertaken by the black market barons or serious political debates. Abrielle's role, as one of the players, had expanded greatly since those early days, and she now was in charge of altering the codes on a regular basis in case any French agents were watching. Her linguistic skills, ever increasing musical abilities, and dramatic flair made her a natural for such a job.

She and Paul should have been happy. They were comfortable, enjoyed one another's companionship, and were growing increasingly wealthy through their ill-gotten gains. But lately the success and security she craved only served to emotionally separate them. Did Paul truly not wish to be with her? They continued to discuss the subject of marriage, but despite their years together, they still refused to embrace it. Now it loomed silently over them, creating doubts and fears about their present and possible future relationship. But there were other things as well.

Though no longer working at the salon, Amelie continued to serve as a rival for Paul's affections. And although she could never prove it, Abrielle believed that Paul had cheated on her with Amelie on more than one occasion. Could he be with her now?

Abrielle shifted uncomfortably in bed. He'd been extremely distant for over a month. Might Amelie be to blame? Sometimes these thoughts obsessed her so that Abrielle had even gone so far as to try to spy on Paul, but quickly concluded that she'd never be good at it. Such things took patience and devotion to the task at hand, and deep down, Abrielle wasn't sure she wanted to know the truth. Paul was all she had in this world. She stretched out her body; the cool air tickled her naked skin. She was hungry.

An unexpected blast of very cold air forced her to seek refuge under the blankets again as Paul rushed into the room bearing a large satchel. She shot him a look of annoyance, which changed when, with great ceremony, he withdrew an apple and brought it close to her lips. She smiled at their personal joke and took a bite. He sat down, turned, and began to unpack more items from the bag. Abrielle brushed her hair's brown strands away from her face and draped her arm over his shoulder, resting a hand on his chest, and kissing his cheek. He kissed her arm but made no further comment.

"Is that fresh?"

"It was twenty minutes ago. It's pretty cold out though, so don't blame me if it's already hard."

Abrielle pressed her fingers to a loaf of bread.

"No," Abrielle shook her head as she chewed another bite of apple. "No, it can't be worse than … than that bread they used serve us on soup day."

"Yeah, soup day," Paul mused. "I'd forgotten about those."

She rolled her eyes.

"One of the cooks told me that those were a week's worth of unsold loaves leftover from one of the Bayonne bakeries. I'm amazed we never chipped any teeth. Oh, did you mail my correspondence?"

"Don't I always?"

"I know you do," she hugged him, "I just enjoy knowing that the D'Aoust's are getting …"

"Stolen money? Black market profits? Ill-gotten gains?"

She hit him lightly.

"It's the least I can do."

"Actually, the least you can do is to send them nothing."

Paul would never understand her connection to the D'Aousts and complained nearly every time she asked him to post a letter laden with money. It was beginning to wear on her. She quickly changed the subject lest it lead to another argument.

"What else did you bring me? What time did you leave anyway?"

"5:30, maybe," he shrugged.

"So early?"

"I had to see someone."

At this, Abrielle abandoned her attempt to maintain a good mood in front of him.

"Who? Amelie?"

"It was just business," he shook his head in annoyance. "I needed some information. I could only work out a trade for some of that silver we picked up from that estate last month, so it took a while to get it all."

"Which pieces?" Her eyes narrowed.

"Ah, let's see, well, two of the platters, a couple of the serving sets, and that tea pot with the little design on the one side."

"Paul! You never even asked me about those. I was planning to use them when we …"

He turned a fraction, his eyebrow arching somewhat. She'd personally taken those pieces so that one day, when they owned their own home, she'd have an elegant serving set.

"I didn't trade the candlesticks," he said by way of apology.

She pulled away from him and wrapped herself in a sheet.

"So what was so important?" she demanded.

"Hhhmm?"

"You said you traded for information. What's so important?"

"Don't worry about it," he said dismissively.

Satisfied with his inventory of the bag's contents, he stood up and let the bag clatter to the floor. As he returned to the bed, she turned her back to him. He tried to kiss her exposed shoulder, but she pulled the sheet up.

"What's wrong with you?"

"Nothing," she said curtly.

"Look I'm sorry about the silver …"

"It's not the silver," Abrielle forcibly asserted.

"Then what?" Paul quietly asked.

She turned to face him.

"It's maddening to be so close to you but to have so little."

Paul blinked.

"What's that supposed to mean?"

"You and your damn secrets; that's what I mean!"

"Oh God, is this about Amelie again? Dammit, I wasn't with her."

He was breathing hard. Abrielle closed her eyes a moment before continuing.

"It's not about me," Abrielle said quietly, "it's about us."

Paul turned away when she opened her eyes. She began to gently massage her temples with her fingertips.

"Maybe I'm protecting you … maybe there are things going on that are bigger than us."

"We lead a dangerous life, and I can accept that as an excuse up to a point, but don't you want more than this? Paul, I'm happy with you. I love you. I'm just not always sure you feel the same."

"What, bringing you breakfast in bed isn't enough?"

She held the sheet over her breasts as she stood up, pushing her hair behind one of her ears. Her sad, troubled eyes gazed searchingly into his. She would not be denied.

"What's troubling you?" she softly asked.

The moment breathed in time unto itself. She took his hand and kissed it.

"Please, Paul."

He sat down with her on the bed and held his head. Abrielle began to rub his back soothingly.

When he finally spoke, he muttered his words so badly, she was compelled to gently prod him to repeat them. There was no mistaking them the second time.

"I think I found my parents."

Her hand came to rest on his back; the only sounds of life in the room came from outside.

Paul shook his head to the unspoken question in her eyes.

"It's complicated … I, I'm not even sure if …"

He looked away, his voice choked with emotion. As his spirit faltered, Abrielle pressed herself against him. He'd finally reached out to her; they would find a way. Love and fear united their passions well into the afternoon.

*

"It was back in August, when we were having problems. I was trying to fence those paintings we stole in June."

"The ones from Agen? Is that how you paid for the dress?"

Paul kissed her tenderly. She grinned at the memory of his expensive gift.

"I used one of Rivard's contacts, strictly a small timer, but very efficient. We met in Limoges, and everything was going well until he set eyes upon one of the paintings. He studied it forever: the frame, the brushstrokes, even the way the light brought out the color. Then bold as anything declared that he knew who the painting belonged to."

"Was he going to blackmail you?"

"That was my first thought, but then he began to study me; my face, that is, and nodded a lot."

"What was in the painting?"

"A portrait of some type; to be honest I didn't even remember taking it. We'd put quite a few already in storage, but I'm fairly certain it came from Agen. Besides, the other paintings all seemed much more valuable to me, so I never really paid much attention to it. Rivard's contact claimed to have once been a servant in the household it was from. He said one of his duties had been to dust all of the paintings, so eventually he remembered each to the last detail."

Abrielle considered the possible validity of this as Paul continued.

"He pointed out some scratches on the frame. He said the marks were made when they'd hurriedly moved the paintings to a country estate just before the Revolution broke out."

"But he wouldn't tell you whose?"

"Exactly, he only said that if I was the one who'd taken it then it was poetic justice. I shouldn't have let him see how interested I was. He offered to tell me more but only if I could get him a large quantity of quality silver for another client of his. That's where I was this morning."

She hugged him.

"Why didn't you tell me?" Her head cupped possessively over his shoulder.

"I wasn't sure what to do. I went back to Agen two weeks ago but had trouble finding the place again."

"Oh, that's right, we robbed that one at night," she recalled as she sat back up.

"Yeah, and apparently it's had more than a few owners since the Revolution."

Abrielle propped her head up with her hand.

"So he told you this morning?"

Paul nodded with vacant eyes.

"How do you know he wasn't lying?" she asked.

"It's the only thing that makes sense," he replied after a prolonged pause.

"What is?"

"Okay. I know you don't like to talk about this, but I have to. The day the Jacobin mob came to the orphanage, Sister Michelle and Sister Annette were gathering us up in the church, right?"

He was right. She never liked talking about that day, but she nodded. She needed to hear this.

"Now I can't remember every name they said, but there were five or six of us, including Marie'. Both Michelle and Annette mentioned that they needed to hide us. Annette even wanted to show them the mass burial grave and all that."

It was coming back to her but slowly. At the time, she'd assumed that they were simply trying to hide any children who they could find, but reflecting on it all now, they had focused primarily on the safety of a few.

"Then out in the courtyard, they asked Sister Annette and Michelle where the aristocratic children were."

"I remember," Abrielle's voice was heavy with breath.

"It was us," Paul finished.

Abrielle's mind couldn't accept this. She sat up and turned from him.

"They lied," Paul asserted.

"What?" she asked incredulously.

"Sister Michelle told them that the records were gone and that all of the kids had been given new names. But what if they didn't destroy the records and our names are our own? Then the Jacobins might have found our names on some list at the orphanage and killed us that day."

Abrielle was barely listening. If all this were true then Sister Michelle had died to save them—to save her. She felt numb and repulsed. She wasn't worth saving; why had Sister Michelle done it? Why hadn't Annette told Abrielle the truth afterward? She'd always pitied the woman after the terrible events of that day and tried to be friendly toward her. Was this betrayal of Abrielle her thanks?

"Rivard's contact told me this morning that the painting belonged to a family called Cheval. They're aristocrats from Tours."

Paul, an aristocrat; could his theory be correct; could all this mean that Abrielle was also French aristocracy? It suddenly seemed possible. But unlike Paul, she'd never been christened with a surname. Why was she so undeserving of one? She thought back to the man and his daughter at the orphanage. What had his surname been … Tierney? They certainly were not nobility. Which was the truth? Could she actually be the daughter of French nobility or could that man have really been her father?

She felt Paul wrap an arm around her bare waist.

"We should get some dinner," she declared as she pushed his arm away.

"I'll go down and get something in a few minutes," Paul promised. "So what do you think?"

"About what?" she absentmindedly replied.

Paul laughed.

"All this," he waved an arm expansively, "it's like a fairy tale. Trade a troll some silver and find out you're a prince."

"Please, Paul, I really am hungry," she intoned.

"Hungry, huh?"

He tried to kiss her, but she pulled away. His levity in the face of all this was unnerving.

"This isn't a story, Paul. Every time the past has come looking for me, it's only brought pain: first Sister Michelle, then those people at the orphanage, and now this."

"It also brought us closer together," he pointed out after a moment.

Abrielle stared at him in disbelief as reality shone. Was he really this stupid?

"You want to find these people, don't you?"

"Why not?" He smirked.

She shook her head, went behind the screen, and began to dress, too upset to continue the conversation. Abrielle could hear Paul following suit on the opposite side.

"You don't want to give up the adventure, right?" he taunted.

The stitching on her dress' sleeve tore as she jammed her arm roughly into it.

"Abrielle, scourge of the law abiding," he declared, raising his voice.

She didn't even bother with stockings; instead, she hastily drove her feet into her shoes and began to tie her hair back. If this didn't stop, she really would murder him some day.

"… Angel of the Underworld," he continued.

"Enough!" Abrielle snapped.

The pain was too close to the surface for her to hold it in. She aggressively charged out from behind the dressing screen.

"They don't want you, Paul. They never did. Don't you see? For over twenty years, they could have come back for you. They didn't. There are no riches waiting for you, no country estate, only pain and rejection."

"How do you know?" he shot back immediately. "Your family came back for you, didn't they? Or half of them did anyway."

She was too stunned to speak. Paul pressed on seemingly indifferent to the effect his words were having.

"You never even found out why they left you there, did you. It's been an excuse to hide behind. It probably never occurred to you that maybe they didn't have a choice." He paused but she said nothing. "Well, I do. I'm going to Tours, and then we'll see what the Chavels have to say."

He stood and left the room, shutting the door firmly behind him. Humbled, Abrielle sank to the bed and stared blankly into the waning fire. She watched it die then sat alone in the dark. Paul did not return to her that night.

*

The rain finally stopped falling but left the sky trapped in a sea of harsh grey clouds. It mirrored the gloom within the small carriage. Abrielle shifted the travel blanket for what felt like the hundredth time. It kept slipping with the vibrations of the horse's hooves over the assortment of terrain they'd encountered. At long last they were near Tours.

"Could we eat before we see them?"

These were the first words either had spoken in several hours. By now they had argued to the point where silence was preferable. Paul did not immediately respond as he pretended to be busy concentrating on the road. She'd never been to Tours and honestly would have preferred to have avoided this trip all together. Uncertain of what to wear, both donned fine clothing, which each had to admit the other looked stunning in. For a time, they even called a truce as they put their differences aside to secure appropriate transportation, in this case, Le Hir's personal carriage.

Actually obtaining it was nothing short of a miracle. Le Hir was one of the most subtly paranoid men she'd ever met and always seemed to think those around him were about to betray him. Consequently, favors of any kind were always greeted with both suspicion and a liberal number of questions. They'd managed to convince him that Abrielle wished to see her great-aunt whose existence she'd only recently learned of. To this end, she'd forged several letters after rejecting the idea of passing off Anne D' Aoust's as evidence of the mythical aunt's existence. Ultimately the paper Anne wrote on was too cheap to make the ploy believable.

Still the carriage was an elegant conveyance with a well-cared-for mount to match. Paul seemed to need his parents to see that he too had made something of himself despite their potential disregard. But to Abrielle, the clothes and the carriage could only maintain the illusion for so long. She feared how he might handle the situation if too many questions were asked.

But then again, she herself was not thinking too clearly right now. In the days leading up to this trip, she'd found sleep all but impossible. Troubled dreams forced her awake and bid her to stay there lest she attempt to sleep and fall prey to their wicked ministrations once more. Her waking mind offered only similar tortures as she was forced to play out, over and over again, her final hour at the orphanage.

The anger, humility, deep sense of betrayal, confusion, bitterness, the desire to love and be loved wrapped themselves around the moment, forcing her to ceaselessly question her actions. She was angry with Paul for doing this, but it was an anger primarily fed by fear. He refused to believe that they wouldn't embrace him again as their own. Would he still need her after today, if his parents accepted him? Would he cast her aside?

Paul finally deigned to answer her question.

"I'll drop you off at a café."

Too hurt to respond, she turned her attentions out the window. The most important moment of his life, and he had no need for her support. Yes, he would cast her aside.

She felt his hand reach out for one of her gloved ones.

"Sorry. I should have stopped earlier," he said by way of apology.

Abrielle made a polite noise but said nothing more.

In twenty minutes, they'd located the Cheval estate. In ten she was standing on a street corner in the damp cold outside of a café, alone.

"Just eat and head back toward the house," Paul suggested.

She nodded.

"What, no kiss for luck?"

Reluctantly she leaned forward and briefly kissed his cheek. Moments later he was gone.

The simple meal of soup and bread was awkward as Abrielle was uncertain if she should take her time eating it or should rush so she could get to the Chevals faster. Much to her dismay, several of the café patrons took more than a passing interest in this unescorted, beautiful, immaculately dressed young woman. By the time she left, a respectable mist began to coat the somber world outside, but fortunately it also seemed to prevent even her most attentive audience members in the café from following her.

Lost in thought, she took several wrong turns and was compelled to retrace her steps in the inclement drizzle. By the time she reached a corner of the main road, the only thing she truly desired was to get out of the incessant mist. Fortunately, the building on this corner was bestowed with a sizeable overhang. Eagerly availing herself of its use, she leaned against the brick wall a moment and closed her eyes.

"Bonjour, mademoiselle, are you all right?"

Abrielle opened her eyes and was surprised to find a rather poorly dressed young blonde girl staring up at her. She carried a basket, which held an assortment of delicately wrapped flowers within it. The petals radiated a warm collage of vibrant colors. On such a drab day in which the world itself felt so weary, the child shone like a beacon of purity.

"Are you lost? You looked frightened just now?"

The genuinely concerned girl, no more than eight by Abrielle's estimate, gazed openly up at her. Abrielle smiled in appreciation of this small act of kindness. It was so rare in life and such a gift freely given to her by one so young. Something about this girl was warm, familiar, and Abrielle felt an abatement of her defenses. She lowered herself closer to the girl's eye level.

"I was heading for the Cheval residence and was lost for a time. Can you tell me if I'm headed the right way now?"

"Oui, it is beyond the bend," the cherub pointed cheerily. Her arm wavered a little as she shivered in the damp, cold air.

"Thank you. Were you on your way home?"

The girl sighed.

"No, I must try to sell these flowers or my father may lose his shop and our home."

"Your father's shop sells flowers?"

"No, Father makes candles but puts most of the money he makes into growing these flowers year round. You should see his gardens."

Abrielle smiled politely.

"Couldn't he just be a candle maker, and then you wouldn't have to be outside on a day like today?"

The girl shook her head.

"No, he lives for his gardens. He would not be happy, and I cannot disappoint him."

Abrielle was not normally one to fall for such stories, but she could sense no duplicity from this child. She began to barter for her flowers, smelling each variety as she chose. Her gloved fingers caressed the delicate petals. They had not wilted since being cut from their stems and exposed to the cold. She hoped it meant that the girl had not been outside for too long then. For her own part, Abrielle was becoming increasingly aware of the falling temperatures and moved to conclude the transaction by handing her a charitable portion of the coins she carried. The girl's eyes lit up.

"Thank you, mademoiselle," she leaned forward and spontaneously kissed the older woman on the cheek in gratitude for such unexpected generosity. The gesture touched Abrielle. Who did she remind her of?

"Go home," Abrielle ordered with a smile. The girl curtsied and began to walk away then stopped and removed the cloth, which protected the flowers in her basket and gave one freely to her benefactor. They'd just finished waving a parting farewell as the girl disappeared around the corner when Abrielle heard her name frantically being yelled.

"Abrielle! Abrielle! Hurry! We must leave!"

Paul was leaning out the side of Le Hir's carriage screaming so harshly that he distorted his words. Confused by both his words and actions, she began to chase after the carriage, which was wobbling wildly as he careened around the corner.

"NNOOO!!!" Abrielle wailed.

The surrounding buildings muffled the sound of the thundering hooves and the yelling. The girl never had time to move or to react with more than a look of shock and astonishment when death came. Abrielle rounded the corner only in time to cry out as she witnessed Paul's carriage run the young flower girl down. His attentions were fixed solely on Abrielle, and it was not until the wheels cleared the girl's fragile body that realization dawned.

Bright coins and colorful flowers highlighted the crimson stain created when the girl was drug first by the trampling hooves of the horse and then the slashing wheels of the carriage; so much blood for one so small. Abrielle's legs refused to move at first, held in place by the abhorrent sight before her.

The next minutes were largely a blur of sensation. Paul trying to restrain her, repeatedly pulling at her and yelling for her to come with him; the sound of running boots and heels, echoing off the stones of the road and the surrounding structures; the cacophony created by voices raised in alarm, grief, and anger; the warmth of the blood as it soaked through the fabric of her cream colored dress when Abrielle threw herself down beside the girl.

Unlike the rest of her body the girl's face was unmarred by the violence that had taken her life. It was tranquility; she was sleeping, just sleeping. It happened just as she'd rounded the corner and seen the girl's face that recognition finally came. This girl's loving manner, those eyes, her expressions, even at the moment of her death were those of another young girl she'd carelessly abandoned four years earlier. And the guilt of that choice rent her asunder. As others gathered around her, Abrielle clasped the bloody child in her arms and wept for the loss of such a sweet soul, for abandoning her sister, and for the first time in years, for herself.

*

"I've come to say good bye," Le Hir repeated. He was the first visitor come to see her in the four months she'd spent in prison and certainly one of the last people she could have foreseen coming to her. She was embarrassed that he'd come to see her. Abrielle was no more than a shadow of her former self. The harsh life of her younger days paled in comparison to this new reality.

She'd bathed no more than three times since her internment; her hair was now a molded mass that crackled when she slept on it. The frigid months and lack of food asserted a marked physical toll upon her as did her fellow prisoners. This morning, for instance, she bore another black eye, another earned in a ceaseless series of fights. She coughed nearly constantly now and itched with flea and rat bites. Worse still was the yawing emptiness within. She would never be happy again.

"Monsieur," she paused to clear her dry throat, "it is most kind of you to make such an effort on my behalf."

He made no response so she continued.

"I must apologize for not being wholly honest with regards to the use of your carriage. Was it very much damaged?"

She could barely meet his eye.

"It is serviceable now, though all the blood soaking the inside necessitated new seating be secured for it from Paris, no less."

Inside? The image of the dead flower girl returned to her. Le Hir waited. She sat up a bit.

"I do not doubt your word, Monsieur Le Hir but I cannot see how … blood from the accident could have soaked your seating."

She didn't get back in the carriage in her bloody dress did she?

"Accident? Good God. Do you think you have been imprisoned all this time because of that child in the street?"

Abrielle fully raised her swollen face to greet that of her former employer.

"Has no one told you that you are to die within less than a month by guillotine?"

Her lips parted in disbelief. Her eyes tore from his and uselessly studied the table they sat at while she fought to process his words. Finally, her own returned.

"If not for the flower girl then … then why am I to die?"

Le Hir leaned forward and looked evenly into her eyes.

"Why, for the murders of Madame and Monsieur Cheval, Abrielle."

CHAPTER 8
ENTERING ELYSIUM

She finished heaving into a bucket. Le Hir offered her his handkerchief. With trembling hands, she ran the cloth over her sweat and tear stained face. She clasped the bucket again, unable to breathe; the last minutes of Sister Michelle's tortured end assaulted her mind.

"I'm innocent," she gasped as Le Hir presented some water to her. She drank it reluctantly, "I know nothing of their deaths, only the child's."

Le Hir looked away, uncertain for the first time since their meeting had begun.

"Paul has testified otherwise," he reported.

Though she still trembled, her mind seized upon that name as a sailor in a tempest raged sea grasps flotsam.

"Paul," she whispered, "He said it was me? That I killed his …"

Le Hir nodded gravely, "Before he escaped two months ago."

For a long moment nothing happened. Then she flung the bucket into the nearby stone wall of the cell, smashing it. Guards rushed into the room, but Le Hir waved them off. She raged, pulled at her shackles, which were bound to the floor, until her wrists bled, and cried out in misery. Le Hir watched all of this silently only speaking again when her energies were largely exhausted.

"Now, I simply came to say good bye," he reminded her.

"Please, you have to help me," the last word was choked by sadness. She was alone. She was going to die. As he stood a change came over him.

"Help you? How could Le Hir help you? You've been dishonest about the nature of your trip; you've led the authorities he's worked so carefully to fool or bribe to his door and exposed his own criminal activities. He has knowledge of your own illicit activities, which could only hurt you further. No, he cannot help you. I already have."

Abrielle's head throbbed. What was he saying?

"What the devil are you talking about? You're Le Hir!"

"Correct. I am Le Hir." He waited a moment but his impatience got the better of him, "Oh come now, Abrielle, have four months here really dulled your mind so rapidly? I expected better."

This was insane.

"You're not Le Hir?"

The man favored her with a tight smile.

"Also correct. But who then is Le Hir, except a name? One of many I use as my purposes warrant. It will soon be discarded until it is needed again. But I still have work left to finish in his guise."

"Who are you?"

The question amused him.

"A surgeon, a butcher, a tavern owner, an artist, a false friend come to the aid of another of his kind; I am above all of these, a loyal servant to my master," the smile vanished, "My most important role, however, is as a shadow, with anonymity as my shield. That is how we survive."

"You're a spy?"

He nodded.

"One who has taken an interest in your talents and abilities. If not for them, you would already have been executed for the murder of the Chevals."

A flicker of hope stumbled through her heart.

"Then you believe me innocent?" she asked weakly.

"You are a known thief, a talented actress, in general as well as in the art of deception, a person who's established past is questionable at best, and your accomplice in crime has provided testimony against you. I have no reason to believe you. You are scheduled to die in two weeks for those deaths."

His pronouncement on her life angered her anew. Why toy with her like this?

"Then kill me! Other than prolonging my anguish, why keep me alive another two weeks?"

He slowly drank from Abrielle's cup of water.

"You maintain that Paul is guilty?" he inquired upon finishing.

"I never said that."

"There was never a need. If you are innocent, then he is guilty. I am giving you two weeks to prove either his guilt or your innocence. After that …," he waved a hand dismissively.

Her hope began to dwindle. How could she prove anything if Paul was gone? She'd only learned of the Chevals' deaths and her imminent end less than half an hour ago. She was no spy. Surely if this man was one, why had he been unable to find Paul during the past two months? What if he was lying about Paul? Who did she trust?

"I'm not sure I can," she shakily asserted.

"Then you offer me nothing and I will say good bye."

He rose to leave, turning his hat thoughtfully in his hands. She needed to be strong.

"I'll do it," the declaration raced from her in desperation.

He smiled thinly.

"You'll be released as soon as you've bathed and eaten. You will be watched so don't try to run. Two weeks."

Le Hir, whoever he truly was, made to leave.

"How will I find you?" Abrielle called to the retreating man.

"I will await you at the salon. If you are successful, we will discuss a new beginning for you. If not, your fate is fixed. Au revoir, Abrielle."

*

Sister Annette genuflected before the cross. The prevalent stiffness in her back made her motions awkward; she couldn't wait for spring to arrive. It was time. The damp days of autumn and winter always made her joints inflexible and those seasons unpleasant. She crossed the church and nodded to the last two of her order as they made for the exit.

As she approached the confessional, Annette reminded herself that she'd have to remember to douse all of the candles before locking up the church. Donations were slow this year, and their supply of candles was all but exhausted. Besides, Sunday services in the spring always seemed to attract more potential parents and she wanted to make certain their initial impressions of the orphanage were positive. Perhaps the priest awaiting her in the confessional would help her extinguish the taller ones.

She pulled aside the dark red curtain and sat down on the hard bench within.

"Bless me, Father, for I have sinned. It's been two weeks since my last confession."

Annette was momentarily distracted as she tried to recall all her recent faults, so the delay in the priest's reply did not register promptly.

"Father?"

Maybe he had stepped out.

"I know you have sinned," a harsh feminine voice suddenly intoned. Annette attempted to peer through the screening.

"Who's there?"

"I have a pistol aimed at you. Don't try to leave."

Annette heard a metallic click as the aforementioned weapon was armed.

"What do you want?" Annette managed after rejecting the notion of fleeing; the risks too great.

"Your confession," the voice cynically sneered.

"You're not a priest. You cannot absolve my sins I … I can't give it to you."

"I'm not interested in forgiving you," the voice said bitterly. "Step outside of the booth. We have sins to discuss."

With measured motions, Sister Annette slowly drew back the curtain and exited the confessional. A tall woman, dressed in red stood before her, the pistol she brandished shook only slightly in her outstretched hand. Her face was obscured by an impenetrable black veil.

"If you run or scream I will shoot," the figure vowed as she sized up Annette. "We're going to your office."

Dumbfounded, Annette turned towards the doors of the church.

"No. The back walkway and stairs will do."

How did this woman know about them? Only the nuns ever accessed them. As she walked, Annette's eyes roved over the burning candles which were familiar, flicking, and indifferent to her situation. The trappings of rituals she had long found comfort and strength in. Would she return to snuff them out? The stranger callously relieved the church of one before they proceeded out the back door.

The short trip proved uneventful. Still, the woman shoved her roughly into the room as soon as Annette finished unlocking the door. Seconds later they were locked within. The lone candle cast a myriad of shifting shadows, which were largely dispelled when the woman lit a lamp behind Annette's desk. Both sat down. The woman seated herself in Annette's desk chair. For a long moment, her unseen eyes studied the room silently. The only thing Sister Annette was studying was the pistol aimed at her.

"Please, my dear, there is no need for that."

The stranger's focus returned to her.

"That's right; you haven't been around many of these … except when the Jacobins came and that man struck you with one."

That voice. Annette's fears wavered as her resolve rose.

"Yes, they came, everyone knows that."

"Does everyone know about Sister Josephine's list?" the woman asked.

"There is no list," Annette promptly asserted.

As the seconds passed without retort, Annette's sense of uneasiness returned. The other woman seemed to relish this discomfort, indulging it fully before responding to the denial.

"Really? I haven't even mentioned what might be on it. I'm sure Josephine kept lists on any number of things, running an orphanage takes a lot of organization. Which list are you denying exists?"

Annette cursed her own lapse.

"It is no concern of yours."

"On the contrary, it is everything to me." The figure's free hand removed her veil. Annette was speechless. The girl looked so ghastly in the lamplight that one could have mistaken her for a ghost. But then again she was a ghost, raised from the past. Her pale complexion, only served to highlight the sickly, sunken eyes, one of which bore the traces of a disquieting bruise.

"Abrielle?"

Sister Annette didn't want to believe it was her. The girl was so changed.

"I want your confession," Abrielle said. "Give me the list."

"Your father's name isn't on it," she said quickly before adding, "he left a letter for you, though."

"I don't care about my father," the younger woman said harshly. "Tell me about the list. Where is it?"

"It won't help you find your mother."

Abrielle stood up and pressed the pistol firmly against the nun's temple. She could feel her pulse throbbing against the cold metal.

"Killing me won't help you."

"They'll kill me in two days if you don't," Abrielle said breathlessly, digging the metal in harder against Annette's head.

"Who? AH! All right, all right."

The pressure eased.

"It's in this room?"

Annette nodded.

"Get it."

Abrielle covered her with the pistol as Sister Annette retrieved the yellowed papers from behind a loose brick in the fireplace. Abrielle grabbed the pages from the nun and desperately searched for the name her life depended on. All her other attempts had failed. If she couldn't prove the connection, they would kill her. The man who continued to follow her every move since her release firmly convinced her of that. Her emotions surged as she read the twelfth name on the list. Paul had been right: he was aristocracy by birth, and he was a Cheval. She released a trembling sigh that echoed through her frame.

With a sense of grim determination, she continued to scan the pages for her own name. When she found it, the entry contained only her first name and the year of her birth; but her last name and the identity of her mother and father were burned from the page. A quick scan of the remaining pages revealed that only her last name had been obliterated.

"Why?"

"Sister Michelle knew …," Annette trailed off apologetically, grieving inwardly for the loss of her friend.

"I wasn't here when this was written, and I don't know why Josephine made that list. I think as the Revolution grew more violent she thought that if we had a record of your backgrounds, it would be easier to protect you. I know she hoped that some of the families who fled France might reconsider what they'd done and send for their children, but they didn't. All of you came to us for different reasons, and I'm sorry to say that some of your families never wanted to be reminded of your existence again."

Sister Annette paused a moment, uncertain if Abrielle was truly listening.

"They paid us to take you, some to annihilate all traces back to you. That may be why your last name is missing. Josephine and Michelle changed some of your names but kept others. Sister Michelle wanted to destroy the list outright but Josephine was reluctant. Michelle was working on memorizing it around the time the Jacobins came. After she was murdered, well, I couldn't bring myself to burn it, so I hid it. I meant to tell each of you about your backgrounds when you decided to leave, but each time it seemed like too much of a burden to unleash upon you as you were starting new lives. After your reaction to your father, I decided never to tell anyone."

Abrielle hardly heard Sister Annette's last words. Her father had at least returned for her. Did her mother's family hate her so much that they'd tried to erase her very existence? Is that what Paul had discovered about his own family, that he was nothing more than an unwelcome reminder of the past?

"Abrielle, what's happened to you?"

"I have to go," Abrielle said quietly, unable to even look at Annette now.

Numbly she requested that Sister Annette unlock the door. She began to do so then paused.

"Wait."

The nun went to her desk and began to hurriedly rifle though a stack of papers. It took several minutes but she managed to retrieve the letter Quinn Tierney had left for her to give to his daughter should she ever return. Abrielle glanced at the words and addresses inside, and without further comment, took it and Sister Josephine's list. She paused in the doorway.

"I was never here," she commanded, then left, determined she should never set foot in that terrible room again.

*

How long was he going to ignore her? Abrielle paced like a caged lion through the empty room. Well, not completely empty. Le Hir sat on stage seemingly untouched by her actions as he ordered the painter to continue crafting the mural he was working on. The artist, however, seemed genuinely relieved when another figure entered the room from backstage and Le Hir lazily waved the painter away. He left without even making eye contact with Abrielle.

The newcomer leaned over Le Hir and began to whisper into his ear. Occasionally both would glance at Abrielle as they spoke of her. The muted conversation must have ended with some type of joke at her expense for they both looked directly at her and exchanged a knowing laugh before the man departed. Le Hir waved for Abrielle to join him on stage.

"Le Hir is redecorating his former establishment," he waved expansively. "What do you think?"

Abrielle looked at the once familiar setting of the salon, now vacant of both its furniture and patrons.

"Interesting, will I get to see it when it's finished?"

Bemused, Le Hir smiled and held out his hand.

"What have you brought me?"

"Why don't you just ask your friend, or is he too busy holding that pistol on me behind the curtain to tell you," she challenged.

This time he laughed. It was the first time she could ever remember the man doing so.

"Call it a final rite of passage. What gave him away?"

"Nothing. I simply don't trust you."

"Good. Never do. But I am pleased you understand our natures."

His companion stepped out from behind the curtain and searched Abrielle for any hidden weapons. He took Josephine's list from her, handed it to his master, and vanished as Le Hir indicated that Abrielle be seated in the vacated artist's chair. He studied the list without commenting. The minutes passed like hours. Anxious to relieve the stress, she began considering the incomplete mural of the spy before her.

"Tell me about the woman you interviewed in Tours," he said without looking up.

"Which one?" Abrielle countered.

She'd spent five frustrating days in the town trying to learn more about what had transpired at the Chevals'. Most of what she uncovered was either hearsay, conflicted with prior information, or only added to her confusion.

"The only one who told you anything of value, the former servant. How did you gain her trust?"

Is that what her shadow had been whispering to him about?

Abrielle tried to recall the details of the conversation, now a week old. The woman in question had been an older servant in the household. With the deaths of her employers, she and most of the staff were either actively looking for work or had already left. One of the worst parts of her mission was trying to devise plausible reasons for her to be asking such questions. A little money for bribery would have been useful, but after leaving prison, she'd returned to Bordeaux only to discover her and Paul's cache of stolen goods empty. She briefly considered writing the D'Aousts requesting a loan but was too embarrassed and worried about what questions being asked. In the end, she'd settled her financial woes by picking pockets as she traveled. Her shadow did nothing to intervene, and she was too desperate to care if he saw. This method, though successful, slowed her progress immensely and ultimately jeopardized Abrielle's chances of completing her mission within the allotted two weeks.

"I told her that I was a servant, acting as an agent on my employer's behalf, to investigate if anyone who'd been serving the Chevals would be worth interviewing for a new position at my master's estate."

"She believed you?"

"I told her what she wanted to hear," Abrielle shrugged, "After that, she talked freely."

"And?"

Abrielle tried to recount the events dispassionately, but it grew more difficult as she spoke.

"She heard more than she saw directly. Her position afforded her only intermittent contact with visitors. Paul ...," this was difficult, "... and another woman in fine clothing arrived around one o'clock."

"Kindly provide me the description of said woman."

It was a profile Abrielle was far too familiar with, and her sense of disgust registered clearly in her tone when she spoke the name.

"It was Amelie."

"How can you be sure?" Le Hir pressed.

"The way the servant described Paul and her acting when she brought them refreshments, the physical description, and the dress she wore."

"Why should the dress be significant?"

Her eyes turned downcast.

"He gave me one just like it seven months ago."

The spy sat up straighter.

"Your conclusions?"

Abrielle's heart flooded with emotion. There was only one rational explanation. The truth had rarely tasted so bitter.

"That he was going to leave me and begin a new life with Amelie using the Chevals' money."

Le Hir nodded solemnly as he studied her.

"And this list you've brought me is supposed to prove his motive for murdering them?"

She smiled awkwardly.

"You know Paul and his temper. I think they…that the Chevals rejected him as a son a second time and he got angry."

She tried not to think about the lurid descriptions the servant had provided regarding the condition of the bodies. It was too brutal.

"Why didn't the servants stop this crime?"

The question refocused Abrielle.

"The woman told me that, at some point in the conversation, Madame Cheval ordered two of the servants to discreetly obtain the authorities and commanded the rest to remain in the kitchen. She must have felt the Chevals could handle the situation until the law arrived."

"Unfortunate for all that, they couldn't," Le Hir commented. "Well, we know what happened next with Paul. What about Amelie?"

He was toying with her now.

"I did what you wanted. I proved Paul's testimony against me is a lie. I don't care what happened to her!"

"Of course you do. Would you like me to tell you?" Le Hir asked coolly.

"You found her?"

"She was executed a month ago; she died most painfully, if it helps."

Abrielle was astonished.

"For this?"

"No, for the murder of our dearly departed friend, Sarah. Poor girl, learned too much too quickly. Amelie got suspicious and put an end to her. Fortunately, she never discovered that Sarah was working for me. If she had it would have ruined the entire purpose behind setting up this salon. I do not take the deaths of my operatives lightly."

Abrielle stared at the mural, as a new and terrible truth descended upon her.

"You used me as bait … bait for your trap."

"To a degree, but I assure you the Cheval murders caught me off guard as well. I never knew the boy had such rage in him. For whatever its worth, I do think that Paul loved you and genuinely tried to be your friend, but ultimately, he was unwilling to trade his true passion for you."

Abrielle drew her eyes away from the painting.

"He wants to lead an uprising against my master," Le Hir explained. "I am charged with ensuring this not happen. Salons were hotbeds of Revolutionary activities and ideas before the monarchy fell so we use them now for our own purposes. By publicly establishing them, I play the piper for the rats, and they all come to me freely and bring about their own destruction. Paul has risen to a position of power within the ranks of those seeking to once again destabilize France. Good God, can you imagine it, a New Terror, more blood in the streets."

Her heart trembled with a new fire. That Paul had once witnessed such brutality and would work to see it happen again was appalling.

"Their funding comes from robbery, extortion, blackmail, trade on the black market," Le Hir explained.

In other words, Abrielle had unwittingly been aiding the birth of a new revolutionary movement.

"What happened to our cache?"

"Oh I'm sure Paul cleaned that out before he vanished, not that I wasn't tempted when I found it. You two had quite the impressive stockpile. By the way …"

Le Hir leaned back as he reached into his coat pocket and retrieved a sizeable sum of francs, which he handed to her. She didn't want his money or his pity.

"What's this for?"

"Those letters you sent to your friends, the one's Paul was supposedly mailing with money enclosed. He never sent them the money. If you still wish them to have it, there it is, or what I estimate you planned to send."

"What?" she breathed incredulously.

"He was using it to help pay for Amelie's living quarters while she helped him continue to organize their forces, most of whom are now dead, jailed, or in hiding. Hence, the emptiness you see around you, and so tomorrow, Le Hir too will vanish and I will begin life anew."

Abrielle felt weak but she must know.

"What about me?"

Le Hir covered his mouth with his hand as he smiled and tapped his upper lip.

"As any good spy, I am always looking for potential assets. Without listing all of my reasons, I believe you to be a natural for this kind of work. And I can offer you one thing you've never really had before."

He waited.

"What's that?"

"Power," he replied.

Abrielle's lips parted minutely as she tasted the word, savored it. All her life she'd suffered and survived. Here at last was a chance for her to embrace destiny by choice and to control her own fate. Slowly a grin crept across her face. The spy master smiled in acceptance.

"Good. Now, if you would be so kind, Abrielle, go outside and try to find our artist friend. I'd like to get this done some time today. And send that money to your friends. I'm sure they will be glad to hear from you. I trust I need not remind you to say nothing of our arrangement to anyone.

She nodded, averting her eyes.

"We will begin your training tomorrow when we will both assume new identities."

"What shall I call you from now on?" Abrielle asked as she stood to leave.

Le Hir seemed to consider the question a moment as if weighing unseen factors in his mind.

"You may call me Bellange."

**

Abrielle considered the small house before her. She could smell the enticing scent of smoke from the fireplace. It would be dark soon. The sun and its warmth always faded so quickly in late November. She'd done all she could to prepare herself for this moment, but still she hesitated. Bellange trusted only her with this mission, she reminded herself. Did he consider this a final test or was this some perverse gift? Indeed, his words had sent her racing across the whole of France in order to get here on time. She was exhausted, having only stopped once in three days, but this was something she had to do, not for Bellange but for herself.

Much as she sometimes admired the spy master, it was doubtful she'd ever come to trust him. She knew far too well how manipulative he was. He would use any advantage he could to gain his true objectives. Abrielle was glad she'd taken the precaution of destroying Quinn Tierney's letter to her before leaving for Bellange's training facility. If she lived beyond this hour, perhaps one day she would use the enclosed addresses she'd memorized, but she refused to give him any more power over her. He craved secrets; her family's existence was one she would deny him.

But this was not about Bellange. With determined steps, she started once more toward the building. Despite her many journeys in the name of the Empire, she'd never actually been in this region of eastern France. How long had he been here? If not for the disastrous loss suffered by the Combined Fleet at Trafalgar over a month ago, she wouldn't even be here. Her talents were to have been employed in occupied England, but instead, fate had destined them to be together once more. Very soon she would know the truth, and regardless of what she discovered, Abrielle knew her life would never be the same.

When she knocked softly on the door, all sounds within ceased. Several seconds passed before a challenge was issued.

"Who's there?" the voice on the other side barked.

Under the circumstances, any sane person would have either answered or ducked in case shot suddenly poured through the wood of the door. But Abrielle did neither. She silently stood her ground. She was resolute that he would come to her, and if she died for that choice, so be it.

Only a diminutive sound alerted her before the door was pulled open. She did not see the gun pointed at her. Instead, Abrielle concentrated on looking into the eye that aimed it.

"Bonsoir, Paul."

Paul kept the shotgun trained on her, clearly unwilling to believe she was truly there.

"No, no you're dead … in prison."

"May I come in?" she requested.

His eyes searched the gathering darkness beyond her. Was she alone? With the gun still hovering, Paul suddenly grabbed her and flung her inside. He briefly checked outside once more before slamming the door shut. He looked thin and haggard. Both Paul and the small house were stained with the strong scent of alcohol. His eyes burned with uncertainty as he examined his old lover.

"The cloak, take off the cloak," he ordered. Abrielle obeyed and allowed him to satisfy himself that she carried no weapons. None would be needed. Finally she lowered her hands as he raced to the windows until he was confident that they were alone.

"What do you want?"

"I want to talk, Paul," she said simply.

"So talk," he barked.

"Please …"

Her eyes darted between his and the gun he still clutched. With obvious reluctance, he finally submitted to her plea and set the shotgun onto the kitchen table. He sighed.

"I've had dreams of this, you know. It's those eyes of yours; ever since we were kids … they kept me honest."

"You know why I've come, so be honest with me now…what happened that day?"

The question seemed to fragment him, and it took Paul a moment to work up his courage.

"The girl I killed, it … *she* was an accident," he began defensively.

"Ssshhhh."

Abrielle shook her head, crossed the room to him in three steps, and put a finger to his lips.

"What happened at the house, Paul?"

His eyes retreated from hers momentarily.

"Yes, I know. Tell me about the house."

When he looked up again, his lips formed a terse line.

"You were right, okay! Is that what you came to hear? I shouldn't have gone. They acted like I'd made the whole thing up, like I was crazy. My own mother claiming she had no son and my…father," Paul shook his head as fought back tears, "I shouldn't have gone. I shouldn't have gone."

Abrielle wrapped her arms around him and he held her. It all was so familiar; the sensation of his body against hers. He choked back sobs as he kissed the top of her head.

"I thought I lost you that day."

Her heart strained against her mind. The memories of their life together were too strong. Her heart ached. In that moment, she didn't care about conspiracies, his crimes or her duty. Even his infidelities with Amelie seemed but dim, unpleasant memories. He still needed her. There was a chance. The moment gave her the strength to ask the question, the only one that mattered. She pulled back from him, wiped away his tears, and gazed deeply into his eyes.

"Did you tell them it was me?"

He looked back at her searchingly.

"At the prison, Paul. Did you tell them that I killed your parents?"

An eternity passed between them with only the words of their souls filling the void. Their expressions did not alter, but her heart did. She knew. At last, she drew back from the abyss.

"Kiss me."

The words were barely past her lips when he pressed his to hers. The passion, once so craved, so well remembered, burned between them. His hands clasped her, and for a moment, one of hers dove into his hair and clutched the strands on the back of his head. Behind her the other hand paused deliberately over the object on the table before she allowed the kiss to end. Without another word, she walked away, tied the black cloak over her shoulders, and opened the door.

"Abrielle."

She paused just outside the doorway.

"How did you find me?"

Abrielle's voice trembled with emotion.

"I always find you."

Then she nodded to the dark figures concealed outside on either side of the door. Her eyes never left Paul's as he watched in horror as the two Imperial Guards she'd brought stepped heavily inside. They never wavered as he reached for the useless gun on the kitchen table, which she had jammed. Only when his eyes turned to her rich with a last desperate plea for mercy did she allow herself to look away.

Her breath escaped in even clouds of steam as she listened to the last moments of Paul's life. When she knew it was over, she began to walk away from the house. There was no need to wait for the guards. Without looking back, she pulled the cloak's black hood up and began up the small but steep incline on the muddy road. Abrielle and the dying embers of the sun disappeared into the heavy gloom.

***

Chapter 9
Fragile

The selection of food before her covered everything from the mundane to the exotic: wines, fine cheeses, tender meats, seafood, steaming soup, fresh fruits, colorful vegetables, a variety of breads, and rich desserts graced the table. Candles shone like small stars over the impressive array of choices. But Abrielle could barely stand to look at any of it, let alone to eat it. She took only a roll as she studied her new, well-lit surroundings. It was not so much a cell as it was a room. Bars remained over the windows, but it seemed more likely that this space was originally intended for use as a storage room than a cell. The room held an opulent dining table, a very comfortable looking bed, clean clothing, a table and mirror, several embroidered chairs, two armed guards, and Chloe.

The lavishly dressed spy also deliberately failed to partake in almost anything that the table had to offer. She sipped a glass of wine and waited for Abrielle to reveal something to her. But Abrielle's eyes were downcast. When she chewed any of the roll, it was very slowly, almost unconsciously. In fact the only thing that her prey seemed to notice was the full moon shining through one of the windows. Chloe had never seen the woman so meek and distant. Was it an act? Or did it tell her something about what might have happened during Abrielle's mysterious absence? Chloe motioned to one of the guards behind her and whispered instructions into the man's ear. He and his companion left immediately to obey. Abrielle never looked up.

No words broke their silence, even when the guards returned with hot water and towels. Under Chloe's orders, they made the unresponsive Abrielle stand then walked her to a nearby canvas chair. They deposited additional items on the table and left, locking the door behind them. One by one, Chloe leisurely removed the expensive gloves from her hands. She crossed the room, removed something from a drawer, and then returned. She met no resistance from Abrielle as she straightened her legs out, forcing her to lean further back in the chair.

Gently, Chloe poured a small amount of hot water over Abrielle's hair then began to rub the soap into the snarled tangle. She took her time as her fingertips loosened both knots and grime. Her light movements were soothing. From her reclined position, Abrielle could see even more of the moon. Her eyes fixed upon it as Chloe's efforts slowly restored her hair to a more familiar state. As time passed, Abrielle shook slightly as the cold night's air played across her damp head. Chloe rang the water from Abrielle's strands as she toweled them off. The drops burst upon the stones of the floor and cascaded out through small drains along the wall. Chloe considered Abrielle's gaze.

"Does he hold your secrets? What does he whisper to you, Abrielle, from such a distant and lonely place?"

Abrielle heard these words, felt the warmth of the speaker near her ear just before Chloe changed the position of her chair. The moon vanished from view.

Chloe eased herself onto Abrielle's legs, the silk of her stockings rubbed invitingly against Abrielle's bare skin. She took a cloth, dipped it into the still relatively warm water, and used it to trace away the dirt on Abrielle's face then neck.

"Such a thing could only be jealous of the warmth between us tonight," Chloe lips parted as she patted Abrielle with a towel. Her breathing slowed. She leaned forward and tenderly kissed Abrielle's cheek then brought her own to rest against it.

"But this won't do. Not tonight. You must give me more."

Chloe slowly withdrew and guided Abrielle out of the canvas chair.

She stood behind Abrielle who heard the hum of the object before she felt its presence over her shoulder. The dull side of the knife blade edged menacingly along the side of her neck, then shifted and sliced below the knot holding her gown up. Cool air rushed over her back and exposed shoulder; her other arm held the cloth over her breasts. Chloe struck quickly at the second knot leaving all of Abrielle's back and shoulders exposed. Abrielle fought to keep her breathing controlled. She could hear Chloe doing the same.

It became more difficult when Chloe lathered her hands with soap then began to run them over Abrielle's back, shoulders, and neck. She caressed the skin, massaged the muscles, and closed the gap between their bodies. As Chloe rinsed Abrielle, she blew hot breath over her damp skin. Abrielle's nerve endings sang. This time she did not bother with the towels, instead Chloe wrapped her arms lovingly around Abrielle as she kissed her exposed shoulders. Abrielle's chin trembled. Chloe held her more tightly and sighed.

"Oh Abrielle, to see you here, like this, saddens me … and excites me," she whispered intimately. One of Chloe's hands moved from around Abrielle's waist and wrapped around the hand Abrielle was using to hold her gown up. She felt Chloe's soft lips caressing her neck. Her fingers worked to lace themselves among Abrielle's own. She laughed lightly at Abrielle's resistance.

"Going to Bellange, that was clever, very clever. I thought you hated him too much to …" Chloe's fingers suddenly began to caress Abrielle's throat.

"Some spies grow too dangerous; so now I hold your life in my hands, not Bellange. And you will not leave this prison until I am satisfied that you are not a traitor." She stepped back now, admiring Abrielle's shivering form.

By now Chloe was herself quite chilled and eager to remove her own damp clothing. To Abrielle's great surprise, she moved a privacy screen between them and placed a dry robe over top of it for her. However, this offered no relief, it taunted her.

It was all part of Chloe's cruel game, and this time, Abrielle could see no way out of the trap. Chloe had her. If she tried to escape from this room, Chloe would kill her. If she killed Chloe, the guards would kill her. So, she was to share Bellange's fate. Abrielle was to be repaid for her own cruelty. Numbly she finished washing herself with the now cold water. As she did so, the room grew progressively dimmer as Chloe extinguished candles. Abrielle prayed silently as she assumed the robe: *Aut viam inveniam aut faciam. Either I shall find a way or I will make one.*

Abrielle emerged from behind the screen to find Chloe waiting for her. She'd changed into a pale blue gown. A lone candle remained alight upon the table and another by the bed. A quiet triumph glowed in Chloe's eyes as she looked into Abrielle's and saw understanding. They sat down upon the foot of the bed. Chloe's hand began to caress her leg. Abrielle couldn't look at her. She closed her eyes. Abrielle hated Chloe, but she hated herself even more.

What good had she ever been to anyone? If she wished, Chloe could probably keep her here forever for her own amusement. Maybe she deserved this. Her own pain and all of the sadness and misery she'd inflicted upon others lay bare before her. And then Chloe was kissing her lips, and Abrielle was kissing her back. For a moment Abrielle lost herself to the sensation of the physical, the pleasure of it. But ultimately it only served to remind her of how alone she really was. When Chloe spoke, she slowly opened her eyes.

"Now," she licked her lips, "my dark, wandering angel, what has taken you from … us, for so long?"

When it happened, it was so unexpected that there was never any hope of stopping it. In the dim flickering light of the candle, Abrielle suddenly saw the two objects, which the guards had placed upon the table. The walls she'd spent a lifetime erecting crumbled. There were no defenses left to her here in this crucible. A few sputtering gasps escaped before the tears came.

"Abrielle, what …?"

And then the torrents of pure grief came, and Chloe could not escape it. The passionate sorrows were unleashed all at once. Bewildered, Chloe attempted to calm Abrielle, only to discover her efforts brought forth even more intense sobs. She was completely inconsolable. Her wails turned to screams then reverted back. She clasped Chloe so hard she was choking her. Heaving breaths and surging emotions made any words she might have been saying completely unintelligible. In the face of such overwhelming grief, Chloe's own defenses lowered and she held Abrielle, for the first time ever, as a friend. Whatever was happening, Chloe knew she was not the cause of it. She held her as wave after wave of unceasing misery wrenched Abrielle apart.

The only person who'd ever truly loved her, who'd accepted her unconditionally from the moment they'd first met was gone.

"Ailis, oh God, Ailis!" Her sister's name brought even more tears. "I watched her die; for weeks … I watched her die … but I couldn't … I couldn't help her! I loved her!"

Her frame trembled uncontrollably as she buried her face into her hands. She'd been strong for so long. She had to be, day after day, as she watched Ailis grow weaker. She'd held together; she'd stayed strong for Ailis, for Tara, the Shaws, for Ernest. Abrielle had always had to be strong. Now as she lay shattered upon the altar of grief, she realized it no longer mattered. For so long, serving that need had kept her from her sister. It turned her into a killer. It had controlled her destiny. But she could not allow it to keep her from saving Tara. Either I shall find a way or I will make one.

She wiped the tears away as best she could. She would surrender herself fully to Chloe. It was the only possible way to regain her freedom. It was the only way to save Tara. Abrielle's lips again found Chloe's, and she struggled to loosen her own robe. They kissed for a moment before Chloe shoved her harshly away.

"How dare you toy with me," Chloe said haughtily.

"No, I want to …"

"NO!" Chloe burned with jealousy and anger. Abrielle was playing her. She didn't care that this Ailis was dead, she hated her. There would be no victory tonight. Chloe ran to the table with the drawer and took out her knife.

Abrielle lay upon the bed, half disrobed, taunting Chloe.

"Please, Chloe, please. I'll do anything you wish, but you must let me go. You must let me save my niece."

"You have no niece, you traitorous cur! And even if you do, I'll see to it that you'll never see her again. Guards! Guards!"

Abrielle had only seconds now.

"Chloe, Bellange was going to help me find the gypsies who are holding her. That's why I went to see him. They're here in France."

The lock turned.

"He was going to help me find the Moon Shadow clan."

The door flew open and the guards entered with weapons drawn. Chloe ignored them. Had there been a flash of recognition across Chloe's face when Abrielle shouted the clan's name? No one moved.

"Chloe?" Abrielle begged.

"Seek comfort in your trinkets," the spy bit out as she left the room, her guards trailing close behind. The door was locked, then all was silent. Abrielle closed her robe and walked across the cold stones to retrieve the objects from the table. Exhausted she took them back to the bed with her. She fell asleep, clutching both Ailis' flute and Tara's blanket like a lost and frightened child.

**

CHAPTER 10
THE DEEP WINTER

She watched the flame as it slowly drank the candle. Fire consisted of such a strange nature. It consumed until it destroyed even itself. If it were a living thing, if it could reason and choose, would it still do so? Would it attempt to adapt in order to avoid such a fatalistic destiny? Or must all things, even when given choice, adhere to their natures?

The little flame did all it could to beat back the darkness, but ultimately it was a doomed battle. The candle would be devoured, the light extinguished, and the darkness would prevail. During her unhappy weeks here, Baseria had found that the darkness always won in this place. Worse still, her own world had grown dark and silent. The last Seer had no power, and she knew she would die in this cold, isolated, bastion of darkness. A draft stole the flame's breath, and the room resumed its natural state.

Absent a twilight glow, there was no true day here and that faint, treasured light had long since transcended the sky. Baseria sat in the blackness and listened. The perpetual sea winds moaned in abject sadness against the stones of the fortress. Why would they wish to penetrate a place so cold and cruel? They were free. If this place possessed a name, she had not learned of it. In a sense, it did not seem to deserve one; it was the absence of everything. The fortress was a long-forgotten sentinel left to guard the polar night in an unyielding wilderness. How her enemies ever found this place at the edge of the world was a mystery. Even before the separation of the clans, her people had never been explorers or sailors. They were stewards to secrets bound to ancient myths and the prophecy. What insanity could have brought them all to this desolate landscape?

Baseria pulled her cloak more tightly around her, too lonely, too sad to question any more. A new sound attracted her attention. At first she took it to be the somber, soothing song of whales she occasionally heard. No, there was more to it than that. Perhaps another bear had come too near the fortress and killed another guard whose mind was numb with cold and empty of spirit. It had already happened twice that she could recall. No, the noise was both from within and without. Her nerves jumped slightly as a knock was issued upon her door.

"Ba? Are you in there?"

"I'm trying to sleep, Etolie," she lied.

The door opened anyway.

"Something's happened. You'd better come," Etolie suggested, ignoring her friend's countenance.

"I don't want to," Baseria replied simply. She was tired, too tired to invest herself in any more woe. Besides, she still could not forgive Etolie. Despite the winds, the noises grew louder. Ignoring her feeble protestations, Etolie grabbed Baseria's shoulder and shook her.

"Wake up. He's here," Etolie proclaimed.

"Who?" Baseria's spirit sank as her thoughts turned to the Moon Shadows' dark Master.

"Frankenstein. He's here," Etolie excitedly affirmed.

For the first time their eyes met. Etolie nodded to her friend's unspoken request for confirmation.

"You've seen him?" Baseria asked.

"Two ships came in. They're offloading new prisoners and the wounded right now. I saw him," Etolie managed a weak smile.

A great weight shifted within Baseria. She did not even try to understand her emotions.

"Where? Where is he?" she demanded as she pushed past Etolie and headed out the door.

"I think they were heading to the chapel … Ba, slow down, Ba!"

She didn't. Etolie could catch up. Here at last a dim flame of hope burned in the darkness. He was here. They had not been abandoned and left for dead.

Baseria barely eyed the row of prisoners being led through the main gate. She slid on fresh snow as she tore across the common area and into another turret, which contained a staircase that would lead her down. By design, fate, or accident the fortress was now claimed equally by both the sea and the land. Portions of it, seemingly unreachable across the frigid water, rose up out of the sea or perched on the rocky cliff-face. At first Baseria had dismissed these as mere ruins, but over time, she'd seen lights ablaze within them above the pounding waves. She could only guess that one might reach them by some, as yet undiscovered means, when the tides were low.

At the bottom of the icy turret, she turned sharply to her left, climbed a short set of stairs, and entered the chapel. The structure was the creation of sheer will, having been forged by hollowing out a portion of the cliff, and was suspended just above the pounding waves below. A small group of men were just finished placing someone onto a long wooden bench.

"Go back," one of them growled when Etolie rushed into the chapel. Apparently none of them immediately noticed Baseria's entrance. She now ignored their command.

"Is he hurt?" she urgently inquired.

The man was about to answer when another voice, deep and terrible, interceded from the doorway.

"You will tend him."

Baseria's heart trembled. He had returned. At some unseen signal, the men vacated the chapel. She felt Etolie clasp her hand.

"Alone."

Baseria was too frightened to turn and gaze upon her abductor whose gigantic form filled the chapel's entryway. The massive shadow receded momentarily as one of the men reentered and drug Etolie from the room. She overheard the creature giving one of the robed figures instructions as the doors closed. Then they were alone.

Baseria tried not to worry about Etolie as she ran towards the form outstretched on the bench. She could only take grim comfort in the thought that until they escaped, none of them were truly safe. She was in just as much danger as her friend.

Ernest was unconscious. Baseria conducted a hasty examination, which was hampered by the dim lighting. They'd wrapped him in heavy blankets, but the clothing underneath was singed and very damp. One of his cheeks was peppered with bits of wooden shrapnel, and his right hand bore a very angry gash. She allowed her fingertip to hover over the wound.

"Jesus," his eyes suddenly shot open and he coughed violently and began to struggle to get up.

"No, no calm down. Everything's …"

He rolled away from her and immediately became sick upon the floor. Baseria patted his shoulder reassuringly.

"Are you all right?" she asked when it was over, but there was no response. He'd lost consciousness again.

The door opened and one of the Moon Shadow gypsies entered, accompanied by one of the robed figures, who remained in the doorway. The gypsy kept a wary eye on her as he lit several of the altar urns. She was grateful for anything that could dispel both the gloom and the chill from the large space.

"The Master asked if you will need anything," the gypsy stated indifferently.

Baseria nodded at Ernest.

"What happened to him?"

The man said nothing. Inwardly, she sighed.

"A few more blankets would be helpful and some water or food, perhaps."

He left without further comment, and the robed guardian again sealed the door behind them.

Baseria pushed another bench near Ernest and sat heavily upon it. She was exhausted. The cold did drain her so. She wished they were closer to the fire, but that would have to wait until Ernest could offer some assistance in the matter. Despite her shivering, she nodded off and awoke hours later to discover that the items she'd requested now lie nearby. Ernest was clasping his head in pain. She stood and laid him fully onto his back. The motion made him wince. Ideally, she should have gotten him out of his damp clothing, but she doubted her efforts would succeed. She piled more blankets on him and placed several under his head.

For the next several hours, he wavered between stomach churning episodes of pain and tranquil slumber. Baseria ate a small portion of the food that the Moon Shadows brought but tried to save most of it for Ernest. As the dark hours passed, the fires gradually faded, compelling her to shelter with Ernest for warmth. Only the dull roar of the surf echoing through the stones beneath and their puffs of breath reminded her that they were not in a tomb. In spite of his deplorable condition, she found Ernest's mere presence an enormous comfort. She pressed herself more tightly to him.

"Where are we?"

The words provoked another fit of coughing. Embarrassed she slid away from him. She was relieved that the water in the bucket was not frozen.

"Slowly," she admonished as he choked unpleasantly while drinking. The flickering glow from the waning fires hurt his eyes and he blotted them out by using his arm as a shield.

"Where are we?" he repeated.

"Are you all right?" she asked in the Germanic tongue.

He considered the question.

"Baseria, please."

It was reassuring that he recognized her at least.

"On an island, somewhere in the Arctic. I don't know much more than that," she admitted.

"Norway," he muttered, "the ship that attacked us was from Norway. That's probably where we are."

"You were attacked?"

He breathed heavily a moment but managed to control himself.

"Military ship. They waited until the storm broke. Both sides sent boarding parties. There was an explosion, and I was blasted into the sea. I don't know what happened after that. How do you know this is an island?"

"I've been here for weeks, and they all know it's an island," she pointed out sarcastically.

He smiled weakly.

"I suppose they do."

"Well, you must have won because Etolie said that two ships docked, and I saw prisoners being led into the fortress."

"Fortress? I thought I'd dreamt that."

Baseria burned with questions. What had become of her family? Why had they been brought to this horrible place? How would any of them ever escape?

But she held back. She didn't want her faint hopes to die too quickly. Unless he'd brought others, escape seemed impossible for it was not the fortress which prevented it but the frigid sea.

"Have they told you why they brought you here?"

He took his arm away from his eyes as he waited for her response. She shook her head and blinked back tears.

"No," her voice strained as her fears surged.

She turned from him. Baseria felt the tips of his fingers touch her lower back through the blanket.

"Baseria … Baseria, do they know… do they know about you?"

The gentleness of the question caught her off guard. She lowered her head.

"They're not sure."

His hand slipped away.

"They can't find out," he whispered after a moment.

She gripped herself.

"I'm so frightened, Ernest."

Again he touched her lightly.

"Where are the others? Are they alive?"

"Etolie, she … tried to kill herself. On the ship, she ... I stopped her."

The dark memory of her passage to this prison tore at her. Her best friend tried to jump overboard, to drown herself, right before Baseria's eyes. She'd come within seconds of succeeding, of dying exactly as Baseria's sister and her cousin had. Baseria stopped her, but the animosity born between them in that moment would not fade.

The incident also unwittingly incited new debate among her captors as to which one of them was the actual Seer. This discussion put Etolie's near abduction prior to the attack on the camp in Hungary into a new light. After the night the prophecy was shared, they apparently hadn't been sure which girl was rumored to be the new Seer, so they'd taken them both. In the minds of their captors, Etolie's attempt to end her life meant that she might have more to hide than Baseria did. And so they waited and watched them both.

If she'd allowed Etolie to jump, it might all be over. By now the Moon Shadows and their dark Master would have drawn their conclusions and carried out their vile plans. But by saving Etolie, she'd stolen her choice and prolonged their mutual suffering. She turned to Ernest, desperate for comfort.

"We have to escape," she declared, "before they … why are you looking at me like that?"

Ernest hid his eyes immediately. He couldn't bear to look at her. If he did she would again see the accusation alive in his eyes and she would ask questions that were too painful for him to answer.

"I'm tired," he said flatly.

"There's food here," she finally replied, feeling suddenly uncertain.

"I just need to rest. We'll talk more, later."

He slept.

*

Something had changed; though he was only half awake, Ernest could sense it.

"At last, you stir, Uncle. Is it still too bright?"

The voice came from the end of the benches Ernest lay upon. He opened his eyes fully and saw the cloaked mass seated there beside him.

"Baseria?"

"The girl has gone back to the others for a time. I wanted to return this to you. It was dropped to the deck as you were thrown overboard." The diseased hand presented Ailis' journal to him. "That it still survives at all is a miracle."

The ardent longing in Ernest's soul reawakened as he took the treasured journal. He'd almost lost her again. The unseen face studied him, the head beneath the cloak turned slightly.

"Why did she love you?"

"You've read it?"

The hidden head nodded thoughtfully.

"I wanted to know my aunt."

"And do you now?" Ernest could not keep the anger from his voice.

The great being answered.

"Enough to understand your pain," he replied.

"You know nothing of my pain!" Ernest's words slapped against the stone walls of the chapel and then echoed in the silence that followed.

"She did."

The violation was too much.

"Get out."

"Answer me," the man's voice was like the hum of a blade, one dedicated to hitting its mark. "Can you feel her presence here among us in this place of worship?"

Ernest turned from the creature who would not be denied.

"She saw something in you. Didn't she? Something kindred, yet wholly unique, a bond that forever enriched her life until ..."

"Please …," Ernest could hear no more.

The thing's enormous hand forced Ernest to turn back. He stared unwillingly upward into the sickening yellow eyes.

"I honor your great sorrow, Uncle, for it is the angels who have sinned. It is for their greed that you suffer, after they fell shamefully from the heavens, claiming in their anguish one so cherished."

"And did your greed cause you to fall from the heavens never to return?"

Gleaming teeth leered at him from the blackness of the hood.

"I wonder if you will ever be prepared to hear my answer. Just as I wonder how you will live now that such a light has passed from this world. Can pages full of her memories preserve her for you? Or will you spend your days in endless lamentation, offering alms, hoping she will hear?"

He leaned closer.

"How will you answer your own child when the day comes and she asks, 'Why did she love you?'"

Ernest wanted to throttle the life from this thing. Ignoring his dizziness, he shot up from the benches and reached for its throat. For a moment the creature offered no resistance for he'd long since ceased to fear his own ending. The concealing hood began to slide off. Then he gripped Ernest's own throat firmly.

"You seek to assert yourself over my domain? Then look upon me! Look upon me, Frankenstein, for I am Death!"

The hood removed, a nightmare of living death towered over Ernest crushing his windpipe.

"You must fight me now, Uncle! Fight Death as you have your whole life. It is the only way you can save her. It is the only way to save yourself."

With a final squeeze, the monster suddenly flung Ernest backward. He sprawled onto the stones, desperate to force air back into his lungs. The harbinger of darkness resumed his hood.

"Why struggle?" he railed, "What keeps you in this bleak world without her? Fear of death?"

"Tara," Ernest rasped, "Tara."

"And yet you abandoned her to come here. Why?"

"The girls you took … I have to," he coughed as the room spun, "take them back, only way to save her."

The shadow knelt and leaned closer.

"But if you succeed, you will still be alone and so will your daughter. Forever, alone. Both of you merely existing without your love, without your soul, without your wife. I know your pain, Uncle, for it is mine also."

"Do not torment me!" Ernest cried.

"I do not. I seek understanding as you do. I rage against death as you must. But you must also accept that she will die. Your daughter will die without you, without her mother. And you are powerless to prevent it. Just as you were for all who have gone before you."

The abyss of his soul rang hollow for the dead. It cried out for forgiveness from the living. But the fiend was right. The hours left to hope were faint. He could think of no means to escape this fortress and the frigid seas it guarded. And what of Abrielle and what of Tara? He had destroyed them by coming here just as he had destroyed Ailis by leaving her.

"We are all that exist, you and I; all that is left of the Frankensteins. But you would reject me, destroy me, and hunt me to the ends of the earth before you would embrace me as family."

Ernest smiled bitterly.

"Before I can do that I must know where your father is. Where is Victor?"

"I told you. He is dead," the other affirmed. "He died on the Arctic ice ten years ago. There was nothing to be done."

"He died by your hand?" It was as much a question as it was an accusation.

"No, by his own choices. He succumbed to the elements while aboard a ship of exploration."

"But he meant to destroy you?"

"Yes," the creature wheezed.

"Why?"

The question was considered.

"Because his madness made it such that he could not bear to know that I lived. All will be made clear to you when I take you to where he now lies."

"It is here?" Ernest whispered after a measure of heartbeats.

"It is within reach. There will be time to discuss my father, but for now, you should know that my forces actively seek to secure your daughter and her safe return. She is family, wrongly taken, and she will be avenged."

The creature seemed to relish this last word, drawing it out in his harsh, rasping voice.

Ernest felt uncertain of what to say but finally settled on a question.

"Why did you bring me here?"

"You chose to come," the shadow reminded him.

"At your behest. You've spoken to me of destiny, that boy dying by the river in Hungary, one of your people. The last words he spoke were of you and immortality. That you awaited me here, with the women you have taken."

"Immortality," the being sighed, "the collective dream of humanity, its great sickness. How could I offer such a thing? There is no permanence in this life. Do you mistake me for a god?"

"Isn't that what your people think, these gypsies here, isn't that what you are to them?"

"Is that what I am to you?" He paused before continuing. "Gods are too lonely. Perhaps that is why death exists, to remind us of them. My people follow me because they believe. I give them hope. I would do the same for you, Uncle, if your mind is open and your heart is willing."

"If what you say about Tara is true, then you have already given me hope. But let these women go. What purpose can there be in holding them in this wasteland?"

The immense creature stood menacingly.

"They cannot go," he declared, "their destiny is fixed. All else depends upon them and the Seer."

"The Seer is dead," Ernest affirmed.

The sneer returned.

"The shell is dead, but the Seer remains and she is here. And I will use her powers to recapture that which was wrongfully taken from me long ago. If you do not interfere; if you aid me in my efforts and embrace me as family, then I will do all within my power to restore that which was so unjustly taken from you."

There was something in his tone that Ernest did not understand. With a swirl of robes, the creature turned to leave.

"Do you speak of my daughter?"
"No, your wife."

Chapter 11
The Third Alliance

Abrielle closed her eyes and sighed. She'd done it again, and this time, she would not be able to hide her crime from the others. It would be worse than before. If only they'd bartered for more in that last town they'd stopped in. Oh well, the burnt fare served them right, she thought, since the others refused to cook and knew by now that she couldn't. Maybe she could still slip back inside before …

"Is that ready?" An unwelcome voice behind her demanded.

She quickly shoved the burnt ham under the eggs on the plate, then turned, and wordlessly handed it to Berryer, easily the most annoying member of the group. He eyed both her and the contents of the plate before he grudgingly sat down. Despite the cold air of the mountains, the cooking fire made her quite warm. Abrielle grabbed the nearest water bladder and tipped it back. No, she would almost enjoy watching him choke on the ham.

"Don't drink that!" Chloe barked as she emerged from the tent.

Abrielle stiffened in surprise. She could see nothing distinguishing about the bladder and aside from the contents smelling slightly stale could detect nothing amiss about the water within. Was Chloe simply trying to make her paranoid?

"What? Are we out of water again?" Berryer whined as a portion of half-chewed egg fell from his mouth.

"Yes," said Chloe without removing her eyes from Abrielle, "go fill the rest of the bladders up."

"I'm eating," Berryer replied dismissively.

"I can get more water," Abrielle offered.

Chloe's visage and stance indicated otherwise. She hadn't allowed Abrielle to leave her sight since their journey began. Suddenly Berryer choked. Abrielle winced as he spit out his food and noisily flung the metal plate back toward her.

"Dammit! I ate better when I had Austrians trying to shoot me!" he thundered, in reference to his previous career as a member of Napoleon's Grande Army.

"I wish one had," Abrielle retorted.

Muttering in anger, Berryer started towards her, but his movement was impeded as Chloe grabbed him and held him in what appeared to be an intimate embrace.

"Touch her and I'll kill you," she hurriedly whispered. "You're causing a scene."

Berryer paused and studied a few of the curious faces, which scrutinized them from the nearby camp.

"I'm playing my role," he asserted defensively. "Do you think they care if another gypsy yells at his wife?"

She held him tighter.

"Imbecile, you almost blew our cover."

"You will now if you don't let me hit her," he countered.

Chloe's eyes touched those of the expectant spectators, her grip relaxed, and he flung her away; then he struck Abrielle. Her eyes burned with resentment as he grinned defiantly back at her. In Berryer's eyes, she was a traitor, and he was more than happy to treat her as she deserved. He stooped and retrieved several of the empty water bladders before leaving. The matter settled, most of the curious members of the Moon Shadow clan began to disperse.

Chloe knelt down and studied Abrielle's face, touching the tender skin where the blow had landed.

"I'm fine," she insisted, turning away from Chloe in anger and humiliation.

"I don't care," Chloe said evenly, "but they have to believe I do, so hold still.

She took the heavy cooking towel, wrapped snow within it, and held it to Abrielle's face. Chloe brushed some loose strands of hair behind her ear.

"Remember, my love, I'm your sister."

Abrielle tried not to look away. That Chloe had chosen this, of all roles, to assume for their mission revolted her to no end, but she could not allow her to know what affect the words she'd just uttered truly had upon Abrielle's heart. She hugged Chloe, who warmly embraced her in return.

For four days after Chloe's failed seduction of her, she was left alone in her gilded prison. Even the guards did not appear. Then on the fifth day, Chloe returned and offered to allow her an hour's time in the prison yard. Though it was freezing outside, the prospect of fresh air thrilled her. Chloe remained at her side, but neither spoke until the final moments before she'd been returned to her cell. All Chloe asked her was where the Moon Shadow gypsies might be. Without mentioning his name, Abrielle described the area where Ernest had been waylaid and taken to the cave.

Chloe returned three days later. A strange, sympathetic softness overcame her demeanor when she informed Abrielle that she had located the clan, here, secure in the towering heights and awesome beauty of the Pyrenees. And despite repeated attempts, Abrielle had been unable to pry from Chloe or any of the others how they'd suddenly learned the whereabouts of the Moon Shadows.

"Preparations have been made to infiltrate them, but before we can proceed, I will need your word. We will be watched by others outside of our group. If you attempt to betray us or escape, they will kill you. I pledge that while we are on this mission, you are under the direct protection of the Emperor. Do I have your word?"

Abrielle considered Chloe's wholly unexpected offer.

"And if we are successful? What will happen to me then?"

A wry grin had spread across Chloe's face.

"Let us be certain that we are successful."

Did they intend to use her to spy on these gypsies for a prolonged period? Would she be returned to prison after they learned what they wished? Or would they simply kill her during the mission? It really didn't matter. As long as she remained locked away, Abrielle could do nothing to save her niece.

Abrielle agreed, and twenty-four hours later they were seated before a campfire with Germanic Romani[10]. Several years earlier, Abrielle had infiltrated another group of Romani gypsies, so many of the customs were, if not familiar, then at least comprehensible. She was now Orfilia, a young, widowed Romani who was accompanied by her older sister, Onella, the alias that Chloe assumed.

At first, Abrielle gave little thought to their cover story and identities. She was so relieved to be free from prison that she readily assumed the role she was to play without question. Berryer had been placed within

---

10 Rom/Romi/Romani – collective terms for primary group of Gypsies in Europe.t

the Romani encampment for several months prior to their arrival. A brief ceremony gave the appearance that they were betrothed and soon after, Berryer got them exiled for violating a host of customs. All of these events were carefully choreographed so that now there was a viable trail, should anyone wish to backtrack them and check on the validity of their cover story. And so the exiles crossed the border into France and headed first south then west. They picked up the other member of their small party in the second to last town they stopped in before entering the demanding Pyrenees.

Abrielle recognized him from two prior missions but his presence brought no reassurance. During both of those, he interacted only with Chloe, and during both, he pursued some secret secondary mission before vanishing. He was younger than any of the other members of the group, but even Chloe seemed to respect this primarily silent addition, as she always had. For this mission, he was called Grenier, a mountain guide they'd hired to take them to the Spanish boarder, looking for work in the war-ravaged Peninsula. Grenier slept in a separate tent, ate his own food, and interacted with them only when the role he was playing compelled him to. He often scouted ahead of them and did seem to know this landscape quite well. The more Abrielle observed of him the more of a paradox he became, one that was both inviting and worrisome.

They had discovered the Moon Shadow camp three days earlier and petitioned to either join or trade with them. The clan did not react favorably to these intruders and all but ignored them the first day, perhaps hoping that they'd just move on. But they hadn't. The second day resulted in a short conversation between members of the groups. On the third they allowed Berryer to trade some items and to briefly enter their encampment. Now they at least had a basic understanding of its organization. What would this morning bring? Would she and Berryer's spat soften their suspicions, confirm them, or had the incident already been dismissed.

Successfully infiltrating any organization required total commitment by all those involved. There must be a rhythm to such things. A moment's hesitation, any perceived inconsistencies, or lack of sincerity in either words or actions could, and for some groups had, brought disastrous results. In an effort to avoid such a fate, all devoted a great deal of time to developing their fictional personas while they traveled.

For a time, they all but disappeared into their respective roles; that was expected. Ironically, by now they knew their fictional selves better than they knew one another in reality.

Since her first return to Abrielle's cell, Chloe had been polite, respectful, and reserved. In short, she'd not been Chloe. What was behind this new kindness? At first, Abrielle struggled to discover what purpose this new act might serve. Did Chloe honestly believe that she was fooled by it? No, she was more intelligent than that, so why do it? As they traveled, she did not once attempt to touch Abrielle and constantly defended her against Berryer's ire. By now, for all appearances, she'd successfully become Orfilia's somewhat protective older sister. But Abrielle came to perceive that Chloe's Onella persona was crafted to serve ulterior motives. It afforded her a subtle, intimate, and inescapable means to continue her interrogation of Abrielle.

It was so insidious that Abrielle failed to recognize it at first. They spent many hours on the road, discussing what type of a life these fictional gypsy sisters would have led. They developed stories about their pasts, plans for their future, even how each would die. The conversation turned to the philosophical, the spiritual, but avoided the personal. Neither ever revealed any links to her past. But there was something now, in Chloe's eyes, when she said the word 'sister' that disturbed her. Abrielle feared that the true purpose of their conversations was actually an attempt to confirm a suspicion Chloe held. Or was it more than that? Chloe was irate when she erroneously concluded that Ailis had been Abrielle's lover. Had she now reasoned who and what Ailis had truly been? How would the knowledge impact Chloe's decisions regarding Abrielle's fate? Would she use the truth to help Abrielle gain permanent freedom or suppress it and use it to keep her a prisoner forever?

Chloe handed her another water bladder.

"I thought we were out of water?"

Chloe picked up the bladder she'd admonished Abrielle not to drink from.

"Don't burn my eggs," she instructed.

Then she disappeared back inside the tent.

*

Pias eyed the four surviving Wild Rose clan fighters bound before him as he tried to ignore the numbness in his fingers. Their method of attack was well-conceived and executed. The wolves hadn't detected their scent. They'd used the surrounding landscape to their full advantage, and by doing so, succeeded in killing half of his men. Pias himself was sent flying down an embankment and into the icy mud of a nearby stream, where one of these men had attempted to drown him. Such spirit and resourcefulness was to be admired, that is, if they'd won. But they hadn't, and now he must use any means necessary to discover the truth quickly or all of his carefully laid plans could fail.

He paced before them. They all averted his gaze. Normally he would have executed the leader, but time elicited a different choice be made. He picked one at random, withdrew his pistol, and shot the man cleanly through the temple. The wolves strained against their leads at the sight of blood upon the snow. He studied the reactions of the remaining three prisoners. None ultimately revealed what he needed.

"Your friend was a brave man …," Pias mocked as he released the wolves that quickly descended upon the carcass. "Look what it got him."

He waited, but none of the others spoke. He shook his head.

"Now… I'll ask again and then the lesson repeats itself. How many more of you are there?" he asked as he reloaded his pistol. No one spoke.

Pias turned to one of his men.

"Take two men back with you. Tell Nicabar where we are and that we need a cart or horses to bring in …," he paused and fired, randomly ending the life of another, "two prisoners."

His men moved quickly to obey their orders.

Pias squatted down and touched the warm barrel of his still smoldering pistol to one of the remaining gypsy's faces. The young man strained not to cry out.

"You must be dead inside. I murder two of your friends, and it means nothing to you." He drove the hot barrel harder into the man's cheek.

Eyes choked with pain and violence suddenly met his.

"I swear I'm gonna kill you," the gypsy vowed.

Pias laughed then became quite sober.

"Brave men don't just let their friends die, nor do real leaders. My father taught me that. Didn't yours, Espen?"

*

Tasaria blinked as she tried to clear her mind. Slowly, the world came back into focus. She was back in her tent. It was a welcome sight. She was never completely comfortable entrusting herself to the chaotic energies of the unseen world, and for several years, all but refused to do so. It was too easy to become overwhelmed while under their influence or to touch forces she could not control. But since the arrival of their Master, there had been little real need for her to seek guidance from the hidden realms. All was as it should be. Besides, in her younger days, too often when that Elemental energy revealed secrets to her, these had only led to great problems or miseries, but then again they had also once led her to greater levels of knowledge and power. Gifts she'd seen fit to use.

Ever since his return, Nicabar insisted that she attempt to access them again.

Even absent his urging, she would have. She'd felt her mother pass long before Nicabar returned and informed her of both the disastrous raid and of her death. Pias was to blame for both. She'd never liked the man, but now she detested him. He was a necessary evil, but now that the war with the Wild Rose clan was all but finished, both she and her husband knew that his usefulness was nearing an end. He was too volatile, too unpredictable. He was a creature of violence and war, but when the Master's work was complete, there would be no place for him. At least, none that Tasaria could foresee. Besides, he was an outsider. How could he possibly understand the great destiny of her people? Then again, if they still lived, could her mother or her sister have truly understood? She doubted it. They'd both adhered too closely to a flawed interpretation of the prophecy, one which offered no hope for a better world.

And now, she was the last Seer. Fate intended it so, and it only re-enforced, in Tasaria's mind, that as regrettable as the outcome of some of her choices, they were also correct. Soon the Moon Shadows would claim immortality for humanity and replace fear with eternal hope. Though her heart was certain of this, her spirit was wary. Something vital remained obscured from her. She could feel it. But did it threaten their success? The energies of the unseen world were growing increasingly erratic, and as they did, that which she sought became even more elusive. Still, an unknown whispered to her. Something was waiting for her. Would she recognize it for what it was when it came?

Suddenly the flap to the tent drew open and a cold rush of mountain air banished any further musings. Nicabar stomped in and threw himself down onto his favorite chair. Despite the fact that he was obviously in a bad temper, Tasaria could not let a long-standing argument rest.

"How many times do I have to yell at you to take off your boots before you come in?"

"I haven't tracked anything in here in months," he snapped.

Tasaria scoffed but allowed the matter to fade. He obviously needed to confide something to her. She took a moment to seal the flap properly then turned to face him.

"What troubles you, Husband?"

*

Abrielle scraped the last remnants of grease from the pan. The water was frigid, and her hands now burned with cold. She stood and plunged them beneath her heavy cloak then against her body for additional heat. Unconsciously her body began to move, as if the motions themselves would generate the warmth she sought. She had to be careful though. The rocks were slick, and this pool was not far from where the mountain stream turned into an impressive waterfall that vanished over the edge of the cliff. Her eyes began to study the terrain. Was she being watched? Despite the cold, it was pretty here. Even winter could not fully mask the lush forests that covered the landscape. It felt warm and familiar. Her thoughts turned to Anne and Noel D'Aoust, tucked away here among the peaks. She turned west and wondered for a moment how long it might take her to reach them if she just began to walk. The flurries, which had begun several hours earlier, seemed to have become more purposeful. Abrielle peered through the waves of snow.

A cold hand gripped her shoulder. She shrieked in surprise, and to her astonishment, found that it was Grenier. He held one finger over his lips. Her questions died on hers.

"Leave the pans," was the only instruction he gave before walking away, in the direction of the waterfall. She followed as quickly as she could, but the flying snow hindered her progress.

He stood upon the precipice where the waters thundered heedlessly over. Unwilling to get too close to either, she finally yelled a question. The wind stole it immediately. With great reluctance, she drew closer to him.

"What are we doing here?"

"I need to show you something," he shouted back over the roar.

She looked down at the rushing water, framed by pine trees that must have been hundreds of feet tall. Swirling winds laden with snow hastened to meet her gaze as she glanced over the edge.

"I can't see anything. Can't it wait?" Abrielle asked with a measure of trepidation.

Grenier shook his head, knelt down then began to clamber over the edge. Was he mad?

"What are you doing?" she demanded.

"It's the best way."

"Do you have ropes?"

Again Grenier shook his head. He was mad.

"This is the best way to avoid their wolves. I can't show you if we go through the camp. This is much shorter and there are good grips. I'll guide you. Now hurry."

He vanished.

Abrielle hated heights.

"Grenier!" she said in a low voice, but there was no response.

For God's sake, why couldn't he just tell her what was so important? Or at least, why couldn't they wait until after it stopped snowing? Could this be how they planned to eliminate her? If she didn't go was the mission over? No, it couldn't end. Not like this. She hiked up her dress, knelt, and lowered herself slowly until her feet located a narrow purchase on the cliff. Grainer was there, affixed as a spider is to its web. The winds howled and buffeted them. And for the first time ever, Grenier actually smiled. He was having fun. Abrielle was not.

The distance, though not great, was agonizing. What on earth could have inspired him to attempt this in the first place? Her hands and feet fought her mind. They wanted to remain where they were. Her mind, however, realized that numb extremities could only result in the very outcome she was determined to avoid. She blinked snow from her eyes, her nose ran, and icy gusts swirled up into her clothing, but she ignored these and concentrated on succeeding each perch that Grenier abandoned as he moved further along the cliff. Only once did her foot slip, but her heart hung in her throat for the rest of the unpleasant journey.

Finally, Grenier began upward again. He pulled her the last few feet, and at last, they stood together on a firm outcropping just below the edge of the cliff. He leaned close to her ear.

"Commit everything you see to memory. Pay close attention to anyone you see. Notice the details for the tents surrounding the one with the guards. Watch for any wolves lurking about the camp. If they spot us, we might as well jump."

He grinned tightly and motioned for her to stand fully upright. Abrielle gingerly raised herself and tried to ignore the obscuring snow as her mind sought details to commit to memory. Several figures darted among the tents, including the one under guard. She tried to establish what might be significant about them, but abandoned the task the moment she spotted a wolf walking beside one of the figures.

Grenier steadied her as she sank back down and again held a finger to his lips. She nodded. With no apparent alarms raised, they took a moment to warm themselves before resuming their journey back to the waterfall. When they were once again by the pool in the stream, Grenier hurriedly issued instructions.

"Meet me in my tent in an hour. They'll want us to leave. Find some way to keep us here. Tell no one what you have seen or that we've spoken."

His orders complete, he disappeared among the snow and the gathering twilight.

Abrielle returned to her tent but dedicated most of her time to figuring out a new excuse to escape it. Chloe was already paranoid about leaving her alone. Cleaning the cooking ware and locating a private location to relieve herself were viable explanations once, but using something similar was bound to raise their suspicions. Besides, how long would her conference with Grenier last? She had to think of something else the others would not want to witness or do.

Much to the consternation of Berryer, she began to play Ailis' flute while she meditated on the problem. While she sat thinking, a Moon Shadow stopped by and suggested that if Spain remained their goal, then leaving in the morning would be advisable. He explained that snows like this could last for many days and make the passes inadvisable for travel.

In that case, they'd be snowed in for an unknown period of time, perhaps even the remainder of winter.

"I'm not staying here 'til spring," Berryer declared the moment the gypsy left.

"I'm sure he's exaggerating," Chloe replied diplomatically.

"And if not, we're stuck here with … shut up that damn noise!" he yelled at Abrielle, who had resumed playing. Actually she'd been playing the same notes over and over again for the last half an hour as if she were trying to recall a tune. It took long enough, but the ploy was finally eliciting the response she'd hoped for.

"Orfilia, please," began Chloe.

"No, it's fine, I can practice outside," Abrielle declared as she threw on her cloak.

Chloe made to follow her lead, determined not to let her slip away again. Or perhaps she was simply anxious not to be left alone with Berryer, a sentiment Abrielle could more than understand. From personal experience, Abrielle knew that Chloe liked to create, what she considered a balanced team for each mission. In light of this fact, Berryer seemed an odd choice from the beginning, and with each of his outbursts, the reasons Chloe selected him became more elusive. Was he simply a convenient asset or were there other reasons? Perhaps this mission was less official than Chloe made it out to be. That would certainly account for the unusual choices in personnel. Maybe Berryer and Grenier were also in trouble with Imperial Intelligence, their presence not by choice.

"Oh, no. Someone is talking to me about leaving or I'm gonna start packing up right now," Berryer affirmed. Chloe was obviously torn. She wanted to keep an eye on Abrielle but was anxious to avoid another scene for the neighbors.

"We'll need more firewood anyway," Abrielle stated as she ducked through the entry before any discussion could take place. Fortunately, no one followed. Still, she gathered firewood as she worked her way to Grenier's tent. For the deception to work, she'd need some when she returned.

"You're late," Grenier observed when she arrived.

"Family matters," she replied by way of explanation. His tent barely looked lived in or was he already packed for a hasty departure? Could he be expecting trouble soon?

"Quickly, tell me what you saw earlier."

Abrielle described the number and arrangements of the tents, and began to provide details about the people she'd seen. Grenier stopped her.

"I've been observing them while they've been busy observing you. A group came in this morning on the far side of the encampment. They bore two prisoners and one body. Their arrival caused quite a stir; soon after they began to patrol the grounds with the wolves."

"Prisoners? Locals?" she questioned.

"No," was the blunt reply.

She was convinced there was more, but Abrielle was also certain Grenier wasn't ready to divulge his secrets regarding them. She switched subjects.

"I haven't seen or heard any wolves."

"They appear well trained, but they have made an effort to keep them away from our area. Probably don't want one of them getting shot or questions raised."

"Why didn't they use their wolves to keep us away initially?"

"I overheard an argument about that, too. There is an enclosure further down on the far side of the mountain. Apparently, the clan leader doesn't like to have them loose; something about a past incident involving an injury to a child. The man you saw leaving the tent, the one with the wolf at his side, also brought the prisoners in and was greatly annoyed by our presence. I have a feeling that had he been present when we arrived, they'd have used the wolves to chase us away. They still might."

"You were right, they did suggest we leave."

"You must prolong your stay?"

"Why should we?" Abrielle challenged, suddenly tired of his ambiguity. "I hung off the side of a cliff for you today, and I'm here at my own peril because I think you've got something important to tell me. Now, what's going on Grenier? I know it has something to do with those prisoners, what is it?"

His eyes departed from hers for only an instant.

"What do you know about the Wild Rose clan?"

Abrielle's lips parted in bewilderment. She'd never mentioned them to anyone in her party. How could Grenier know anything about them?

His face was a mask.

"Why?" The question seemed the safest option, though she was certain her delay had been telling.

Grenier paused and checked outside for a moment before continuing. Did he hear something?

"The prisoners, you must talk to them," he declared.

"How?"

"I've shown you the way. They rotate the guards, just watch for the wolves. Have you found an excuse to remain, yet?"

Abrielle shook her head. Grenier retrieved a water bladder and handed it to her.

"Don't drink from it, but make sure at least one of the others do. Hide it or destroy it after you've done so."

Abrielle locked her eyes with his.

"Why are you helping me?"

His secrets remained guarded.

"You should get back," was the only answer she received. He held the tent's flap open. "Make sure you're not observed by your companions, anyone else will just think you've been discussing leaving with your guide."

"Can you spare some firewood? I'm supposed to be gathering some."

He pointed to a stack nearby.

"Take it. I won't need it." The flap descended without further preamble.

He wouldn't need it? By now nightfall, the snow pack, and the winds conspired to send the temperatures plummeting. Abrielle planned to sleep as close to the fire as possible tonight. How exactly did Grenier plan to avoid freezing to death? She hid the mysterious water bladder on her person, took what firewood she could carry, and began a circuitous route back to her own tent. She hoped that Chloe and Berryer were settled down.

Questions raced through her mind. Why were Wild Rose clan members here in France? Ernest said they lived in Hungary. Were they here by accident or had Jack been captured and revealed her plans to infiltrate the Moon Shadows to them? She thought back to the gypsy who spoke to her in French the night Tara was taken. Could these Wild Rose prisoners actually be spies? Why hadn't Grenier simply slipped into the camp and talked to the prisoners already? He certainly possessed the skills to do so, yet he'd entrusted this task to her. Could all of this be part of a set up?

Before putting it away, she sniffed the contents of the water bladder and was again unable to ascertain what drinking the contents might do. Would she poison someone if she gave the contents to them? If she did, and she was being watched as Chloe warned, what happened to her then? Would Chloe have actually risked her life and her career on a mission unsanctioned by Imperial Intelligence to enable Abrielle a chance to clear her name and find her niece?

Why was Grenier so determined that she talk to the Wild Rose gypsy prisoners? What was his hidden agenda? Was he spying on everyone? Again Bellange's cryptic warnings about conspiracies flashed through her thoughts. Alone, uncertain of her own actions, surrounded by potential enemies, and confronted by a host of questions impossible for her to answer, while the lives of both she and her niece hung in the balance, his warning was never more vivid.

*

Nicabar rubbed the polished wood between his fingers. He'd put so much care into shaping it, dedicated his heart to the task, and she had loved it. She had loved him. His daughter had been such a sweet child. His fingers traced the solid form of the toy wagon he made for her so long ago. He'd used one of the fragments from the project to carve her a little wooden rose, which he attached to string and fashioned her a necklace.

In a state of abject despair when he retrieved her body from the river, he'd searched for it. He'd been frantic to find the necklace. It was a symbol of the special bond between him and his child. But it was lost forever, either during her descent or to the churning waters of the river. Just like his daughter. It was strange that the loss of such a trinket should still disturb him. But it did. He carefully replaced the cloth around the toy before he returned it to the chest and locked it securely within.

Perhaps the loss of the necklace still troubled him because trinkets and memories were all that were left of Jucika. Nicabar reflected on all the lonely years of pain and loss. All the miseries the war had unleashed. But if the Master was successful in his great purpose then such sacrifices would be rewarded. A new reality would be born, one which promised to banish his grief and to finally heal both him and Tasaria.

It was their inability to move beyond Jucika's loss at the hands of her cousin which troubled him now. His wife's hatred of her sister's family became more embittered over time. Nicabar would never forgive Baseria, but he could not bring himself to condemn her fully. She too had lost a sister that day, and Tasaria's actions towards her niece were shameful. Her relationship with her mother had been equally unbalanced, both craving her approval and guidance while rejecting them. Yet, Nicabar never doubted that somewhere, deep within her, his wife loved them both. But which of the conflicting emotions would she embrace in the end?

There was no longer a choice to be made regarding her mother. Pias' killing of Nasi left Tasaria as the lone Seer. Or she should have been. She'd never completed her studies. After Baseria healed Nasi, he'd tried to barter a peace, to enable the knowledge of the Seer to be passed on but those talks had failed. There was too much resentment on both sides to make it feasible. It was impossible to comprehend all that was now lost with her death.

Time and time again, the Master asserted that the Seer would play a vital role in creating what must be, but now the true Seer was gone and the burden fell to Tasaria. Was she ready? Did she have the knowledge, skills, and natural abilities to ensure that providence was properly fulfilled? Or would all that they had fought and suffered for perish now that Nasi was dead? Nicabar rubbed a hand over his bald head. The future was coming too fast. He was losing control.

The problems were now coming more rapidly than he could calculate solutions. After years in hiding, members of the Wild Rose clan had located them, and there was no way of knowing if some had escaped to seek re-enforcement. Fear of an attack ran rampant through the encampment. His nephew still refused to say anything. It could cost the boy his life. Pias and Tasaria were particularly adamant that he talk and were prepared to use any means necessary to pry vital information from him. Nicabar, though sympathetic to both the plight of his people and Espen, had even larger problems to worry about than the discovery of the raiding party or the presence of his nephew.

A directive had arrived from the Master several days before Pias brought in his prisoners. It instructed him to locate Jal and somehow safely retrieve the infant daughter of Ernest Frankenstein from him. The message provided no insights into why Jal took the girl, but insisted that the matter be dealt with immediately.

Why did the Master continue to trouble himself with this Frankenstein? They'd secured the journals the Master sought by using him, but that should have been the end of it. How was he to make decisions without any information? It was maddening.

Communications with the base in the north often grew erratic during the winter months. That was not unusual, but other trends were beginning to alarm him. He hadn't seen the Master since before the raid on Jal's camp. He sent word of Nasi's death, but received no response. Before their attack, the Master repeatedly ordered that communication and even contact be carried out only in the direst emergency. The loss of the Seer would seem to qualify as it directly threatened their plans, but he took no apparent notice of it. Instead, he was suddenly concerned about the fate of some insignificant infant. And there was still more.

Nicabar could not recall the last time one of his people had returned from the fortress in the Arctic. What was going on up there? In the early days of establishing the outpost, there was a shared sense of purpose and free movement between the Moon Shadow encampment and the fortress. Nicabar had been there himself several times, but now he'd lost track of nearly a fourth of his clan. They were spread throughout Europe on missions, sailed ships into battle, or remained in the frozen wilds of the Arctic serving the Master's will. Moon Shadow losses in recent engagements in Hungary, Slovenia, and other raids were mounting rapidly. After the battle in Hungary, his men scattered and several parties still hadn't returned. Were they still eluding pursuers or could they have been captured or killed?

And now, with the threat of an imminent attack, he was supposed to again seek out the Wild Rose clan and involve his people in some cryptic rescue mission? Nicabar was short of men, material, and time. It could take months to locate where Jal had taken refuge, to say nothing of how he might secure Frankenstein's offspring if Jal was reluctant to bargain for her safe return. To even invite such a discussion meant he would be negotiating from a weakened position. Pias asserted that they could trade Espen for the child, but Nicabar knew better. Espen and Jal were of the same ilk. Each would rather sacrifice himself than endanger others. Jal would not bargain for his son. They might at least be able to get Espen to tell them where the Wild Rose clan was hiding and attack the camp directly, however, that might produce unfortunate consequences. Why would Jal take the baby? Did it have something to do with the women they'd taken from the Wild Rose clan? Probably. Pias was trying to discover that now. He and Tasaria would join him as soon as she completed the mixture for her truth potion.

"Excuse me, Tasaria?"

The voice came from just outside the tent's entryway. Both Nicabar and his wife uttered a collective sigh. What could be wrong now?

"Enter," Tasaria said simply.

Hebba entered with a hasty bow of acknowledgement to them both. She was definitely agitated about something.

"Well?" Tasaria was anxious to return to her work.

"One of the Rom women came to see me about twenty minutes ago. Wanted to know if I had any medicine she could use."

"They haven't left?" Nicabar asked incredulously.

"No, sir. Well, that is to say, not all of them."

"Go on, Hebba," Tasaria instructed.

"Woman said her husband is too sick to travel, but their guide left sometime in the night."

"Incredible," Nicabar shook his head. As if he didn't have enough problems.

"How long has he been sick?" Tasaria's eyes narrowed.

"He seemed well enough all day yesterday but kept screaming about all sorts of things, even last night. My husband did as you asked and suggested they leave, then suddenly this morning, she shows up insisting he might be dying. I told them I'd ask around for medicine."

"Dying of what?" Nicabar questioned.

Hebba made a face.

"He is in a bad way. Probably best if one of you just comes and sees."

"How soon until you are ready, my wife?"

"I am ready now," Tasaria declared as she closed a pouch containing her mixture.

"Deal with the situation, Hebba, as best you can. Keep them outside of the encampment. We can't risk something spreading. We'll come see for ourselves after we've completed our talk with the prisoners," Nicabar commanded.

*

Nicabar and Tasaria entered the guarded prison tent eager to finally complete the interrogation. Decisions needed to be made and quickly. To their mutual surprise, Pias was not there, nor was one of the prisoners, but a generous trail of blood bore testament to his ultimate fate. Espen was obviously beaten badly and was barely conscious. A gasp escaped Tasaria at the sight of his beleaguered condition.

"Nicabar, there was no need for this," she bit, angrily shaking the pouch she carried. "How could you order it?"

Nicabar was silent. He hadn't ordered this, and such an act infuriated him.

"I'll find Pias," he declared, resolute in his purpose.

"No, stay,' his wife commanded. "In his present condition, this will not take long. And I don't want Pias here when he speaks."

Nicabar nodded as she set the pouch alight. They vacated the tent for several minutes while the smoke took effect, then returned after ordering the guards to send Pias to their tent immediately. Tasaria knelt beside Espen who was shackled and bound to a tent pole. His head hung to one side; she leaned in close and began to speak.

At first the voice didn't touch him, he was too traumatized, but slowly he became aware of its existence. It was a voice he recognized, but the accent puzzled him. Who was speaking? It was a mixture of the east and the west.

"Etolie?" he asked weakly.

She must know that Kelv was dead. Thank God she was safe. How could he begin to explain? It was his fault. She would hate him, forever.

"No," the voice said gently, "I need to know where Etolie is."

That's right. She'd been taken.

"I don't know," he cried, "We must find her."

"We will," the voice said reassuringly. "Is she with your father?"

"She was taken. I promised I would find her," he frantically explained.

"We must tell your father that she is not here. Help me to find him."

It was difficult to think.

"I don't know where he is," Espen confessed.

"He is not with his people?" the woman's voice inquired.

"No."

"Where then?" the other pressed.

"I don't know. He left."

There was a pause. Espen tried to raise his head, but the motion made the world spin. One eye seemed to be swollen shut. He could only make out two murky outlines hovering nearby. The air was thick with smoke.

"Why is he not with his people? The infant?"

Espen's head drooped again.

"What? There is no infant. We have to save them."

He heard a whisper.

"Why is your father not with his people?" The voice was more forceful this time. Espen tried to remember.

"He left to get her back."

"Etolie?"

"Yes. No. Not …"

It was so hard to focus. Espen struggled to remain in the moment.

"The infant?" the other pressed.

"No. Baseria," that was it. "She was taken. He left to get Baseria."

The name breathed in the silence for a moment, and then he heard a frantic whispering. Was it angry? Scared? He couldn't focus. Who was talking to him?

"Etolie? Baseria?" he asked.

But there was only silence, and when he was again able to lift his head, the figures had fled.

*

They managed to retain their composure long enough to re-enter their own tent a short distance away.

"It can't be true," Nicabar muttered frantically as the flap closed behind him. He would never be as foolish as to get Baseria directly involved. The end result could only be something disastrous like this. In fact, he'd made a point, even with the Master that she was not to be taken with the others. There were simply too many negative variables regarding Jal's reaction,and too many unknowns about the Master's ultimate purpose concerning them.

His goal with the raid in Hungary was to secure Nasi and to bring her here to complete Tasaria's training. The abduction of the women was to have served as a distraction while they secured and escaped with the Seer. But the Master needed them for another purpose as well and had taken at least two to the fortress in the Arctic. Could he have somehow taken more there without Nicabar knowing; and if so, for what intent? The Master never violated his trust like this. It was not his way. But it was Pias'. The thought suddenly burned like a flame within him. Tasaria paced feverishly too angry to speak.

The tent flap was barely opened when Nicabar lunged at the visitor and hurtled him to the ground. He kicked Pias viciously, who gasped for air as Nicabar repeated the offense.

"You murderous traitor! You're no better than your wolves. What have you done?!"

Nicabar struck him again. Pias shielded his mid-section to a degree before he attempted to reply. His voice was hoarse.

"You wanted information. I did what I had to."

"No, you did as you wanted to, as you always do!" Tasaria charged.

"One less enemy," he defiantly asserted.

"Is that what you thought when you arranged to kidnap my niece and the others?" Nicabar asked before he struck him again. Pias tried to laugh, but it quickly deteriorated into a fit of coughing.

"How many were taken?"

"Five. The Master ordered it."

"You lie," Tasaria proclaimed glaring down at the prone figure beneath her.

"No," he wheezed, "there is a step which must be taken if the Master's promise is to be fulfilled. Your husband would have impeded it, so he entrusted the task to me."

"You lie." It was Nicabar's turn to make the accusation.

"Do not … blame me for your self-deception. The Master believes that one of them has been trained in the knowledge of the Seer."

"I am the Seer!" Tasaria shouted. "There is no other now than me."

A strange, disquieting smile crept across Pias' face.

"Are you willing to sacrifice the future because of your pride?"

Tasaria stormed from the tent after issuing a final, vicious curse. For several minutes neither spoke nor moved, but gradually, Nicabar's anger abated a degree. The leader of the Moon Shadow clan considered this new information. If it was true, it explained much. Pias slowly sat up.

"Do you want me to get her back?"

Nicabar turned his head slowly to face his disgraced lieutenant, who spit out a small amount of blood.

"Your niece. Do you want me to go to the fortress and retrieve her? By now the Master must know if she is the Seer or not."

After a moment's consideration, Nicabar turned away from him.

"We need you here. If the others should attack ..."

"They won't," Pias waved a hand dismissively. "At least not immediately. The other one said enough before the end to convince me."

There was no reaction from Nicabar. Pias pressed the matter.

"The Wild Rose clan is in disarray. We should strike. End it, now."

"No."

"Nicabar ..."

"No," the Moon Shadow leader said adamantly. "The Master sent me a pressing directive several days ago. Jal has taken Frankenstein's daughter. He's ordered we secure her. Until that is accomplished an attack is out of the question."

It was Pias' turn to think.

"Why should the Master care if Jal has ...?"

"I don't know," Nicabar cut him off harshly.

Pias paused before asking his next question.

"Then why would Jal take Frankenstein's daughter?"

Nicabar smiled tightly. Now that he knew Baseria had been taken, the answer was relatively obvious.

"There are ancient traditions among my people, Pias, regarding honor, which Jal adheres to quite seriously." His gaze drifted to the younger man, "If you were not an outsider, it would be easier to explain."

Pias chose to allow the insult to stand unchallenged. There would be another time.

"Trade him his son for the infant then," Pias advocated with strained patience.

"No," Nicabar nodded to himself. "No, it must be Baseria. It is the only way."

Pias shrugged.

"But what if she is a new Seer?"

"Then Tasaria is best qualified to deal with her," Nicabar rejoined. "Besides," he added hastily, "if the Master's work has successfully progressed, she will be needed there anyway."

Nicabar worked to suppress his fears. Of all his options, this seemed to present the least amount of risk, which wasn't saying much. He should be the one to go, but current circumstances made that impossible. He was the clan's leader, and despite his compatriot's reassurances, the Moon Shadow camp remained vulnerable. If the gypsy Pias had killed was lying, then Jal could appear at any time. He could not abandon his people, nor could he consign them to the protection of another. Pias alone could not be trusted to return Baseria safely, but could Tasaria? What choices would the battle within her soul lead her to? Which emotion regarding Baseria was the stronger?

In their absence, he would have to continue to pursue other options to secure Frankenstein's child. There must be another way, but for the moment, it eluded him. Pias broke into his thoughts.

"What of Espen?"

"He will remain here as our prisoner."

"A fine plan, and if he should escape? Jal will bring whatever is left of his forces and annihilate this camp."

Nicabar smirked.

"For the time being, we will use my wife's skills to gain as much information from him as we can. If your mission is successful, he will be useful to us as a guide or emissary when we seek out Jal."

"And if he has already killed Frankenstein's child, we waste precious time and resources for nothing. There is too much at stake for this nonsense."

"This," Nicabar paused to emphasize the word, "is the Master's command. Our faith demands that we obey it. After you leave, I will pursue arrangement for the trade with Jal. You'll have to keep in close contact if this is to work."

"A thing not easily done from the Arctic," Pias observed.

The Moon Shadow leader nodded.

"Yes, but everything now depends upon it. When can you be ready to leave?"

Pias considered the question a moment.

"In two days, if you send a messenger ahead to my ship immediately. Your wife must be ready to depart."

"I will speak with her," Nicabar promised.

*

"Don't touch me! I know one of you did this ..."

Berryer never finished his thought as another wave of the inexplicable illness again overtook him. His muscles locked in a spasm, and he clawed for the bucket. Abrielle handed it to him just in time. She turned away from her crime. She'd known whatever was in the water bladder would likely make anyone who drank it sick, but she hadn't expected it to be so severe. In fact, at first, she found it rather amusing, after all Berryer's posturing and abuse, to see him suffer a little. But now she worried that he might not leave this tent alive. What had she given him? And where had Grenier obtained it?

She'd managed to substitute her water bladder with his and stayed awake late into the night, feigning sleep, waiting for him to rouse and take his nightly drink. After she felt certain he again slept, she tossed the bladder into the fire, along with several logs. By now, all that remained of it was ash. Still with the onset of both dawn and Berryer's violent illness, Chloe took the time to check the water bladders. Her earlier admonition of Abrielle seemed to indicate that a similar substance was most likely hidden in one. She'd either been verifying that the contents of her water bladder could be accounted for or making certain that they couldn't be used against her; ultimately, she dumped the contents outside and burned the container. To make matters worse, Grenier had apparently vanished in the night. His sudden absence was ominous.

Berryer's head flopped back down onto his bedroll. The stench from the bucket was overwhelming. Reluctantly, Abrielle grabbed it and made to dump its contents outside. She was leery of again setting foot outside should the man with the wolf reappear. He'd come from the woods an hour earlier when Chloe and Abrielle were outside. His eyes were piercing, delving into them, cruel. Only once or twice before could she recall being casually studied by eyes so malicious. His wolf did not approve of them either, and only its growls broke the hypnotic embrace of his gaze. She couldn't be certain, her mind too preoccupied by the encounter to know for sure, but had she seen Chloe give the slightest nod towards the man? A nod of familiarity? Could he be one of her secret observers? Could he have been searching for the missing Grenier? His eyes paused for a time on Abrielle's scarred right hand; had he been marking her for some purpose?

Despite her misgivings, the fresh air outside did revive her. Chloe was returning from her conversation with the abrasive woman from the Moon Shadow camp. A look of annoyance was etched upon her features.

"Vile woman," she spit contemptuously.

"Is she their doctor?"

"More than that I'm sure; more importantly she also seems to be the only one who might help us. How is he?"

Abrielle lifted the now empty bucket and shrugged.

"About the same."

They slipped back inside. Berryer was fast asleep.

"What did you tell her?" Abrielle asked quietly.

"That my poor sister's husband would die without aid," Chloe responded as she cast about for something.

"She didn't want to examine him?"

"No, she was too suspicious of us to come inside alone, but she did promise to make some type of medicine to treat the symptoms I described. She was quite adamant that we remain here until she's ready."

"I guess that makes sense. Are they looking for Grenier?"

Chloe ignored the question as she located a small pouch.

"We're going through firewood too quickly. I'll gather some more before it gets dark. If this Tasaria should reappear while I'm gone, explain to her where I've gone and that I'll be back soon."

Abrielle nodded, Chloe paused in the entryway, the pouch in her hand.

"Orfilia, I needn't tell you what must be done if they come for you and your husband?"

No, there was only one option if the gypsies acted on their suspicions. Whether she died by her own hand or died fighting them, she and Berryer, must surely die rather than be coerced into revealing their true identities.

*

Abrielle wrapped the scarf more tightly around her face. Too much of her breath was still being made visible in the frosty night air. By now she was anxious for this to be over. She'd waited for hours, but Chloe hadn't returned to their tent. Berryer seemed closer than ever to achieving his final reward, which meant that tonight might be her last opportunity to gain access to the prisoners.

Though she'd managed to return to the cliff side perch Grenier had shown her, she still didn't have a real plan. Abrielle should have felt relieved that she'd made it even this far, but her success only deepened her doubts. It was too easy. With the mysterious Grenier, Chloe's unseen observers, the now missing Chloe, and an armed encampment of gypsies, someone should have happened to stop her, but they hadn't. Could anyone observing her leaving actually believe she was simply gathering firewood?

After resolving to go, she gathered a few supplies, mindful to limit herself to the basics: matches, a knife; she'd looked for a pistol but been unable to locate one. Naturally, Chloe hid them somewhere outside to prevent her reluctant charges from gaining any tactical advantage. She tied a measure of rope around her waist and affixed Tara's blanket beneath it. Her attire was dark in color, heavy, but not so much that it restricted her movements. After careful consideration, she stowed Ailis' flute beneath a rock near the tent as she left. Any flash of light off the metal might reveal her. It should be safe until her return, and she could now retrieve it without re-entering the tent. Any food or water would freeze outside, and she was unwilling to have any on her lest the sound of sloshing water or scent of food betray her to the wolves.

Abrielle's fingers caressed the cold rock at the lip of the cliff as she tried to reassure herself. This was something she must do. In her mind, she'd already selected the route she could take to the prison tent. Now she would have to see if fate would permit it. Slowly she drew herself upward and began to cautiously survey the Moon Shadow encampment. To her great relief she saw no wolves stalking around the encampment. Even more encouraging, she did not see the dangerous man with the piercing gaze. However, to her surprise she saw no guards outside the tent, which was supposed to house the Wild Rose prisoners. Few gypsies lingered outside. Most darted among tents, happy to remain inside on such a frigid night. But her instincts and experience made her wary. It was too easy, and she did not trust coincidence. Still, if she didn't try she'd probably never have another chance to speak to these men, and she might lose Tara forever.

Her muscles tensed at the thought. Her fears evaporated. Abrielle took a moment to breath and was just about to raise herself up onto the frosty ground when she saw the smoke and dim light. Her body froze. The prison tent flap opened and a bald headed man and the intense woman who'd promised Chloe medicine emerged along with a thick haze of smoke. Both coughed as they drew in the cold night's air. Were they tending the prisoners, giving them medical attention? Could that explain the woman's delay in returning to give Chloe medicine? Even more importantly, could this somehow validate Chloe's own absence? Why was there so much smoke? She dimly overheard a remark between them about time before they unexpectedly walked away and disappeared into another tent nearby. Without further hesitation, she rose and began to delicately make her way towards the unguarded prison tent. She met no resistance and withdrew her blade only when she was two steps away from the tent's flaps. If another guard remained inside, he would have to be dealt with swiftly. As she drew back the flap, Abrielle suppressed the urge first to cough and then to scream.

Her foot hovered a moment over the object of her terror, but there was no reaction from it to her presence. Her heart raced as it sank. The tent was not unguarded. Through the haze she now perceived more of them strewn about inside, along with a single, semi-conscious prisoner tied to a pole in the center of the tent.

A mad determination surged through her as she willed her foot to gingerly complete the step over the sleeping wolf. The animal stirred minutely as the tent flaps closed behind her. Whatever happened now she was committed. The smoke stung her eyes and sapped her strength. Each measured step became increasingly difficult as her focus and will abated in the haze. What could this miasma be? She looked down at her feet. Whatever it was, the wolves must be drugged in some manner. It seemed the only rational explanation for their behavior. Her thick scarf must be protecting her to a degree but it was only a question of time before she too succumbed to the smoke's effects. Each step portended doom. The wolves shifted their bodies, ears twitched, soft whines escaped them, and one even barred its teeth briefly. Abrielle pressed on knowing it would take only one to bring about disaster.

When she finally reached him, she made a quick assessment of the man's status. He was badly beaten; his mind and energies seemed to slip in and out of focus as the smoke worked on his senses. Talking to him here was out of the question. Any utterance could awaken the powerful canines all about them. But could she get him out of here safely? And if so, what then? Her pulse thundered in her ears. Awkwardly, her fingers reached under her garments and began to loosen the rope about her waist. The process seemed to take an eternity. When would the others return? At last it was free, and she set the coiled mass over one of her shoulders as she retrieved the object beneath. Abrielle pressed Tara's blanket to the man's face and prayed it could filter the smoke's effects swiftly enough for him to regain his senses.

She heard the noise outside a few seconds before the tent flap was drawn open. Without thinking she hid the rope and blanket beneath her as she pressed herself immediately to the ground. A slumbering wolf lay mere inches from her face. The Wild Rose prisoner's body hid most of hers, but if someone entered, her attempt to pass herself as a wolf wouldn't last long.

As the figure in the door hovered in the entry, the wolf before her slowly opened one yellow eye. She stared into it, frozen in terror, certain it would strike. Her soul cried out, unwilling to embrace death, but she remained motionless. Endless seconds passed. Then, casually, the wolf's tongue worked a measure of moisture back into its mouth as it lazily resumed its tranquil state. The shadow disappeared from the entry and the flap closed. Abrielle shook with fear, but she managed to gingerly raise herself back up.

The fresh air let in by the now-absent visitor and Abrielle's own efforts prior to their arrival seemed to have revived the prisoner to a degree. His lips parted to speak, but she pushed Tara's blanket roughly against his face and shook her head. She motioned for him to breathe deeply as she resumed the rope over her shoulder. The gloss in his eyes began to clear. As he regained lucidity, his manacles rattled, but she lacked the means to remove them. He'd just have to hold the chain joining them taut to silence them as best he could. She took her knife and deftly sliced though the ropes binding him to the pole.

Abrielle tied Tara's blanket to her midsection again then helped the gypsy to stand. They began their treacherous journey toward the entry. Twice wolves sat up. Apparently the fresh air had also revived them to a degree, but each time, they bedded back down without further menace.

Upon reaching outside, both she and the prisoner replenished their lungs with clean air before racing for the cliff's edge. She all but jumped back down to the small ledge. The gypsy followed at a less suicidal pace, shaking in the cold night's air. Again she indicated he be silent as she raised herself up and surveyed the camp.

Nothing, neither man nor beast, stirred. They'd done it. She settled back down and a quaking breath finally escaped. The man squeezed her forearm in gratitude. She nodded in relief then indicated the direction they must travel. She began to loosen the rope, but the gypsy touched her again and shook his head. He could make it without assistance. Ten agonizing minutes later they crawled back over the cliff's edge by the waterfall. There, they rested a moment.

What now? She hadn't gone intending to free anyone nor would she entertain his inevitable request to return and free his companion. She certainly couldn't remain with the others now, but could she risk returning to the tent for supplies? Time was essential. Frigid air teased her senses. No, they'd die in the mountains without food or water. But where could they go? The man asked her a question, but she couldn't understand him. He tried again in English.

"What now?"

She swallowed before answering the question echoed by her own thoughts moments earlier.

"I have to get supplies. Wait here."

He gripped her.

"I need a weapon."

"Find a rock," she replied sarcastically. She certainly wasn't going to arm this man. He, however, took the suggestion literally and quickly secured a formidable rock in one of his hands. It seemed desperate, but then again, after what he'd been through though, Abrielle couldn't blame him. Any defense was better than none. She nodded and began to make her way back toward her tent, oblivious at first, that he'd begun to shadow her. His iron manacles betrayed his presence to her.

"Go back," she whispered, angrily. What did he think he was doing?

He continued to follow her almost to within sight of her tent. She rounded on him furiously.

"Take one more step, and I'll kill you myself. You're not that valuable to me. No one must see us together or we'll both be killed, understand?"

"You're not that valuable to me either," he chided. "I want to know what's going on."

"There isn't time to explain," she blinked and shook her head, "And if you want to escape, you'll just have to trust me."

"You're not Moon Shadow?"

"No."

"Or Rom?"

She drew down the heavy scarf, which largely obscured her face.

"No. Now shut up and wait here."

He shifted, clearly at odds with himself. He didn't trust her and she didn't have to time convince him. But if he followed and was spotted, all of her efforts and hopes would be wasted and she would still lose Tara.

"Dammit," she withdrew her knife. He raised the rock to bludgeon her but stopped mid-motion as she held the hilt towards him.

"We have to leave here. Take it and stop wasting time."

The man hesitated only a moment before he dropped the rock and took the proffered weapon. Abrielle cut him off before he could say anything.

"At least cover me if anyone follows," she admonished as she stalked away. Their short argument cost her valuable time. As soon as she could get information from this man, she was going her separate way.

As she approached the backside of the tent, she became aware of raised voices outside the entrance; one of which she recognized as Chloe's. Had the gypsy woman come to deliver the medicine she'd pledged only to discover the sick man's wife was missing? Where had Chloe been and what type of story might she be using to cover Abrielle's actions? Would her sudden reappearance help or hinder the unfolding situation?

A flicker of motion in the nearby woods caught her attention, but as she studied it, Abrielle could detect no further movement. Her nerves danced in the icy night air. She should leave. The voices in the front were becoming more intense, but she couldn't make out the words, which were obscured by the intervening tent. She began to back away. Perhaps she could at least locate Chloe's weapon's cache before departing. It must be around here someplace.

Suddenly a hand gripped her forearm. Stunned, she turned to find Berryer clasping her. Both his iron hold and sure stance offered no testimony to his recent, and by all appearances, near fatal illness. How was this possible?

"Here," he bellowed into the night with a deep, steady cry. It was cut off almost immediately. Abrielle viciously throttled his windpipe, silencing him and knocking him panting to the ground.

But the damage was done. She looked up to see Chloe, the cruel-eyed gypsy, the Moon Shadow medicine woman, and several others staring back at her. The silence echoed between them. Then the unthinkable happened.

"She's a spy!" Chloe cried out, triumph etched upon her false sister's face.

Abrielle heard herself gasp. Berryer lunged for her leg and, she pivoted to avoid him, while striking him in the head. She heard a pistol ball whistle past her ear and pass through the spot where she'd stood a moment earlier. Smoke swirled from a spot in front of one of the gypsies while another now tracked her movements. A shot from the woods unexpectedly dropped him dead. Only chaos could follow.

The cruel-eyed gypsy whistled and several wolves raced from behind the tent toward her. Before she turned to flee she heard more shots being exchanged between the gypsies and the attacker from the woods, several wild shots also impacted off rocks buried in the snow near her.

The snow hindered her progress, but it also slowed her inhuman pursuers; however, the ultimate outcome was obvious. They would overtake her. Her only chance was to go back over the edge of the cliff. The prisoner she'd freed must have come to the same conclusion for he waited only long enough to hurtle the blade at the lead wolf's hind leg before he too began to flee back to the cliff. Though the injury to the leader slowed him down, the other wolves never broke stride. Twice she nearly lost her footing, a move which would surely prove fatal, but she managed to keep moving.

They were beyond the pool now and nearing the waterfall rapidly.

Abrielle's lips felt frozen to her teeth as the frigid air raked her lungs. There wouldn't be time to secure the rope to anything on the top of the cliff. How far was it to the bottom? Would the gypsies follow and simply pick them off from atop?

She could hear the wolves closing behind her, but she didn't dare turn to look. If she did, they would have her. The lone figure on the edge of the abyss before her suddenly turned, stooped, and held aloft a large rock. He apparently intended to use it to cover her when she reached the edge rather than save himself. The thunder of the waterfall now filled the air, and she could no longer hear the wolves. The next few seconds would bring either life or death. She slowed a degree as she reached him.

A flash from the woods across the wide mountain stream appeared seconds before something impacted directly into her back. She never heard the gunshot. She only felt its results, and for a moment, knew its tragic consequences.

The wolf must have been leaping up to finish her when the shot killed it. Its momentum, however, carried the body onward. The dead weight pushed her off her feet and into the gypsy. The rock he bore in her defense now sealed their mutual fate as he toppled backward.

For a moment they clutched frantically for each other in blind horror, but their fingertips never met. Her body touched only air as she sailed over the cliff's edge. The winds buffeted her as they fell towards the waterfall, framed by its towering wood sentinels. Impenetrable mist swirled below them. Then Abrielle's head struck an outstretched branch, and her senses tumbled into blackness.

CHAPTER 12
MORALITY PLAYS

She was on the ground looking up at them. It was foggy this morning or was that smoke? Why did they study her so? She was as she'd always been. Then she remembered—she was dead. No, not dead, but she wasn't there either. She was everywhere. The men looked sad, defeated, scared; the destruction of lives and the remains of the encampment they stood within were dimly present in the background. If only they could understand.

"Baseria?"

One of them whispered to her.

"Baseria," the voice was more insistent, more frightened. If only he could understand. And then the vision was gone.

"*Firinnie*," she replied in Gaelic.

"What?"

"Isn't that what you asked me to say?"

Ernest did not reply immediately, at least, not with words. But that same look he worked so hard to conceal returned for an instant before he was able to suppress it.

"No. Are you all right?" he asked hesitantly.

"Yes, why?"

He gazed at her a moment longer then stood and wiped a hand over his eyes.

"We've been at this too long. Let's take a break."

She absently played with her fingers.

"Ernest, I'm fine. My mind must have just drifted."

He ignored her statement as he filled two cups with water, handing her one. Ernest began to pace the length of the frigid chapel as he sipped his own. Why was he so agitated all of the sudden, she wondered. Today's lesson had been going well.

Baseria's teeth crunched on some frozen ice chips. She was pleased with her progress, even if her tutor was not. It was gratifying to know that their efforts were proving fruitful. His Hungarian was coming along nicely, as was her Gaelic. Soon they should each have a working knowledge of their respective languages. The long idle hours made learning them both practical, and now they realized, essential.

If they were ever to have any hope of planning for their escape from this unbearable incarceration, they must be able to outmaneuver their captors. This would require both trust and subtly, so they learned the nuances of their respective languages, working to learn enough to develop an oral code. Written plans were impractical for their possessions were often searched while they slept. And then there was the presence they both sensed, here, in this place, and the knowledge that the unseen watched.

Ernest had only been allowed to leave the chapel once since his arrival, and her visits were erratic and enforced. Though when they were allowed to be together, it was often for generous amounts of time. Obviously, their enemies felt their relationship would serve some as yet unknown purpose. Perhaps they hoped it would expose the truth about whether she or Etolie was the Seer. Or maybe it had something to do with whatever had happened to Ernest before his arrival.

Baseria finished her drink. Despite several attempts, she'd been unable to learn what events had transpired after her abduction in Hungary to bring him here.

"Oh, wait, it was *leabhar*. You pointed at the book on the altar, right?"

She smiled at her own silly mistake. He solemnly nodded.

"What did I call it?"

He paused and took a breath as he finished his own water.

"You said *firinnie*."

She searched her memory as she mouthed the word but there was nothing.

"What does that mean? It doesn't sound familiar."

Ernest averted his eyes.

"It means truth. It doesn't sound familiar because I haven't taught it to you yet."

"You must have …"

Her smile faded as he turned and faced her.

"No. I didn't."

Only the echoing waves below filled the void that followed. These long, tense silences were becoming increasingly familiar and unwelcome.

He was mistaken. Ernest must have said it at some point and simply forgotten. How else could she know the word? There was one way. She looked away as an unwelcome reality began to dawn.

"It's nothing," she said, attempting to regain her smile. "We should continue."

His lips moved to speak but stopped short of issuing an utterance as his eyes roved over the stone walls. The presence might hear them. He crossed to her and leaned in close to Baseria's ear.

"Have they returned," his tight voice demanded "Have your powers returned?"

She leaned away from him.

"No," she answered firmly. The word, the daydream a moment ago, they were nothing. She felt no different than she had for endless weeks now.

"Are you sure?" he asked her in French, his voice shaking.

Baseria's face hardened.

"I told you not to speak to me in that tongue," she admonished.

"It is my native tongue ...," his voice rose.

"It is the enemy's tongue! Yours is Gaelic."

"My wife's was Gaelic!"

He turned from her and hurtled the wooden cup into a distant stone wall. It clattered loudly across the floor, the harsh syllables of each impact reverberated throughout the dim chapel.

"She died because of you."

Baseria closed her eyes as his words gripped her heart and mercilessly scarred. It wasn't true. Baseria clenched her jaw so hard it felt as if the bones would shatter. Please let it not be true.

Baseria's body still recalled the exquisite pain the woman had suffered in her visions. Her soul crying out in longing and bitter sadness as she endured physical agony beyond description, but beneath it all had been such love for another. A love so deep, Baseria could barely comprehend it. Why hadn't she said something sooner? Silent tears began to trace across her porcelain cold cheeks. Her lips and chin quivered. She covered her mouth.

"… didn't know," she sobbed, but Ernest was relentless. The emotional wall that protected them both now lay in ruins.

"Yes, you did!" He roared.

"No," Baseria shook her head emphatically. "Only later, that final day in Hungary ..."

Ernest gripped her and Baseria's eyes could not turn away.

"You spoke truth to me a moment ago; speak it now! Did she die for your prophecy? This great destiny of yours? Is that why my child must die too? Do they all die for you, Baseria?"

Frozen breath mingled between them as did their wild surge of emotions.

"Your child?" Her voice broke.

Each sought truth in the other's eyes but found only questions and guilt reflected back. The horrible moment faded. Ernest's grip relaxed, and she slapped his hands away and wept openly. She hated him and she loathed herself. It was her fault; just as it was with Patia, just as it was with Jucika. She could only bring death to others.

There was a shout in the hallway, followed by a pistol's report, then an unnatural wail. As the shriek died, Baseria and Ernest froze in alarm. A pounding began against the door then suddenly ceased. Keys rattled in the lock, and Ernest moved in front of Baseria to shield her from view. The door burst open, was slammed shut, and then locked. The key squealed in protest as it was lodged to seal them in.

The man turned. He was wild with terror. His face was concealed by grime and a thick, unkempt beard. The tattered remains of his uniform testified to a once well-ordered life, as well as, to what the life was that succeeded it. His eyes both pleaded and condemned. He hobbled as he stalked forward, blood pouring freely from several fatal wounds. Baseria moved, anxious to see who approached them, and screamed as her eyes finally beheld him. Frightened by the unexpected movement, the man repeatedly pulled the trigger of the pistol in his hand but no shot followed. He drew another from his belt and held it on them as he completed his approach. Whoever these people were, they too seemed to be prisoners. They were not like the others. The thought soothed him. He relaxed a degree and proceeded to the altar.

It was becoming difficult to breathe. As the strangers edged cautiously forward, he took comfort knowing that he would not die alone. More importantly that he would not die like the others. But if these people were indeed prisoners, then they must be made to understand, so their fates could be different. He spoke but neither seemed to comprehend his words. He sighed and laughed slightly, ill fortune no longer fazed him.

He leaned back against the altar and studied his surroundings. Was this a chapel? A wave of pain shot through his frame and the pistol slipped from his grasp. The shot discharged uselessly into a stone wall. The others jumped but after several tense moments began again to draw nearer. As the woman's face came even with his own, he gazed upon her. It was obvious she had been crying. Why should one so young, so beautiful be so sad?

He tried to smile. He was truly sorry he'd tried to shoot her. Again she spoke, but he could only nod slightly in frustration. Her companion, who hovered far overhead, said something to her. She was growing dimmer in his vision. The book! He'd seen a book on the altar. If he was in a chapel …

The dying man suddenly pointed upward and folded his hands as if in prayer. Baseria looked to Ernest in puzzlement.

"Heaven? Does he want us to pray for him?"

"Or he might want this."

Ernest passed the Bible from the altar down to her. The man nodded weakly as he accepted it. Maybe the book would bring him comfort in his last moments. He placed the book on the floor and flipped pages awkwardly. What did he seek; a favorite passage? Suddenly he stopped. He whispered something to Baseria who leaned closer to hear as Ernest studied the illustration his fingertips tapped. His work finished, his eyes shut, forever.

Across the chapel there was a new pounding at the door. Ernest knelt down. There wasn't much time.

"He must have been one of those Norwegian sailors they captured. What did he say?"

"It was short and in Latin," Baseria explained distractedly as she concentrated to translate the man's final words.

"Could you understand it? My Latin's not that strong."

"I think so," she turned as a crack was heard at the far end of the room. The wooden door was giving way.

"Baseria?"

"What did he point to?" she asked as her attention returned to Ernest.

Wordlessly, he held up the illustration, now tinged with bloody fingerprints.

"*Hostis humani generic*," she repeated the dead man's words breathlessly.

The door was seconds from shattering.

"What does that mean?" Ernest demanded.

With a final harsh splinter, the door collapsed and Moon Shadow gypsies poured into the room followed by their dark Master. Baseria stole one final glance at the demonic figure cruelly staring back from the illustration.

"Enemy of the human race," she translated. Her eyes fixed on Victor's unholy son.

The agents of the gigantic menacing figure fanned out, seizing the pistols, shoving Ernest toward a bench, checking the dead man, and restraining Baseria who struggled as they pulled her away from the corpse. No one spoke as the grim figure glided silently to the altar. He lowered himself and studied the body carefully before finally retrieving the still open Bible. His reaction to the illustration was marred by the shadows of the concealing hood. He closed the book and returned it to the altar then nodded to his subordinates who began to remove the body.

"Gently," he admonished as his gaze found Baseria who immediately looked away. A decrepit hand motioned those who guarded her to leave. Ernest stirred to intervene but was restrained upon the bench. He watched helplessly as the towering figure stood before the frightened girl.

"Do you weep for one you hardly knew?" he asked in French.

Baseria breathed heavily as she looked to Ernest for a moment.

"No, for your cruelty," she finally answered.

Defiantly she raised her head, though she still shook in his presence.

"Then know my compassion," the towering shadow said. "Your companions await you in the reading room. You may go to them unescorted."

His hand rose slightly as if to touch her cheek, and then faltered.

"Take comfort child. Our long night is almost at an end."

He delayed a moment longer before turning his attentions to Ernest. Baseria quietly slipped away, only pausing to stare at the corpse of the robed figure that had been shot while guarding the door. Precious little remained of its face.

"An unfortunate business," the creature commented after she'd gone.

"Yes," Ernest agreed quietly.

"You must forgive my extended absence, Uncle. I have not meant to ignore you. I hope the girl has proven adequate companionship. You seem quite taken with one another."

Ernest shifted uncomfortably.

"I would hate to be deprived of her companionship," he said after a moment.

A trace of brilliant enamel flashed in the shadow of the hood, the cruel hint of a smile.

"That is her decision ... and yours."

"Mine?"

The creature moved to the entry.

"Please, there is much to discuss."

Ernest eyed the waiting shadow, wary of what was to come. Restless fingers absently rubbed against the scar on his right hand. He stood and followed.

*

Sparks showered the fireplace for a moment as Etolie threw in another log. The heat the flames radiated was seductive. She stood and turned to allow the pulsing waves of warmth, carried by cooler air currents, to wash over her legs and back. The reading room, as they'd come to call it, was an oddity within the fortress. What its original purpose might have been she couldn't fathom, but now it served as a type of sanctuary for her and the other Wild Rose prisoners.

Opposite the wall with the large fireplace was another covered entirely by bookshelves and divided by a balcony. They contained a surprising variety of literature that covered a host of subjects. The books were written primarily in French, but there were also enough copies in other languages, spread throughout the collection, to make many of the works accessible to her non-French speaking companions. Unlike everywhere else in the fortress, there were comfortable sofas and chairs in the room. Perhaps it had always been a type of library, but not one easy to reach.

One gained access to it either by using a remote turret or by passing through a maze of corridors and stairwells. However it had come to be, at least it was away from their quarters, was one of the only places they were allowed to gather together, and above all, despite its icy perch, relatively warm.

The sound of the doorway from the corridor being drawn open stirred Etolie from her reverie. The expression worn by the girl who passed through the entry already answered her unspoken question, but nonetheless she felt the need to ask anyway.

"Sebbi?"

Isyll shook her head and closed the door, anxious to warm herself before the fire. Etolie removed her warmer blanket and draped it over a grateful Isyll's shoulders. She trembled visibly as she spoke.

"I looked everywhere I could, but no one claims to have seen her today. Of course the Old One who was following me everywhere might have had something to do with their answers. I could tell some wanted to say more."

Etolie nodded in reflection.

"And there's no way she could have been taken from your room while you slept?"

The younger woman shook her head.

"We've been sharing a bed. It's far too cold alone. I would have felt her being taken, if for no other reason, than the loss of her body heat. I can't understand it," Isyll said, lost in her fears.

"What's there to understand? I see no point in debating this further," a new voice asserted from a nearby chair. "However it happened, she's gone."

Vochallet closed the book she'd been reading and leaned forward in her chair.

"So we should abandon her?" Isyll demanded incredulously. "Would you like us to do the same if they took you?"

"Isyll," Etolie placed a hand on her shorter friend's shoulder. The young woman was closer to Sebbi than anyone, even before they'd been captured and brought here.

"They will take me," Vochallet declared coldly, "just as they'll take you. Who knows, perhaps they plan to steal you from your bed tonight; just as they did Sebbi. People don't just vanish."

"Enough," Etolie began.

"No, it's not enough," Vochallet said passionately. "You know we're going to die here. They brought us to this wilderness for some hideous purpose. We've all seen things. We've all heard things. The only mystery for me is why they prolong our misery. At least it's over for Sebbi."

"You're wrong," Isyll shook her head, tears in the corners of her eyes.

"You're scaring her, Vochallet." Etolie admonished.

"And you've been giving her false hope. You and Baseria. Is that any less cruel? We can't escape," the eldest among them affirmed.

Only the dimly heard noises from the dock far below intruded among the silence. Isyll hung her head. Etolie squeezed her shoulder reassuringly.

"Hope is never cruel," Etolie said softly, "And it's all we've got left…besides each other."

Vochallet turned away. She released an inner sigh as she walked. Etolie felt her own sorrows cry out. What if Vochallet was right? She returned her attentions to the fire and momentarily lost herself among the flames. The fight wasn't anyone's fault. Fear drove it. They were all scared, and Sebbi's disappearance only heightened their fears and reawakened the despair and helplessness they suffered as isolated prisoners in this frozen bastion.

Etolie's thoughts turned to her distant home. She could almost feel Kelv's touch, the sun's warmth on her skin. Her thoughts dwelled on nights spent with friends singing and laughing around the fire.

Etolie pushed her thoughts away. She had to. If she was going to survive, she must. It was she whom they looked to for guidance. Baseria had isolated herself, Vochallet was too self-absorbed, and Isyll too inexperienced, Sebbi too quiet, so, ironically, the woman who had tried to kill herself to escape imprisonment had become the peacekeeper and even caretaker of them all. Maybe this was her penance for her utter loss of hope while at sea. Then she'd felt alone, now her only concern was for her companions and to be reunited with her husband. If she stopped believing there was hope now, then it didn't matter what the Moon Shadows did. They'd be dead long before the enemy destroyed them. She must not let that happen.

But she was so frightened. Despite the arrival of Frankenstein and Baseria's reassurances, Vochallet was right. They might never escape. But how much longer could they endure in this place? None of them had slept well in months. The Moon Shadows seemed to constantly change their schedule, and with no true sun to guide them, night seemed eternal.

Etolie tried to reassure herself. How many of the bizarre occurrences might be nothing more than waking nightmares? She wished they were all but shadows of the mind. But hadn't they all fancied similar things: strange noises from the walls, lamentings heard in the unyielding depths of night, lights which appeared in the sunken portion of the fortress, and an intermittent pressure on the body's senses which came and went without warning. Then there was the queer nature of those robed figures the Moon Shadows referred to as Old Ones. They were certainly real enough, and alarmingly, there seemed to be more of them now than when they'd arrived. She'd noted that their presence even seemed to disturb the Moon Shadows themselves. But who were they?

Etolie massaged her temples. How could she lead others if she could not contain her own fears? Isyll extended the blanket back around Etolie and smiled warmly as she hugged her lightly.

"I should have brought back some tea or something."

"I could use something stronger than tea right now," Etolie quipped.

Isyll nodded in quiet agreement.

"But tea never makes me come over in a fit," Isyll added, referring to the seizures, which occasionally paralyzed her.

"Is it my imagination or does it seem brighter in here?" Vochallet suddenly asked aloud. Almost unconsciously, the others turned and swiveled their heads slowly. It did seem brighter.

The door from the turret opened without preamble as a familiar figure crossed the threshold into the room. Baseria stood transfixed, though not by anything in the reading room. Instead, she studied the spiraling stairwell from which she'd just come. The others shared glances of puzzlement as the new visitor made no move to shut the door. Other than swirls of icy breath escaping her in great quantities, she was motionless.

"You're letting all the heat out," Vochallet finally said with strained patience. Still Baseria did not move.

Etolie abandoned the blanket to Isyll and hurriedly crossed the room. She was forced to physically turn Baseria away from the stairwell.

"Ba? Ba! What is it?"

The pale girl leaned on the doorframe and blinked. Her distressed reply escaped as a thin whisper.

"I've just seen a ghost."

*

The remnants of the meal, which they'd passed nearly in silence, were now cleared from the heavy oak table, only their drinks remained. Ernest wondered if the lengths of timber they'd eaten upon could have once belonged to a ship. Where was her crew now? A massive fireplace filled the wall behind the hooded figure who sat opposite him. A soft, shifting glow burned behind the high-backed chair he sat on.

"Tell me of your life, Uncle," the being presumptuously requested.

Ernest's hands met as he set his elbows upon the table.

"You've attempted to read my wife's journals, spied on me, listened to my conversations with others, what more is there is to say?"

"A great deal," the creature's voice said flatly before he took a sip from his mug.

"What then?" Ernest implored.

"I wish to know morc about your life beyond the confines of Europe."

Ernest turned his eyes to the piercing yellow ones.

"Why?"

"It is the one topic of conversation you were willing to omit when you spoke with Christiansen in Geneva. I want to understand why. What happened to you out there?"

"How can it possibly affect you?" Ernest asked turning his eyes away.

"If we are to be family in more than name I must understand you."

"And I you," Ernest retorted. "Why do you keep prisoners?"

"You would prefer I destroy them?"

"I would have you set them free. If you understood anything about the family you wish to connect with, you'd know that your ancestors would be appalled by your actions."

"Yes, the charitable nature of the Frankensteins," he mocked. "And what makes you think I deny that nature?"

"There is nothing natural to any of this."

"I am merely doing as all enlightened beings must, embracing my own nature so that I might enlighten others."

"And how does killing people bring them or you to enlightenment?" Ernest demanded.

"The living are always walking among the dead. Only time alters our perception between the two states." He leaned back. "I wonder what will become of humanity when it believes it has solved all mysteries."

Ernest longed to be free from this fiend.

"What are you?"

"I'm not human in your eyes? What then do you believe me to be, beside a murderer?"

What did Ernest believe? Was this thing a man, a god, some form of eternal evil, or could it be all of these things. He longed to press the matter, but he also recognized the danger inherent in the question. His impressions, once stated, could be turned against him. Or if he brought up the prophecy, it might endanger Baseria, then again the subject might provide some much needed answers. How much of the prophecy did the Moon Shadows already know?

"You fear to answer the question?" the cloaked figure needlessly asked.

By now it must be obvious that Ernest did.

"Will you provide an answer if I do?" Ernest countered.

"As much as I am able," the other answered coolly.

Ernest felt the moisture leave his mouth.

"You claim to be my brother's son; yet, he would have been a child when you were conceived."

"How old do you believe me to be?"

Again Ernest struggled to respond. What should he say? Ageless? Besides, the diseased condition of the abhorrent being only served to further distort clarity of fact, but Ernest's impression, that the figure who sat across from him was older than he, was unshakeable.

"From what I've seen of your physical state, I'd say over forty."

Simmering white teeth seemed to ridicule the notion.

"I am both far older and far younger, Uncle, than you perceive."

"You answer me in riddles."

"I answer in truths," the creature declared.

Ernest would not be dissuaded.

"Then explain how you can be both?"

The other paused only a moment before responding.

"A paradox, born of two separate but entangled truths. It has taken me most of my existence to understand it. You also must be given time before you are ready to embrace the full meaning of my revelation."

"How much time?"

Again the question served to amuse.

"Uncle, you are not a prisoner. I do not detain your steps in this world. Tell me where you wish to go and I shall take you there."

It was frustrating to be toyed with in this manner.

"You know I can't leave," Ernest reminded the dark being.

"Ah, yes, take solace, Uncle. My forces seek your child even now. She will be found shortly."

"So you have said," Ernest challenged.

"You doubt my word?"

Ernest shook his head as he too sat back in his chair.

"No. I have seen the devotion of your followers. If you say they are attempting to locate her, I have no reservations that your words are true."

"Would you care to join them?"

The question caught Ernest off guard.

"I thought I was being protected here?"

The creature sighed.

"It seems I have failed in that promise already. I must admit, the incident in the chapel has disturbed me. If you wish to leave, I can allow several of the women to go with you as well."

Ernest silently debated the idea. Was this a genuine offer? If so, who exactly did the creature intend to retain? Would Ernest be forced to chose? No, the image of the monster's half-extended hand in the chapel and the abduction in Hungary returned to him. Ernest knew who he intended to keep.

"But you won't release Baseria?"

The beast shook his head as he drew another draught. Ernest could feel his pulse quicken. He stammered slightly.

"Why … why must she remain and not the others?

"If your child is found after you depart, I must be ready to offer her in trade. And I find her of, unique interest. There is much I could learn from her … in time."

Of all the words that had passed between them since the bizarre conversation began, these last disturbed Ernest more than any uttered prior. What was he saying? Did he know that she was the Seer or were his interests purely carnal? Ernest felt an unpleasant buzzing in his mind, his body felt light.

"The others present no interest for you?"

"I forget that you have seen only her. No, each of the others is blessed with an abundance of talents and beauty worthy of great admiration, but the girl's presence is vital if I am to be reunited with my mate and restore yours to you. I owe you that much."

"You…owe me?" Ernest muttered in bewilderment.

The cloaked head nodded.

"Yes, as retribution for Father's crimes. His madness has taken much from us."

Ernest looked away as he put a hand to his forehead, sickened by these games.

"My wife's dead," he said softly.

"I know," the other replied sympathetically.

"She's dead!" Ernest repeated forcefully. The words echoed in the chamber before fading to memory in the silence.

"So was I."

*

"Just breathe," Etolie instructed as she sat Baseria down on one of the reading room's soft chairs.

"What do you mean you saw a ghost?" Vochallet demanded, her emotions wavering between alarm and outright disbelief.

"Give her a minute," Isyll pled with an outstretched arm.

Etolie perched on one of the chair's arms and wrapped an arm around Baseria's neck, drawing her closer, as her hand stroked her friend's hair. Isyll placed her blanket over Baseria's legs and remained hovering nearby. Vochallet wrapped her own blanket more tightly about her shoulders as she opened the door to the turret and disappeared.

"It was on the step just below the fourth landing," Baseria stated in a daze, "I only saw it for an instant."

"Are you sure it wasn't just a person?" Isyll asked hopefully, though all knew the possibility was remote. This particular turret had no other doors except one leading to its roof and one at its base. Unless Baseria was lying completely, it seemed unlikely that any random individual would have chosen to lie in wait in the frigid staircase; unless they had been spying on the women in the reading room.

"There isn't anything in there," Vochallet reported as she closed the door behind her, rubbing her upper arms for warmth.

"What exactly did you see, Ba?" Etolie asked.

Baseria's wits seemed stronger.

"Well, it was a shimmer. I glanced up and saw it in front of the window."

"Was it a person?" Isyll inquired earnestly.

"I … no, it was," Baseria sighed and shook her head; the memory was too hard to articulate.

"It was probably just snow that got in," Vochallet asserted.

"Maybe," Baseria said flatly.

"Then why would it shimmer?" Isyll asked.

"Because the sun is rising," Etolie said in wonder as the light from the high windows sent beams radiating down to touch sections of the room.

"I was about to point that out," Vochallet said with a smile. "Should we try to get to the roof?"

Baseria gripped Etolie's arm.

"There was a presence. I could feel it."

"Well, I didn't feel anything down there when I went to check except cold," Vochallet volunteered.

"Good," Baseria said in genuine relief.

"Maybe someone was there, I mean a real person," Isyll said.

"What?" Vochallet asked.

"Sorry, I was thinking out loud. The Old One who followed me earlier, it was spying on me. Why wouldn't they want to spy on us here? They do everywhere else. They still rifle through my room at odd hours."

It made sense and they'd only climbed through the tower twice previously. Could there be a hidden door someplace in the stairwell? Maybe the Moon Shadow spy was simply careless.

"Then where did the spy go?" Vochallet pointed out.

"Ba, maybe you startled him and he ran up the stairs," Etolie suggested.

"He could be up there right now," Isyll breathed as her eyes turned to scan the ceiling.

"Or maybe I did see a phantom," Baseria interjected.

A wicked crack broke their train of thought as Vochallet kicked out one of the spindles on the staircase that led up to the balcony. She repeated the assault three more times, then handed a spindle to each of her companions.

"Let's go find out."

"But he could have run back down by now," Isyll fretted.

The others ignored her.

"Two up, two down?" Etolie asked the group.

"I don't want to go back out there," Baseria said anxiously.

"We all go up," Vochallet decided.

After a few more feeble protests from Isyll, the group wrapped themselves in blankets and entered the turret. Frigid air bellowed up from below, but there was no sign of life. Slowly they climbed the remaining stairs until they came to the latched doorway at the top. They glanced nervously at one another.

"What do we do if someone is out there?" Isyll whispered.

"That's their problem," Vochallet answered as she hefted her spindle.

The latch was sprung and they tumbled through the entry into a cold, relatively narrow space. Walls continued to rise around them and another short staircase to their left led to a platform above. Vochallet led them as they crept upward.

It was windy at the top. It was also empty. A shared sense of relief brought smiles to their cold faces, brilliant beams of sunlight through the clouds brought joy. How long had it been?

It was too cold to remain in the open for very long, but the wind and the sun brought with them a desperately needed sense of freedom. They had survived perpetual night. Etolie and Baseria looked to one another, and the smoldering resentment between them abated a measure. The moment needed no words. The wounds between them could be healed, though they would never be forgotten. The women huddled together for warmth near the ramparts and finally gazed upon the beautiful expanses of total desolation of their Arctic prison.

It was a wild place, serene and bedazzling at the same time. Dark, tumbling waters stretched all around them. In places huge icebergs rose and fell among the waves, at a greater distance, though, they seemed to glide peacefully across the unseen currents. The women were too high to see much directly below them. The turret was probably designed to spot invaders when they were still far out at sea, at least on a clear day.

The sun illuminated a rolling stock of clouds, uniform in shape, to the east. The west held an island, all but consumed by dark clouds, which were imposing more snow on the rocky mountains that were already thoroughly blanketed. A single, brilliant shaft of sunlight reflected brightly off the white snow. The north was obscured by fog and mist, while the south held more remote, mountainous islands.

A sense of great loneliness descended upon the prisoners, and they huddled closer. They would have to go back down soon. There, together in the sunlight, with her fears held at bay, Baseria finally noticed the absence of an important presence among them.

"Where's Sebbi?

CHAPTER 13
SERENITY'S NEW CREATION

The driving pain rushed through her all at once. Her body felt shattered. She couldn't breath, she couldn't turn. All she could do was pray for unconsciousness to seize her again. Abrielle could hear herself fighting to draw each raspy breath. Then a new, unpleasant sensation assaulted her lungs. She coughed up fluid rich with a nasty iron taste. The blood clung to her lips. What had happened to her? Abrielle tried to look down. She felt certain her eyes were open but still saw only blackness. She was blind. She was blind!

"Oh God, help. No. Oh God, help me," she pleaded quietly in terror.

She could feel the unmistakable texture of a powdery snow beneath her. Abrielle's fingers probed the ground. Who had done this to her? Chloe? No, she was on top of the mountain … back with the others. Her searching fingers touched something soft, and then withdrew in terror. She began to crawl backwards.

No! Her mind screamed. She didn't know where she was. She could plunge further into the abyss of the waterfall if she moved. If she didn't though, the wolf she'd just touched would kill her. Why hadn't it?

Abrielle attempted to rise up on her hands and knees only to feel her senses tumbling through darkness. A wave of nausea overtook her, and the spasm it brought forced her to cough up more blood. Why hadn't the wolf struck? She screamed as strong hands pulled her to her feet. Her head was pushed back and fingers pulled each of her eyes open. She had to get away.

"Stop struggling or you'll break more of your ribs or puncture a lung," a voice commanded her in English.

"The wolf will kill us," Abrielle insisted as she pushed against any resistance offered.

"It's dead," the other urgently said. "So are the other two that followed us over."

Abrielle ceased her struggles and concentrated on breathing.

"You're sure?" she gasped.

"I'm sure. You're all right. The one by us was shot up top, one went into the waterfall, and I had to break the other's neck to end its suffering. Can you stand long enough for me to bind you?"

"What?" She couldn't think.

"It will help your breathing. Don't move, we're close to the edge."

She could hear fabric being torn and her body moved into a specific position. Abrielle felt the gypsy's hands wrapping lengths of it around her chest and torso.

"I can't see," she admitted humbly as he worked.

"I noticed. Your eyes didn't react at all when I checked them."

"Why?" she asked as a jumble of memories assaulted her mind.

"Can't you remember? No, don't touch your face," the man admonished.

"What?"

"That tree branch you hit cut you up pretty badly. That or the rocks did."

She stopped his motions and tried to touch his face.

"Are you all right?"

Abrielle jumped slightly when he took her hand and squeezed it.

"My leg is lame, but I think it's just sprained. I have a few other injuries, but I'll manage."

Espen didn't add that given their current situation there really wasn't really much of a choice. If they remained here, they died. If their enemies and their wolves didn't finish them, then the cold and lack of food and shelter would.

He'd fashioned a splint, which did an effective job of immobilizing the injury, but it did hamper his movements. He'd been sliced by branches, stabbed by rocks, and was fairly certain several of his ribs were either cracked or severely bruised; to say nothing of the injuries he'd received prior to their fall. Given the circumstances, though, he was grateful just to be alive.

His mysterious benefactor seemed to have actually fared much worse than he. She sank appreciatively to the ground as soon as he completed his task. What skin he could see that wasn't obscured by clothing was rent with cuts, covered in blood, or by bruises displayed a greenish hue. Still her breath did seem to be coming easier.

Their uncontrolled descent had carried them through numerous pine tree branches; offering glancing blows from rough, solid trunks, bouncing them off the cliff face, and landing them on a thick mound of snow by the bank of the waterfall. The drift was probably built up from snow blown off the mountain top and the surrounding trees. Only its existence had spared their lives.

The Moon Shadows most likely believed they'd perished, but his uncle wasn't one to leave such things to chance. Nicabar would send scouts down, eventually. Espen was certain that only the treacherous terrain and obscuring fog had, thus far, prevented their arrival.

"Where are we?" the woman asked as she shook with cold.

"Someplace we can't stay. Can you walk?" Espen urgently inquired.

"I need a minute."

It was painful to look at her. Abrielle's lower teeth and lips glistened crimson with blood. One eye would soon be swollen completely shut, and both bore angry purple hued bruises. Grated patterns raked her forehead where she'd struck the branch and dried blood caked one of her ears. Given the force of the impact, it was amazing she hadn't snapped her neck.

If only Baseria or Nasi were here. They'd have been able to heal her. But he was alone, bereft of their presence. Espen turned his head just in time to see the woman slumping over unconscious, her head barely clearing a nearby rock.

"Mademoiselle, hey," he repeated as he reached her and fanned the air around her face.

Slowly her eyelids opened to reveal vacant orbs. He rubbed her chest, she needed to stay warm or she could go into shock. Her eyelids fluttered.

"Come on. Hey. Talk to me. You've got to stay awake."

"Where am I? I need some water," her eyes cast about uselessly as she fought to hold another coughing fit at bay.

Espen left her, cupped his hands, and brought her a small quantity of water from the nearby stream. She sipped some then swatted his hands away.

"No, the poison. It's poisoned." Again she tried to move away from him. He restrained her.

"I just got it from the stream. It's mountain water. It's clean."

She calmed herself again, her energy clearly waning.

"Need to sleep," she said in a husky tone. "Can't tell when I'm dreaming or awake," she confessed.

"You can sleep. I'll let you, but first you must help me get you someplace warm and safe," Espen bid.

"Fire? But I'm warm."

She must be running a fever. He had to get her to some type of shelter.

"We don't have a fire. There isn't enough wood here," he lied. Actually their fall brought down a number of branches, which under other circumstances would have proved useful. However, a fire was impractical with the enemy so near. In her delusional state the lie was the best truth.

"Anne and Noel … they'll have fire," she wheezed.

"We can't go back up to the others," he reminded her.

She smiled faintly.

"No, go west."

"Stay awake," he admonished as her eyes drooped.

A tiny tremor shook her shoulders as she attempted to obey. It was starting to snow again. Espen's instincts were urging him to head east. It was the only sensible option if they were to safely leave France and return to his clan. West only took them further into enemy territory.

"How far away are they?"

"I don't know. Miles."

He silently cursed, then tried to recollect his composure.

"You've got to give me something to go off of, otherwise, we'll wander in these mountains until we die."

"Is it snowing?"

"What? Yes. Why?" he asked with a mixture of concern and vexation.

"The flakes are sticking to the blood on my lips." Her fingers delicately touched, traced her lips and the cuts on her chin. "We should go."

She began to struggle to gain her feet. Espen helped her up.

"How far do you think you can walk?"

"Just guide me," she commanded resolutely.

Their progress proved to be agonizingly slow. It took over an hour just to find a place where they could cross the wide, fast moving stream. The snow fell more purposely. Wherever these people she sought lived, Espen knew there would be no chance of reaching them tonight. He began to train his eyes on possible locations to shelter. They spoke little;

instead, each concentrated on simply moving their badly abused bodies onward.

Dark shadows grew thicker on the valley walls; still they discovered no sign of human intrusion in the lonely valleys. Espen's hopes dwindled. The woman was stumbling more readily now, even with his assistance. They must rest soon. But if they sat down, would they ever rise again? Their extremities were numb with cold, their bodies parched with fatigue. Left in the open, it seemed certain they would perish. And then there was the increasingly intense snow to contend with.

"Wait … stop," he instructed.

"Did you find something? Can I sit?" she inquired wearily.

He helped lower her to the ground.

"I don't think I can go any further."

"You won't have to," Espen said distractedly, annoyed with himself for not thinking of the idea sooner.

He waded into a mound of snow and began to pack it down. He tried to remember what Kelv had taught him about properly constructing one while he attempted not to recall his friend's brutal demise. The structure he hoped to create crumbled twice before he finished. Then he dug out some fallen pine branches to pile overhead. His bare hands burned as he retrieved Abrielle.

"Wait, where are you taking me?" she asked as her hands touched the sides of the portal.

"It's a snow cave. It'll keep us warm," Espen said reassuringly. It did not allay her fears.

"What? It'll collapse. We'll suffocate."

"We might if it snows on us in the open tonight. Come on."

Abrielle was too tired to argue the matter further. She didn't protest as he lowered her gingerly down into the hollowed out space. Nor did she comment when she heard him manipulating the pine branches, showering her in sticky needles. And she was fast asleep by the time he wrapped his arms around her, as their hearts worked in tandem, fighting to keep out icy whispers of death.

*

"Oh my God," Anne D'Aoust said softly as she lowered her musket.

Noel's vacillated a fraction but remained trained on the strange man before them.

"Put her on ground," Anne commanded. The man hesitated but relented without protest. He backed several steps towards the horse they'd arrived on. Anne bent down and quickly examined the unconscious, beaten woman. When the task was completed, both her temper and her weapon went up.

"Noel, get her in the house. Watch her ribs. I'll show this one and his mount to the barn."

Noel studied the man then motioned to his wife that he felt their roles should be reversed. A disparaging look from Anne would have ended the conversation for most, but Noel was used to her fire.

"I can't carry her myself, you great ox. Besides, I can handle this one," she motioned with her weapon's barrel to the man adorned in gypsy garb. More than anything he looked like he wanted to collapse. She doubted he'd be much trouble.

After locking both horse and rider into the barn, she eagerly returned to the cabin. Noel removed the younger woman's shoes and placed a heavy blanket over her. Anne gently caressed the bruises. They were more than two days old she guessed, with the exception of the apparently self-inflicted wound on her right hand.

"Well, don't just stand there idly, loomin' Noel. Get some hot water and towels so we can clean all this blood and dirt off the poor child."

She fought to keep her emotions steady. The instruction was a necessary step, but Anne mainly gave it so that Noel would leave and not see her tears. He retreated without comment.

"Saints have mercy on us all," she said softly as she wiped them away.

How many years had it been since she and Abrielle last sat together in this room? Not that it really mattered. Not a day passed that Anne didn't think of this girl, a daughter to her in all but name. Strange that she should feel so much for one who'd remained so distant. Her letters were always friendly but guarded, preferring to react more to what Anne previously stated in her own rather than to share details about her life.

Anne studied the mysterious woman's face. The features were older, the sadness that had always graced her spirit seemed to be etched deeper.

"Anne?" Abrielle breathed the name gently.

"Oh," Anne gasped in relief as she took held her friend's hand. "Abrielle."

She touched her feverish skin lightly. The younger woman smiled weakly, her eyes remained closed. When she spoke, the words felt heavy and they took a long time to say.

"Where's the gypsy?"

"I locked the big brute up in the barn. He's not going anywhere."

"You've … he needs your help too," Abrielle explained, much to Anne's surprise.

"Did he do this to you?" Anne demanded harshly.

"No … he saved me. He's injured," she coughed. Anne waited for the fit to subside then coaxed a small amount of water into her patient.

"Maybe you should rest for awhile," she suggested. "We can clean you up later."

"No … no, don't leave me. I have to know. Am I going to remain blind?"

Anne stared at her incredulously.

"Blind? Lord, Abrielle what's happened to you?"

She finally opened her eyes, or opened them as best she could. One remained a slit, swollen mostly shut. Anne bent over her, studying Abrielle's eyes. She couldn't observe any response from them when she waved or when she altered the level of light around them.

"He said my head hit a branch. I don't remember. It could have been rocks."

Noel returned with towels and a steaming basin. He touched Abrielle's shoulder gently before turning to leave.

"Noel, my love, be a dear and check on our guest outside would you. Take the shotgun, and some food and water."

He nodded, silent as always, then closed the door behind him. Taking great care, Anne began to dab at Abrielle's various contusions. This was going to take a long time. The soap and water stung tremendously. Abrielle winced every time she was touched.

"It's gonna hurt, Abrielle, there's nothing we can do about it. Talk to me. Tell me about how you supposedly hit the branch or whatever?"

Abrielle's vacant eyes opened wider, and she struggled to sit up, despair hanging about her frame.

"Oh, no." She blinked uselessly, as if the action would banish the realization.

Anne tried to restrain her.

"What? What is it?"

"No, no, no, her flute … I left it up on the cliff," Abrielle was starting to panic. Her wheezing breaths became more labored. How could she have forgotten it? It was all she had left of her sister.

"Ssshhshsh. Calm down. We'll find it later."

"No, we … we can't go back, Chloe …"

Chloe had her sister's flute. And she could not go back for it. She could never go back. Her life as she'd known it was over.

"Abrielle?"

Though Anne still held her, this new understanding deafened Abrielle's senses. She was alone, now, truly alone. Any unacknowledged hopes it could be otherwise, perished. Only what Abrielle had chosen to become remained. How could this epiphany have eluded her? Everything she'd fought and suffered for since leaving the loving arms of Anne and Noel D'Aoust had been taken from her or was now gone forever. There was no future. She was an orphan again. No. No, she was a changeling. The orphan Anne once knew and loved was an innocent. What she tried to comfort now was not. The person she'd been was dead.

"I'm a murderer."

The gentle humming stopped. The comforting hands lay upon her like dead things. The words came.

"I'm a coward. I … I'm a spy."

Abrielle's eyes stared out into the eternal darkness. She could imagine Anne's expression as each hurtful word of Abrielle's confession destroyed what was left of herself and obliterated Anne's illusions of her. There were no lies left to protect, no secrets to guard, no power to fight for.

Abrielle's face was wet with tears. She didn't deserve those, they were selfish. But so was telling Anne, who loved her as a daughter, from whom she'd hidden the truth for years. Her last great betrayal was complete.

The hands withdrew. The familiar presence drifted away. If Anne had ever truly loved her, she would destroy Abrielle now. Kill the changeling that masqueraded in the guise of the girl she'd known and cared for. Annihilate her to preserve the memory of what she'd once been. The stillness consumed her heart. Abrielle prayed to hear her own death scream. She was wretched. She prayed for anything to slay the silence and the blackness all around her. But it never came. There was no absolution. The door to the room opened, and then quietly shut. And the darkness remained.

"*Maman*[11]," she whispered.

*

Espen's eyes shot open, and for a moment, he forgot where he was. His eyes searched frantically for the butcher, the phantom from his dreams, but slowly the waking life asserted its stark realities once more. The barn did not hold his foe.

He sat up on the mound of hay, casting aside the blanket he'd been given. The dream was the phantom, but the man in it was very much of this reality. He'd tortured Espen, murdered his friends, slain Kelv before him, and mercilessly burned his grandmother alive. Twice Espen possessed the upper hand, and now twice, he'd failed. Espen didn't sleep well anymore. Since his rescue by the mysterious woman, sleep only found him for a few hours each night. But the nightmares followed him into the day.

In a matter of months, he'd lost his sister, witnessed his grandmother's murder, and suffered mere steps away as his best friend since his boyhood days was tortured and executed. The emotional wounds were far deeper than the physical ones, now beginning to heal. How could he ever face Etolie?

She'd been a friend of his long before she married Kelv. How could he tell her that she would never see her husband again? Worse, would he ever have the opportunity? The thought was too painful to bear.

Desperate for something new to ponder, he considered his own failures. What would his father say? It would have been a merciful end if the fall from atop the cliff had killed him. But it hadn't. Every single man who'd nobly joined Espen to find the kidnapped women of their clan was now dead—save him. The butcher taunted him with this fact. Espen's father would never have made such mistakes. If he had, he would have

---

11 French. Mom

made certain that he alone paid for his failures, not others.

By now Jal was probably home, Baseria was safe, and the other women found alive and well. His thoughts returned to Etolie. If only he knew the fate of his friends and family, then the sacrifices made by so many might be justified.

After their escape, ensuring that his benefactor survived was his only concern. During the two days spent in this new incarceration, he'd heard no news of her condition. Then again, how could he? His only company, aside from the horse he'd stolen from another farm, had been a giant man who never seemed to speak. He brought Espen food and water, gave him supplies to tend to his wounds, and even stayed to hold brief contests involving their throwing apples into a basket, but that was all.

Espen pondered the woman's connection to these people. Were they also spies? Could they have trained her? Did they know what she was? He still was having difficulty believing the woman who'd rescued him could be one. If not for the other woman's screams before the wolves attacked, he might never have considered the possibility. Spies were shadows, mysterious and all-knowing figures, not fragile young women who needed to be rescued.

Still there were questions about her and talents she'd displayed that were not easy to dismiss. Why was she at the Moon Shadow encampment in the first place? What concern could his capture have been to her that would necessitate any ordinary individual to take such insane risks to rescue him? Her memory was astonishing. Even blind, with only his muddled descriptions to guide her, she'd managed to direct him to this place. Her skills with language seemed equally impressive. As she grew weaker, she'd spoken to him in a wide variety, one he didn't even recognize. She was strong, physically and spiritually. Few people could have sustained such severe injuries and then completed such an agonizing journey over mountainous terrain primarily on foot. Most would simply have given up and died. Yes, there were many qualities about her Espen found admirable. If only he felt he could trust her.

Footsteps halted outside the barn's door, and moments later, the couple who owned the structure stood before him. The man was armed as usual, but the woman was not. He'd only seen her briefly when they arrived, but still he perceived a change in her demeanor. During their initial encounter, her actions and words were direct and purposeful. But as she approached him now, she seemed uncertain, hesitant, even scared. Had the young woman died? She pulled up a small milking stool and sat opposite him, each silently regarding the other. Then she spoke to him in French. Espen remained silent.

*

Anne repeated the directive more slowly.

"I need to know how you met her."

The man's eyes seemed to convey that he understood, his expression did not. What was he hiding? Then again why should he answer, especially if what he disclosed betrayed that he had anything to do with Abrielle's injuries? He might get past her in an escape attempt, but Noel was sure to drop him. He seemed to be weighing his options. She would wait.

It had taken her more than a day to gather the courage to face him. Meanwhile, poor Noel was left to tend to his needs, while she tended to the now all but silent Abrielle. He had such a good heart. What would she ever do without the man? She spoke little to him about what bothered her. She couldn't bring herself to. She didn't want to believe anything Abrielle said was true.

Anne had all but convinced herself it wasn't true. It was the fever talking. The blow Abrielle received to her head was causing her to hallucinate. She just needed rest, and then she would be able to recognize truth again. They'd laugh about the incident later. It was all so ridiculous. It simply wasn't possible. Anne knew in her heart it wasn't true.

But the doubts could not be silenced. They gnawed at her spirit, denied her rest, and drove her to hover in Abrielle's doorway while the girl slept and ponder if indeed a killer did lay asleep before her. As she watched her labored breathing, Abrielle seemed so fragile, just as she had when they'd first met. Even in slumber, she still possessed that same warmth of spirit crying out for someone to embrace. Abrielle could blind herself to it, but Anne could feel it, even more so now than before. She was terrified. What had happened to her? In time, Anne's insatiable desire for answers abated her fears enough for her to seek them. But they would not come from Abrielle.

*

The gypsy gave Noel one final look of appraisal then he spoke.

"I was a prisoner. She freed me. She was injured in our escape," he explained.

Anne shot Noel a look of surprise that the provided response was in English, and then continued her questioning in French.

"Why were you a prisoner?"

"The war," the gypsy said.

"Are your people fighting in Spain?" Anne probed.

Could he be another refugee fleeing the brutal fighting in the Peninsula War? She and Noel certainly had enough of them stop to ask for food or shelter during the last several years.

"No, my people are at war."

Anne pondered this statement a moment before asking her next question.

"And how does your war involve her?"

"It doesn't," he said directly.

"Then why would she risk her life to rescue you?"

Espen's eyes shifted between Anne and Noel. He seemed to seek an answer to the question from them. The truth was there before her now, but neither she nor the gypsy could speak it or fully accept it. Anne hung her head. The gypsy kicked lightly at the hay as he repositioned his leg.

"Is she better?" he quietly asked.

Anne nodded but said nothing. She could ask more. Who was Chloe? Why was the flute so important? Where had they come from? But he'd already told her what she needed to know. Abrielle hadn't saved him out of friendship or love. His look began as expectant then slowly changed to puzzlement. He'd anticipated they knew why she'd saved him. The assumption could mean only one thing. He thought they were something they were not, only because of what Abrielle was.

"Are you well enough to travel?" Anne asked calmly.

There was no longer any need to keep him locked up. The man seemed surprised but pleased at the sudden turn of events.

"I would ask you for some supplies and another day to rest."

Noel lowered his gun.

"We'll see what we can do," Anne assured the gypsy as she stood, lost in thought.

Espen studied her face.

"You did not know what is she?" the gypsy asked in genuine surprise as he read Anne's wounded expression. There was no need to answer. She turned from him, nodded a wordless request for her husband to see to the man's needs, then disappeared back into the cabin.

*

At first, she only felt its presence. The unmistakable warmth of the sun through the window recalled her mind to days now past. She replayed images of other sunlit days, and soon the light became real. Eternal night was lifting its black veil, but its grasp was slow to fade. Eventually the light resolved into shapes. She could dimly perceive the walls surrounding her, the blankets piled atop her, and the quiet shadow that watched over her. She would not speak to it. Anne tended her now out of a sense of duty. Not love. How could she love Abrielle? For her, night and day blended as time ebbed and flowed with prolonged and welcome passages of sleep.

Her dreams were simple, often tranquil. She could rest now, finally rest. Abrielle's body was moving beyond the pain as a new strength filled her. Breathing was becoming easier, the coughing fits ceased, the host of abrasions though still quite tender did not impede her movements as they once had. And each time she awoke, her vision was stronger, the details more vibrant. The bed felt safe, her spirit at peace. It was quiet here in the mountains. She embraced simply being.

Occasionally she was fully aware of gentle hands shifting her blankets, carefully inspecting her host of injuries or just holding her hand. Once she even felt Anne's lips kissing her forehead. Abrielle permitted herself only the most fleeting of glances as she withdrew. Anne's face was tired, stressed, but her eyes were alive with concern. Though it touched her aching heart, Abrielle would not allow herself to believe that she'd been forgiven. She couldn't. She could never forgive herself, so how could Anne?

The look on Anne's face could have been worn for many reasons besides Abrielle's condition. Perhaps she was still simply repulsed at what lay in her home, the kiss an unspoken regret for what Abrielle had become. Coming here was a mistake. How could she have ever hoped to have brought Anne or Noel anything other than pain? But Ailis had taken more than that from Abrielle. She'd always seen something beautiful in her sister. But then again, Abrielle never told her what she truly was. Abrielle's thoughts returned for a time to those dark months in Ireland.

Why hadn't Anne left the room? Abrielle feared to open her eyes a second time. She could not bear the thought. Then she heard the hushed words. They were slow, rhythmic, and ageless. She existed beyond grace to hear them. She would not have to open her eyes. But now she had to see. Abrielle needed to know it was not a dream.

The dim light from the candles hurt at first, but her eyes adjusted to the sight they beheld. Anne knelt, her back turned to Abrielle, her hands folded in prayer. Her voice was low, and Abrielle did not hear all of the words, but she heard enough to know that this was not a dream. Anne prayed for her. Anne still loved her.

Abrielle was too stunned to speak, too overwhelmed to move. She watched as Anne D'Aoust crossed herself, stood, and quietly left the room. Abrielle closed her eyes and curled her knees closer to her chest. She was loved. Someone still loved her. She was not alone. Her thoughts returned to Ailis.

"Thank you," she whispered, "thank you."

*

There must be a reason. There was always a reason. Anne pondered the thought as she finished preparing breakfast.

"Stolen? You're sure?" she asked as she placed a third bowl of oatmeal before her husband. Noel nodded absently as he began to devour the bowl's steaming contents.

"Well, you should have at least checked with the Blanquis' before you just gave that gypsy Maggie. Did you ever re-shoe her?"

He shook his head. Anne scowled at him.

The animal in question, a horse, had been left to them by Noel's aunt a year earlier. Maggie, as Anne called her, never adjusted well to the thinner air of the mountains. She was slow to travel on and not wholly reliable when used for plowing either. It made sense that Noel would have been willing to part with her. Of the three horses they owned, she did the least and ate the most.

Still Anne wasn't completely sure she believed her husband. That he could so easily recognize, at random, one horse from a distant neighbor's farm seemed too incredible to believe. It was much more likely that Noel simply saw an opportunity to gain a more reliable horse and took it. No doubt he thought himself quite clever.

"Wicked oaf," she admonished as she threw a towel onto the table.

Noel smugly used it to wipe his mouth then stood and snuck up behind her. She shrieked as he grabbed her playfully. Their pretend struggle was momentary as it changed quickly into a hug. She needed one. Anne twisted in his arms and kissed him lovingly.

"You're still an oaf," she teased.

It was good to see her smile. He kissed her again and grinned.

"Don't suppose I could talk you into cleaning up the dishes while I check on Abrielle?"

Noel pretended to think the matter over carefully then issued a mock salute. This time she did hit him with the towel.

"You're so bad. Do a good job this time and maybe I'll make you that rabbit stew you like so much."

He gave her a quizzical look.

"The one with the celery," she reminded him patiently as she left the kitchen.

The image that greeted Anne upon entering Abrielle's room was so different from the one she'd expected that the moment ceased to exist. Abrielle sat up in her bed, the blanket the gypsy had given Anne to return to Abrielle cradled on her lap, but her eyes clearly focused on Anne. She could see. But it was what lay within Abrielle's eyes that brought joy to Anne's heart.

For the first time since her return, Anne saw the girl she'd known there in the battered woman's body. The shy vulnerability, the indomitable spirit, the unspoken longing for acceptance still shone in her eyes. Whatever corruption the world had brought upon her, she was still Abrielle. She was still Anne's adopted daughter. The moment needed no words. They embraced as family, as mother and daughter.

"I'm sorry. I'm sorry, I got so lost," Abrielle sobbed.

Anne pressed her close.

"You were never lost to me," Anne assured her. "I prayed for you every day."

Abrielle shuddered as she held her even more tightly.

"I love you," Abrielle confessed.

"I know, girl. I know. And we love you."

She shook her head.

"No. No, after what I've done …"

"Ssshhh. Hush."

Anne rubbed Abrielle's back. There would be a time for such things, but it was not now. They sat together and allowed a measure of peace to be restored.

"You know," Anne began, "I'm a coward, too. I could have reached out more. All these years, I knew you were in pain."

"You knew I wouldn't let you," Abrielle said humbly.

"I still could have tried," Anne said regretfully. "I could have told you that Noel and I are no better."

"What do you mean?"

"We've both been compelled to kill. Noel when he served in the army …"

Her words drifted away. Abrielle would have to ask.

"And you?" She finally breathed.

Anne swallowed.

"Once at the hospital I worked in … I'd been there for years, alone, the orphan who would be a saint. Who cares for the caregivers? I was young. I watched as men lived. I suffered when they died. You think you're there to do good, to help, but after awhile, the sights, the smells, the suffering inflicted to prolong life," she winced at the disturbing memories before continuing.

"There was a patient of mine, a man I didn't really know, a man who was very badly injured. I … he might have lived, but I'd already seen so many suffer needlessly as he did, only to die weeks, even months later. He had blue eyes. They were kind eyes. But there was so much pain." She couldn't go on. Silence descended between them.

"You killed him."

Anne nodded slowly.

"I couldn't let him suffer as I'd allowed so many others to … so much death. They worked us so hard," her eyes grew distant.

Abrielle squeezed her hand, returning her to the present.

"Well, anyway, that was a long time ago. It was soon after that I met Noel. We married, and then settled here—far away from such things. But the guilt remains with me to this day. I often wonder what kind of a life he would have had if I hadn't made the choice I did."

"But you've done so many good things," Abrielle began.

"Yes. But I can never be forgiven for my actions. I'm no saint. I can only work to make the sufferings of others less. That is my penance. That is my choice: to try to become something better than I was; to love, not to judge."

How could Abrielle learn to live with her own crimes?

"Does your husband know?"

Anne nodded.

"He knows."

"I never told my sister," Abrielle hung her head. "I never told her what I was before she died."

It was difficult for Anne to choose which revelation was more shocking. In all their years of correspondence, Abrielle had never even hinted at the existence of a sibling. Again she held her as Abrielle's sorrows momentarily overwhelmed her.

"Maybe … maybe all she needed to know was that she had a sister who loved her." Anne's fingers trialed through Abrielle's hair.

"She was so beautiful to me, even when she was dying," Abrielle said.

The gentle motion of Anne's hand gliding through her strands was soothing. Abrielle's eyelids fluttered slightly.

"Of course she was," Anne assured her.

"I could never replace her for … never be as good as she was."

Anne shifted slightly.

"How long ago did she pass?"

Abrielle's eyes slipped out of focus momentarily.

"A few months, I guess. Time, I … I lost her flute."

"What?"

"On the mountain with the gypsy. I lost Ailis' flute." She looked away from Anne.

No further comment passed between them. The object was now gone, and it was a poor substitute for she who had once owned it. Abrielle gripped the blanket she held more tightly. The action did not escape

Anne's attention.

"Your gypsy friend gave me that to return to you. Apparently you dropped it at some point and didn't notice. He kept it for you. I should probably wash it. No telling what it's been through in that barn."

Abrielle didn't seem to hear her as the tips of her fingers caressed the blanket. It was still here.

"The gypsy is recovering?" she asked after a long silent moment.

Anne hesitated before answering. There was no use in hiding the truth from Abrielle. She felt comfortable that she'd done the right thing.

"He left yesterday afternoon."

*

Noel had just finished washing the last of the dishes when the noise caught his attention. At first he dismissed it. His ability to perceive sound had grown so erratic over the years that he no longer trusted his hearing. Perhaps his mind compensated for the near loss of the sense by creating false echoes. He was not altogether deaf, yet what noises he could hear were distant, muffled, or simply drowned out by the incessant ringing in his ears.

It was probably nothing but still he headed towards Abrielle's room. As he approached, the vibrations in the walls made it abundantly clear that the noise he'd heard was quite real this time. He opened the door to discover Anne and Abrielle alternately shouting and pleading for forgiveness from one another.

Noel hovered in the doorway as he tried to make sense of the bewildering scene playing out before him. The exasperated women flew rapidly between a host of emotions as both gestured wildly with their hands, their voices scaling and dropping in pitch and volume, as they surged after each other around the room. One moment Anne was shaking her head, the next Abrielle was doing the same as she clutched the dirty blanket the gypsy had given them to return to her. Over the din, three words uttered by Abrielle brought the argument to an immediate halt. The room bristled with silence.

Anne slumped to the bed dumbstruck. For his own sake, Noel wasn't certain he'd heard her right. Abrielle was so transfixed on Anne that she hadn't even noticed him until he stepped fully into the room and tapped her shoulder. She spun towards him in alarm. He cupped his arms and made a rocking motion with them, a mixture of concern and puzzlement on his face. Abrielle gazed at him intensely for a moment longer then her face broke into a smile. Her tensions abated as she began to laugh. Abrielle flung her arms wildly around him. She could see him and he'd heard her.

Anne seemed to slowly be regaining her senses. Noel looked to her for insight but found little written upon her face. He returned his attentions to the younger woman who still held him. Those last words she'd spoken, that he'd heard clearly, echoed in his mind. Who, he wondered, had "'… stole her baby'"?

Chapter 14
The Wolves and the Sunflower

"She didn't love you!"

Baseria yelled, cutting him off. Her anger burnt as a torch. She was furious. She'd believed in him. She'd championed the others to believe as well, but those hopes were false. Baseria had moved beyond the fear and the wounds caused by his own prior accusation. He seemed unable or unwilling to save them. What use was he?

"If she loved you, she would have told you she was sick! She would have told you she was dying! She didn't! She was selfish! She was stupid! And I wish to God that she had told you because then we never would have met! I hope you die here, alone!"

As these last searing words escaped through visible wisps of breath, her body trembled with rage. He didn't care about her, he never had. All he cared about was his own selfish needs. For the first time since she'd encountered one of them, she was comforted by the thought that one of the Old Ones stood only a few feet away, visible but silent. She stood before Ernest a moment longer then retreated. His expression never altered. It was as frozen as his heart.

She was halfway to the top of the dark turret, which led to the courtyard when she heard the voice.

"Baseria," it whispered.

She spun wildly, seeking the speaker. No Old One followed and she was certain the voice did not come from above or below. It must be here, beside her the young woman decided. But she was alone. Baseria fought her instinct to flee. Her tormentor was here. They must be. She would wait for the voice to speak again.

Without warning the flame of the candle she carried vanished from existence. She shuddered. The small hairs on her skin rose. There was a presence here now. One she'd not sensed before. It was behind her on the stair. She was sure of it. Her jaw shivered uncontrollably. It was here. She was afraid to breathe, even more frightened to move. What would happen to her if she did? She felt as if eyes were boring into the back of her, waiting for her to turn and look into them.

"Baseria," it whispered again, practically, directly into her ear.

She screamed.

Her flight was manic, her motions uncoordinated. Several times she slipped on the icy steps, bruising her legs as she groped through the darkness in search of escape. She burst through the entryway of the turret and across the empty courtyard. She did not pause before the great fireplace in the entry hall to warm herself. Even here in the lit portion of the fortress she feared the voice would find her. Baseria's eyes tore madly all around her as she continued to make her way back to the others in the reading room. What stalked her in this place? She sought only the reassuring presence of her companions.

As she rounded a corner, her head swung around to find Him towering over her. She gasped in his presence as her eyes looked away. His breath rattled in his lungs. He seemed harried.

"What is wrong?" the harsh voice demanded of her.

"Noth … nothing. I'm fine."

She could sense his unyielding gaze bearing down on her. He wanted something from her. He wanted it very badly. She could feel it. The imposing being took a step closer.

"You are startled."

"I … you …"

"It was not me," he interrupted. "Speak. What has troubled you, girl?"

For an instant, Baseria genuinely wanted to tell him. Something in the voice betrayed kindness. Why would he show her that? Her thoughts momentarily returned to his treatment of her in the chapel, after the escaped prisoner had died. There was a moment then when she did not fear him. She wanted to ask him what had happened to poor Sebbi? But in her heart, she already knew. They all knew.

With every nerve in her body uttering in protest she turned her gaze upward and once more endured those sickening yellow eyes.

"I heard a noise." It was a foolish admission. What if he questioned her about it further?

"… and you did startle me," she hastened to add.

His head turned downward as he studied her for deception. Baseria managed to endure the scrutiny.

"You are returning to the reading room?"

It was not really a question. She nodded in assent. He looked upon her a moment longer then brushed his massive, black-cloaked form past her and stalked away. When he vanished from sight, Baseria leaned her back against the wall and drew in, what felt like, the first ragged breath she'd taken in for many hours. Her nerves hummed.

Were those merciless orbs the last things poor Sebbi saw? Would they be hers? It was maddening to constantly live in such terror, to feel so helpless. Baseria shook her head and suppressed her tears. She held her head up. She was going to die here, but not without a fight. She was Baseria Nalie, daughter of Jal and Mayte, trained in the ancient arts of the Seer by her grandmother. It was against her very nature to give up. She must find a way to save the others. By the time she reached the reading room, fear had once again been vanquished by anger.

As soon as she stepped into the room, her spirit faltered at the sight before her.

"What happened?"

Etolie was holding Isyll, whose left eye was bruising. Vochallet loomed behind them, wielding one of the spindles she'd knocked loose. Blood trickled from a wound on her forearm. She lowered the weapon slowly. Fear burnt in the eyes of all three. No one spoke. Could they have turned on each other? Perhaps Isyll had suffered a seizure and fallen.

Baseria closed the door behind her.

"I told you we should have barricaded it," Vochallet declared to the others. They ignored her.

Baseria cautiously knelt before Isyll and studied her eye.

"Who hit you?"

Isyll gripped Etolie and turned away in pain and shame.

"Who did this?" Baseria demanded of the others. Etolie and Vochallet seemed to engage in a silent conversation as their eyes and expressions rapidly altered. What were they hiding?

"Not here," Etolie finally answered. "We shouldn't talk about this here."

"What? You think it's any safer some place else?" Vochallet scoffed. "Personally, I don't plan to ever go back to my room. We should all stay together … for safety."

"We were together when this happened. Look where it got us," Etolie pointed out.

"So what? You want to obey them now? It won't make any difference."

"Of course not," Etolie protested.

"Then don't talk as if you do," Vochallet admonished.

"Please don't leave me alone," Isyll pled.

Vochallet shot an icy look of reproach at Etolie before she began to fiddle with a makeshift tourniquet for her arm. Baseria rose and tried to help her, but Vochallet waved her off. Etolie cooed reassuringly to Isyll that it would never happen again and that they weren't going to leave her.

"How can they be so cruel?" Isyll wondered aloud.

"I don't know," Etolie confessed. Her eyes were burdened with anguished tears yet to be shed.

"Don't we?" Vochallet challenged as she glared at Baseria.

"Are you all right, Vochallet?" Isyll sniffed and tried to smile up at the older woman who proudly displayed her wound as she knelt down.

"What this? You should try childbirth sometime, puts little scratches like this into perspective."

She smiled reassuringly.

"What was his answer, Baseria?"

"Huh?" Baseria was so engrossed by the drama playing out before her that she failed at first to recognize what Etolie was asking her.

"What did Frankenstein say?"

The women gazed at her with longing looks of both fear and hope. She felt naked before them. She'd placed her faith in Ernest, and they'd done so in her.

"He said …," she took a deep breath; the words seemed too terrible to be spoken aloud. "He says he can't help us."

Shock eventually gave way to fear as Isyll began to weep quietly. Etolie closed her eyes, a pained expression etched on her features. Vochallet swore viciously. Baseria had never felt like such a traitor. She sat down quietly in a nearby chair as a weighty silence bore testament to the depths of her betrayal.

"Why?" Isyll sobbed. "Why won't he help us? He has to help us."

Baseria shook her head.

"He wouldn't tell me, only …"

"What, Ba? Only what?" Etolie demanded as she pulled at her hair in unbridled frustration.

Baseria felt tired, very tired as she responded.

"I don't understand it. He said he can't lose his wife again."

"You told us she was dead," Vochallet said accusingly.

"That's what he told me," Baseria replied as she attempted to suppress the memory of his accusation. "I told you, I don't understand what he meant."

Vochallet seemed unmoved.

"Maybe she's a prisoner too," Etolie wondered aloud.

The others considered this possibility.

"If he thought she'd been brought here …," Vochallet rejoined.

"Maybe that's why he came," Etolie finished the thought.

Baseria's heart sank. So he hadn't come for them at all. He hadn't come for her.

"He has to," Isyll repeated softly as she stared at nothing. "He has to help us. Baseria, go back to him."

Baseria rested her fingertips against her cool forehead.

"Please go back to him."

She closed her eyes. She could say nothing. The others waited. Their eyes silently probed for her soul. Baseria turned it further inward, away from their prying. She could not go back. The silence was interrupted by Vochallet.

"We should search this place. If his wife is here then we've got something to bargain with."

"But how can we?" Isyll asked. "I mean, we've been here for months, and I've barely seen any of this fortress."

"It was dark before, now with the light …," Vochallet optimistically began.

"Light won't get us past guards and into areas we haven't seen," Etolie remonstrated.

"No, don't make the guards angry," Isyll begged Etolie.

"Better yet, we should bargain with him as if his wife is here, without searching. It's safer that way," Vochallet asserted.

"That's shameful," Etolie admonished.

"It's practical," Vochallet fired back.

"I think Baseria said something," Isyll said quietly.

The others paused, but Baseria did not stir.

"Ba?"

"Oh. Leave her out of this, Etolie. What use has she been?" Vochallet challenged.

"What did she say?" Etolie asked Isyll who shrugged.

"Ba?"

"Look, just forget about her. Who's going to talk to Frankenstein?" Vochallet anxiously demanded.

"You can't just use him like that," Etolie began to protest.

"No, let her talk," Isyll insisted.

Vochallet seized the moment, her voice rising steadily with emotion as she spoke.

"There's no escape over land. We've seen this for ourselves. He's the only one among us who knows how to sail a ship. We can't do this without him. You all know it. You're just scared of using him, of hurting his precious feelings or whatever. So what if we lie? We'll all die if we don't—his wife too, if she's actually here. And my children are not going to be raised without their mother! So to blazes with Frankenstein and his miserable feelings!"

A strange, unnatural sound suddenly silenced them. Nerves stressed beyond reason forced their fearful eyes to turn reluctantly towards the source. It was Baseria. She was laughing uncontrollably, though the sound she emanated was barely to be recognized as such. It was strained in such a manner that any true mirth drowned in her unspoken sorrows. The dim, bitter tones reduced the women to mere statues as the horrid noise filled the great room. Had she gone insane?

She drew in short, heavy breaths as tears crossed her face. Each of her companions looked to the others for insight or to see if they would be the one to confront her. What was the joke, if any existed at all? She began to wheeze perceptively as the sound like salt cutting glass diminished somewhat. For a moment she covered her face then wrapped her arms around her body and began rocking. The others waited.

"I can't remember the last time one of our talks had a happy ending," Baseria sniffed.

No one spoke so she continued.

"They want to kill us. He's going to let them kill us because I …." For a moment her face was awash with fear and sadness, then it contorted as another spasm of mirthless laughter gripped her.

"Isyll?" Baseria asked when the fit ended.

"Yes," Isyll's voice broke in reply.

"What happened to your face? Tell me," she coaxed.

Isyll looked to others for guidance but they left the choice with her. She swallowed hard.

"I … well, he …," she shook her head, let the words die stillborn, and looked away in shame.

Vochallet rested a reassuring hand on her and answered in her stead.

"One of those Moon Shadow devils barged in here and demanded to know which of you is the Seer. Said he wouldn't leave without the truth. Threatened to cut Isyll's tongue out if she didn't talk. Threatened to do other things, too."

Baseria looked at Vochallet's arm.

"He hurt you too?"

Though she knew the answer she needed to hear it.

"He tried," Vochallet said darkly. "Doesn't have much of a jaw left now. Fled down the turret before I could finish the job."

Baseria's breathing was rapid as she rocked. She closed her eyes.

"Please tell me you told him," she begged. "It's a worthless secret."

She needed the great burden removed.

"Ba, no," Etolie replied in shock. "Do you imagine for one instant that telling them would help us? Any of us?" She added the later statement with emphasis so the implication would not be lost on the others.

"But they're hurting all of you because of me," Baseria contended forcefully.

She felt fingers lightly touching her hand then her chin. Her eyes opened and met Etolie's.

"They're hurting us because we haven't given them what they want. They haven't driven us apart. And we're stronger than them for it."

Isyll suddenly wailed.

"But Sebbi … I saw him looking at her from across the room at dinner the night before she was ... oh, I didn't say anything, and now she's dead because of me."

"No, she isn't," Vochallet raised Isyll to her feet and held her. "No."

"I miss her," Isyll sobbed through ashen tears.

"We all do, Isyll. We all do," Vochallet affirmed in soft tones as she led the distraught young woman away from the others. She needed to rest.

Etolie seated herself next to her friend.

"Baseria, tell me what happened with Frankenstein."

"I told you."

"No, you started to say he wasn't going to help us because of something you did. I need to know what you meant."

Baseria bit her lip and fixed her eyes upon a beam far above in the ceiling. The muted glow of a red dawn highlighted the cracks along the lengths of the well-aged wood. She ignored Etolie as her emotions tossed her mind and spirit in a vast tempest. Etolie shook her shoulder.

"Ba, please," she implored. "We may not have a lot of time."

Slowly, Baseria's eyes withdrew from the ceiling. She looked with pity upon her friend. How could she ever understand what Baseria had done?

"Do you know what my life is like, Etolie? Really know what it is to live day after day of emptiness—of knowing no love, but bearing witness to others' happiness all around me. Knowing that it can never be a happiness I too can have. Always questioning why—why no one will have me—the unclean thing who can never know love."

Etolie made no attempt to answer. Baseria's position in the clan was such that, unlike her peers, all were dissuaded from courting her. The inclusion of her into one's family could only bring shame and scorn upon them. The girl was cursed, everyone knew that. Even Etolie endured ridicule for befriending the outcast. Some of the younger girls like Isyll did not share the animosity towards Baseria that older members of the clan possessed, but they too were wary of befriending the girl who many blamed for starting the war.

Baseria turned away but not before betraying her heart's unspoken desire.

"What can you know of loneliness?"

Etolie studied her friend. The troubling certainty now before her held her momentarily at bay. The emotion she must now confront was such a powerful, yet fragile thing. One Baseria possessed but had almost no real experience in dealing with. Would she deny it? In a different time and place such dreams might take root, encourage nourishing growth and transformation. But here, such things were impossible.

Time afforded Etolie no choice. If they were to survive, they must have Frankenstein's help, even if that help came at a terrible personal price.

"Baseria, he doesn't love you."

Etolie waited through the silent heartbeats.

"He could," Baseria insisted flatly a moment before she stood to flee across the room from her companion. Etolie could not allow her refuge. The only way to save them was to destroy Baseria's illusions.

"You want him to. You need him to, but he can't. His wife ...," she called out as she pursued her.

Baseria unexpectedly turned on her friend, her face livid with emotion.

"You don't know anything! But you always talk as if you do. You don't know our hearts. You don't know what's passed between us."

Etolie paused only a moment as Baseria's words brought forth a new revelation.

"I never pretended to understand your grandmother's magics."

"I'm not talking about the healing union!" Baseria cried.

"No, but I am," Etolie replied evenly.

With a look of disgust, Baseria again darted away. There was more between them than that, she knew it. How many months had she been without her power? Yet he still came, but then again so had his wife's spirit.

"What did you do, Ba?" Etolie persisted.

Baseria shut her eyes tightly as haunting words flooded her mind. They were her last hateful words to Ernest. Etolie would draw them out of her. She knew it, just as she had surmised Baseria's unspoken desires. Those words now gleamed in the dark like a bright blade. One she would rather fall on than expose to the light again. Etolie said something to her, touched her again, but Baseria dove inward. However, she was not alone this time.

The sensation overwhelmed her, partially because it was so wholly unexpected, and partially because of the sheer power that flowed into her. It felt as though she'd never breathed until now. The winds of the world surged in her anew. What was happening to her?

Again she felt someone's hand touching her skin. The words came as a tidal wave, one which rose from the depths to commanding heights as it worked its will upon the sea. As each succeeding wave rose to break over the previous one, she began to chant them. Over and over the words were spoken, though she was unable to discern if they reverberated only in her mind. Other voices seemed to echo them back to her. At last, as the final wave broke, her eyes shot open.

"She's dead!"

A face she'd never expected to set eyes upon again hovered before her.

*

Tasaria blinked at the unresponsive girl. Baseria's lips moved minutely, but otherwise, it were as if she was in a trance. The new Seer indeed. She seemed entirely unaware of their entry into the reading room. After grasping her twice and yielding no results, Tasaria decided that patience was the best option. If her niece wanted to continue this little game for a few more minutes, so be it. It would change nothing. Baseria was not the Seer.

Standing before her, the absurdity of her mission to this frozen wasteland brought a fresh wave of anger to Tasaria. She should be in France, with her husband, protecting their people. Instead she was isolated in a crumbling fortress at the frigid edge of the world. The trip made her uncomfortable, and she was eager to complete her task and return. However, she was anxious to question the Master as to why he'd brought Baseria here in the first place. It was a secret she'd been unable to pry from Pias during their journey. As she waited, Tasaria began to study the girl.

Baseria was all but a child the last time her aunt had seen her so many years ago. What had Mayte's nickname for her youngest been? Tasaria concentrated, having long since forgotten it. Still she tried to recall it from a host of buried memories. How like her mother she appeared. Mayte would have undoubtedly treasured this fact. Patia had certainly favored Jal, in both appearance and disposition, while Espen possessed his parents' physical traits equally. Tasaria's thoughts tended a moment more on her long dead sister, on Mayte's deceased daughter, and finally to her own dead child.

All of them were gone, now but dust and memory. And yet, this miserable, useless girl remained. Her very presence mocked Tasaria's tragic loss. What would her child have looked like at Baseria's age? Thanks to this girl, Tasaria could only imagine. She would never know. Baseria's eyes suddenly flashed open, and as Tasaria gazed into them, she no longer beheld her niece, now she only saw the face of Jucika's murderer.

"She's dead!"

Tasaria was too stunned to speak. Baseria looked around, frightened and clearly confused as recognition dawned as to whom exactly stood across from her.

"Etolie?"

The young woman she turned to said nothing. Pias stood clutching her from behind, a sinister expression of anticipation on his face, as he began to whisper something into her ear. Neither Isyll nor Vochallet moved. The younger of the two looked terrified, while the hatred smoldering in the older one's eyes could have reduced the Moon Shadows in the room to ashes.

Only the slightest of doubts crossed Tasaria's mind as she moved to strike Baseria, the little wretch. Yes, Jucika was dead, and it was her fault. All of this was her fault.

Just as Tasaria finished her few steps forward, Etolie suddenly emitted a bloodcurdling scream of pure agony as she began to collapse to the ground. Pias bore a look of pure malevolence and delight. What had he said to her?

As Tasaria turned her head back to face her niece, a discordant sound beyond the girl attracted her aunt's attention. It blended momentarily with Etolie's screams. Tasaria's blood turned to ice at both the sound and at what appeared in the red light beneath the window seconds before the glass panes shattered. The shards flew across the room, propelled by the howling winds, which rushed through the gap. Several people, including Tasaria, were hit with the debris, but she barely noticed. She focused only on the spot, where for an instant, her mother had stood.

CHAPTER 15
A TRUCE OF TRUST

Abrielle rubbed the dirt between her fingertips and inhaled the rich, damp scent. Her keen eyes quickly studied every inch of the terrain over the hoof print that captured her attention. Though still muted it was gratifying to see that the land at these lower elevations was definitely close to revealing the approach of real spring. Infinitesimal buds and a few pockets of bright color bore testimony to the great transformation the landscape was about to enjoy. Inwardly she sighed. The arrival of spring brought a sobering reflection. How many months had Tara been gone now? What had they done to her?

Unconsciously Abrielle turned her face towards the eastern horizon. The brilliant assortment of orange, red, and purple hues among the towering bands of clouds indicated that the sun would be devoured by the earth soon. This was all taking too long. She dumped the dirt back upon the ground and gingerly straightened up.

Her body did everything it could to remind her that she still had a lot of healing to do. She bit her lip as nerves and tender cuts grated against each other. Abrielle paused a moment longer as the echoes of pain slowly subsided, knowing, unfortunately, that they'd soon return. The past several days served as yet another endurance test. She doubted even Bellange's villainous intelligence instructors could have improvised a more grueling physical trial, although several of those they'd designed came close.

The knot in her neck now returned, and despite her best efforts, it often prevented her from turning her head fully. As her fingers worked to loosen it, she walked back to her mount and gave one of his ears a reassuring rub. It was time to move on. She took up the reigns and began to guide him up another steep incline.

By now she'd decided there was simply no good way of going about this. At first she'd tried to ride the horse that Noel and Anne had lent her. However, Abrielle's various injuries still brought waves of nausea and occasionally made her extremely dizzy. Clambering up or down to constantly search the ground for clues as to the gypsy's path only worsened the problem. If there was any blessing to be found in all of this, it was that the gypsy wisely chose to remain away from towns and even most roads.

This was of benefit to Abrielle in several ways: fewer people meant less attention would be paid to the single woman, covered in cuts and bruises, riding alone, positioned fully astride her mount, rather than side-saddle. Ironically, it also made him easier for her to track. Normally this would not have been the case. Had he opted for speed rather than stealth, his tracks would probably have been erased by other travelers on a busy road. Noel's failure to re-shoe Maggie gave her a distinct gate and a hoof print pattern that was easy to recognize. Riding in relative isolation, the gypsy unwittingly allowed this pattern to be clearly stamped across the countryside.

Another factor that should have worked in her favor was that Maggie, by her very nature, possessed the distinction of being notoriously slow. Still, after days of pursuit, Abrielle had not caught up. The gypsy skillfully chose to travel over terrain that made spotting telltale marks of his passage difficult.

Abrielle's painful injuries compelled her to walk, rather than ride, and to sleep longer than she normally would. She'd fully expected to reach him two days ago but he'd changed his tactics and begun a series of backtracking measures, perhaps fearing he was being pursued or simply to try and prevent it from happening. Both her limited food supply and time were running low now. And although she was hesitant to admit it, her stamina was also wavering. If she did not find him soon, she might never catch him. If that happened, her only chance of finding Tara might lay with Jack's autonomous efforts to locate the Wild Rose clan.

The ground finally leveled out and Abrielle paused to survey the area. A vast forest spread out before her, pitted with looming outcroppings of rocks. The sky darkened with the final setting of the sun, which only added to the gloom of the woods. It would be all but impossible to locate any additional tracks tonight, still she made an attempt. The extra effort might yield another clue to the gypsy's whereabouts and through him, Tara.

She found nothing. Where should she sleep tonight? The very thought of establishing yet another camp made her tired. The outcroppings would do an adequate job of shielding light from her cooking fire, but the idea of sleeping on them made her bones ache. Besides, there was another factor that must be considered. One she remained mindful of throughout the day. She reached up and stroked her companion's long nose. The horse whinnied softly in acknowledgement.

"So, be honest. Where do you think we should sleep?"

Abrielle leaned closer as if the horse was about to make a serious contribution to their one-sided discussion.

"What was that? Oh, a lady with expensive tastes I see. Yes, Versailles does sound inviting, but it's murder to get on the guest list this time of year. Don't you like roughing it?"

The animal strained in protest at her reigns.

"Well, you're right. At least there we wouldn't have to worry about them finding us."

She patted the black mane to calm the animal.

"No, just me," a voice said from behind her in English.

Abrielle jerked her head towards the intruder, but discovered once again that she could turn it only a fraction of what she needed to. Pain coursed through her shoulder, neck, behind her eyes, and up to the top of her head. Her hand again began to rub the offending knot as she winced in pain, slowly turning her entire body to face her quarry. She heard a loud clattering sound before the gypsy spoke.

"You're still hurt," he said by way of greeting.

"Nice to see you, too," Abrielle absently remarked as she continued to work on the knot in her neck.

The gypsy gave no response.

"I did fall off the top of a mountain, so yes, I'm still hurt. Aren't you? God, don't just sneak up on me like that," Abrielle demanded.

She tried rolling her head. Something had to work this loose. The gypsy was unmoved by her plight.

"You've been the one who has been trying to sneak up on me," he charged pointing accusingly at her. It was Abrielle's turn to be indifferent.

"Learn to hide yourself better then if you don't like company. Have you even checked your horse's shoes? Just be grateful I found you before someone else did."

He paused a moment before continuing.

"What are you doing here?"

She ceased trying to massage her neck and looked him directly in the eye.

"Just conversing with my horse about the sleeping accommodations for tonight," Abrielle quipped. "What do you think I'm here for?"

Her eyes momentarily followed his to the ground. She looked up at him in surprise.

"You were going to hit me with that, weren't you?"

Espen looked away.

"No, I wasn't," he protested, simultaneously dropping the offending object.

"Yes, you were. You were going to hit me in the head with that rock."

"No."

He gave a casual shrug. Abrielle wasn't ready to dismiss the matter.

"What is it with you and rocks?"

Espen stiffened.

"Well … I had to be sure it was you. Besides," he added haughtily, "I still don't trust you."

She stared at him. What else would it take to convince him?

"We've saved each other's lives," she reminded him.

"You're a spy," Espen said distastefully, "and you can never trust a spy."

Abrielle pursed her lips in annoyance.

"Fine," she agreed. "You're right. I was a spy. But I'm not anymore. Or did you miss the part where they fired me?"

"Spies deal in deception," the gypsy observed unabated. "All of it could have been nothing more than that, an elaborate trick to get me to trust you."

Abrielle released a long sigh as she pushed back her hair from her eyes.

"Look, I'm not here to spy on you. I'm not going to take you as some type of prisoner. I just need to talk to you. I swear that's all."

The gypsy appeared to carefully consider her words. She met his gaze.

"I'm Abrielle, by the way."

She stretched out her scared right hand. Finally, reservedly, he took it.

"Kelv," Espen lied. She would have to fully earn his trust before he told her his true name.

She nodded, thoroughly exhausted. It was a fragile truce; one that could collapse if additional steps were not taken soon to validate their trust. She tried to smile reassuringly at him. The pain behind her eyes was blinding. All she wanted to do was lay down.

"I don't suppose you've already set up camp?"

Espen studied her a moment, then wordlessly guided her to her horse and helped her up. He took up the reigns and began to slowly lead the animal into the forest. Abrielle allowed her mind to wander as her eyes passively took note of her surroundings. At least she didn't have to worry about looking for hoof prints anymore. Tomorrow they would have to either re-shoe Maggie or abandon her. In her current state she was too much of a liability. If Abrielle could find Espen, their enemies could as well.

"Did you hear them last night?"

The gypsy partially turned his head and nodded.

"We are still in the mountains. There's bound to be a native population."

"But can you tell the difference between them and the Moon Shadows' wolf pack?"

"No," he admitted.

The howls last night sounded distant, but sound did reflect differently in the mountainous foothills. Abrielle slept little the previous night, scared of what she might discover when she awoke. She trembled unconsciously with the memory of their haunting bale. Espen tried to remain positive.

"Even if they did belong to the Moon Shadows, shouldn't they believe us dead?"

Momentarily Chloe's face swam into her mind.

"No, I promise you someone climbed down to check and make sure."

"Unless they thought we fell in the river," Espen suggested.

But no one could have made such a mistake. Their blood must have been everywhere, undoubtedly, winding a trail behind them as they'd fled; at least until snow covered it. Certainly Chloe would not have made such a mistake; she was too well trained to have left without verifying Abrielle's demise; unless of course, she herself was now dead. Espen shrugged, obviously worn out as well.

"Let them come."

It was not a sentiment which Abrielle shared. She feared she would not survive another encounter with the Moon Shadows' trained wolves.

**

"You are to be as immortal as the State, as silent as sin, and loyal beyond question. Fail in these and you'll likely be either dead or worse. Assuage your illusions for power functions in no other way. It would be best if you forget what you have been and embrace what you now are.

In the ordinary, such as relationships, you will find both peril and a useful means of exploitation to successfully conduct missions through to the end. But never doubt that friendship can be your undoing. We're spies. We have no true friends, only passing allies in an ever-shifting landscape of allegiances. You are ghosts whose presence must be felt and feared when needed and invisible, yet ever vigilant, for threats from within and from without.

Here you will learn to survive, to communicate, and to conquer. As you grow more successful, we will teach you more. Stagnate and I promise you will come to fear us. We are the first and the last to be honored. There is no place for personal ambition. Failure does not exist.

Your decision is final. Your choice must be made. If anything I have said has elicited even the slightest doubt, then now is the time you must walk away. This is not the life for you. For doubt can only led to death. If you chose to remain, you embrace us and through us you will come to know true power. You will wield it as your own. You will ensure that which must be. You will summon the future for our nation. Now, for the honor of France and the glory of Napoleon, make your choice."

**

It was the rhythmic dance of rain against the stones that drew her back to consciousness. Abrielle's eyes slowly opened and she lay mesmerized by the nearby drips of water as they continuously pulsed out of existence before her.

"What were you dreaming of?"

Her neck still hurt so she didn't turn to face Espen.

"Why does it matter?" she asked evenly.

"It doesn't. You just seemed restless."

"Oh," she paused awkwardly. "What time is it?"

"Afternoon. I don't know exactly," he admitted.

"What?" she said in surprise.

She sat up, regretting the motion within seconds as ripples of pain raced outward from the knot in her neck.

"Don't worry, everything is fine," Espen assured her as he leaned forward to help.

She waved him away.

"The hell it is. Why'd you let me sleep so long?"

Espen turned his eyes from her and poked a stick at their campfire.

"Because you needed the rest," he said honestly.

Abrielle studied him for a moment. Was he actually concerned about her?

"I can manage."

He shook his head and met her gaze.

"There's no need. I tried to wake you several hours ago. You felt feverish. We talked for a time, remember?"

Actually, it did seem familiar.

"It rained all night and hasn't let up," he continued. "The mud will only slow us, the horses have good shelter here, and our scents have been dissipated by the rain so we're relatively safe from any wolves that might be out tracking us. Relax," he handed her a plate of food.

"Thank you," she muttered humbly as she accepted it.

He was right of course. She took several bites.

"Did you check on the horses?"

The gypsy nodded.

"They're fine. I even took care of my horse's shoe issue," he added.

Abrielle paused her chewing.

"How?" she managed.

A sly grin slowly spread over his face, even his eyes seemed to twinkle with mischief.

"An old trick my father taught me. He's quite knowledgeable about horses."

He waited for his words to register with his companion. When they did, Abrielle stared at him in disbelief.

"You knew about it the whole time. You could have taken that shoe off at any point. You wanted me to follow you."

Espen's smiled turned to one of self-satisfaction. His smugness only added to her irritation.

"Are you insane?"

"You're here, so no," he arrogantly replied.

"You could've been killed, you idiot," Abrielle snapped in exasperation.

He shook his head, still smiling.

"No, it was a good risk to take. I had to know why you rescued me and if you really were a spy. Besides, if another had tracked me I would have dealt with them. I had to make sure I wasn't leading anyone to my people."

"And am I a spy?"

Their eyes locked. She'd meant the question as a challenge, but something in his look made her turn away. It was as if he knew the answer to a secret she wasn't prepared to discuss. Was she blushing?

Last night was the second time since they'd met that they'd been compelled to keep their bodies very close together. The first time was for warmth and a desperate attempt at survival, last night because of limited space. Still the intimacy it created was not lost on either of them.

Abrielle cleared her throat and resumed eating her food. She studied the view from their perch high atop one of the rocky outcroppings. It was a niche in the rocks, almost like a small cave. An overhang protected them from the rain and winds, and an open recess in the back provided a wonderful place for their small cooking fire. The ceiling provided enough clearance for them to sit up comfortably and to move about the confined area. Undoubtedly the rain-soaked rocks were now more treacherous to climb, but not impossible to navigate.

She quietly finished her meal then lay back down. Espen leaned back against the solid stone wall. For a long time they simply listened to the rain. The silence, accompanied by stolen glances, eventually grew uncomfortable, but when one tried to speak, the other did also which led to a series of polite apologies, followed by repeated entreaties that the other say what they wanted to say. Another awkward silence descended upon them.

"Ehem, so," Abrielle finally began, "what were we talking about this morning? I really don't recall."

"It was a short conversation," Espen acknowledged. "I asked you about how one becomes a spy. You muttered something about training then fell back asleep."

Well, at least that explained the subject of her dream. She wondered why she'd been dreaming of her first formal training with Bellange.

"You look troubled," Espen observed.

"What? No, it's fine. I was just remembering something my mentor once told me. I guess I didn't fully appreciate it at the time," she reflected.

"Did he order your friends to turn on you?"

A sadness touched her beautiful features.

"Spies don't really have friends. At least, not many true ones. I doubt my mentor was in a position to order anything. He learned something he shouldn't have, and they took him away."

"Is that why the woman you were with betrayed you?"

The image of Chloe's expression of triumph reached out from Abrielle's memory.

"It's … a little more complex than that. But that might have been a factor. I really don't know."

She turned her gaze to the mass of rock suspended above her. There were any number of reasons why Chloe might have tried to have her eliminated, but why did she choose to reveal the truth to the Moon Shadows when she did? Why had she vanished for so long before Abrielle decided to go and rescue Espen? If Chloe survived, who else might be searching for her?

"You have friends," Espen noted.

"What?"

She rose slightly

"Or were those your parents? At the farm?"

Abrielle pondered the best response.

"I guess they're both," she decided as she lay back down.

The rain filled the silence.

"They did not know what you were."

How had he learned that?

"No," she said quietly.

"They are … good people," Espen declared.

She silently agreed for emotion would have choked off her voice. They were good people, who now might be in terrible danger because of her. It was not impossible that Chloe could follow her and Espen's trail through the mountains and bring Imperial Intelligence directly to the D'Aoust's doorstep. Despite her warnings about this, they'd remained more concerned about her, especially once she revealed that members of Espen's clan had stolen her deceased sister's child. Anne was beside herself that she'd let Espen go. Noel practically ran from the house to the barn and began to saddle a horse to follow him immediately.

It required no small amount of pleading to convince them that she was best qualified to locate him, in spite of her physical condition. She made them memorize two addresses before leaving: Christiansen's in Geneva and the Shaws' in Ireland, though she recommended them as a last resort. Besides, though Ernest had alluded to them that it might be otherwise, officially, according to local Irish law enforcement, she was dead. The D'Aoust's promised to leave and visit friends spread across half of France and to leave letters with Christiansen as they traveled. She gave them basic instructions on how to remain inconspicuous in public, though with Noel's size and Anne's personality, she doubted how effective her techniques would prove. Under such extreme pressures, this was the best she could manage. All she could do now was to pray for their safety. Espen interrupted her musings with a thoughtful but amusing question.

"Does the man ever speak?"

Abrielle smiled but didn't answer as she also suppressed the urge to giggle. Espen was fascinated by her, and as the damp hours wore on, she began to speak more freely about the life she'd left behind. In most cases she never spoke to anyone about her experiences, other than select members of the intelligence community. Unlike her conversations with Anne, this was a different type of confessional. Reflecting upon her experiences, it was astonishing to realize all she had learned.

In many ways it was thrilling to share her stories with someone who had no concept of what her life had truly been. Espen listened with the wonder of a child to stories too fantastic to believe. She did not divulge all of the details. How could she? But even the more general stories she chose to share held him in sway. For Espen, it was amazing that she was still alive at all. How could she have willingly embraced such an unforgiving existence?

"So, each time you completed a mission successfully, they augmented your skill sets?"

"Not every time, we'd never have been in the field if that were the case. Training wasn't always announced or even recognized as such. More often than not, it just sort of happened."

"What do you mean?" Espen asked in puzzlement.

Abrielle delicately drank a mouthful of water.

"Our superiors were constantly tutoring us, but the lessons usually took place in the field. I might be assigned to track an individual but be provided with only basic information about my prey. How I went about finding that person, if they even truly existed, was left up to me. But in the course of doing so, I might be presented with an analytical problem, like which road might this person chose. I'd have to take what I knew about their background and personality, evaluate why I'd been assigned to find them, what the ultimate purpose of their flight might be, and make my decision. An observer might be following me and would later debrief me on my choices involving decisions, methods, and tactics, good or bad."

"Doesn't sound any different from guessing to me," Espen quipped.

"It was more detailed than that because multiple skills were tested at once. I might assume an alternate persona, which I'd have to creditably maintain as I tracked a person across fifty miles of country in less than a day and enter a shop thinking I had them cornered. But the shopkeeper, under orders, might choose to hold the conversation only in English or Spanish or even blend the two. If I wasn't able to converse with them, my target might use the opportunity to flee, and my mission would fail."

"And what happened when you failed?"

Her answer was not boastful, but still it was chilling to hear.

"I never did."

She touched upon a host of topics and skills developed by years of incessant training: tailing or tracking a subject, the study of a multitude of languages, working with ciphers for coding and decoding, infiltration tactics and methods, learning to deal with the military and other officials who technically outranked her, lifestyle adjustments, survival techniques, endless endurance trials, physical and mental discipline training, gaining an in-depth knowledge of cultures and the arts, learning to use topography to her advantage, refining combat skills, counterespionage practices, analytical reasoning, developing a repertoire of social skills that extended across all levels of class, and the diplomatic skill of negotiation. As impressive as all of it was, Bellange had been right.

"So what mission has brought us together? Why do you need me?" Espen prompted.

He saw pain in her eyes, which she quickly tried to mask.

"It isn't ...," she tried to shake her head. "It isn't a mission."

It was too soon to tell him about Tara. Building trust between them was a slow process. He might be completely innocent of the knowledge of what had been taken from her. Such an accusation against members of his clan before he was ready to listen to hear it might mean a permanent end to their truce. Tara would be lost to her. She would have to confide in him shortly but not yet.

"It's personal," Espen said quietly, as if reading her thoughts.

She nodded stiffly, clearly unwilling to say more.

"Does it involve saving your mentor?"

Abrielle's reaction was unduly hostile.

"My mentor's been dead to me for a long time," she bit angrily, as her face grew pale. "Ever since he used me to …," she cut herself off, her heart desperate to escape the guilt of Paul's death. Bellange's words again echoed in her memory. He'd said them to her that late November day as she left for what was to be her final confrontation with her former friend and lover.

"*'No amount of training will ever prepare you for the most personal choices you must make.'*"

In that moment he'd spoken of loyalty, of the fragility of the human heart; the one thing the spymaster could not always control. But he'd worked to be able to control hers. It wasn't until after Paul's execution that she learned the truth, that Bellange had manipulated facts to suit his needs. Paul didn't escape from prison. Bellange quietly arranged for his release. When he felt Abrielle was ready, he'd arranged one final test of his most devoted and promising prodigy. The final decision was hers, but the situation could not have existed without Bellange, and she would always hate him for it. He had destroyed her heart, and she hadn't spoken to him again until the night the soldiers came and took them both away.

"Where are you going?"

She sat up too fast, the motion made her dizzy as pain again coursed outward from her neck.

"I just … I need to be alone for a while."

A gentle touch made her pause as his hand guided her back down.

"No. I'll go. The horses should be checked anyway," Espen said almost apologetically.

He moved closer to the edge as she settled back down without protest.

"Abrielle, I will not help you until you tell me why you saved me."

He did not see her tears. By the time she turned to speak he was already gone.

*

Home seemed very far away.

"What am I doing here," he muttered half to himself. The horse closest to him appeared wholly disinterested in his plight as it eyed him momentarily then resumed munching on the feed grain Espen had stolen from a farm several days earlier. What should he do next?

He wasn't certain if he admired Abrielle or was completely frightened by her. She was obviously talented and strikingly beautiful, despite the cuts and bruises. But it was also apparent that she was capable of doing nearly anything if she deemed it necessary. Her moral ambivalence, as he saw it, engendered an attractive vulnerability and a dangerous certitude. After hours together he still was left with the basic question that he needed to answer: Could he trust her? He'd grown more comfortable with the idea that she was being truthful, but what did she hope to gain by it?

It surprised him that she hadn't asked him where he was going. Did she already know? Could this delay allow some of her compatriots to reach his people before they did? What could her mentor have learned, if anything, which would cause him to become such a threat that those he'd once controlled had turned on him? What had he 'used' Abrielle for? Did she share in this secret? Is that why her own people had tried to kill her?

Additional thoughts also made Espen uneasy. She'd made no real effort to learn about him. There were no questions as to why he'd been a prisoner, about the fate of his other companions, or his people. Abrielle spoke a lot and asked very little, which to Espen, seemed most unusual for someone with her background. If the unspoken matter was so important that she risked her life and now her health to speak with him, why delay gaining information about him, unless, of course, she already knew most of the answers. If that was the case, then why was she so interested in him?

For a moment, Espen tried to imagine what his sister or grandmother would have thought about Abrielle. Actually, they probably would have simply warned him to stay away from her once they knew what she was. Well, maybe not Baseria.

Etolie, on the other hand, probably would have found her most interesting. She'd lived in France for a time with her parents before the Moon Shadows separated from the clan. What events had she witnessed, which Abrielle, or others like her, might have played a role in creating? Espen kicked mindlessly at a rock, his own deep sense of guilt returning. Etolie. He shouldn't have chosen Kelv's name to use as cover with Abrielle. It was disingenuous to his memory.

He needed to get home. It began to rain harder. After one final check that the horses would be safely secured for the night, Espen darted out into the deluge. He was grateful when he returned to the outcropping that Abrielle had cooked them dinner. He tried to warm himself by the fire as he ate.

It was a quiet meal, with each of them lost to their own private reflections, as they watched the ceaseless drops descend from the heavens. Abrielle thought of the dead. Espen worried about the living. Suddenly she cried out in pain, practically dropping her food. The knot in her neck was pulsing again. Her teeth clenched in agony. She closed her eyes, knowing the pulsating assault would move behind them soon. Would this never end?

She felt strong fingers massaging the offending muscles. Surprised, Abrielle began to utter a protest, but a gentle, "ssshhh," in her ear silenced her. Did she want this to happen? She was so tired of running.

The rhythmic motion of his fingers over her exposed skin calmed her. She began to take deep breaths as the pain slowly subsided. She trusted his touch. The hands upon her moved, one still applied a soothing pressure to the knot, the other now worked to delicately unlace the knot on the back of her dress. Her nerves danced as she sensed it give way, her soft brown eyes gradually opened.

Espen repositioned his body directly behind hers, his legs on either side of her own. His fingers now roamed freely across her back and down to her hips. With each small contact, promises were exchanged. Abrielle began to emit short gasps as the tension in her body faded. He moved closer, one hand continued to trace her form while the other held her. He tentatively touched his lips to the tingling skin of her neck. Her head lolled back towards him, and she smiled at the pleasure of the sensation. He whispered in her ear, and her hands released the front of her dress.

Espen's own breathing had deepened as her body responded to his touch. Lacing them with her own fingers, she drew his hands to her breasts. Abrielle moaned lightly as her hands bid his caresses to continue. She wanted him to know her body.

One of his hands traveled upwards and caressed her neck. The other moved down past her muscular abdomen. Her lips kissed his wrist hungrily. She could feel his warm chest pressing against her back. Feel his fingers probing her. His fingers traced her lips. She smiled as they withdrew and began to touch the soft, toned length of her inner thigh. Abrielle pressed her breasts against him as she turned to kiss him. Desire and need overtook them. Neither noticed what time the rain stopped falling.

*

The frontier lay illuminated under the early morning sun. Shadows and mists, snow and rock, river and meadow all wove across the majestic, eternal landscape before her. Soft mountain breezes played with her long, unbound hair. Her senses worked to identify every scent they carried. It was all so vivid.

After so many months spent in darkness, blindness, or isolation, the abundance of beauty surrounding her, coupled with the warm reassurance of the sun and these refreshing breezes dancing across her skin, Abrielle should have been happy. These last four days, she had been happy, but today would change that. If she was to save Tara, it must. The specter of time stalked her joy. She didn't want the dream to end. It was all so vivid, her peaceful mind repeated.

The coffee she'd made was now cooled considerably but she wasn't ready to abandon it. She pulled the blanket closer around her shoulders and in so doing beheld a sight which gave her pause.

Abrielle reached down to touch the delicate bud growing out of what appeared to be sheer rock. Such miracles were all too often easily dismissed. Its survival seemed impossible that it should be able to grow, even thrive here. Its very existence filled her with hope for she saw herself reflected in it. For her, France had been the rock, she the fragile flower, and Kelv now served as the sun bidding her to reach upward and grow. With all she'd suffered since her return to French soil, nothing of her should have been able to survive, let alone to grow in such a harsh, unyielding environment. But something did. She gazed upon the young bud a moment longer. What color would it be when nature called it forth? What shape had the universe destined its petals to take?

For four days they'd traveled, bearing witness to vistas of exquisite magnificence. Peaks rose and fell, spring again begrudgingly adorned the earth with color, stands of mighty trees whispered in light breezes, and the sun only abandoned the clear sky at night.

Aside from selling Maggie and procuring some fresh supplies, they all but existed outside of humanity during their journey together. They were free, and they embraced their passions without reservation. To them, it did not matter if it was love or if it was need.

They spoke only when absolutely necessary, each fearing that words would only invite reality to intrude. Near silence protected the fragile dream. This was a gift, one not to be questioned but enjoyed. Nothing was confusing. Sometimes, Abrielle felt that the only time she truly existed was when she lived in the moment. By stepping outside of one's reality, one could come to understand the myriad complexities that life offered and to appreciate them. But sitting here, an hour or so from being able to cross into Switzerland, reality assaulted her.

Abrielle set her cold cup down and studied the scar on her right hand. Several times Kelv commented on her habit of deliberating upon it. When exactly had it become a habit? She said nothing to satiate his curiosity regarding either its presence or her fascination with it. He didn't need to understand. It was a part of her, as was the promise it symbolized.

Her middle finger traced its length down her palm. Her thoughts turned to the man who bore this Gemini mark. At the thought of him, her eyes grew sad. For some reason, it upset her to realize that she hadn't really thought about him in weeks. Where was Ernest?

She drew her legs up to her chest, hugged them with her arms, and laid her head on her knees. She sighed. They could reach Geneva in two days—but what then? Had Christiansen and Jack given her up for dead? Did any of them really care? By now, did they know Ernest's fate? How might her life be changed by what she learned there? What was her life to be?

She sensed his approach moments before he bent over to kiss her. This morning there was only the slightest hesitation between them before their lips met. Did he perceive her pensive mood or did his own thoughts intercede?

They smiled at one another as he sat down beside her, and she extended the blanket around them. He'd brought Tara's blanket and wordlessly draped it across Abrielle's lap. For several minutes neither spoke. It was not an uncomfortable silence, rather one that simply required no words. Kelv nodded at her cup.

"Any of that left?"

"It's cold," she cautioned as he reached for it.

"Better than nothing," he noted.

"I can brew more."

He downed the cup's contents in one gulp.

"I'll make you some," he grinned, kissed her cheek, and began to loosen the blanket to leave.

"No, stay." The words escaped her before she realized she'd spoken them. The request surprised him somewhat as well. It had seemed as though she wanted to be alone.

Without comment, he wrapped an arm around her. She leaned against his shoulder and placed a hand against his chest. His face did not betray the tension she sensed in his muscles. He, too, was troubled.

For a long time they did not speak. Shadows shifted across the landscape as time silently marked its own passing. She did not want the dream to end. At last, Kelv kissed her forehead.

"What do you see out there?"

Abrielle did not respond immediately. The moment had come. She didn't want to let go.

"The future," she said quietly.

Abrielle felt the worn fabric of Tara's blanket beneath her fingers. The blanket she and her sister had created together. The tip of her middle finger again traced the scar on her hand, touched the promise living in her soul. She slowly pulled away from him.

Suddenly it seemed awkward that they should be so close. Abrielle began to speak as she looked down at Tara's blanket.

"Anne told me that you saved this for me when I was blind. Kelv," her eyes rose to meet his. "I never really thanked you for …"

Abrielle's lips parted as a chilling realization dawned upon her. The words left her—the expression on his face. A lifetime before, on the face of another lover, she'd seen that expression. She knew what it meant. Her heart leapt, uncertain of what to do.

"Abrielle … I have to tell you something. I haven't been honest, and before you say anything else, I need to be. I'm not …," he looked away for an instant. "My name isn't Kelv."

His voice fluctuated slightly.

"When I told you that it was I still wasn't sure if I could trust you. I thought I was protecting myself or that you already knew my real name so I haven't told you the truth." He hung his head.

She said nothing. Paul, her mind repeated. His expression looked like Paul's, just as it had before she'd …

"It was a mistake. I realize that. I've been trying to think of a better way than this to tell you the truth, but I haven't found it. I'm sorry."

He released a deep breath and raised his head.

"My real name is Espen Nalie."

The only thing she was certain of was that her heart was still beating. The pulse of it echoed in her ears. Her mind worked independent of her will as the name was located in her memory. Nalie. Ernest had spoken the name. It was one she'd memorized sitting beside the stone hearth of the fireplace in the front room of his home, sitting beside an empty cradle. Jal Nalie took the infant who should have been resting there, safe and loved. He stole her niece. Ernest's words returned to her.

'His son, Espen, was taking some of the clan's warriors to try to find Baseria and the others.'

She was staring into Espen's eyes, not Kelv's, staring into Paul's eyes, begging for forgiveness, for understanding, asking again that she respect the need to betray her.

Abrielle felt warm everywhere, dizzy. The memories of their bodies touching, the sensation of being needed, desired by him now filled her with guilt. She wanted to cry, but she couldn't. Without realizing it, her hand moved for the place where she kept her knife. Except this time it wasn't there. She hadn't brought it with her this morning because of him, because she felt safe in his presence. What did she want to do with it now?

In horror she began to stagger away from Espen but did not make it very far. Paul's final cries, she could hear them. The spinning ground met her knees; she became sick. Her nails scratched the bare, cool rocks with the force of her exertions. It seemed it would never end.

She felt his hand holding her hair back, could hear his voice saying her name. By now the tears had come. They were the only thing that felt real. His family had destroyed hers.

"Don't touch me!" she cried out in French as she shoved him away.

The motion caused a spasm in her already exhausted abdomen muscles. She clutched at them in pain and fought to regain her breath. She could do it; she didn't need a knife. Abrielle could kill him. His remains might lay in this idyllic setting for years before someone found his bleached bones.

Her heart despaired and her emotions surged at the repugnant thought. No. She didn't want to kill him, despite what his family had done. Abrielle couldn't. He had saved her life. But more importantly, if she destroyed him, as she had Paul, she would destroy herself. She struggled within her tempest of emotions.

"*Use him,*" her mind ordered. The professional spy in her awoke —"*Use him.*"

Something within her resisted the suggestion. She did have feelings for him, and she knew he had them for her. She'd witnessed them in his eyes, knew they existed within his heart. Was it right to pervert those?

He handed her a water bladder, and she immediately rinsed and expelled the coarse, distasteful, film from her mouth. Too tired to move, she leaned against the reassuring stones. She must find Jal. If Espen could be used for that purpose—if he would chose to become an ally—then safely freeing Tara might be possible.

She must move cautiously, but the final outcome must never be in question. It began to dawn upon Abrielle what a gracious and unexpected gift that fate now bestowed upon her. She would use the son against the father. A man whose destiny, when they met, was unavoidable. That was justice. If, however, she was unable to manipulate Espen to help her or if he fully supported his father's choice, she must be prepared to incapacitate him and use him in trade for Tara.

Abrielle's eyes searched the wild beauty around them. Not, here, she thought. If at all possible, it must not take place here. If the need did arise for her to capture him then she would have to transport him and keep him immobilized for two days on her own. In that case, the safe confines of Christiansen's office would be much more practical. Espen was warily studying her shifting expressions. What was she thinking?

"I once had a lover who betrayed me and left me for dead," she sniffed.

Espen's face remained calm, his eyes did not.

"He also betrayed my master, who bid me to locate and deal with him."

The young gypsy hesitated.

"And did you?"

She turned her eyes to his.

"He was never honest with me," she replied, "but neither was my master."

"And did you kill him too?" Espen's voice rose slightly.

"No," Abrielle held his gaze. "I told you, I don't know his fate, though I doubt it was any different than Paul's. Tell me, Espen, is there anything else you feel you need to be honest with me about?"

The question was posed as a means of intimidation. Espen, however, refused to be baited.

"Yes," he answered sharply. "When I said my real name, you recognized it."

She nodded.

"How?" he demanded as she awkwardly began to rise from the ground. Abrielle paused before answering.

"Because we share a mutual friend, if he's still alive," she explained simply as she began to walk away.

"Wait. Where are you going? Who is this person?"

"We should pack. It's two days until we reach Geneva, and we have much to discuss."

"Who is in Geneva?" he demanded.
"I hope my brother-in-law, and perhaps, your sister."

CHAPTER 16
THE VALLEY OF SHADOWS

Baseria studied her arms. They burned with a soft scarlet translucence, but they were not bathed in blood; rather, the hue that shone upon them came through the window. It was the red light of dawn. It cast her in silhouette, framed her before the destroyed window. Though she stood closest to it, all of the glass had passed her. She was unmarred. Hundreds of shards had sailed on the winds which now whipped at her clothing. Her garments, unlike her body, hadn't been spared, and the seemingly infinite gouges and holes bore testimony to the singular violence of the explosion.

A power she'd touched only once before now raced through her form. Her spirit begged to relinquish control to its seductive allure. It was intoxicating. It was dangerous. She worked to suppress the euphoric sensation that accompanied it, fought to control her breathing. Baseria tried to ignore the new and powerful senses that were trying to awaken deep within. They craved to touch the power that called to her. What was happening to her? Only sheer will held them back. She focused on the moment. Others around her suffered. She must concentrate on this and this alone. The longings abated slowly as she beheld the scene before her.

They all bled—Moon Shadow and Wild Rose alike. The injuries varied in location, severity, and their aftermath. Some would heal quickly, others seemed certain to prove fatal. The cruel man who'd already caused Etolie such pain hovered over her, holding a pistol on Baseria. His cold eyes left no doubt; he would not hesitate to kill. Her friend lay unconscious at his feet, an ugly bruise, half hidden by her hair, marked where the handle of his weapon had struck her. A new cry attracted her attention, but it was not Etolie who screamed now but Isyll.

The girl was covered in blood, though how much of it came from her was impossible to tell.

"Help her! Help her!" she wailed to the others who all stood dumbstruck at the sight before them. Vochallet's eyes were open, but only the involuntary motion of the lids betrayed life within. The orbs were vacant, her neck slit open by flying glass. Blood burbled from the wound. Her right index and middle fingers were trying to hold it shut. The pallor of her face stood in stark contrast to the slowly spreading pool of blood beneath her.

"Help her! Help her for God's sake!"

Isyll was clutching desperately at Tasaria who crouched on the ground nearby. Baseria's aunt was only slowly beginning to realize what exactly had happened. She looked to her niece with a mixture of astonishment and uncertainty.

"Pell, fetch others," Pias commanded to the gypsy who'd threatened Isyll earlier.

Pell hesitated only a moment.

"Now!"

Pias watched his underling as he departed but never allowed his attention to waiver from Baseria for more than a few seconds. An impression of motion caught his eye.

"What are you doing?" he demanded of Tasaria as she crawled over to the dying Wild Rose woman. "She can't be saved, let her die."

Tasaria ignored him as she examined the other woman's neck. The windpipe did not appear to have been severed, nor the jugular. But if the bleeding wasn't stopped immediately none of that mattered.

"Please, please, don't let her die," Isyll implored as she stroked Vochallet's hair with trembling fingers. Though they really hadn't known one another before, without realizing it, Vochallet had become a mother figure and friend to her, especially after the disappearance of Sebbi. It was she who was willing to fight back, not Etolie, and certainly not Baseria.

Isyll turned pleading eyes to Tasaria, who began to tear a length of Vochallet's dress. Eager to do something to help, Isyll began to do likewise to her own clothing. Baseria took half a step forward to help. Pias immediately raised his weapon. She stepped warily back. Almost instinctively her thoughts told her to summon the winds. She could do it. Use them to blast the pistol from the man's hand, force him into submission. Is that what she had done before?

Her eyes again swept over Etolie's unconscious form. Was she responsible for shattering the glass and injuring the others? They seized upon Vochallet and the crimson flood that Isyll and her aunt worked feverishly to control. Baseria's hands rose to cover her mouth in silent horror. She had done this. She was to blame, just as she was for Jucika and Patia's deaths.

"You're going to be fine," Isyll whispered reassuringly to Vochallet as she and Tasaria pressed the lengths of cloth against her throat and held them there. Each strip was quickly overwhelmed with blood.

"It's not stopping," Tasaria tersely observed as she mopped more blood away from the wound. The Wild Rose woman's breathing was becoming shallower, her color ashen.

"No, no, stay with me. You've got to stay with me," Isyll gently shook Vochallet as her eyelids began to droop. The action revived her to a degree.

Pias watched all of this play out with annoyed detachment. According to the scant intelligence he'd learned from Pell, it seemed highly unlikely that this woman had any value to their cause whatsoever. She was not an asset but an extra. One the "Master" decided to bring to this place of his own volition, a choice Pias himself disagreed with from the beginning.

She was also, apparently, the most troublesome of the lot, attempting to inspire the others to rebel against their captors. She was a liability, one that ultimately only contributed to the loss of time and effort, neither of which could be spared. Events had conspired to force his presence here, yet others were unfolding back on the Continent that might forever jeopardize his plans. Complex schemes he'd fought long and hard to ensure would prove ultimately successful. Besides, he meant what he said to Tasaria. The wound seemed fatal. Why struggle against what must be?

He turned his attentions again to the girl near the window. She'd sunk to the floor, tears in her eyes. For the moment she seemed to have forgotten about the man holding a pistol on her. If he was going to act, it must be now. Decisively, he strode the few steps needed to obtain a clear shot. It was time to end this nonsense.

"Move, Tasaria," Pias commanded.

The older woman paused in her ministrations and stared at him in disbelief.

"No!" Isyll shrieked as she attempted to shield her dying friend from Pias' pistol.

"No!" He heard Tasaria's niece wail.

"It isn't up to you," Tasaria declared. "The Master …"

"Isn't here," he snapped. "Move!"

Pias raised his gun to line up his shot and suddenly found himself flying through the air. It all happened so quickly that, for an instant, true terror gripped his senses. What had happened?

He recovered to find his own windpipe was slowing being crushed in a vice-like grip. The diseased hand that clutched his neck also held him precariously over the edge of the open window. Pias struggled against the unholy thing. He longed for the frigid air racing across his skin to fill his lungs. Those horrible, yellow eyes bore into him from above. They were bereft of mercy, as was the mummified death mask of a face that possessed the misfortune of holding them. Anger burned within those eyes unlike any he'd witnessed there before. Pias felt his weight shifting dangerously close to sending him into the crashing, ice-laden waves below. He gripped the creature's concealed forearm for dear life. If this was the end, he would not die begging to live.

His vision ebbed towards blackness. The bones in his neck strained as he struggled to utter each syllable.

"It's … good to…,"

His air was almost gone, still the fingers pressed even more tightly. Pias summoned a final supreme effort to complete his thought. The words barely escaped.

"… see … you …, … Master …"

For a moment, Pias hovered close to nonexistence. Then the world suddenly spun as he was hurtled roughly by his neck back into the room. He landed unceremoniously in a heap several feet away from the massive shadow that had just spared his life. Pias was oblivious to the shards of glass digging into his arms as he greedily gasped for oxygen. His burning lungs choked on the icy air, and he coughed and gagged uncontrollably.

Pias was not angry, for each time he faced death and survived, it validated that his path was true. It was as his beloved always told him. It meant the universe wanted him to succeed. That thought alone made the pain tolerable.

The black presence paused beside Baseria for only a moment before continuing towards the dying woman and those tending her. The nightmarish eyes studied her injury. Then he leaned forward and placed two of his wretched fingers and a thumb against Tasaria's neck. She recoiled involuntarily to his touch. She could feel the pointed bones beneath the shallow flesh.

"The pressure must be placed down here, well below the wound."

The creature turned his eyes on Isyll who immediately looked away but placed her fingers on Vochallet's neck as he'd demonstrated. Tasaria recovered and pressed a new piece of torn dress cloth over the gash. All were silent as they waited for fate. Only the creature moved as he stalked over to Etolie who had yet to regain her senses. A group of gypsies and two Old Ones stood near the doorway patiently awaiting orders. After what they'd seen the Master do to Pias, no one was especially anxious to upset him.

"I think it's working," Tasaria finally stated.

The pronouncement seemed to draw the creature back from his reverie. For several minutes now his attentions wavered between studying Etolie and Baseria. Pias sat up, gingerly pulling bits of glass out from beneath his skin. His shaking fingers made the task more difficult. The frozen air pouring over him was a shock to his system. The Master motioned to his underlings. All but the Old Ones, who remained at their posts by the door, complied.

"The window must be covered and sealed, the women returned to their rooms, and anyone who is wounded tended to. You will have to be careful when you move them. Tell Pias and Tasaria I will meet them in the dining chamber in two hours. Show them where they are to be quartered during their stay. The Old Ones are to observe them with discretion. No more."

Everyone nodded in acknowledgement of the Master's commands. His orders complete, the creature moved towards the door as the others quickly organized themselves to fulfill his wishes. As he left, Baseria finally staggered towards Etolie who was just beginning to come around. Her friend moaned as Baseria touched her softly.

"Etolie?" She whispered her name.

The young woman's eyelids fluttered but did not open.

*

It was abysmally cold when she entered the room. Baseria pulled the lone chair within closer to the bed. The dim lighting, combined with the heavy blankets all but obscured its slumbering occupant. It was quiet in the room, the first real quiet Baseria had experienced in hours, though in truth seemed more like days.

Etolie wept uncontrollably during the last hour after she'd regained consciousness. And despite repeated attempts by Baseria to comfort her friend she would say nothing of her grief, the source of which could only have been caused by something the cruel gypsy said. It must be. And Baseria could think of only one subject which might cause such inconsolable heartache. The only alternative was that the months of ceaseless stress and darkness had finally broken her—that Etolie had lost her mind. If that was the case, she wasn't the only one.

Maybe Isyll would have better luck. Though it was something of a relief to be alone, it was at the same time unnerving. Baseria stole a quick glance around the room, praying her ghostly tormentor would not appear. No phantoms materialized, only the baleful sound of yet another storm intruded. She dug under the blankets and took up one of Vochallet's hands. It was callous but relatively warm. She gripped the hand somewhat awkwardly at first. She'd never felt particularly close to the older woman. In fact, once when Baseria was younger, Vochallet had publicly blamed her for causing the clan's separation. Espen, of course, defended her against the accusation. Jal had not. He rarely did when such incidents occurred. She tried to banish the painful memories of her father's remoteness.

Baseria avoided interacting with Vochallet for years afterward, and during their months together, incarcerated in this frozen purgatory, neither ever spoke of it. There was no need. Everything was different here, and in time, all things past became a treasure, the present a soul-crushing burden, and the future something to behold with dread. It seemed all but certain that none of them would ever have a future—only torment and death.

Vochallet's pale face was peaceful as she slept, untroubled. Only the red hue, which stained the wrapping about her neck, betrayed the illusion. The faintest traces of a smile momentarily moved across her lips. Baseria hoped that Vochallet's children were comforting their mother in her dreams. She couldn't begin to imagine how much being separated from them day after day was hurting her. And now she might be slowly dying. And once again, Baseria was to blame.

Baseria hunched her shoulders against the cold. It seemed impossible that one could ever recover in this unhappy place. Hadn't they all been slowly dying in this hellish fortress for months? It was only during those first days after Frankenstein's arrival that there'd been any real hope that they might live to see a future beyond this.

Before that it was Vochallet's spirit that challenged them not to give up, to fight for hope. She'd sustained them by urging them to struggle against their captors' wishes. This woman's spirit was strong. Baseria could only pray that it still was strong enough.

The strain on that spirit was increasingly apparent lately as Vochallet progressively relied more and more on Isyll and Etolie to help sustain her as well. She was tired of the fight. They all were. How long could they cling to false hopes merely to survive in a state of abject terror? As she studied the older woman's face, Baseria discovered an elegance about it which she'd never really appreciated before. She didn't deserve this. Baseria raised Vochallet's hand to her lips and softly pressed them to it. As she lowered it, Baseria hung her head and wept.

*

"You have to do it. There isn't another way, Isyll."

The terrified girl shook her head in refusal. All of this was too much for her.

"There is. We'll find one. Frankenstein might …," Isyll began hopefully.

"Isyll, there isn't another way," Etolie repeated quietly as their eyes met. "You know I'm right." The look of regret on Isyll's face made it clear that a part of her did, but everything else within her fought against Etolie's suggestion.

"I don't care if you're right," she said bitterly. "How could you ask me to do that?"

"Isyll," Etolie shook her head in sympathy.

"No, it doesn't matter," she asserted. "I won't do it. I … I'll stay."

Etolie waited a moment before continuing. She knew this was difficult.

"That won't help."

"And how does this?" Isyll demanded bluntly, her voice rising passionately.

Etolie looked away.

"Because this is the only way the rest of you can live."

Isyll was angry. This was the second time in as many hours another had instructed her to play God with the lives of others. She resented their demands and feared to do so. Who was she to be asked to make such choices? Life and death was not her purview exclusively. The decision was made worse by the knowledge that no matter what she chose, it would result in another's end.

"But how could I live knowing that I caused your death?"

"You didn't," Etolie explained quietly. "That man who asked you to betray us did."

Isyll closed her eyes. She felt guilty and ashamed.

"He didn't ask me," Isyll lied but Etolie persisted.

"I heard him while they were carrying me. They thought I was asleep, but I heard what they asked you to do."

Tears began to trickle from the corners of Isyll's eyes. That her salvation must lie in the destruction of another whom she loved and respected sickened her. Maybe it was her relentless fears, or the months of uncertainty, or perhaps her overpowering desire to save Vochallet's life, but Etolie's argument was beginning to make sense. Still she resisted.

"Please … don't ask me to do this, Etolie. Please."

Etolie leaned forward and cupped her hands tenderly around Isyll's damp face. Slowly the girl's eyes opened. They were filled with fear and pain.

"He could be lying," Isyll pleaded.

Etolie's own courage wavered as her emotions overwhelmed her. The nightmare of Kelv's death played out silently behind her eyes.

"He's not lying. I've shown you that he's not," she choked as she attempted to regain a degree of her composure. "You're strong, Isyll, more so than you realize. Look into your heart, as I have. You know the answer you need is there."

Etolie clasped the girl's shaking hands into her own. Isyll turned her wounded expression upon her, but there was no fight left in her. Etolie held her.

"I couldn't save him, but I can save you. If you do this, we can save the others. Please, help me."

*

Pias' thoughts swirled like the myriad of snowflakes hurtling past the window of the dining chamber. What was truly going on here? He needed answers. If his plans were in jeopardy, if his betrayal was imminent, then he must quickly grasp the scope of what was happening at this fortress, else all be lost. He rubbed at his neck, which felt as if it had been twisted beyond his body's ability to heal it. Would he survive another direct confrontation? Of course he would. He always did, regardless of the opponent.

Unlike the reading room, the windows here were lower and not really much more than slits, probably once used as concealed firing ports by whoever had originally embraced the insane notion of constructing the massive fortress in such a desolate place. Still, he felt a unique reverence for the structure itself.

As he peered through the slit, he pondered its existence. Pias was not one given to fancy, however, the foreboding presence one sensed from the fortress always conveyed impressions of immense power and death. Perhaps that was why he felt at ease here. He knew that except when it had been abandoned to the winds, this structure had known no peace.

He scowled in frustration as he drew his head away from the slit. Were it not for the intense fire burning in the immense fireplace, which took up half the room behind them, the temperature would be unbearable.

"I can't see a blasted thing, Pell."

He tried to blink warmth back into his eyes and did nothing to mask his annoyance with his subordinate. His underling stiffened, no doubt worried that Pias would take out his frustrations on him.

"You will," the other promised sincerely. "Keep watching, sir. They work them even in conditions like these, no matter how brutal."

Pias concealed his smirk to himself as he turned back to the slit. It was wise for Pell to be nervous in the presence of his true master. Especially since he knew he was out of favor with his lord.

"Indeed, how unfortunate that we docked on the other side."

He could dimly perceive movement in the blizzard but little else. The dock and the ship along side it were masked by the gale, one they themselves thankfully had missed being caught in by a matter of hours.

Actually, Pias was relieved to have docked at all. Pressing matters kept him away from this abysmal place for several years. Finding it again proved more difficult than he'd anticipated. The fortress was constructed in such a manner that it all but vanished at certain angles when viewed from the sea. And several of the land markers Pias had used in the past to navigate by were completely obscured by storms or fog. It was primarily random chance, rather than skill, that allowed them to relocate the fortress.

Of course, he only had himself to blame for this journey. Pias glowered. It was a mistake to allow the "Master" to create his own dominion. A rare lapse in judgment for Pias enabled the tactical error, but it was one of increasingly vital import. Affairs now played out across vast distances, involving intricate plots that required careful nurturing and manipulation. Initially establishing the isolated outpost was primarily meant to keep the creature away from Pias' carefully conceived schemes, however, it instead accomplished far more than that. It helped to define the fiend's identity, projected an image of power to those who served him, and as such had established a dark temple of worship for one wholly undeserving of such considerations. If only they knew. Most important though, it made it difficult for Pias to monitor the other's activities.

As he sought substance in the shifting shadows of the storm, Pias knew that they passed through an hour of great change. He also recognized that if matters were not handled properly, events would rapidly transcend his ability to control them, if they had not already. He turned to speak with Pell and froze. An enormous black mass blocked most of the light from the fireplace. When had he entered? Pias looked to Pell who seemed equally surprised at the unexpected appearance of the fortress' dark Master. Apparently he too had failed to notice his presence until now. Pias nodded for Pell to leave.

"No," the creature's harsh tone halted the man in his tracks.

A shadow stirred beyond the fireplace and the smaller, hooded form of an Old One came fully into the light. Pias again masked his surprise. Had they spoken of anything that might compromise their position? He quickly replayed the last few minutes in his mind.

The Old One whispered into his lord's ear—one demon to another.

When the disquieting conference concluded, the creature again rose to his full, commanding stature and fixed Pell under a relentless gaze.

"Your cunning is admirable, Pell. Praiseworthy, indeed."

The sentiment was uttered without any real emotion. Pell hesitated a moment before responding.

"Thank you, Master?" His tone did little to conceal either his confusion or nervousness at receiving such praise. The yellow eyes continued to bore down into him.

"My friend will convey you safely to your afternoon watch station at the main gate." The head demon nodded to the Old One who began to stalk toward Pell. "May I suggest you maintain your vigilance. The polar bear the morning watch reported likely remains close by concealed in the storm. It would be a shame to lose you now."

Pell's eyes flashed only the briefest gaze towards Pias, and then he and the Old One vacated through the room's set of great, creaking doors. They closed loudly, and for a moment, the only sounds heard in the room were the crackling of fire, howl of wind, and the unnatural breath rattling beneath the cloaked figure's hood.

"An interesting choice for your spy," the creature finally noted. "Especially in light of Pell's recent treatment of my prisoner, Isyll. Such actions typically breed contempt, not capitulation."

Pell was loyal beyond question, which was part of the reason Pias had left him to oversee his affairs here, but sometimes that sense of duty overrode reason. Undoubtedly he'd learned of his true master's imminent arrival and panicked that after so many months, he still did not know for certain the Seer's true identity. The creature was right, of course. Pell's stupidity could still work against them. But Pias also trusted his instincts.

"She was an obvious choice. She still perceives she has something to lose. That makes her vulnerable. You saw firsthand how she defended the fallen woman. The others all have more important personal concerns."

"Interesting conclusions. Do you think she will talk?"

Pias allowed himself to relax a degree. Yes, he was sure. From her perspective there was everything to be gained and little to lose.

"It's a simple enough ploy, and those are often the most effective," Pias explained as he stepped over the bench to seat himself at the dining table.

"Personally," he continued, "I'm curious as to why you have not attempted to employ such a direct method of subterfuge yourself."

He pulled the bench closer to the table and gazed up questioningly at the cloaked face.

"I prefer other, more subtle methods," the creature explained.

"Of course," Pias smiled. "I guess we will have to see then whose method ultimately proves to be more efficient and successful, unless you care to share your conclusions now?"

It was the shadow's turn to grin. He turned away from the other man. By now Pias' devious little mind was undoubtedly weighing if he should voice his suspicions.

"Speak, Pias."

"You keep them under surveillance at all times, do you?"

"The Old Ones must be taught," the dark form responded by way of an answer.

"And, ah, what else do you teach them?"

The response was slower this time but no less cryptic.

"We teach each other."

Pias rolled his eyes.

"Will they be ready?"

"They are. For your purposes, they are," the other said somberly.

Pias' eyes shone. The pronouncement, if true, was both fortuitous and timely. An hour of great change, indeed, his future arrived at last. He felt emboldened.

"And just when did you intend to tell me?"

The creature rounded on him.

"I received Nicabar's missive of your impending arrival only hours before you did. Tell me, did you seek me out immediately to address the serious situation in France or did you instead go to your spy and attempt to undermine my vital efforts?"

Pias fired back immediately.

"If you knew Pell was my spy then you should have dealt with him. If he was one of yours, I would have. Don't fault me for your mistakes."

Most likely the creature had been well aware of Pell's loyalties and intended to use the man to gain information about Pias' own plans and directives. Only he hadn't gotten to him in time.

"You got greedy," Pias asserted.

"As if your own greed knows limits, Pias," the creature began.

"All right, yes, there are other spies here. Undoubtedly you've attempted to use yours against me as well. But for the moment, let's move beyond that. She'll be here soon, and there is much we still must discuss."

The anger in the yellow orbs did not diminish but the reality of the statement did seem to refocus the great being. Pias pressed the advantage.

"Your other work?"

"Has progressed more rapidly due to recent events," the other responded.

"Such as?" Pias inquired suspiciously.

"I will have to show you. How long do you plan to remain?"

"I can spare no more than three days. The situation in France is more dangerous than Nicabar is willing to admit, at least in any letter to you. But on one point I must agree with him. Tasking him to waste time and manpower to locate Frankenstein's infant is absurd. There is too much at risk."

"He is here," the creature responded simply. The declaration turned Pias' gaze to ice.

"Here?" Pias asked incredulously. "Frankenstein is here?"

A loud bang and creak issued from the entryway interrupted before either had an opportunity to fill the void with words. Pias worked to control his rage. As she entered, Tasaria looked tired, and the myriad of gashes on her hands and face did nothing to aid her appearance. The creature graciously guided her to one of the table's lone chairs. Pias crossed his arms.

"You must rest when our discussion concludes."

"Thank you for your concern, Master, but I will be fine. My apologies for being late. It took longer than I'd anticipated to move the woman and to clean my wounds. I must admit, however, I am fatigued. Perhaps it's the cold."

"We should eat then, before our sister retires," Pias suggested with a fake smile.

The creature hesitated then raised his voice.

"We shall do so then."

Apparently the Wild Rose clan prisoners were not the only ones being observed. The door opened a few moments later, and one of the

Moon Shadow women appeared.

"Prepare an afternoon meal for our guests. Ensure their quarters' fires are kept alight."

The servant bowed then shut the door behind her.

Pias shifted his attention back to Tasaria.

"Will the prisoner live?"

Tasaria returned a venomous look to him before addressing her answer to the creature.

"The bleeding seems to be under control for the moment, however, there is swelling all around her windpipe. It may eventually asphyxiate her."

"I admire such compassion for your enemies," Pias sarcastically interjected.

"Better than the cold, cruelty of your heart, Pias," Tasaria hotly affirmed.

He leered at her, enjoying himself until the other interceded.

"Enough," he said quietly. "Tell me, how did the window's glass come to shatter?"

The question elicited looks of mutual reproach and puzzlement from Pias and Tasaria, neither wanted to answer.

"It must have been the wind from the storm," Pias began.

"It wasn't the wind," Tasaria asserted as she cut him off. "Not entirely."

Fierce yellow eyes demanded answers.

"What then?"

Tasaria was reluctant to answer but knew that she must. Of the image of her mother's spirit, she would say nothing.

"It was the power of the Seer."

Pias snickered.

"The power of the Seer, no less," he said. "So you cut your own face by summoning the wind?"

"No."

"Well, how else could it have happened?" Pias continued. "I mean you claim to be the Seer, so if it wasn't you, then who was it? Your niece then, perhaps?"

"No, it was not her," Tasaria's eyes became unfocused for an instant, then narrowed, and suddenly she seized the offensive from Pias. "What did you say to that woman before she screamed? The window shattered a moment after you upset her."

It was Pias' turn to hesitate.

"Answer," the hooded form demanded.

Pell had identified the women for him when they entered the room. The opportunity that arose when he recognized Etolie's name was too much to resist.

"I merely passed along my condolences for the unfortunate loss of that woman's poor husband back in France," Pias explained in a sympathetic tone.

"What's her name?" Tasaria asked, and then abandoned the question as the realization of what Pias had done dawned upon her.

"The Wild Rose prisoner? Pias, you didn't?" Tasaria felt ill, and her hatred of the man grew. Pias only nodded in self satisfaction.

Their meal arrived. Pias tore a section of the bread and began to calmly chew it.

"And that news caused the window to break?" the shadow asked.

"She screamed," Tasaria answered, the observation a thinly veiled accusation.

The creature turned to Pias, who sat up just a little straighter.

"I returned her husband's necklace to her and she screamed, yes. I assume you would have preferred that I'd hidden his death from her, Tasaria? This is somehow less cruel than what I did?"

She was not given an opportunity to respond.

"So Pias, you are responsible for their injuries?" The creature challenged.

Pias glared at him and sat up even straighter. Wasn't he a victim too? Hadn't he been cut by flying glass also?

"Hardly," he shot back. "If it was the Seer, as Tasaria maintains, then undoubtedly, it is her niece who is responsible."

"Impossible," the woman's denial was instantaneous, as was Pias' reply.

"Why? Because you refuse to believe that your mother would train her? Something that you would never do. A bit simple-minded, isn't that?"

He leaned forward and jabbed a finger in her direction.

"Don't allow your own prejudices to blind you to truth. Don't you people have any butter?"

Tasaria was furious as she stabbed a finger back at him.

"You provoked the attack by telling Etolie about how you murdered her husband. I'd try to kill you, too."

"You're right. You're right. It was an attack, not an emotional outburst. But what were you about to do to your niece just before that glass went flying?"

Pias had her. The older woman clasped her jaw shut in righteous indignation. Who was he to question her actions or her feelings?

"It was far less than she deserves!"

"You provoked Baseria?" The creature asked flatly.

"I never touched her," Tasaria protested.

"No, the glass got to you before you got to her," Pias informed the hooded figure smugly. "And she was the only one I saw who didn't seem to be injured in any way."

"She's not the Seer!" Tasaria declared in a booming voice, her fist slamming firmly into the table. "Mother may have begun training another before she died but her power has passed to me. I felt it when you killed her. I am the Seer."

She expected another challenge from Pias, at the very least a demand that she prove her power to them this instant. Instead, an embarrassed silence descended upon them, one that over time allowed tensions to slowly ease. The creature began to pace. Pias chewed absentmindedly while Tasaria poured herself a drink and then raised the mug to her lips.

"Tasaria," the creature began softly, "you once mentioned to me that when your mother initially trained you, she saw fit to train your sister simultaneously. Is that not so?"

Mayte's face broke through the gates of memory. Tasaria set the mug back down and calmly nodded, then met her Master's eyes. The implication was clear enough.

"You think she repeated that … that she was training both of those girls?" Pias postulated. Even if it wasn't true, he began to consider how he might use such a notion to his advantage.

Tasaria wanted to refute such nonsense outright. It was too painful for her to contemplate. Yes, she and Mayte had been trained together, but at what cost? Instead of uniting the clan, the decision had destroyed it. After Mayte's death, Nasi refused to continue Tasaria's training. By then her mother considered her surviving daughter to be too dangerous. The thought of her entrusting such vital secrets, skills, and power to these girls was outrageous; especially if she truly had favored Baseria, the most unworthy member of the entire Nalie clan. Still, the past did set a precedent, which was difficult to ignore.

"It is … possible," she conceded at long last.

A tentative knock, so muffled, and gentle that it could barely be heard over the fury of the storm raging outside brought their conversation to an abrupt halt. They listened as it was repeated. Tasaria, silently grateful for the interruption, crossed the room and drew the heavy door open. The hinges moaned in strained protest, the metal wailing through the echoing chamber. Outside in the hallway, stood the young girl who'd protected the eldest of the Wild Rose clan women after she was injured. She was accompanied by an Old One and stood before Tasaria visibly quaking from either cold or fear.

"Allow her in," the creature commanded. His tone betrayed no surprise at her sudden appearance. Tasaria stood to the side and motioned for Isyll to enter. The girl had to will her legs to move and she jumped when Tasaria closed the solid door firmly behind her. Tears clung to her eyes and she struggled to control her breathing. No one spoke. For a moment it appeared as though the girl was about to faint but she recovered herself. Then in a quivering voice, she spoke.

"I know who the Seer is."

Chapter 17
The Favor

Dusk clung to the streets of Geneva, the air laden with chill. There would be fog from the lake tonight Christiansen noted as he hurried towards his destination. For the fifth time since leaving his office, he again felt for the reassuring weight of the pistol concealed in his right coat pocket. His head swiveled, in what he hoped was a casual manner, as he watched for signs of pursuit. At least two weeks had passed since he'd last perceived being watched, but the clandestine rendezvous that beckoned him to step among the lengthening shadows of twilight tonight only heightened his awareness of their apparent absence. He must remain vigilant.

His wife hated him carrying a gun. Despite his repeated reassurances, she was convinced that sooner or later he'd only end up shooting himself. He smiled as he inwardly acknowledged that she may be right. The weapon was really more for show than for any skill he might apply to its use. If it came to actually fighting, then his cane would make a much more effective weapon. Undoubtedly, she would worry when he did not arrive home at the expected hour, but under the circumstances, such an oversight was unavoidable. He'd sent word that he would be working late but provided no further details. Christiansen hoped his note to her would bring reassurance rather than alarm.

For his part, he was not certain which of these emotions he currently felt regarding the missive he had himself received. Since his first meeting with her, this woman elicited both emotions equally from him, and now she'd returned. That was, of course, if this was not all part of a trap. He resisted the temptation to reach into his left coat pocket and retrieve the paper there within. By now he'd memorized any detail worth noting. Normally, such news about one so long absent would have been reason to celebrate. And he was pleased to hear from Abrielle but apprehensive to learn what had transpired during her prolonged disappearance. Did her return herald fortunes for good or ill? Where had she been these long months? What if she'd found Ernest dead or that Tara had been killed? Could she have resumed her former life as a spy? How would she respond to Jack's news? Not well, he decided.

Christiansen desperately wanted to stop and light a cigarette to help calm his nerves, but the sky was growing increasingly dark, and he was not in the best of districts. So he pressed on. Besides, the tavern he sought couldn't be too much further. His mind worked ceaselessly to control them, but his fears refused to be silenced. What if this was a trap? He should have brought someone with him. He certainly had connections with enough people in the justice community that he could have easily have had ten guards surrounding him right now if he wished. But that would have aroused unwelcome questions, ones best left in the imagination and not to the open scrutiny of others. Of course, Abrielle's note provided him with plenty of difficulties already.

It appeared on his office desk that afternoon while he was out at court. No one who worked in his office could apparently recall seeing a woman fitting her description either enter or exit the edifice all day. The content of the note was simple: the tavern's address, a date, a time, and the word home, translated into Gaelic beneath it. Before leaving, Abrielle spent some time working out a simple system of code with him. One of their recognition signs was the date of Tara's birth. The other involved the use of seven words, translated into Gaelic, that were meant to indicate the sender's status. But for the life of him, Christiansen could not recall if they'd decided that 'home' meant fortunes were favorable or ill. It had all happened so rapidly months earlier. And he was afraid to write anything down in case his office was searched. The fact that they'd also debated several dissimilar systems, each using the seven basic words differently, didn't help the current situation either. So he was left to guess.

Bells began to call out the hour, and Christiansen paused to check his timepiece. He was late. He quickened his pace but slowed when he heard a sharp, short whistle emitted from somewhere behind him. His senses tingled as he clumsily retrieved his weapon. Was a trap about to be sprung? He turned and looked quickly all about him but discovered that no one was close by. Moments passed but the street and its limited number of occupants remained quite calm and ordinary.

Embarrassed by the odd glances his actions summoned, he carefully returned the pistol back to his coat pocket. His nerves were getting to him. This time he did stop and lit up a cigarette. He inhaled deeply, and after a moment, continued onward. Next he'd be jumping at his own shadow. People whistled for all sorts of reasons, he reminded himself: calling one's dog, attracting the attention of a friend, or to issue simple non-verbal orders. This final thought was just entering his mind when he rounded a corner and came to a dead halt.

He'd successfully located the squat, disreputable tavern he sought, but the taller, apparently abandoned building next to it belched thick clouds of roiling smoke from the cracked second story windows. His eyes began to search frantically for help.

"Fire … fire, FIRE! FIRE!" he began to yell.

The buildings were very close together. If it spread, it might quickly set the entire block ablaze. His cries were being joined by others now as more and more of the locals began to arrive each time he yelled. Some men began to form lines to pass water buckets along. That this particular street backed up directly to the lake was fortuitous. Some families decided it best to flee the area until it was safe. The once nearly-empty street was rapidly flooding with people as everyone sprung into action at once.

"Have you seen any flames?" a harried voice asked over the growing din.

Christiansen did not hear the reply as bells began to ring, alerting the whole district to the danger. It was once the deafening chaos of noise and fear firmly established its hold on the masses that it happened.

The crowd shifted, and Christiansen was forced to step back towards a narrow alleyway. The hand that grabbed him and pulled him into the dark recess was quickly joined by a companion that covered his mouth. In his surprise, Christiansen dropped his cane. His arm was pinned so tightly behind him that any motion to free himself would only cause it to be broken. He was being rapidly hauled backward, down the dim expanse. The man who held him was strong, and the force he applied to the arm made it clear that breaking it would not be a problem. He was relieved of his pistol and suddenly a heavy bag was thrust over his head. He was being picked up, spun. His feet kicked uselessly at open air for a moment, then clattered against wood. The rest of his body followed and the sinking, rocking motion beneath him left no doubt that he'd been thrown aboard a boat. He kept trying to yell, but the bag's material was so thick, he doubted if anyone could actually hear him. His cries were most likely being drowned out by the chaos created by the fire. Still the bag was pulled tighter around his head. Apparently his captors weren't willing to chance him being heard.

Muffled voices whispered urgently to one another as his hands and feet were bound. At points, the bag loosened as more urgent matters prevented one of them from holding it completely closed. But as soon as Christiansen began to yell, the pressure returned and silenced him. The boat shook violently a moment, and then they were moving. Merciful heavens above! Did they intend to drown him?

He began to struggle against his bonds. That is until he felt the blade at his throat. It remained there until he calmed then it vanished. Christiansen remained stock still, even as the craft that carried him shifted with the winds. One thought silenced his terror. Escape appeared impossible. Still he must be certain to create an opportunity to make a final plea for the safety of his family.

The bag was itching him badly by the time it was finally removed. How long had he been in it? He blinked as the fresh, night air whisked into his eyes. No, it wasn't just the air he realized. They were moving through a great fog bank. He could hear distant sounds from the shore, mostly animals calling into the night, and could see the occasional lamp through the veil of mist, but the vessel he sailed upon was kept dark.

"Please, you must not harm …," he began but stopped, startled, as another's hand suddenly touched his.

"SSShhhh. Your voice is carrying Christiansen," a woman's hushed voice admonished.

Several heartbeats passed.

"Abrielle?"

"Yes."

His tone betrayed both annoyance and relief.

"Good Lord, I should have known."

It was too dark to be certain, but he could imagine her smiling at his reaction. On second thought, had he ever seen her smile? Once, perhaps.

"What's the meaning of all this nonsense? Untie me."

"Not yet," she answered calmly.

"What? What do you mean 'not yet?'" Christiansen stammered.

A burst of unexpected light blinded him. He blinked frantically to clear his vision. She held the lit match between them, then lowered it practically into her lap, walls of fog shimmered all about them. The dancing shadows echoed across her stern face. A series of fading bruises adorned it. She was not smiling.

"Your voice is carrying well across the water to the shore, and I just went through an awful lot of trouble to cover your disappearance from our enemies. I know you're not a foolish man, so please stop acting like one."

Abrielle allowed the light to die, but her eyes never wavered from his. Christiansen cleared his throat.

"Sorry," he whispered.

"Better," she praised flatly.

They paused and attempted to start their conversation over.

"Abrielle, while I am grateful to see you, did you have to endanger an entire neighborhood just to speak to me?"

"What do you mean?"

"I mean, I assume you are responsible for the fire."

She laughed lightly.

"There wasn't any fire."

"Yes, there was. I …"

She touched him again and his voice dropped back to whisper.

"What, I suppose you just didn't see the smoke?" he asked sarcastically.

"Of course I saw it. I made it. But there was never any fire."

For a moment he silently stared into the mist beyond the bow.

"A trick," he nodded to himself.

"A simple diversion, a knowledge of basic chemistry has its uses," she admitted. "Wouldn't you say?" This time he knew she was smiling. Too bad he couldn't actually see it.

"Have you heard from Ernest?" he asked.

At this the figure next to him looked down at her hands, one deliberately began tracing the palm of the other. He definitely heard a sigh.

"I was hoping you had," she admitted, the regret in her voice plain.

"I'm sorry."

There was nothing more to say.

Christiansen's curiosity got the better of him.

"Are you all right? Your face …?"

Abrielle straightened back up and cleared her own throat.

"There were … complications in France."

Christiansen waited patiently.

"Such as?" he prompted.

"The details will have to wait, but let's just say it's prudent for me to keep a low profile," she distractedly responded.

He needed more than that.

"I thought that's what spies normally do," he stated.

"Former ones, too," she said mirthlessly.

He could suddenly feel the mist as it clung to the inside of his open mouth.

"Imperial Intelligence forced you out?" he asked with unguarded surprise.

"Imperial Intelligence would seem to want me dead, but as I've said, the details will have to wait. Have you heard from Jack?"

Christiansen squirmed uncomfortably in his seat. This was a subject he'd hoped to avoid a while longer.

"I *heard* from Jack, yes."

The nuance of his statement was not lost on Abrielle. Even in the dark he could tell she was scowling.

"Heard? Is he all right?"

"I don't know," Christiansen admitted. "His initial letter sounded promising, but his second requested that none of us contact him."

"When was that?"

"Well, I burned both immediately, you understand, but I'd say almost a month ago. Never received anything like that second one from him before. Can't imagine what it means."

"What did the first one say?" Abrielle asked anxiously.

Christiansen pursed his lips in concentration. Though the letters were short, he wanted to be certain he didn't forget any minute clues.

"Essentially that he'd tracked your gypsies and said he'd report further details later."

"Are you certain the second letter was his?" Abrielle pressed.

Christiansen squared his shoulders.

"My dear, I've known that boy since he first learned to walk. Believe me, inexplicable as it may be, the second letter was in his hand."

They grew silent again. The boat rocked gently as it rode upon the dark waters.

"Tara?" she whispered hopefully.

"I'm sorry, no, he didn't say anything about her," Christiansen sighed. She clasped her head. He allowed her a moment before continuing. He was eager to hear her appraisal of the situation.

"What do you make of the matter?"

Abrielle's mind was rapidly progressing through the possible reasons for such a communiqué. Could Jack have been coerced, his family threatened, acted impetuously, become ill, leaving false information, discovered Tara was dead and didn't want to share that knowledge. Was he a prisoner? Whatever the reason, it did sound quite the opposite tone from his earlier sentiments and would seem to indicate that Jack was in over his head.

"Where does he live?"

Christiansen hesitated a moment before answering. He had a bad feeling.

"Salzburg."

"Well, we have to head that direction anyway, so we'll just pay Jack a visit."

The older man shook his head. Abrielle's was studying the hazy outline of the shore.

"I suppose we're leaving now, right?"

"Yes. No, not exactly. What time is it?" she asked in a distracted manner.

"A bit hard for me to answer that at the moment seeing as how I'm being kidnapped."

Christiansen held his bound arms up hoping she'd be able to see them. Without preamble, she began to search his pockets, and then relieved him of his watch.

"You're welcome," he muttered as she got down close to the deck and struck another match over the timepiece which she quickly extinguished.

"Good. We're early," she commented as she shoved the watch unceremoniously back into Christiansen's pocket.

"I doubt you'd care to enlighten me as to what exactly we are early for, so allow me merely to ask if you plan to untie me sometime tonight?" he inquired with fain patience.

The blade she wielded moved so expertly and rapidly across his bonds that they were already upon the deck before he realized what had happened. He blew a breath of relief that she hadn't accidentally sliced him to ribbons in the darkness.

"We're waiting for a friend," she explained as she scanned the shore through the mists. Abrielle was glad he couldn't see her face. She still couldn't decide the best way to address the subject of Espen to him. Maybe she didn't want to.

"Another spy?" Christiansen asked suspiciously as he rubbed his wrists.

"Let's just call this field training," she answered wryly after a long pause.

They waited silently as they floated in the damp night air. How many minutes had it been since she checked the time? Christiansen's frustrations grew.

"Could you at least tell me what we're looking for?"

"Home," she replied cryptically. Inwardly, he rolled his eyes.

In the absence of any additional information, Christiansen decided to simply study the shore and see if it revealed any clues as to their whereabouts. Unfortunately the fog made this task quite difficult. For a long time, it grew deadly quiet between them.

"Do you think he's still alive?" Abrielle asked into the shrouded void, her back fully turned to Christiansen. The question did not startle him, but the manner in which it was posed did. There was such an open sense of bare need in her voice.

"Have you reason to believe otherwise?"

He knew they both did.

"I asked you," she said quietly as her head turned towards his. "Do you believe?"

She needed an answer, not a discussion. He could feel her eyes upon him, but each of their faces was invisible to the other in the gloom of night. He searched his heart.

"I refuse to believe that my godson is dead to us," Christiansen answered directly and, he hoped, reassuringly.

The silhouette of her head slowly turned away from him as her gaze returned to the shore and hung there wordlessly for a minute or so until something captured her attention.

"There he is," she said, perking up a measure.

"He?"

For a moment Christiansen was too confused to comprehend that it was not Ernest to whom she referred, but rather to a spot of light, a lantern, which rose and fell at regular intervals from the shore. The signal must be her 'friend.' Abrielle fumbled with the matches and lit a small lamp of her own, then rose awkwardly and repeated the motion back to the sender several times. Then both lights were doused, but not before Christiansen noticed that Abrielle's cheeks were wet with silent tears she'd tried to conceal from him. Where they for Ernest or relief that they'd found her compatriot? He decided they were for Ernest.

Christiansen could feel his own heart soften towards her. It seemed that this woman had lost much already. What would become of her if she did lose Ernest or Tara? Suddenly Christiansen felt oddly protective of her. He reached out and wordlessly placed a reassuring hand on her shoulder. It lingered there a moment before she patted it and nodded. They stood and together began to draw the sails up the mast. Thin winds caught them and slowly began to return them to land.

"Do you plan that the winds or the roads should carry us to Salzburg?"

"A little of both, actually," she commented as she trimmed the sails.

"Whose boat is this anyway?" Christiansen wondered aloud, only to receive a mild shrug in reply. If his mutterings of disapproval about her means of obtaining the boat were any indication, it would seem to be best that she not mention who exactly awaited them onshore. Better that he make the discovery for himself.

The fog bank began to grow thick again, and both parties were compelled to reignite their lanterns for a time. Abrielle's tension level rose. She was still worried about striking rocks near the shore, but equally worried that the more they used the lanterns, the greater the possibility that someone would take an active interest and investigate. Christiansen's curiosity also deepened as they drew near the shore. Who waited for them? He couldn't begin to imagine the type of company a woman like Abrielle kept. The lantern upon the land began to appear intermittently, as a beacon. Now it was Abrielle's turn to mutter in disapproval. Christiansen also noted that something about the shore began to seem familiar. He peered into the shifting mists.

"Good God. Why have you brought us here?" he exclaimed as recognition dawned. Abrielle said nothing as she concentrated on slowing their momentum. The old dock was tantalizingly close. As it turned out, too close. But aside from one loud bang as the bow met the boards of the landing, they were able to secure the boat without incident. Both of the mariners breathed a sigh of relief.

After tying up the boat and taking down the sails, they preceded past a decaying boathouse and several storage buildings. Christiansen's apprehensions mounted with each step. This was crazy. Where was Abrielle's mysterious friend? Why risk coming here, a place they both knew had been watched by the enemy before? It seemed a foolish chance, for no profit he could possibly fathom, for this was a place best left to ghosts.

As they approached a great oak, a short, oddly familiar whistle was issued, and an instant later, another dark silhouette joined them. Abrielle held a hasty conference with the phantom, in of all languages, English. She then vanished towards the foreboding, long-silent house, abandoning the strangers to the whims of the night.

At first the two sat awkwardly in the dark together, hoping Abrielle's mysterious errand would not take too long. But as the minutes echoed and died, it became clear they should not expect her immediate return. The large shadow stirred and pretended to study the gloom. There was nothing to see. The combination of night's broad cloak and the fog prevented that. Christiansen studied the nearby presence. Eventually the other sensed his interest, knelt, and began to fiddle with the lantern.

"Why did she cry?"

It took Christiansen a moment to translate the words into French. English always seemed easier when he heard it than when he spoke it.

"How did you know that?" Christiansen asked in surprise.

"English, please," the other emphatically requested.

"I don't speak it well."

There was no reply. Now what was all this about? Even Christiansen could tell that English was not this man's native tongue. Why was he so insistent that it be used? He shrugged off his annoyance and concentrated on translating his words into the cumbersome language.

"I don't speak it well," he repeated slowly, this time in English.

"Not well," the voice agreed, with a hint of amusement. "But well enough. I did not harm you earlier?"

Had Christiansen heard him correctly—harm him? Then he realized what the question meant.

"I'm fine but I'd prefer that you not drag me down anymore alleys or toss me into anymore boats," he said gruffly. The shadow raised hands in a manner that suggested that these acts weren't his idea. They paused a moment before continuing.

"How did you know she'd been crying?" It was certainly too dark for the man to have seen her cheeks.

"The sadness in her voice," he explained. "I've come to know it. You could not hear it?"

Christiansen took note of this. So they were familiar with one another's company. He wished he knew if this were a good or bad thing.

"I see," he replied noncommittally. "Do you know why we've come to this house?"

The silhouette shook its head.

"I was hoping you could tell me."

After a moment, they shared in a moment of muted, knowing laughter. They both understood the woman they were with. It felt reassuring to know that a measure of equality, even if it was mutual ignorance of their purpose here, stood between them. A large hand suddenly swam awkwardly out of the darkness before him.

"Espen Nalie," the voice said.

Christiansen took it, and they began to shake. As he did so, an odd feeling began to settle over him. The name seemed familiar to him. Something wasn't right. But Espen was full of questions so Christiansen was left to wrestle with his worries as the other continued their conversation.

"Christiansen, I am most eager to learn, have you heard anything from them?"

He opened his mouth to answer but closed it as he realized he was too puzzled to respond. What were the words in English?

"To whom are you referring?"

"From Frankenstein or my sister," the other said.

A new and terrible certainty flooded over Christiansen. His sister. Nalie! The older man reacted as if an electrical charge suddenly surged through him. Their hands parted instantly. Why would Abrielle bring him here? What should he do? Christiansen made a noise as if to answer the question, though, in truth, he had no idea what to say.

From the darkness came rushing footsteps and the hushed whisper of a hem across the grass; Abrielle appeared from the fog, pausing only an instant.

"Let's go."

"Trouble?" Espen asked as he scooped up his lantern, following fast on her heels.

"Not yet," she commented over her shoulder as she kept moving.

Christiansen sprinted to catch up to her.

"I've got to talk to you," he labored to say in French. When was the last time he'd had to run like this?

"Not now, on the boat," she answered dismissively.

"No, now," he insisted. She ignored him. "Do you know who he is?"

"On the boat," she repeated tersely.

He wanted to argue with her. He wanted to tell her that her stubbornness was about to get them killed, but instead, the young woman easily outpaced him; he wheezed hoarsely as he continued to pursue her.

By the time he reached the boat, Espen was already cutting the lines, and she was working on the sails, motioning for him to get aboard. Christiansen threw one backward glance in the direction of the Frankenstein estate then boarded the craft a moment before Espen pushed it away from the dock and climbed on. No one spoke again until the first rays of light began to appear in the sky.

Christiansen ran his fingers over his temples and across his balding head. He was exhausted and felt trapped. When was the last time he'd eaten? His wife would kill him when she found out what insanity he'd gotten himself involved in this time.

"Something still on your mind, monsieur?" Abrielle inquired.

He snorted in derision, then his eyes involuntarily moved to the gypsy seated nearby who looked to be fast asleep. Christiansen motioned towards him, mouthing a desperate warning to Abrielle. This was Baseria's brother, Jal's son, the man who'd taken her niece. She nodded serenely and even a fleeting smile graced her features. He couldn't bear it any longer.

"Are you completely insane?!" Christiansen's voice echoed across the empty waters.

Espen jolted awake. Christiansen didn't notice, but Abrielle did. It was time. Inwardly, she tried to brace herself for what must happen. She hated using Christiansen in this way, but she must discover the truth about Espen. And she was too emotionally involved to trust her own judgment.

"You believe me to be infirm in my faculties?" she asked evenly, intent on angering the older man. He scowled.

"If he's here, then yes. After what his father did to you and Ernest and you call him a friend? Where did you even find him?"

"France," a new voice joined the conversation. "We met in France."

Christiansen looked dumbfounded and horrified as he stared over at the gypsy who'd spoken in their native tongue.

"He can understand us?" Christiansen remarked in surprise.

"Of course," Abrielle calmly stated. "Espen's clan simply refuses to speak French for it is the language their enemies have adopted. I did tell you to keep your voice down."

Christiansen's temper flared as he stood and gripped the mast. He was tired of these games.

"Was he a part of it?"

Espen stood and glared back at Christiansen, though he was uncertain as to why the other man suddenly grew so passionate.

"Does he share in his father's crime, Abrielle?"

Christiansen turned, annoyed she was not pressing the gypsy for answers as well. Her face instantly revealed why. Her impassive mask had shattered. She was seconds from falling to pieces, emotionally. Her eyes pleaded for understanding. With one last angry look at Espen, Christiansen abandoned the confrontation and turned his attentions to consoling Abrielle. She didn't want to hear Espen's answer. If he'd had a hand in taking Tara …

Espen's face bore only empathy and confusion for her sorrows and resentment for Christiansen's accusations.

"What about my father?" he demanded.

"You know perfectly well what he did!" Christiansen thundered. Abrielle clasped him harder.

"I've not seen my father in months," Espen began to counter.

"And thanks to him, we have not seen her niece in months!"

Espen tore his eyes from Christiansen. He tried to kneel down and touch Abrielle. She would not face him.

"Please … please, Abrielle, I don't understand. What's happened?"

Christiansen batted his hand away.

"Your father steals an infant, tries to murder my godson, and you dare to claim ignorance," Christiansen incredulously began.

"My father would never do such things!"

Espen stood ready to strike the old man, only Abrielle's proximity prevented it. He would not endure such slanders. Christiansen reached behind Abrielle and retrieved an object, brandishing it like a weapon. Espen stared at the familiar sight with new eyes.

"Where is she?! Dead? Sold for profit to some ..."

Espen punched Christiansen squarely in the jaw. Tara's blanket dropped from his hand to the deck.

"He wouldn't do that!" he screamed as the older man worked to recover his senses.

Abrielle let go of Christiansen, but he waved off her attempts to check on him. Then with trembling hands, she reached down and retrieved the blanket. As Espen watched her tender motions towards the object, his own heart crumbled. It wanted to rebel against the thoughts in his mind, ones that weighed Christiansen's words, and his own knowledge and feelings about the woman before him. He said nothing but looked into her pain-filled eyes. His own closed in shame as the impossible became truth.

*

Abrielle jumped as the hand that gripped her was removed.

"We're here," Christiansen's tired voice declared.

It took her a moment to regain her bearings as she nodded and attempted to rub the sleep from her eyes.

"What time is it?" she asked as she stretched.

She heard him withdraw his pocket watch and snap the case shut.

"About eleven in the morning," Christiansen announced.

That was a good time, early enough to ensure that those they sought should still be at home, but not so early that their visit should be viewed as an intrusion. She cleared her throat and looked around the cramped compartment of the coach.

"Where is my hat?" she asked, sleep still thick in her voice.

With a look of strained patience, Christiansen reached under her seat and handed it to her.

"You were smashing it again."

It did appear now to be somewhat asymmetrical. Still she did her best to try and make sure that it fit properly. He probably thought it served her right. After locating them, she began to put her gloves on. Christiansen's fingers drummed absentmindedly against the seat. Maybe it was the sudden absence of hoof beats that made his mind feel the need to recreate them after so many days spent in their presence.

"Now, what is our story again?" he sighed.

She finished snuggling the second glove securely over her fingers.

"You're you. I'm me. Espen's our driver. I'll fill in the rest."

Abrielle scooted across her bench, opened the door, and inhaled deeply. The unpolluted air was a welcome change, at least to her.

"I don't suppose you could splurge and get me some proper cigarette tobacco here, could you?" Christiansen intoned as she stepped down from the coach.

She reached back in and patted his hand.

"If Jack doesn't have any, I'll buy you four pouches of tobacco."

She turned to talk to Espen who was just clambering down from the driver's seat.

"And what about my eye? What's our cover story for that?" Christiansen sourly shouted as she began to walk away.

She considered this minor problem for only an instant before replying.

"Jack will love it."

Espen was petting one of the horses' long noses, clearly unwilling to get too close to the passenger's compartment still. He and Christiansen had done their best to avoid one another's presence these past few days. Purchasing the coach and horses made doing so easier, but now that they'd arrived in Salzburg, it was time to begin mending their rift. She would need all of them.

"He's not complaining about my driving again, is he?" Espen asked in English.

"No," she smiled reassuringly. "I still think you look nice in those."

He blushed as she brushed dirt off his black driver's uniform.

"I look foolish. How do people wear such things?"

He began to pat his own clothing as she readjusted her gloves. She could sympathize with his plight. The lace felt odd against her fingers. Hopefully in another day or so she wouldn't have to wear them anymore. But for now she must look as respectable as possible. The Clervals would be instantly suspicious of her connections to Christiansen otherwise. And she needed time to properly assess the situation without additional interference from Salzburg's socialites. The last thing she needed was to inadvertently destroy Christiansen's reputation for integrity. Therefore, she was to pose as a niece he rarely saw, but one who he'd often mentioned to the Clervals in the past.

The new clothing, coach, and team of horses were still a sore subject for Christiansen. He did not object to their usefulness, rather, it was the source of the funds used to obtain them. Before they left Ireland, Ernest had entrusted her with a family secret, one he'd instructed her to use as she saw fit, though it was also obvious that he'd intended this option primarily for dire contingencies. They'd arrived in Geneva, three days before obtaining Christiansen, with only a few coins but left for Salzburg bearing a hefty amount of currency, which she'd retrieved from the old, very well-hidden Frankenstein family safe. Though he knew that Abrielle acted as Ernest's emissary, he still was having a difficult time rationalizing what he viewed as theft.

Most likely, Christiansen planned to reimburse the money she spent to Ernest quietly at some later date. But for the moment, circumstances were forcing him to live off the Frankenstein fortune as well. Given the district of Geneva he'd been asked to meet Abrielle in, he'd taken the precaution of carrying very little cash. However, it irked him that by making the correct decision at the time, it now forced him into sanctioning Abrielle's actions. Still, doing so was better than going hungry.

"Remember just let the clothes speak for you," Abrielle advised Espen as she turned to talk to Christiansen, but he was nowhere to be found. The gypsy tapped her shoulder and pointed to the Clerval's front door where a servant was just leaving Christiansen to wait. Abrielle suppressed a grimace and joined him.

"You were supposed to wait for me," she whispered as they stood patiently before the now-closed door. Did she hear someone shouting inside?

"You were behaving out of character," Christiansen admonished in return. "I had to do something to cover it, so I presented my card and may have mentioned offhandedly that my niece has a particular obsession for tidiness."

She blushed. Abrielle didn't bother to deny it. Christiansen was right, of course. It was a foolish oversight. Normally, a lady would not be talking to a driver and certainly wouldn't have been getting her gloves soiled patting dust from the driver's uniform. She never made such obvious mistakes. Then again, her past missions were almost always professional, not personal, with the exception of Paul. She cleared her throat as she regained her composure, summoning her professional experience. She would simply turn the moment of weakness into a strength. It was good for characters to have some limited, unique qualities. It made them more believable, as long as the chosen trait did not attract unwanted scrutiny. She would do better.

The door opened, and the dour-faced servant returned Christiansen's card.

"I am very sorry, but the lady says she will not see you."

The passive face of the servant was unreadable, however, his body language was not. He was eager for them to leave. Christiansen looked to Abrielle.

"But we have traveled so far, Uncle," she observed in French. "And I was so hoping to meet your friends."

Christiansen recovered.

"Indeed, yes. Everyone here is well, I trust?" he asked casually.

The servant's eyes surveyed both of them a moment before he responded.

"Yes, everyone here is well."

"I see. Well, if the lady does not wish to visit, perhaps her husband, Jack, would care to."

A look of uncertainty flashed across the servant's face.

"If you please, sir, the gentleman is …"

Suddenly an object exploded on the ground next to Abrielle, followed quickly by another, then another. She pressed herself against the wall.

"He is no gentleman!!! I told you, be gone!" a livid voice ordered.

They all looked up, but only for a moment, as the crazed woman leaning out the window above began to hurtle another round of sharp, breakable objects towards a protesting Christiansen.

"Madame, please!"

As he tried to protect himself from the onslaught, he inadvertently knocked Abrielle's tormented hat from her head. The attack stopped for a moment. Abrielle looked up into eyes suddenly filled with the white hot rage of jealousy.

"Run!" she yelled to Christiansen seconds before a new round of both objects and insults were hurtled in their direction as they fled.

"Harlot! Swine! No talent wretch!"

The woman was openly wailing as she failed to cleanly hit Abrielle. Christiansen began to help a dazed Abrielle back into the coach. Espen, however, fled towards the door, held a brief conference with the servant, and then returned to the coach dodging a hail of fire from above. A potted plant narrowly missed striking a fatal blow to his cranium, yet, he was grinning as he ascended to the driver's seat. As they pulled away they caught a glimpse of the woman trying to force her way past her servant. All sighed in relief when they turned the first corner.

"Was that …?" Abrielle gasped.

Christiansen nodded.

"Jack's wife," he confirmed.

Espen stopped the carriage a few blocks later on a secluded street.

"I'm beginning to wish we'd heeded Jack's advice," Christiansen commented as Espen opened the door.

"Turn around," Abrielle ordered as she began swiping potting soil off the back of Espen's clothing.

"Are you insane? What possessed you to do that?" she demanded when she'd finished.

"39 Gnigler Strasse," Espen answered by way of explanation.

"Gnigler Strasse?" a bewildered Christiansen chimed in.

"Is where your Jack friend is," Espen beamed as he turned around to face them.

They stared blankly back in return.

"The doorman just told you?" Abrielle asked incredulously. The fellow didn't seem like the giving type. Espen rubbed his fingers together and pointed to the pillow were Abrielle kept their stash of money.

"Well, let's go then," Christiansen prompted, slapping the younger man on the shoulder in approval. Espen moved to obey then halted.

"Which way?"

Christiansen dug into his pocket, hastily wrote down the street's name, and then advised Espen to find a shop where they could purchase a map or inquire about directions. Abrielle tried to inconspicuously check their funds. She sighed as the coach began to move again.

"What's wrong?" Christiansen asked.

She shook her head.

"That servant just tripled his salary for the year."

*

"Stop knockin' already," Jack Clerval roared as he flung the door to his apartments open. He reeked of alcohol and tobacco. His clothes were so wrinkled and disheveled it was hard to guess the last time he might have worn anything else. He squinted against the light.

"Jesus, Christiansen. Can't a man rest in peace? You have any idea what time it is?"

"It's a bit past noon, Jack."

"Exactly my point, far too early for some of us," Jack explained as he rubbed a stubby-fingered hand over his scruffy face. "Besides, I told you not to come."

"That's actually why we're here. We were concerned about you," the older man explained.

Jack smiled roguishly as he tried to loosen his neck muscles.

"We?"

Christiansen stepped aside a measure and revealed the others who'd been hidden from Jack's view.

"Aw," Jack staggered away from the door, leaving it open for the others to follow. He was already pouring a drink by the time they were all inside the rather dark, noxious bode.

"Anyone else want one?" he asked without turning around. No one spoke up, so he downed the contents of his in one gulp, then collapsed into a chair by the fireplace and began to work on lighting a cigar. After he finally managed to get it lit, he drew on it for a moment as he studied the others' expressions, and then leaned his head into his hand.

"I really hope you brought her along to kill me," he moaned in self-pity.

"That depends," Abrielle interjected, displeased by the insult.

Jack smiled weakly from behind his hand.

"Deadly and beautiful, that's my type."

"We noticed," Espen commented dryly.

Jack raised his head from his hand and glared at the young gypsy.

"Who's this jerk?" he asked of the room's other occupants.

"Jack, what happened?" Christiansen demanded, tired of the posturing.

"No, seriously, who are you?"

"Jack! Where's Tara?" Abrielle snapped loudly.

Jack winced and momentarily held his head again, blinking his eyes against the pain of his hangover.

"I was getting to that," he promised through gritted teeth. "Hungary. Romania. Back, forth. Who knows by now?"

He turned to Christiansen.

"What happened is that I did my part with tracking your crazy, no good, dirty gypsies, and I did it so well that Stanza left me."

He launched the cigar into the fireplace, showering the bricks in sparks.

"Curse the lot of those thievin', lyin', double-crossin' gypsies. Lousy, useless heathens," he ranted.

Abrielle moved to intercept Espen before he even had a chance to stand fully, but he was almost as fast as she was. He was shrieking Hungarian curses back at Jack as he fought against her restraining grasp. Amused, Jack stood and continued to try and exacerbate the situation until Abrielle took him up on one of his suggestions and released Espen.

"Aw, let him go. Talk or fight ya …," Espen clubbed Jack's jaw before he could finish. Abrielle grabbed him by the ear, while Christiansen forced a swaying Jack back into his chair.

"Outside," she commanded the vehemently protesting Espen, who she practically had to push out the door as Jack began to taunt him anew.

"Wait at the coach," she clarified before slamming the door shut and locking it. He pounded on the door for another minute before departing.

"I told you this was a bad idea," Christiansen reminded her as she crossed the room.

"Don't start," she shook her head.

"Sensitive, isn't he?" Jack said sarcastically a moment before Abrielle stalked up to his chair and drove her knee into his crotch. Air hissed out of his lungs. Christiansen winced. She grabbed Jack's rumpled shirt.

"We're all sensitive about certain things. Now sober up and tell me where my niece is," she backed away.

It took him a moment before he could speak.

"Well, now that's the point, isn't it? Had to leave to find them, right? That took time, damn good at hiding those people. So I find them in Romania, send word to Christiansen. You're missing. I wait like I'm told but start to worry about the time that's passing, so I leave again. They've moved. Have to track 'em again, but they've gone back into Hungary this time. Worried I might have been observed but also concerned 'bout them leavin' if that's the case. I go out a third time. Stanza's getting suspicious. Where are you going? Why won't you talk to me? Well, I couldn't tell her the truth. She wouldn't let me go if she knew the truth, so I had to start lying to her, see. Gypsies vanished again, my wife's furious, and you're nowhere to be found, Ern's little girl's in danger, and I'm … I'm blasted useless."

Jack's head fell into his hands. Christiansen and Abrielle exchanged mutual looks of reproach. Christiansen tried to cover for his distraught friend.

"So you sent the second letter because you were worried you'd been spotted."

"No," Jack sniffled, "I sent it because I didn't want you to see me like this."

He blew loudly into a tattered handkerchief.

"I mean this isn't my proudest moment here."

Given Jack's colorful life, this was indeed a significant statement.

"I thought Ernest said they broke up before," Abrielle noted to Christiansen.

"Oh, it's different this time," Jack spouted. "She isn't even trying to have an affair. Nothing. Just over, done."

"Okay, I'm lost. Isn't it good that she isn't having an affair?" Abrielle's head hurt.

"Not if she believes I am and she doesn't bother to try to start one herself," Jack began to stuff the handkerchief back into his pocket, but got frustrated and tossed it into the fire.

"And other than precedent, why would she think that you're involved in one now?" Christiansen asked.

The faintest trace of guilt flashed across Jack's face as he looked momentarily at Abrielle as he ignited a new cigar. He readjusted his wrinkled clothing and sat up a little straighter before declaring, "I may have let Abrielle's name slip…once or twice."

"You what?!"

The question broke from the others simultaneously.

"Ah, not so loud, please. It was in my diary. Stanza must have been snoopin' around and seen it."

"Oh, Jack," Abrielle scowled and looked away.

"What did you say in the entry?" Christiansen prodded.

"Nothing detailed. just the date, the compass readin' for where the gypsies were, and a reminder to write Abrielle. Oh, and a question mark by the word France."

"And that made your wife think that you're having an affair?" Abrielle asked.

"Stanza's the jealous type," Jack grinned.

"With your mutual track records I wonder why?" Christiansen quipped.

Jack shushed him and continued.

"We've been going through another rough patch as of late, and you're right. She's got reasons not to trust my unexplained absences. But her accusations this time got me a little hot, especially since that wasn't what I was doin'… but I still couldn't tell her the truth either. So I just let her fill in the gaps," he expelled a foul cloud of smoke into the room.

"That you're having an affair with a French woman named Abrielle?"

Her patience with this man was wearing thin.

"A French opera singer named Abrielle," Jack corrected, raising his cigar for emphasis.

"I don't believe this," Abrielle muttered in disgust as she turned to face Christiansen.

"It would seem to explain our warm reception earlier if she thought you were the other woman," he observed.

"I am the other woman, remember."

"You saw Stanza? How is she?" Jack asked sweetly.

"Unhinged," Abrielle replied immediately.

Jack swung his hopeful face to Christiansen.

"Let's just say if we all survive this madness that I won't be sending you anymore breakable items as gifts, Jack," Christiansen announced diplomatically.

"What?"

"Never mind," Christiansen waved dismissively.

"I'm not sure where this leaves us," Abrielle admitted.

Christiansen was silent as he considered the matter. Abrielle's eyes grew distant. Jack cleared his throat.

"I have an idea. A plan, really."

"I don't think we need anymore of your plans, Jack. They seem to cause more problems than they solve," Christiansen paused as Abrielle gently laid a hand on his arm as she sat on the edge of the seat opposite Ernest's friend.

"Jack, how do you know for certain that you found the Wild Rose clan?" She asked softly. He gazed back into her brown eyes.

"I just followed what you said. Look, I really need you to help me with this plan."

She nodded and stood.

"Where are you going?" Christiansen asked in confusion as she began towards the door.

"We have to be sure. I'm going to get Espen. Jack, you can tell us your plan when I come back; just don't make anymore crude remarks about gypsies."

"Who's this Espen anyway?"

Christiansen sighed.

"Would you believe a Wild Rose clan gypsy?"

The smoldering cigar almost fell out of Jack's mouth. Christiansen decided it was best not to mention his exact relationship to the clan as Jack choked on his own smoke before dashing yet another cigar into the fireplace.

"I need a drink."

CHAPTER 18
BROTHERHOOD OF THE NECROMANCER

Tasaria looked frantically about the room but failed to locate the presence she expected to be there. How could she be there? Still the memory was fresh. Her nerves still tingled with the sensation left where the spectral hand had pressed against her chest, and the words echoed in her mind. It would be impossible for her to go back to sleep now. She rose and gathered her garments about her, illuminating candles to dispel the darkness as she moved. The room was frigid. Hopefully the water in the basin wasn't frozen completely.

It nearly was. She chipped at it, shook it until something useful spilled into her mug, which she took with her back to the bed. At least the residual heat from it was better than nothing. She huddled under the blankets.

As she loudly crunched the ice, the rough edges of which bit into her cheeks and tongue, Tasaria's thoughts turned to her husband and home. What was happening there? Was he safe? When she meditated on him, the energies of the unseen world revealed nothing to her. More than anything right now, she wished he was here for her to talk to. Perhaps he'd already fulfilled the Master's mission with regards to the infant and was spiriting her here this very minute. The thought of seeing his face again momentarily cheered her, then she remembered the spy who had escaped with Espen and her thoughts again darkened. She hated this place. How on earth did the other Moon Shadows who lived here, in some cases years now, tolerate such an abysmal existence, cut off from the rest of the world?

'They will betray you, my child.'

Tasaria tried to banish the thought from her mind, but it was insidious. Was this thought her own or her mother's? She rose to get more ice and momentarily caught a glimpse of her reflection in the nearby mirror. Her eyes fixated on the image suspended before her: the ever increasing wrinkles in the face, the silver highlights streaking through the once coal-black hair, the world-weary look in the eyes. She had always resembled her mother, but as she aged, the similarities became more striking.

She need fear no phantom for her mother already stood before her in earthly form. Tasaria completed her task then returned once more to the security of the bed.

Perhaps it was the troubling nature of this place that relentlessly worked on her imagination—the isolation, the unexplained noises she sometimes heard. Or maybe it was the fact she was compelled to work with the man who was directly responsible for Nasi's death. Hadn't Pias already betrayed them all by killing her? She crunched down on the ice so hard, she felt certain she'd chipped a tooth.

But despite this, he was still here. Nicabar tolerated him, and though it was obvious that he didn't trust him either. The Master and Pias spent hours together now talking in private and touring the fortress. Why did they keep her from such discussions?

'They will betray you, my child,' the voice from her dream whispered again.

What was going on here? Few of the Moon Shadows she attempted to engage in conversation would speak with her at length, and she was shadowed nearly everywhere by one of the Old Ones. Had she done something wrong? Did they deem her untrustworthy for some reason? Her hand began to trace her breastbone. This was the place her mother used to rest her hand when she sang her to sleep as a child. Tasaria had always found the combination of weight and warmth in that spot comforting. And this was where the ghost in her dream had touched her before issuing her warning. Was she still dreaming when the visitation occurred? Nothing made sense.

She set down the mug. Something was changing. The forces of the unseen world were dimmer as of late. Each time she engaged them, they seemed more remote. It was not the first time such a thing had occurred, but it disturbed her that they seemed to be abandoning her now at a time she already felt isolated, her faith shaken.

It also added to her mounting uncertainty about what to do with her niece. Could there be any validity to Pias' contention that Baseria, and perhaps this Etolie, now wielded the power of the Seer? Damn Pias. The thought still revolted her, but he was right, this was an issue she could no longer afford to ignore.

She could see no other reasonable explanation for the incident in the reading room. And what of the youngest Wild Rose girl's confession that

Etolie was the Seer? Could she be responsible for Tasaria's obstruction to the powers? Or was Baseria to blame? The only certainty in her mind about the event in the reading room was that it did not revolve around mere coincidence. But had the attack come from Baseria, this Etolie girl, or a supernatural force?

There was a crisp knock at the door. Tasaria gathered her wits, climbed from the bed, and bid the visitor to enter. It was the Master. She bowed reverently in his presence.

"Rise, Tasaria. We must move quickly, and I can only entrust you with this task."

She hesitated only a moment before responding.

"I am ready to serve your will as always, Master," she asserted.

He waved a hand over his shoulder and stalked into the room. He was immediately followed by three Old Ones who bore an obscure figure wrapped in a shroud of white. The outline of the form revealed that a woman lay beneath the coverings. Tasaria dismissed her concerns that they were placing a corpse onto her bed when she noticed the chest of the figure was slowly rising and falling. Her own heart beat faster. The cloaked shadow spoke.

"Tasaria, you must listen carefully to every word I say. It is vital that you remember these instructions. I have kept Pias busy for now, but I do not want to arouse his suspicions by being conspicuously absent for any length of time. Do you understand?"

Tasaria nodded in assent, though her eyes drifted involuntarily to the shrouded form on her bed.

"Good," he replied curtly, "then look briefly upon the girl so that your mind will be clear as we proceed." He drew back a portion of the shroud.

It took Tasaria's mind a moment to process the sight before her. The girl looked so weak and pathetic. Tasaria turned to face the menacing shadow in horrified awe.

"Master ... why?"

The voice of Death answered.

"It is necessary if I am to fulfill my promise to your people," he contended as she bent back down over the girl's swollen visage. Her mouth was parted, her lips ablaze against the pallor of her complexion.

"She will be in pain when she awakens in several hours, but she is not permanently damaged," the odious speaker said.

Tasaria's fingertips traced a path over the stubble where Isyll's hair had been and over the symbols and equations that were now forcibly and irrevocably tattooed into her flesh. Were these everywhere on her body? The Master covered the poor girl before Tasaria could ask.

He towered over her, his yellow eyes searing hers with a furious intensity.

"No one must ever learn of this."

Utterly intimidated by his intensity, Tasaria took a step backwards, nodding in agreement as she did so. He held his gaze upon her a moment longer then turned to the Old Ones who stood silently in a row behind him.

"Two of them will accompany the girl on her voyage and remain with her. The other will remain but will need to have its mind purged of these events. To that end, I am placing all three under your direct control for the time being."

The creature began to utter words, short phrases, which sounded like a blending of Latin and Ancient Greek, yet was of neither tongue. Tasaria did her best to both hear and remember these, but he spoke in a low, rapid tone.

He grabbed her shoulder and conducted her to the opposite side of the room. There he informed her that a vessel stood ready, of its destination, and outlined the basic instructions the small party was to follow, many of which struck her as downright bizarre, not because of their complexity but rather the opposite. Apparently it was vital to be extremely specific, even down to remembering to eat.

Precautions were in place to clear a path for her so that she might move quickly through the fortress to the ship, unobserved. The Master related how the remaining Old One's mind was to be purged before they reentered and then instructed her to come to the dining chamber when all his commandments were fulfilled.

"I have received word from your husband that I wish to share with you," he growled

She bowed deeply as he swept from the room.

As she rose, Tasaria's eyes hovered over the shrouded, unconscious form on her bed. Isyll's face forever etched in her memory. Her heart twisted with pity. Could she do this?

'They will betray you, my child,' the voice of her enemy promised.

Tasaria banished the warning from her mind and embraced her faith. The Master said he could only entrust her with this task. Besides, it was so little to ask if indeed it somehow brought them closer to achieving their great purpose. She repeated the two word root Latin/Greek command he'd given her. The Old Ones' cloaked heads turned in unison to listen to her instructions. She could see nothing beneath their obscuring hoods.

"Grab the girl and follow me," she ordered. They obeyed without hesitation.

"Gently," she admonished as a sad little moan issued from Isyll. Tasaria refused to allow her heart to be moved by it. The ghastly party moved like shadows through the silent corridors.

*

Pias' fingers tapped against the unyielding stone wall as he gazed downward from the lofts of his concealed perch. The original creators of this fortress must have either been tactical geniuses or delusional madmen he mused.

"Something on your mind, Pias?" the creature asked.

"A great deal, as always," Pias replied casually as he turned to face him.

The dark, cramped passageway afforded him only a view of the creature's menacing eyes. The statement was true enough, still he settled on the mundane. His companion, thus far, had shown him much, but remained cautiously evasive as to what truly lay behind the substance of what he was seeing. Was this tour simply to assuage Pias' concerns or was it meant to serve as a distraction? Perhaps it was both.

"When did you discover all of these," he waved his hand to indicate the hidden passageway in which they stood.

"I am still finding them," the other answered dryly.

Pias decided not to press the matter for the time being. He knew he would get no further. Still it was logical to assume that there were others similar to this one intricately laced and hidden throughout the rest of the fortress. Besides, their conversations were often conducted in such a fashion, each reticent that the other should learn too much. New, but familiar, shapes were suddenly, rudely pressed into his hands. His fingers probed their form. He'd forgotten momentarily that he'd handed the journals to the creature.

"Thank you," Pias exclaimed coolly. "I am eager to see how these tally with each of our mutual calculations."

"I believe you will find quite well," the other proclaimed in a matching tone. "Shall we retire to the dining chamber so that you may study them?"

The other turned to leave. Pias remained still.

"No. Not yet. I want to meet him."

The creature paused without turning fully as he straightened.

"For what purpose?" The suspicion was plain in his voice. One yellow eye gleamed in the darkness over his shoulder.

The fool knew perfectly well what Pias was after—information or mischief.

"You can see and hear for yourself if you like," Pias stated smoothly as he indicated the vantage point he'd just abandoned. It was simple power struggles like these that would ultimately make the difference.

"Then follow," the great being commanded after several tense moments.

When they arrived outside the door, the Old One guarding it whispered something to its Lord, who did likewise in return.

"My presence is required elsewhere, Pias. When you have finished, you will be escorted to the dining chamber. It seems Nicabar has sent us news."

"Indeed," Pias responded calmly. This was potentially interesting if valid. If the missive contained the proper information, it could mean that his intricate plans could finally be put into action. He cautiously reveled at the thought.

Or this could be a minor subterfuge, the intent of which was to allow him to believe that the creature was elsewhere rather than spying on Pias' conversation, childish if true. One thing the tour did make clear was that the usefulness of their alliance was nearing its conclusion. A fact the other must have perceived by now as well.

The Old One stood to the side of the entry as the creature departed. Pias considered the journals in his hand a moment before he entered the chapel. Nicabar's letter could change everything. He probably would never have such a fortuitous opportunity again.

The man within did not even respond to the noise of the door opening and closing. The only sounds in the echoing chamber were the dull roar of the waves below and the crackle from torches burning on the walls. Pias' footsteps reverberated against the cold stones as he crossed the length of the room to face its sole occupant. His curiosity and anticipation of the moment to come rose with each step.

He sat down on the freezing bench opposite the man, who still gave no acknowledgement of his presence. He looked tired and defeated. A sadness marked him beyond his years. It was ironic, Pias noted, that by now he probably understood aspects of this man's life better than he did. But then again he'd long ago accepted revelations Ernest was beginning to learn. It would be interesting to see how the creature's corruption of this man's view of reality was progressing.

"Faber est suae quisque fortunae," Pias said quietly.

There was still no response.

"Every man is the artisan of his own fortune," Pias translated into French as he set the journals next to Ernest one by one. Neither broke the silence.

The other's eyes finally moved and looked upon the worn journals as if from a great distance.

"Your brother was a great man, Ernest Frankenstein … as his offspring hopes to become." Pias leaned back and waited.

Slowly Ernest's gaze drifted from the aged journals to Pias' face. Each was uncertain of what he saw reflected in the other's eyes.

"I hear you've been spending some quality family time together. I can't help but wonder where it will lead you."

Ernest looked away from the cruel face, disinterested. Pias rose and sat beside him on the bench.

"Don't believe his lies, don't be fooled by his promises," Pias advised quietly. "In fact…it might be wise to destroy him completely before he has the chance to do the same to you. Isn't that what your brother set out to accomplish? Isn't that why you're here?"

Pias waited. Ernest did not move. The other rose.

"What? Nothing?" Pias asked in mock astonishment. "Do you even know what those are?" He pointed to the journals. "Has he not seen fit to show you the future he summons?"

These last words faded into the echoing chapel. Ernest's face betrayed no emotion as Pias retrieved the volumes, whispered urgently in his ear, and crossed halfway across the chapel before he called back to the man who still sat silently in the flickering light of the torches.

"Fate will not allow you both to succeed."

He lingered a moment longer and hoped the creature had heard him sowing the seeds of discourse within Frankenstein. Whatever dark purpose drove the 'Master's' attempts to corrupt this man, Pias was determined to openly deny him success. It was always best to leave your enemy watching their back. He only could hope that Ernest's melancholy abated before his time ran out. As he reached the door, he laughed lightly to himself at the thought of the creature and Ernest's mutual annihilation.

*

Etolie's face rubbed against the fabric of the blanket. She blinked. It was light outside, but was it morning or afternoon? Gingerly, she drew back from Vochallet's sleeping form. It had taken hours to calm her enough to get her to rest. She'd finally resorted to begging the Moon Shadows for some alcohol. What they gave her was immensely strong, both to smell and to drink, but it did the job. After Vochallet passed out, Etolie also used it to clean and rebandage the egregious wound. The muscles in Vochallet's neck were swollen horribly, constricting her windpipe. Etolie listened to her labored, raspy breaths. They seemed regular enough. The icy, unforgiving air bit into her skin as she slid out from under the blankets, slipped back into her shoes, and quietly escaped into the hallway. It wasn't much warmer.

She hurriedly checked the other rooms but found them empty. What should she do? Baseria must have left to find Isyll hours ago. Etolie began pacing, uncertain what she should do. If she left and something happened to her as well, no one would be left to protect Vochallet. She rubbed her temples. The throbbing in her head from where the Moon Shadow had struck her wouldn't abate. The generous portion of alcohol she'd consumed didn't help either. The pain kept distracting her. She was contemplating confronting one of their guardians at the bottom of the staircase when a sound from around the corner of the hallway caught her attention. It could only be coming from one place—the pocket chapel.

The pocket chapel, as they'd termed it, was really little more than a recessed area off the main hallway. It was adorned with tiered racks of candles that they often lit and even prayed before. And it was here that Etolie found Baseria.

She was half-kneeling, half-crumpled against the wall. All of the candles burned before her. She was muttering numbly to herself. Etolie was worried she'd frighten the girl, so she attempted to announce herself.

"Ba?"

The soft mumbling continued. Etolie stepped closer and rested her hand gently on Baseria's shoulder. Quivering fingers rose to meet hers and gripped them tightly. The incoherent sounds continued.

"Ba," she repeated.

Etolie knelt down against the wall and drew her friend to her. Baseria's body was freezing. How long had she been like this?

"Baseria," Etolie whispered softly. "Baseria," she said more firmly. The muttering finally ceased, and she looked at Etolie as if she was only just now become fully aware of her friend's presence.

"I can't find her," Baseria said in a dead voice. "I looked … but she's … I looked," her voice broke in anguish.

Etolie felt her heart shudder and die. Not Isyll. Her head lolled to the side as silent tears began to mark her cheeks. The gentle girl's face swam before her. That she should be dead and Etolie still lived. Just like Kelv.

Etolie meant to save her, and all she'd succeeded in doing was to send the girl to her death. Etolie fought the lump in her throat. She tried to grasp some memory to keep the darkness from consuming her.

"Do you remember those apple trees we found two summers ago?" she asked Baseria. The question gave her something to concentrate on.

Slowly, Baseria nodded. The pleasant remembrance brought comfort that their lives had once been different. She wanted to live inside the warm memory. Her eyes focused on nothing. She could feel the touch of cool air in the shade of the trees, smell the grass, tinged with the perfume of flowers.

She was home. Etolie's fingers began to unconsciously play over the girl's hair as she too lost herself to the past.

"It was so green," Baseria remembered wistfully.

Her heart danced with the memory of living things growing in the warm sunlight as swirls of their frozen breath mingled.

Etolie began to laugh softly at first and then more openly.

"What?" her friend asked.

"Isyll and those brambles … she was so funny."

They looked at one another and suddenly dissolved into uncontrollable laughter as the two recalled their friend's efforts to get to the trees. They grew near the edge of a hillside, extending their branches partially over a deep ravine. Their trunks surrounded by a thick, nasty patch of the sharp weeds. An obstacle that would stop most, but not Isyll.

"She was a maniac. Even the boys wouldn't follow her in," Baseria smiled.

"Her armored soles helped," Etolie laughed.

Isyll had waded into the tangled mass barefoot, stomping the brambles down. She'd always been particular about wearing shoes, even in the winter, and was well-known for having the toughest skin known to man on the bottoms of her feet. Their laughter subsided somewhat as the present reality threatened anew. Baseria tried to save the moment.

"Thank God she didn't fall into the ravine. 'Course, I thought she was going to knock someone else in the way she kept firing those apples down from there."

"She wasn't coming down until she'd picked every apple off of those trees ..."

Etolie's strength faltered. The memory evaporated and there was nothing to save them from their grief. They clung to each other more tightly as first Etolie and then Baseria broke down, mourning the loss of another friend.

*

Pias was no longer smiling, though what he was seeing should have delighted him. He worked to resolve the conflict within. It was difficult. There were too many inexplicable breakthroughs for so short a period of time. What could explain it? But if the information on the pages were true, then all he'd dreamt of in the depths of his heart and soul was indeed possible, which is why he distrusted it. It must be a mirage.

Still it might be possible now, more than possible. He bit at the inside of his cheek. His eyes drifted to the Old Ones who stood silent watch near the entry to the dining chamber. There must be a flaw—somewhere.

He closed the journal, rose, walked to the guardians, drew back the hood of one, and studied what lie beneath. He shook his head.

"These final pages …"

"It is precisely what we agreed upon, your cure," the powerful hooded menace at the table rumbled, impatiently. "For once you will simply have to trust me. I have risked much and suffered greatly to discover it."

"For your own benefit," Pias shot back as he replaced the Old One's hood. He would never trust the fiend.

"Like most humans, I have a natural distrust of the unknown, and of you," Pias shot. "Have you tested these new equations? They seem too fantastic to believe."

The other rose, offended.

"They will grant you what you seek, but if they are indeed valueless to you, then put them to the fire. Find your own answers and leave me to discover mine."

The creature was toying with him, and he'd had quite enough of it. He had forgotten his place. And Pias had embraced his role as the underling for far too long. It was time to end his servant's illusions of power.

The other vital notations he required still resided in Pias' possession, far from this place. And aside from the recently added entries, he no longer cared what happened to these relics. With very deliberate motions, Pias opened one of the journals and tore the final six pages from within. Then without breaking his gaze with those disgusting yellow eyes, he handed them over. Then he uttered a command to the Old Ones, each of whom drew a sword and held it squarely to either side of the creature's throat.

"Kneel," Pias commanded the creature; his tone ice.

The other did as was bidden of him, the weapons hovering mere inches away, tracking him.

"Never dare ask me to trust you, for your treachery knows no limits, and neither does my vengeance. You serve, you do not rule," Pias warned, his voice ringing with authority.

"Yes, Master," the wretched thing bent humbly down and waited. Pias forced him to wait a long time as he pondered his next course of action.

"So you taunt me to destroy the recorded essence of what you truly are. I wonder how this factors into your plans for after I depart."

"You have always known my heart and the true purpose of my work," the other professed.

Pias rounded on him.

"And you feel you are that close to achieving it, suddenly, after all these years? Even if that is true, you must face facts, my dark friend; you have become too close to the Moon Shadows and that compromises everything."

The creature chose his words carefully.

"There is no reason to break my promise to them. We can both still achieve our goals without their destruction."

"I doubt you'll much care what happens to them if you succeed in your goal," Pias commented dryly as he paced around the genuflected being. "They've had their uses, but ultimately, they're a liability. They know too much already, and since that spy escaped in France, who knows what action Napoleon is contemplating. This is a dangerous time, and our enemies must be crushed if we are to rule."

"The Moon Shadows are loyal allies," the creature's gaze finally turned up to meet Pias', "as am I, Master."

Pias studied them carefully but read no deception in those cursed orbs. For the time being, he would accept his counsel.

"Then rise and purge yourself of an unhappy past."

With the utterance of a simple word, the Old Ones sheathed their swords and resumed their post. Without a trace of hesitation, the creature proceeded to the fireplace and set alight the journals of Victor Frankenstein. As he watched the pages peel and burn, Victor's offspring wondered if their destruction made him more or less human. The fire was rapidly reducing them to ash. He turned once again to Pias who was hunched over the table writing.

Though extremely rare, there were moments when the creature genuinely appreciated Pias. In many ways, he was a worthy companion. Their encounters were always complex, as each endlessly attempted to outmaneuver the other in pursuit of their own selfish, secretive agendas.

Though each planned to eventually eliminate the other, they did still work well together. Pias could have used the journals to blackmail the creature, but instead, by permitting their destruction, he was acknowledging that a measure of loyalty and even respect did exist between them. It was also freeing, to a degree, for it left the question of the Moon

Shadows' fate open and gave their carefully woven web of lies a new life. All this Pias gave, but his ruthless, calculating nature also preserved his upper hand. For as long as he possessed his grandfather's journals, the option to expose the creature for what he truly was, still existed. But the symbolic act was important. It re-established, if not a measure of trust between them, then at least it temporarily smoothed over their association.

For the creature, the burning, while cathartic, also afforded him additional benefits. In their mutual struggle for power over the years, he'd often found it useful to turn Pias' pride against him. Actually, by now he was quite practiced in it, as it served a key purpose. It helped the other take less of an interfering interest in his "underling's" business.

They'd both said enough during this visit to reveal to the other that a period of great change was at hand. It was important, before Pias left, to allow him to feel secure in his control over the other and challenging his perceived authority was the only way to ensure this occurred. It was almost expected. Besides, his own uses for Pias were not yet at an end. In fact, the success of Pias' own ambitions, was of vital import to the creature's own carefully conceived plans.

"You may find this useful," Pias noted as he handed the creature a sheet of paper with a single formulaic equation on it. The shadow studied it carefully with increasing interest.

"A new theory?"

Pias was not allowed an opportunity to respond.

The paper vanished under the creature's cloak at the sound of Tasaria's arrival. She looked anxious and cold as she joined her Master in front of the fire.

"Please forgive my tardiness to your summons, Master," she intoned as she bowed slightly. "I was tending to my patient."

"Oh, have you buried her in the snow?" Pias asked sarcastically as he pointed to her damp cloak, which a few flakes still clung to.

Tasaria hesitated only a moment, but her look of uncertainty did not escape Pias' notice.

"I cut across the courtyard," she snapped.

The creature intervened.

"I trust your patient is resting comfortably?"

"Yes, she is quite comfortable for the time being," Tasaria responded awkwardly, as she shed a layer of clothing, grateful to finally be warm. She seemed distracted, Pias decided.

"Perhaps a brandy to warm you?" Pias offered as he seated himself at the table and poured one.

"Yes, thank you." Tasaria imbibed the first mug quickly, eager to purge her guilt, and to warm herself. Pias gave her another as he began to sip his own. A single look from the Master, as he sat at the head of the table, slowed Tasaria's consumption of the second. Everyone knew she talked far too freely after a drink or two.

The creature reached within his heavy cloak and withdrew an envelope, which he handed to Tasaria. She devoured the words as quickly as she'd downed her first drink.

"Surely this news could not be better," she crowed as both the words she read and the alcohol took hold.

It was good news: their encampment in France had suffered no attacks, Nicabar was well, and most importantly, he'd succeeded in negotiating a truce with Jal so that they might meet to discuss trading Baseria for Frankenstein's daughter. Most important of all though, the news meant that she was going home. She handed the letter to an anxious Pias, who nodded more soberly at the information.

"How are we to proceed, Master?" he asked, returning the letter to the wraith.

"Your ship is being prepared as we speak, though this storm will slow loading the provisions. You sail at dawn. I have sent word to Nicabar to expect your arrival with the girl in ten days or less at the secondary landing site. He will handle the negotiations and bring the infant here. That is all."

Tasaria waited for the usual protests from Pias, but strangely none were forthcoming. They all stood. She felt flush from the brandy. It was acting upon her more rapidly than she'd anticipated.

"Shall I inform my niece?" Tasaria inquired.

"No," her Master responded quietly without looking at her.

She tried again.

"Well, should any special preparations be made for transporting the injured Wild Rose woman?"

"No."

The first time she heard the word she was willing to accept it without comment, but not the second.

"But Master, her life…," the words died as he turned and stared silently down on her.

"Watch over that life tonight," he commanded.

Tasaria's mouth worked uselessly a moment before she awkwardly bowed and left. He turned his back to Pias and again gazed into the fire. No trace remained of the journals.

"When do you plan to tell Tasaria?" Pias asked behind him.

"When it is too late for her to change anything," The other sighed. "You will leave tonight."

"Nicabar will not be happy," Pias noted.

"He will accept my decision."

"I see. And how long do you anticipate your new labors will take you?"

The hulking shadow vilely whispered.

"*Fortitudine vincimus*—It only matters that I am successful."

Pias paused and took a step back in the direction of the creature.

"And if you are as close as you claim, which girl do you intend to send with me? Or must they all die?" he asked thoughtfully.

It mattered not to Pias, for aside from torturing whomever the creature chose for information during the return voyage, his plans would not be affected by the other's choice. It was not so for Victor's offspring though. The crackling flames drummed at the cold air, but there was no answer. Pias turned to leave.

"Take Pell with you. He is of no further use here," the creature asserted without turning.

"As you wish, Master," Pias smirked as he left.

*

How could this happen again? Baseria practically molded herself to Etolie's shoulder as the other lit every candle in Vochallet's room.

"Faster," she bid, "faster."

Etolie blew out the match.

"They're all lit, Ba. It's all right," Etolie reassured her.

"It's not bright enough," Baseria shook her head frantically.

"Well, it'll have to do," her friend declared. "All these candles are frozen to their stands. Maybe they'll melt if the heat works down to them in awhile."

"Too dark. It's too dark over there, and over there."

Baseria was crumbling. Etolie struggled to maintain her emotions as she sought to comfort her friend.

"Ba, look at me. Look at me. You've got to calm down. When's the last time you slept?"

Baseria's hand stuttered shakily through her hair, she smiled awkwardly a moment and then it vanished.

"I don't know." Her expression suddenly shifted, "I … I didn't imagine it, Etolie. She's here."

"Ssshhh. Sit down and tell me," Etolie pulled Baseria to the room's unoccupied bed. So far, Vochallet had not stirred, and Etolie hoped to keep it that way. The poor woman's fever seemed to be rising.

"Now," she said calmly, "what happened at the cistern?"

The small water cistern for this section of the fortress was located at the far end of the hall, down a short, cramped stairwell, hewn out of the living rock. It was by far the coldest room in this wing of the fortress, and as such, the water it contained was often frozen; however, time and practice had revealed that a thin slush could be coaxed from the fountain head that fed it if one chipped ice in the proper places. Baseria had begun such a task in order to get fresh water for the night.

"And then … and then his wife was there … standing behind me. I could see her form reflected in the ice, feel her gazing down at me," Baseria's nerves danced at the terrifying memory of the phantom.

"You're certain it was her?"

Baseria paused a moment before she answered.

"It felt the same, yes."

If Ernest's wife was here, then that explained much, but Baseria's answer did not.

"You didn't turn to face her?"

Baseria shook her head.

"No, no, but she called to me," her haunted voice continued, "just like before."

Etolie's own heart was racing now as Baseria's experience began to crystallize.

"Before? You've seen her in the fortress before now?"

"Her ghost, Etolie, remember—the first time, in the turret stairwell outside the reading room?" Baseria whispered urgently. "And there was a second time, in the dark, coming back from the chapel after I left Frankenstein, she …"

Baseria covered her mouth and looked wildly around the room as if certain talking about the ghost would cause it to materialize. Without realizing it, Etolie too began to concentrate on the areas of the room left to shadow by the flicking light of the candles. She swallowed hard before she spoke.

"Ba … Ba, listen. I believe you … that you saw something, but I think you need to lie down and rest for awhile."

"NO!" Baseria's eyes flashed. "No, no, she wants to hurt me." She gripped Etolie's forearms tightly, manic with fear. "I didn't mean what I said in the chapel," she cried.

"Ssshhh, no, no," Etolie cooed gently to her until the ardent grasp began to relax. "Just breathe for a minute, okay? Just breathe," Etolie instructed.

Baseria's senses began to return as she breathed deeply. Was Etolie right? Was she imagining it all? Baseria was exhausted. Maybe her own sense of guilt was responsible for the manifestation. Slowly, some of the tension began to fade from her face. Etolie's own expression grew distant and pained as she calmed her friend. Finally, it resolved into almost a look of tranquility.

"Kelv's dead, Baseria," she said softly. "My husband is dead."

The statement was so unexpected and so jolting that, for a moment, all of Baseria's fears became shadows as disbelief and sadness filled her heart. Etolie withdrew the man's necklace from her pocket, providing the answer to the unspoken question that burned in Baseria's eyes. Her worst fears of what the gypsy in the reading room had whispered to Etolie were confirmed.

But the moment brought only peace to Etolie. She felt relieved at having finally told Baseria, whom she leaned forward to and embraced. She could feel her friend's tears against her own cheek. Neither spoke for a long time.

"You know," Etolie finally remarked, numbly, "I've always believed that the dead remember us just as we remember them. And that's why they walk the Earth. I'd give anything to see him again, anything to have a chance to say goodbye. Maybe, if she is a ghost, that's all Frankenstein's wife wants—a chance to say goodbye."

Baseria pulled back and stared dumbstruck.

"But why," she sighed, "why does she keep coming to me then?" She wiped the moisture, now partially frozen to her cheeks, away.

The discussion seemed to be reviving them both to a degree.

"Do you remember what you told me about the energies of the unseen world? How chaotic they can be."

Baseria nodded.

"Well, maybe the world beyond this one is like that," Etolie postulated. "Maybe she got lost looking for him, but instead, because of the healing trance, she found you. Maybe she's hoping that you can lead her to him or that she can tell you what she needs to tell him."

The two women quietly pondered their own thoughts. Was it possible? Could the bond forged by the healing trance have accidentally drawn the wayward spirit to her? Might his wife simply be looking for peace, not vengeance? Baseria did not fully accept the idea, but it did help to calm her fears. Vochallet moaned softly, she was beginning to awaken.

Baseria's eyes turned to her companion. It was time for a confession of her own. She leaned closer to Etolie, afraid to be overheard.

"Etolie, I think I …," it was difficult to say the words, "I think, what happened to Vochallet, that it was my fault."

Etolie shook her head immediately.

"No, Ba. That was the wind, nothing more. You mustn't blame yourself," she began to pull back, but Baseria grabbed her wrist and stopped her.

"That's just it," she gazed intently into her friend's eyes. "There is more now, much more. And I don't think I can control it."

"What do you mean?" Etolie asked in utter bewilderment, before the meaning became clear. "Has your power returned?"

Baseria nodded fervently.

"Just before the glass shattered," she confirmed. "I think I somehow summoned it."

Etolie looked away for a moment, and then her expression altered as a new hope filled her heart, one which blinded her to her friend's fears.

"But Ba, this is wonderful news. It means you can heal her," Etolie smiled with relief.

Baseria's eyes shifted away in defeat.

"I can't."

"Yes, you can," Etolie asserted cheerfully, "you've done it before."

Baseria shook her head.

"No. I told you, I can't control it. I might harm her again."

The smile slowly faded from Etolie's face and an embarrassed silence grew between them for a time as each looked away from the other in despair.

"How do you know?" Etolie suddenly challenged defiantly.

"What?"

"How do you know you'll hurt her? You've never harmed people before. Maybe what happened was just an accident."

Baseria's eyes fixed momentarily on Vochallet, listened to her fighting for each breath she took. She was unwilling to risk anymore accidents.

She turned away as another series of pitiable sounds drew Etolie's attentions firmly to Vochallet. Even before she touched her, Etolie could tell that she was running a high fever. Fortunately, Vochallet was only partially conscious. Etolie dabbed a cool cloth against her patient's exposed skin, wiping the moisture away before it could begin to freeze. An intense resolve grew within her as each pain-filled minute passed, until she could contain it no longer. She stood, marched over, and shoved Baseria's shoulder, forcing her startled friend's head to snap upward.

"How can you just sit there when…don't look away!" Etolie grabbed Baseria's face and forced her to gaze at the suffering form of Vochallet.

"If you truly did that, then you have to help her. That is balance. That is who we are. I know you didn't hurt her on purpose, Ba, but you can help her now. You can save her. I know it. You're just scared, but you can do it. You have to," she pleaded as she released Baseria's head.

Etolie's breaths were escaping in great clouds of icy mist as she waited for Baseria to respond. It took a solid minute before the look of shock etched on her features began to fade into something more thoughtful.

"But I don't have the stones," Baseria protested.

"We're surrounded by them."

"It's not the same," Baseria contended angrily as she stood, clenching her fists. Etolie could not understand what she was asking Baseria to do.

"Well, you're the one with all the power, figure it out!" Etolie barked, her patience gone. "You saved yourself, you saved Frankenstein, now save her!"

As Baseria began to pace, the power residing inside of her seemed to leer back, daring her to embrace it. Her recent prolonged moments of sheer despair and abject terror had made it easier for her to ignore its possessive allure. But as her frustrations mounted, so did the temptation to use it. She was powerful. Why shouldn't she use it?

The surging energy seemed to pulse through her, and she gasped with the pleasurable sensation of touching it. She nodded inwardly to the seductive whispers inside her head. If Elemental Earth was not practical, then use Elemental Fire. And for the first time since their mysterious return, Baseria lost herself to the powers of the unseen world.

Her consciousness bled into the flames surrounding her; their collective energies merging and exchanging. Nasi had always discouraged her from interacting with this element. When Baseria questioned her reasoning for this, her grandmother had simply described the element as too distracting. It was to be something she worked with after she'd mastered her interactions with the other elements. But Nasi was gone, and those lessons would never happen. Still, Nasi had left her power, a power the new Seer must try and use.

Her passions rose rapidly as she played and interacted with the energies, each mesmerized by the other. She'd never felt such freedom, such control when interacting with any Elemental energy. Shadows and light began to dance to her whim, lighthearted at first. Her cravings grew. She wanted more. But in this maelstrom, one source of energy resisted her charms. She tightened her focus, but still the energy refused to obey. The swirl of light and shadows seemed to mock her inability to harness the rogue source. Her passions surged, and then suddenly she was back in the room. Etolie was shrieking and shaking her violently.

"Ba! Stop it! Stop it !!!"

Vochallet was gasping as if a great weight lay upon her chest; the noise of life being drawn from her body was sickening to hear. But the energy of Elemental Fire still burned within Baseria, and the power inside of her lusted for it. Still she had to stop before she killed Vochallet. How did she stop? She had to stop!

And then her desperation found form as the soft flickers on the candles began to grow into towering flames before they ferociously burst from existence. The roar was terrifying as each flame exploded before dying. The soaring flames scorched and blackened the stones, nipped at clothing, singed bedding and their flesh. Then as suddenly as it began, it ended, and absolute darkness claimed the room. Eventually, even the screams died.

CHAPTER 19
OPUS OF INTRIGUE

Abrielle slammed the door behind her as she began to feverishly pace the length of the small balcony. Idiot, she screamed in her mind. Though at this point, the label could easily be applied to either her or Jack. How had she ever allowed herself to be talked into this?

She stopped pacing and clamped her hands down harshly on the railing, swearing to herself that if Jack followed her out here this time, she'd throw him over it and down into the street. Abrielle nursed her anger a moment longer then allowed it to fade. Her head drooped, and she sighed dramatically. The cool evening breezes were a welcome change from the poisonous, smoke-filled atmosphere inside the apartments. She began to study the street below, searching for anything to distract her.

After several more minutes alone, she heard the door open tentatively, and then close quietly behind her. She made no motion to acknowledge the older gentleman who'd passed through it. Christiansen was wise enough not to speak until spoken to and calmly took a seat in one of the balcony's chairs. He too seemed to be in need of a moment of relative peace. For a time, they enjoyed it together.

"I never should have kidnapped you," Abrielle finally quipped without turning.

Christiansen chuckled.

"I suppose we all pay for our crimes sooner or later."

"Well, I'm glad you find this so amusing," she rejoined, turning and spreading her arms out behind her along the railing.

He grinned wryly as he began to roll a cigarette.

"It wasn't my idea to come to Salzburg."

"No, but as Jack's friend, eventually you would have. Please, no more smoke," she begged tiredly. He looked longingly at the half-completed creation then abandoned it with a nod. Abrielle whisked her hair behind her ear and sat down in the other chair. Initially, her gaze remained upon the city.

"I don't know what he expects," she said shaking her head.

Christiansen shrugged.

"He expects you to become the toast of the Continent in a matter of days."

"But that's insane," she asserted, looking back to him once more.

"So is Jack," Christiansen acknowledged apologetically. "He also expects this whole sordid affair is going to work—somehow."

"It's stupid," Abrielle pouted, crossing her arms like a child.

She'd actually had dreams the past two nights in which Ernest arrived and saved her from his lunatic friend. She wished someone would. Her companion nodded.

"Typically where Jack's plans are concerned, my best advice is to simply try and survive them."

"He'll be lucky if he survives me," she mused threateningly.

"Now, now, until Espen returns. there really isn't much we can do. So we might as well keep to our word and try to help Jack, misguided as his attempts may be," he added as he stood.

"Do you think you can be ready in two days?" he asked.

Abrielle waved away the question as if it were nothing but a common nuisance. She'd been studying and practicing for endless hours, encased within equally mind-numbing days. How much more prepared could one person be to do something they barely understood?

"Good. Then I'll go in and suggest to Jack, both for the ultimate success of his plan and for his own safety, that we continue the training tomorrow."

He paused.

"That is, of course, unless you wish to continue tonight?"

She mulled his dare over, not bothering to point out that it was already tomorrow.

"What about his neighbors?"

"I don't think there will be any love lost between Jack and them if we continue. Besides, I believe you have survived worse than this," Christiansen added significantly.

Abrielle closed her eyes. Bellange, prison, Chloe, massive injuries, an unexpected romantic entanglement, wolves, pistol shots, blindness, confessing to Anne, thievery, the death of Ailis, the loss of Tara. Yes, she had survived worse. She sighed. Jack was also partially correct that she did share some measure of responsibility for the current situation between him and his wife. He had remained loyal, could she afford to do any less?

"Only one more hour, after that he takes his life into his own hands," she warned. "Give me a minute. And tell him I don't want to choke on anymore of his smoke."

Christiansen inclined his head respectfully then stepped back inside.

"What'd she say?" Jack bellowed anxiously before he closed the door. She heard Christiansen raise his voice for an instant, which was followed immediately by the sound of windows being thrown open.

Abrielle shook her head and looked up at the stars, which sparkled serenely in the blackness. Her mind went blank. They were lovely. As she watched their dull, irregular pulses, she absentmindedly began to hum the tune of a song she'd been taught as a child. All she could recall from it were a few lines about stars twinkling and their power to bring a person luck. She stopped humming. She felt very small. Two days from now she would need all of the luck heaven could spare her.

*

"I'm a genius," Jack declared as they rode in his carriage two evenings later.

Abrielle raised an eyebrow to this assessment. The man was many things, but genius was not a word she would have chosen.

"Well, I mean just look at you," he gawked at her expression. "You're stunning, absolutely stunning."

Abrielle was about to remind him that his own efforts had nothing to do with her appearance, but instead she looked out the window and shifted uncomfortably on the bench seat. This time it was far from true. She'd rarely worn clothing or jewelry that was this fine and expensive. In fact, Abrielle didn't even want to know how much the ensemble she wore had cost Jack. He generously declared that regardless of how the next few hours transpired, it was understood that these luxurious gifts were now hers.

Jack's eyes continued to rove over her pleasing form. She'd decided several days ago that she might as well get used to this for her role. Still, the attention made her uncomfortable, as did going out nightly and flirting openly with Jack in the company of others. She wondered why. It certainly wasn't the first time she'd been compelled to behave in such a manner, and after all, it was only part of Jack's plan.

Finally satisfied, Jack crossed his arms and grinned. By now he knew exactly what fashions other women wore. This annoyed his wife to no end, and so he'd dressed Abrielle accordingly tonight.

"Perfect. Stanza's really gonna do her best to embarrass the hell out of you tonight, when she sees ..."

"Jack," Christiansen admonished sharply.

"What? Oh, sorry. I'm just sayin'."

"Then please stop," Christiansen suggested with admirable patience.

Jack looked at him a moment then lapsed into silence. Everyone was restless for the uncomfortable ride to be over, everyone except Abrielle.

When Jack first asked her to help, all he was interested in was whether or not she could sing. She could but she hadn't appreciated the intricacies of the art that she would be required to perform tonight. The majority of her singing experience came from playing in taverns, often to drunks, or in small local theaters, as a cover for her espionage activities.

But her audience this evening would be far less forgiving of even her minor mistakes. She was French, and though Salzburg's ties with the Austrian Empire remained strong, recent treaties with Napoleon had annexed it to the Confederation of the Rhine, a fact that many found difficult to overlook. Still Jack adamantly refused Christiansen's suggestion that they should pass her as a Swiss. Come what may, she would stand before them as an Imperial. Abrielle's hand nervously checked her hair again. She rarely wore it up. Mercifully it hadn't shifted.

"You still nervous? You need more air?" Jack asked the questions in quick succession as he began to fiddle with the window.

She shook her head, and he immediately stopped. It was a sign of either Christiansen's subtle influence or Jack's developing respect for Abrielle that he'd suddenly abandoned smoking altogether in her presence. He hadn't touched a cigar in two days and even gone out and bought new dress clothes for himself, as his others were heavily saturated with smoke. However, he'd substituted one habit with another, becoming fixated with attempts to ensure that Abrielle always had plenty of fresh air. It was rather sweet—at first. Her bedroom the past several mornings was freezing, as he now refused to close the windows at night.

"Hopefully by now the word's spread and Stanza believes that we're together. We'll have to make sure she believes it," Jack noted, "or all this will be for nothin'."

"Wouldn't that be a shame," Christiansen noted dryly.

Jack ignored him.

"I know, Jack," Abrielle said flatly.

She was glad Espen was gone. Jack and he probably would have knocked each other senseless over her by now. Their jealousy-fueled confrontations quickly became so distracting that after a single day of it, when Espen suggested an alternate use of his time spent far away from the others, she'd immediately seized the opportunity to separate them, perhaps against her better judgment.

"I can't believe he keeps making advances towards you," Espen growled when she bid him farewell. "I thought you were all doing this to save his marriage."

She'd had similar thoughts, but as Christiansen pointed out, Jack needed to save face after the miserable state they'd found him in. Abrielle was far from unattractive, and he knew his attentions towards her irritated Espen to no end. Put more simply, Jack was still Jack.

"Duke's got to believe you're legitimate, too. Long as you sing well, that shouldn't be a problem. I really sold him on you, the great, mysterious rising star of the Imperial stage," Jack commented casually as he took a nip from his flask, offering it to the others who both refused. His fingers were shaking as he resealed the cap.

Abrielle could feel her stomach turning into a hard knot. She kept trying to hide her nervousness, but tonight she found it nearly impossible. All of them did. The odds were stacked decidedly against them. Her voice was pleasant enough, but she was no singer, and if she still retained one true phobia, it was singing, alone, in front of a large audience.

Abrielle never knew what her voice would do. Sometimes she was brilliant, but other experiences had been disastrous. One atrocious performance at Le Hir's salon almost resulted in her complete dismissal when her voice suddenly went completely off-key, distracting the secret business dealings being conducted. Another time she'd been laughed offstage during a solo, when her voice had unrepentantly given out.

She improved over the years but hadn't sung in a solo capacity onstage since. For days, Abrielle kept telling herself that everything would be fine, kept reminding herself that Jack needed her. But tonight she felt little confidence that she'd actually succeed. And with all of the grueling practices these past few days, it seemed even less likely that her voice would survive any real demands she placed on it.

To her companions' surprise, she suddenly opened the window, waving the air in with her fan.

"Are you all right, my dear?" Christiansen's concern plain in his voice.

"How many people again?" she asked, ignoring him, and turning to Jack.

"What, singin' or total?"

"Both."

Jack's face contorted as he performed some personal calculations.

"Huh, well, let's see. For a sponsorship competition at this level, I would guess no more than six ladies singing and oh … say … forty people in the audience, maximum," Jack promised. "Nothing to worry about, trust me."

*

Abrielle stopped counting heads when she reached one hundred and thirty. Worse yet, there were still more arriving and joining the receiving line at the door. Christiansen stopped her from downing a glass of champagne, which she liberated from a passing tray, while Jack concluded conversing with their host. Abrielle's own conversation with the Duke being kept as brief as possible. There was something in the Duke's eye she didn't like, and she received an even cooler greeting from his son. But if the Duke suspected she was a fraud, then why would he allow her to participate in such an important sponsorship event? The winner of which would go on to an exclusive engagement at the most prestigious theatre in Vienna. No small prize.

"… expected you'd want to arrive here hours ago. The performances will start very shortly," the Duke was remarking.

"Apologies, your Lordship, just wanted to ensure that nobody was intrudin' on anyone else's practice space, but I assure you the Mademoiselle is ready," Jack beamed.

"Of course," the Duke smiled politely, but his eyes bore a different expression. "The others are preparing upstairs. Marta, conduct her to them," he signaled to one of her servants.

Jack bowed formally then quickly intercepted Abrielle and Marta.

"Just one moment if you would," he requested, blocking their path.

"Sir," Marta glided over to one the hallway's marble staircases and waited patiently.

Christiansen had followed them, but was immediately shooed away by Jack.

"Mingle, mingle," Jack instructed him hastily, "your niece is about to perform for the rich and the powerful. Go play the proud uncle."

"Tonight I am proud, regardless."

The older man patted Abrielle's gloved hand reassuringly then left. Her rising sense of panic did not diminish as her eyes surveyed the ever-growing crowd.

"Jack. I don't know if I can go through with this," she said plaintively.

"I know. I know. I wasn't expecting this big a crowd either. Didn't figure the old fox would pull something like this," Jack commented.

"Like what?" She demanded breathlessly.

Jack rubbed the back of his neck as he ushered her over to a nearby wall.

"Ah, well, yeah … see, the thing is the Duke doesn't really like me, but he admires Costanza, a lot, would like to marry her, in fact, were she to become officially available. Her family has money, he needs money 'cause of gamblin', and I'm in the way of him solving these issues. So we're holding a, ah, gentleman's wager, high stakes, if you follow. He probably expects I'm gonna make an ass of myself."

She touched his arm lightly, too nervous to ask the question. What had he gotten her into? Jack's upper lipped jutted outward a moment as his lower one pushed up tightly against it.

"If the Duke wins our wager, I've agreed to forgive his son's gamblin' debts to me. If I win, he's convinced that I'm going to divorce Stanza, marry you, and leave Salzburg, forever."

Abrielle could feel herself going pale as the blood drained from her face. It took her several tense moments before she could speak.

"Who decides who wins?"

"We've taken ourselves out of the equation. The reaction of the audience makes the final determination," Jack voice was strained. "That was our agreement. I figure that's why he invited so many people this time."

"But he could control a smaller group more effectively."

"Yeah, but he probably didn't want me to be able to accuse him of manipulating things to his advantage later," Jack leaned in, "Now here's what I need you to do."

"Excuse me, mademoiselle," Marta interrupted loudly. "But we will begin tonight's performances in a matter of minutes. If you do not hurry, you will not have any time left to prepare."

Abrielle nodded then turned back to Jack, but he, too, was now cornered. The Duke and his son had interceded between them. There was no way for her to reach Jack. As she slowly ascended the stairs, a horrible realization suddenly occurred to her. Abrielle had no idea who Jack had bet on to win.

*

The women in the room strutted in a manner that reminded her of exotic birds. They fussed and preened and surveyed their territory endlessly. All turned in unison when the intruder came. Abrielle, after a brief trip to the dressing room upstairs, had come back down to join the other would-be divas in the drawing room adjacent the ballroom. After their initial response to her arrival, all five of the women began to react differently to her presence. One completely ignored her. Another began to whisper furiously to her nearest companion, each laughing obnoxiously as they studied her. One continued to practice her scales, and one, whom Abrielle recalled very well, put down the small dog she was stroking and stormed over to Marta.

"No, no, no! A thousand times, I say, No! I will not suffer this humiliation, I tell you! Get her out of here!"

"Mistress Clerval, please, I have no control over whom the Duke invites to sing," Marta begged as Jack's estranged wife grabbed her.

"Then find me someone who does!" Costanza shrieked, pushing the woman towards the door. Abrielle doubted she needed any extra encouragement to leave.

Without any further acknowledgement of Abrielle's presence, Costanza returned to her dog and cooed softly to it. Abrielle could feel herself perspiring, and she strode across the room and poured a glass of water from a carafe. Another servant entered from the ballroom and announced the name of the woman who'd been ignoring Abrielle. All the other women grew silent, and the void was only filled once the woman in the ballroom began to sing. Abrielle sipped at her water and listened to the melodic harmonies emanating from the room next door. Since she was already near them, she set the glass of water down and peeked through the doors to the ballroom.

The room was opulent, impressive in scope, and adorned with warm colors. The spacious floor held rows of people. A pillar-supported walkway encircled the room and was lined with additional spectators. The combination of sounds created by both the singer and the accompanying musicians seemed to mesmerize the large, well-dressed audience. It took some time before Abrielle finally managed to locate Christiansen, but Jack was not with him. The servant's return forced her to step back. He seamlessly timed the announcement of the next performer's name as the appreciative applause concluded for the first one's aria. She bowed and exchanged places with the next performer, the woman who'd been practicing her scales. The musicians began to play the aria anew.

There were to be three rounds to the competition. The first two required all of them to sing their own interpretations of musical selections specified by the Duke. After each round, they were to go back out into the ballroom for the final judgment of the audience. Two would be eliminated in each round. The concluding round would call upon the final two to perform a selection from a work of her own choosing. Jack's brilliant plan had afforded her only five days to learn, not only the works she was to perform, but also the language and techniques of operatic presentation. It was torturous to assimilate so much knowledge in so short a period of time.

In this, both her previous experiences in life, and Jack's surprisingly knowledgeable instruction were invaluable. Her various missions made her accustomed to working under extreme deadlines. As such, she'd developed certain techniques to aid and even enhance her memory retention. Her daily exercise regimen and previous stage performances both emphasized motor and breath control. Recognizing her firmly established goal was critical, she was not attempting to become an actual opera singer, only a close enough approximation to complete the task before her. If she'd been called upon to participate as the lead in a full operatic performance, there would have been no hope, but since the competition focused on only a few key musical pieces, it allowed her a fighting chance to succeed. She was additionally aided by the fact that Jack knew his audience well enough to instruct her on appropriate presentation techniques that catered to their tastes. And as she watched and listened to the second performer of the evening, she began to attentively analyze the woman's presentation.

The *mezzo soprano*[12] was singing an Italian aria using the smooth, gliding legato[13] technique. It was pleasant, but added little to differentiate her from the previous performer. Were they using this technique because they saw it as a safe means to engage their audience or to mask limited skills? Too much embellishment early on might alienate them from the crowd. Then again, it might help one forge a strong connection with them. Should she began conservatively or try to impress them early on? Regardless of Jack's bet, she needed to survive into at least the second round. Hopefully, by then, they would have an opportunity to speak, and she would know what was expected of her.

As she weighed her options, she became aware of the fact that the other ladies were beginning to openly tear into her. Apparently they either did not think she understood the Austrian tongue or they simply didn't care if she did.

"It looks like your husband picked out her clothes," one observed mockingly to Costanza, whose only reaction was a short, sharp little laugh as she continued to pet her dog.

"Where do you think he found her?" another asked.

"Probably in a brothel," her companion cruelly postulated to the amusement of the others.

"Do the French have brothels?"

"They'd better. After all, what chance does Napoleon have of fathering an appropriate heir without them?"

They laughed as the performers traded places yet again. Abrielle did her best to block them out and concentrate on each performance and the audience's reaction to them.

The women continued their verbal jabs unabated until it was Costanza's turn.

---

12 female vocal range between soprano and contralto (high to low) range.

13 identifies that musical piece to be played slowly; gliding style.

"You should ask her to watch your dog while you sing," one suggested as Stanza began towards the door and Abrielle. Up until this point, the woman had said little, only issued appreciative sounds to the others biting insults. This time, however, she did not pass up the opportunity.

"No, my dear, she is better suited for picking up after animals," Stanza remarked haughtily as she opened the door.

"You would know," Abrielle rejoined in Austrian just as she was about to go onstage.

Costanza hesitated only a moment, resisting the temptation to respond, before she stepped through the portal. Abrielle smiled to herself and for a time the insults of the others grew more muted. She was beginning to get the sense that collectively these women were not normally friendly, but all resented her presence enough to gang up on her.

Stanza's performance was easily the strongest she'd heard yet, but she did detect two minor flaws, one at the beginning and one at the end. Perhaps Abrielle's parting comment or continued presence was distracting Costanza's mind. She thundered back into the room when she was finished. The others engaged in light attempts at praise which she whisked away and resumed petting her dog in isolation, staring icily towards Abrielle, who turned and pretended to study the books on a nearby shelf. Then before she realized it, the servant was beside her prompting Abrielle for her name.

"Just announce me as Mademoiselle Christiansen," she instructed, her pulse suddenly racing.

If there were anymore insults lobbed at her before she left the drawing room, Abrielle was unaware of it. Time seemed to slow as she walked in a reserved fashion towards the musicians. She could hear the stir racing through the crowd upon her entry, feel what felt like a thousand eyes crawling all over her, waiting to see how she would respond. Abrielle finally spotted Jack who was seated next to the Duke and his son. His fingers drummed incessantly on his trouser legs. He cleared his throat into the suddenly silent ballroom and dabbed at his forehead with a handkerchief.

As she took her place, Abrielle wanted to sink through the floor. Right now she'd rather be facing Moon Shadow wolves than this. Jack motioned a reminder to her and she bowed, she hoped, gracefully to the Duke. Why did he keep flashing grins at her like an idiot? Oh right, she'd forgotten to smile.

The familiar music began several moments after she rose from her bow, and at first, though her lips moved, no sound seemed to be coming forth from her mouth. She could feel her face growing red. Then she heard it. Had she been singing all along? The words sounded like the right ones for the notes she was singing. It felt surreal to be standing before this many silent people, all assiduously critiquing her. Early on in the performance, any thoughts she'd formed as to stylistic choices or operatic technique vanished as her mind worked to catch up with her body. As she concluded, she surprised herself by suddenly ending *vibrato*—her voice wavering, then holding for effect. Then, it was over. She bowed and left the room to polite applause.

The others said nothing as she re-entered the drawing room. They waited patiently in line as Abrielle guzzled down a glass of water. Her body felt like it was shaking apart. The unfortunate Marta was retrieved to watch Costanza's dog, which seemed none too fond of her.

"Mademoiselle," Marta nodded her head towards the door, which the other singers had just finished passing through to be greeted by applause for their collective efforts. Abrielle slammed the glass down and rushed to join them. She made it just in time for all of them to bow together, and then each performer bowed individually. Abrielle walked numbly back into the drawing room with the others when this was over.

They'd reached the first of the twenty-minute intermissions. Abrielle did not wait to see how the news impacted the others. She slipped from the room immediately. Desperate for a moment alone, she wondered out onto the house's rear promenade. It was at least relatively quiet here. She wished there was more of a breeze. Her body felt feverish.

"Mademoiselle?" an ancient voice behind her suddenly beckoned.

Abrielle turned to discover an aged Austrian aristocratic woman and her husband.

"I just wanted to tell you that was a most interesting interpretation," the woman sincerely stated.

"Yes, the introduction in particular," the old gentleman noted, his wife nodded in agreement.

"You're very kind," Abrielle smiled awkwardly. The performance was nothing short of a disaster in her mind. She couldn't fathom why she hadn't been dismissed.

"I must admit that when I heard we had an Imperial singing, I was intrigued but not enthusiastic."

"But you have surprised us," the woman finished her husband's thought as older couples are wont to do and began to lead him away. "We look forward to your next performance," she smiled warmly.

Abrielle curtsied briefly then headed rapidly in the opposite direction from the couple. The hem of her dress scratched rhythmically along the stones. She needed to find Jack.

Her hasty search for him ultimately proved fruitless, however, she did manage to find Christiansen in the grand hallway. She cut his praise short, happy simply to have found one of them in the mass of people.

"Thank God. Where's Jack?"

"Probably still with the Duke, fellow seems to be watching him like a hawk," Christiansen replied uncertainly. "Is something wrong?"

Everything about being here was wrong. Abrielle's eyes wove among the crowd, but failed to find either man.

"What time is it?" she demanded as people began to head back into the ballroom. Christiansen consulted his watch. Only a couple of minutes remained before the next round.

"Look, did Jack mention anything to you about some wager he and the Duke made?"

Christiansen choked a bit on his champagne. She dabbed at his jacket.

"Wager?" he managed.

They were nearly out of time.

"Something about money and marriage and divorce, but he didn't finish telling me what I'm supposed to do to win this bet of his," she explained.

"Oh dear," Christiansen set the glass down on the nearest table, straightened his jacket, and began to leave. "Jack likes to play long odds, but he may have outfoxed himself," he muttered.

"Wait, wait, wait," Abrielle pleaded chasing after him, "What am I supposed to do?"

Christiansen paused.

"Just worry about your performance. I'll worry about Jack," he advised.

*

In many ways, the second performance was even harder. Abrielle went first this time, which afforded Christiansen no opportunity to speak with Jack before it began. She was beset by indecision as she sang the somber cantata about Christ's suffering. This was her least favorite piece, and though she frequently looked to Jack for some hint as to what she should do, he sat very still and impassive. Was this a sign that she was not supposed to lose in the second round? Or was he simply being watched too carefully?

As her performance dragged on, she could feel her voice getting tighter, her breaths shorter, until by the very end her voice cracked on the last note. Her inner turmoil having bled into her performance, she barely remembered to bow before she left the ballroom.

She returned to the drawing room, sat, and did not move until the last performer was onstage. After the first round, the second performer and one of her gossiping tormentors, who'd sung fourth, had been eliminated. The room was quieter this time, but certainly not bereft of unkind comments and harsh glances. Abrielle never responded to these as her eyes fixed on the pattern of the floor tiles as she replayed her own performance over and over in her mind.

*

Apparently, the second round was not particularly kind to anyone except for Costanza, who received a thunderous applause of approval when the time came. The other three women received a polite but not overly-enthusiastic reception. In fact, the response was so even that the audience was forced to repeat their assessment twice more to determine who the other finalist would be. By the faintest of margins, Abrielle was chosen. Perhaps it had been the poignant emotion in her voice during her performance, or maybe it was the fascination a foreigner presented, but most likely everyone simply wanted to see if it would be Jack's wife or mistress who remained in Salzburg.

*

The women paced ceaselessly about the drawing room. Unlike the previous intermission, neither was allowed to leave before the final performance. They were to take the stage together. Costanza looked as if she would boil over with emotion. Abrielle felt as if she was drowning in it.

Neither Christiansen nor Jack sent word on how she was to resolve her conflict. Perhaps it was already too late to win. Occasionally, the women's eyes would lock together, each seething with mutual contempt. Abrielle knew this woman was not truly her enemy, but after hours of enduring her intolerable insults, her patience was spent. Stanza's look become pure venom as resentment turned to smoldering rage.

In theory, Costanza was vulnerable, if Abrielle didn't make the wrong choice in the final round.

"Jack will never pick you," Stanza finally spat.

"He already has," Abrielle asserted smugly.

Her tone elicited the hoped-for effect as Costanza launched herself at Abrielle, who could have ended the struggle in a matter of seconds, but decided to toy with her adversary instead by blocking her frenzied assault. The insufferable woman deserved it, and Abrielle did have a moment of fun, at least until Stanza began to pull her hair.

"*Comprimario!*[14]" Costanza screamed in Italian.

"*Terza Donna!*[15]" Abrielle cried as she too began pulling hair.

A loud banging noise returned them to their senses as a servant entered and used the heavy, decorative staff he carried to call them to attention. He was shaking his head, his mouth agape. They released the twisted clumps of each other's hair and attempted to restore their respective strands back to the previous, more stylized fashions they'd worn all evening. Abrielle gave up and allowed hers to hang in its natural manner. Stanza was more persistent, but it ended up lopsided and became more so each time she walked. Each also worked to smooth rumpled, somewhat damaged clothing, all the while smiling sweetly to the servant as if nothing had happened.

He seemed uncertain about what to do until another servant appeared in the doorway and waved frantically at him to bring them out. He shook his head, but the other only did likewise in return. The Duke was not

---

14 secondary role for a singer in an opera; a supporting singer.

15 third most important female opera singer in a cast.

interested in problems, so the servant proceeded. The women stood side-by-side as he announced the performers for the final time. Each serenely proceeded through the door to be greeted by a silent audience, many of whom looked aghast at the performers' disheveled appearance. Only Jack looked amused.

Costanza elected to sing first. Both the Duke and Jack sat straighter in their chairs. The room descended into silence as she took her place, her arms swept upward in a dramatic manner. The *bel canto*[16] she began to sing was presented so honestly, so *cantabile*—sweetly—that even Abrielle ceased searching the crowd for any sign of Christiansen and listened. It was unlike any performance she'd witnessed thus far. She had no idea what the selection was, nor did she care, for Costanza's soul seemed to breathe for it. The words became her own as a quiet, sincere passion captivated the audience. It was a song about love, about a woman who'd been wronged by her husband, and the choice she now faced as to their fate. Her eyes never wavered from Jack's. Her arms alternately reached for him then drew away, as the music emulated her tortured state.

Jack's expression was haunted while the Duke wore one of astonishment. The music changed as determination briefly soared from singer and score alike, rising to an emotional crescendo; then it descended, ending *sotto voce*—in barely a whisper, as her arms clasped themselves protectively to her body as she sank to the floor.

Absent those who tended to their tears, the room remained enchanted by silence. The spell was only broken when wave upon wave of clapping and cries of approval began to ring through the ballroom. Costanza slowly rose from her collapsed pose and greeted her audience. The applause grew louder as the audience rose as one to meet her. She bowed and blew them kisses for what felt like several minutes.

It was during this time that Abrielle's eyes finally seized upon Christiansen. He looked extremely anxious but was largely obscured by the spectators around him. Stanza turned and bowed to Jack and the Duke, then with a final wave or two to the masses, she crossed back over the performance space to rejoin Abrielle. Her eyes flashed, as her head jerked in a short, obviously defiant motion, the taunt clear to her rival.

---

16 traditional art of Italian vocal performance; elegant.

Abrielle coolly responded to Stanza's gaze by deliberately turning from her and crossing the stage to the starting position. As she did so, Jack finally offered Abrielle some guidance. His body language would have been enough, but both the look in his eyes and the manner in which he twisted his head as he feigned adjusting his bow tie left no room for doubt. She was not to win. After what she'd just witnessed, this came as something of a relief. Abrielle would sing well enough for the competition to remain competitive, but she could finally afford to relax a measure. The nightmare was almost over. She stepped to her mark.

"Prima Donna, of France!" a voice unexpectedly yelled in French from somewhere above on the walkway. Heads turned as people sought to identify the rude speaker, but the cry was not repeated. A low buzz of conversation began as the audience commented, speculated, and joked about the distraction. Abrielle found it somewhat amusing, at least until she looked again to Christiansen. His fingers, which had been tracing his lips, parted and his mouth briefly, but clearly, formed one vital word: win.

She blinked. Her eyes darted back to Jack then once more to Christiansen who nodded a confirmation. Yes, he wanted her to win. Abrielle shook her head slightly, but he repeated the affirmation.

Her pulse thundered in her ears. She wanted to scream; she couldn't win and lose at the same time, there had to be a mistake. Maybe Christiansen hadn't had a chance to talk to Jack and was merely playing a hunch. Or could the two of them have spoken and Jack changed his mind after Costanza's performance?

The servant's plea for silence now calmed the crowd, and the musicians patiently awaited a signal from Abrielle that she was ready to begin. She took a moment and tried to clear her mind, nodded, uncertain what she was about to do, and then allowed the musical notes and her voice to become one as her final performance for the night began.

The song she'd selected was also about love, but unlike Costanza's, hers focused on its promise, joys, and gifts rather than its harsher aspects. It was a rousing celebration of the emotion, one she passionately embraced, and as she did so, a grand sense of freedom surged through her consciousness. She was singing for herself, not for Jack or Christiansen, both of whom continued to try to attract her attention as she moved about the stage. Jack looked mortified, while Christiansen beamed in approval of what she was doing.

Abrielle aggressively improvised with an array of embellishments. Mischief and energy radiated from her as she finally began to have fun. When she reached the *cadenza*[17], her voice became light, the volume low, as she employed the *mezza voce*[18] technique for dramatic effect. The music began to build around the effect as Abrielle neared the end of her performance. Her voice suddenly surged forth to catch the smoldering notes, and as the two met, a power and resonance unlike any she'd produced before erupted from her. The joy and energy of the music and the singer reached a resounding climax. Her *staccato*[19] phrasing, placed so closely together, resolved into a *polyphony*[20] effect, and for a few seconds, it sounded as if not one singer but two performed.

And then it was over. Her arms spread outward, as her torso and head bent into a stately bow. Abrielle's chest heaved as if she'd just completed one of her exercise regimens. The tips of her fingers felt light. Her emotions were running wild. What had she just done? She waited as cool rivulets of sweat crept slowly down her spine to the base of her back.

The audience was slow to react, uncertain if they enjoyed the rather unorthodox performance they'd just witnessed or not. Sporadic clapping began to be heard. Abrielle waited. Was that it? Should she stand? No, it was building; more audience members suddenly seemed to be applauding her.

By the time Abrielle finally rose, the entire ballroom reverberated with clapping and even a few spontaneous cheers. Her face again flushed both with relief and embarrassment. She had won. She bowed again to her audience and to the musicians. Finally she turned and bowed to the Duke. But Abrielle's smile faded as she glanced at Jack. He looked completely devastated.

Costanza was unabashedly distraught. Christiansen was attempting to comfort the inconsolable woman, whose hair had finally collapsed into a tangled mass of loose knots, which played about her shoulders. Marta's effort to placate her was even less successful. She walked up to the pair with Costanza's dog and uttered only one word as she held out the white

---

17 medium voice, lowers volume to emphasize emotion.

18 improvised section of the aria that features the skills of a vocalist.

19 short, sharp presentation of music or vocal notes.

20 combining a host of separate but harmonized sounds (a counterpoint).

ball of fur to her owner, "Bitch." Christiansen waved her and the whimpering dog away.

The Duke rose theatrically from his seat and presented Abrielle with a bouquet of roses, kissing her on each cheek.

"A most impressive performance, Mademoiselle Christiansen," he stated, inclining his head slightly. "I'm certain audiences in Vienna will soon agree."

She curtseyed.

"Your Lordship honors me greatly and I thank him for his generous compliments," she devoutly affirmed.

"Congratulations."

The Duke began to walk away towards Costanza. In desperation, Abrielle rushed around him and bowed.

"Mademoiselle?" he asked.

"My Lord, I mean no offense to the great honor you have seen fit to bestow upon me, but I would humbly suggest that Madame Clerval would be a more appropriate …"

"Madame Clerval," he said stiffly, "has lost. She will, therefore, continue her training in Salzburg. Have no fears, mademoiselle, she will be cared for I assure you."

The nobleman smiled unpleasantly as he took Abrielle's hand, a signal she was to rise.

"As I'm sure Jack will continue to do for you," he whispered, before he kissed her gloved hand and resumed his pursuit of Costanza.

Abrielle felt numb. All this was for nothing. Suddenly an arm wrapped around her waist, and Jack leaned in close to her ear.

"Follow me in about ten seconds and get ready to faint. Might want to work up some tears too," he suggested as he released her.

"Tears? Jack?"

"That's a good start, keep goin'," he grinned and headed into the drawing room after the others.

Abrielle counted to fifteen as she concentrated on trying to summon tears on command. It was not something she'd ever been particularly good at. She entered the drawing room just as the conversation was getting interesting.

"Didn't you just see me award her the flowers? Of course she won and will go on to perform in Vienna just as I promised," the Duke said defensively.

"Glad to hear it," Jack commented as he wrapped an arm protectively around his wife. "It's been an interestin' night, your Lordship, but if you don't terribly mind, I think my wife needs to go home and rest."

Both the Duke and Costanza were about to offer protests when Jack suddenly halted.

"I won that little wager of ours, too, didn't I?"

The Duke, clearly caught unaware, took a moment to recover.

"Wager, Jack? What are you wagering on now?" Costanza threw up her hands in exasperation. Jack put on a look of innocent surprise.

"What, the Duke here didn't tell you?"

"Jack, I'm sure we can settle this quietly before you leave. It was after all a *gentlemen's wager*," the Duke stated, emphasizing the final words.

"Jack?" Abrielle weighed in, the name wrought with confusion as the tears she'd worked to summon began to materialize.

"Oh dear," Jack said solemnly and nodded to Christiansen who moved closer to Abrielle. Jack took her hand and looked apologetically into her eyes.

"Mademoiselle Christiansen, it has been an honor to assist your family, my dear friends, in your collective efforts to help introduce your immeasurable talents to the people of Austria, and I am overjoyed that you'll now have an opportunity to share them on the stages of Vienna, but you know my heart is here, with my beloved Costanza."

Abrielle's tears began to flow freely.

"Jack ...," she sobbed pitifully.

"Please Jack," Christiansen began as he laid a restraining hand on Abrielle's shoulder, "I must apologize for my niece's continued unseemly behavior. You have been most patient and understanding these past few months. She is young and ..."

"No, no," Abrielle protested weakly. "Jack, I sang for you. I did this for you."

"So did my wife," Jack observed as he too kissed Abrielle's hand.

"But I love you," Abrielle's voice trembled with emotion.

"I'm sorry but there can never be more than this between us," Jack stated matter-of-factly. His eyes flashed at hers, and seconds after receiving his signal, she collapsed into a heap upon the floor.

"Oh my. Make room please. Give her some air," Christiansen commanded as he knelt beside her.

The Duke signaled to a servant who fetched some water. As the others worked to revive Abrielle, Costanza gently reached out and touched her husband's face. Their eyes met. He took her hand, kissed it tenderly, and held it within his own.

"Stanza, my dear Stanza. You were amazing tonight."

"Oh, Jack," she gushed.

The Duke was red-faced with anger.

"Sir! Explain yourself," he roared at Jack.

"The fault is mine, your Lordship," Christiansen announced, bowing as he interceded. "As you have heard tonight, my niece is immensely talented, but troubled when it comes to governing her heart. Her French father left her all but penniless, and I was desperate to provide a better life for her. I knew one could be guaranteed her in Austria. I turned to Jack because I trusted him and needed his wisdom and experience. I'm afraid this caused his prolonged absences from Salzburg. But your Lordship, Madame Clerval, I assure you, Jack has remained faithful."

No one spoke. Jack beamed and cleared his throat. Then he reached into his jacket pocket and withdrew a cigar.

"But you bet against her," the Duke's eyes narrowed as he nodded towards Costanza. Jack lit his cigar, calmly blew out the match, and inhaled deeply.

"Actually, your Lordship, I believe you'll find I bet very much for her." The words escaped in a cloud of smoke, most of which wafted into the Duke's face. "Now, if you please, I would very much appreciate it if you would quietly honor your part of our agreement."

The livid Duke left without another word, his servants trailing behind him.

Jack smiled. Constanza smacked him.

"Owho, what was that for?"

"You bet against me?"

"Did you or did you not just have the greatest performance of your life? Besides, we aren't leavin' here empty-handed. Remember how I always said me playin' cards with nobles would pay off someday? Well, guess how much the Duke owes."

Christiansen knelt down as the Clervals whispered anxiously to one another.

"You were brilliant, Abrielle. Just lie still until we're in the carriage," he whispered. That would be difficult. She wasn't certain how much longer she could hold back the urge to laugh.

"Really?" Costanza suddenly burst out joyously as she jumped into her husband's arms and began to kiss him passionately. "Oh Jack!"

*

General de Corps d' A'rmee Ouellet was a practical man, a fact which had both hindered and helped his military career. He was respected, but not well understood. For instance, many on his staff failed to appreciate why he would forgo his dress uniform on those rare occasions when he sought local entertainment. His personal aide, Tellier, was among his critics of this practice. Of course he was probably also self-conscious about being ordered to dress as a civilian. True, it was a breech of etiquette, but such social occasions did afford Ouellet the opportunity to interact informally with the locals, some of whom recognized him and others who did not, which gave him an advantage. People were often more free with their thoughts and conversations when no uniform was present. It made him more approachable. And as Imperial military attaché to this region, it was important that he maintain such perceptions. It helped keep one's senses from being dulled by months spent in this respectable but lackluster posting. Though he longed to be once more on the battlefield, he doubted that he'd ever have the opportunity again. He was too perfect a fit for this job—an experienced commander, but one whose record was far from unblemished.

He believed that subtlety was a key factor in one's ability to maintain power, a notion not always shared by his superiors. And as his carriage finally departed the Duke's impressive residence, his superiors were foremost on his mind.

"Clerval certainly keeps things interesting around here," his aide noted after they'd been riding in silence for several minutes.

"Players in the black market often do," Ouellet remarked distractedly. Was there any significance to the fact that the two were linked? Could Clerval be aware of whom she was? Was Intelligence getting ready to shut down Clerval's activities or merely monitoring them? He hoped the latter.

Jack Clerval was no threat. He catered to all sides equally and was a known entity. If removed, who could predict what sort would succeed him or how it might shift the balance of power. How did this Christiansen factor into it all?

Ouellet always disliked dealing with Imperial Intelligence. They invariably made life more difficult. And things were progressively becoming worse with the retirement of its enigmatic head and the Empire's expansion.

"Apparently," Tellier continued, "there was some type of altercation between the Duke and Clerval after the performance. I heard he ended up sending Clerval and his wife home in his personal carriage."

Ouellet smirked.

"Yes, I'd heard something to that effect."

It did explain the Duke's sour demeanor as they were leaving. His longstanding interests in Costanza Clerval were far from a secret in Salzburg. Tellier nodded.

"Surprising after the way Clerval's been displaying his mistress all over Salzburg this week."

Ouellet only grunted a noncommittal noise. Tellier pressed on. He was keen to discover why his superior seemed so distracted this evening, and why he'd ordered Tellier to conceal himself in a stairwell and shout that the lady was the Prima Donna of France.

"Perhaps the change has something to do with Mademoiselle Christiansen's collapse after the performance," the military aide postulated. He was pleased when his innocent comment elicited a response.

The General de Corps had been uncertain if the beautiful French singer was indeed the same young woman who he'd sat in several intelligence debriefings with years earlier. Her guise and demeanor were quite different then. It wasn't until she appeared with her hair down and looked up to the balcony when Tellier had shouted his pronouncement that he felt certain she was. As such, he'd lingered in the grand hallway conversing after the final performance hoping to reintroduce himself, and that in doing so, he'd be able to eventually learn why she was here.

"I was not aware of this," Ouellet sternly stated.

"Yes, the Mademoiselle was carried out the back and put into another coach with her uncle. I only learned of it myself shortly before we left. Apologies, sir, I thought you knew," Tellier rapidly explained.

Ouellet clenched his jaw and glared out the window. Damn Imperial Intelligence and their secrets. They'd already caused him enough misery in his life. If they were running an operation, one that led to destabilization in this key sector, it would not be the espionage experts who suffered for the consequences. Past experience in dealing with these types had already taught him that bitter lesson. He turned and wagged a finger at his aide.

"For the time being, Tellier, this matter will not go beyond us, understand?"

His surprised and confused aide nodded.

"Good. I have reason to suspect that Intelligence is running an operation absent of our knowledge, and believe me when I tell you they are experts on shifting the blame to the ignorant when such operations fail."

Tellier blinked as he tried to follow the reasoning behind his superior's speculations. Was the older man simply desperate to make up for past mistakes or could there really be substance to his reasoning—real danger? He certainly did not wish to be assigned to this post forever, labeled incompetent as his superior officer already had. He could think of only one possibility for this sudden paranoia.

"The Christiansen woman? An Imperial spy?"

Ouellet nodded.

"How do you know this?"

"I dealt with her before, years ago, smart, that one. I was hoping to have a word with her before she left, clarify the situation, but she'll likely vanish now. Their type always does."

They were silent a moment.

"I'll pull our recent communiqués, but offhand, I don't recall any impending Intelligence operations being mentioned," Tellier pondered. "Should we try to shadow any of them? The woman, the Clervals …?"

"No, no. If there is something going on and we interfere, there will be hell to pay. Intelligence has no tact, but they always expect us to, and we lost our opportunity to approach her casually tonight."

"Then what should we do, sir?"

Ouellet considered the matter a moment.

"We'll handle this delicately. Too many have already bled for this land. We're just being cautious. I still have one or two contacts in the intelligence community. I'll try to contact them, see what they can tell us. In the meantime, start to take a closer look into the Duke's activities, the Clervals, and this Christiansen character. They're probably linked, somehow."

It felt good to be giving meaningful orders again. Suddenly the carriage drew to a halt, marking their arrival at the barracks.

"And the woman?" Tellier inquired.

Ouelett shook his head.

"At the moment I can't remember her name. But it will come to me."

*

CHAPTER 20
THORNS

She looked tranquil, and to his great surprise, hardly stirred when he entered the room. He half expected to be greeted by a knife flying through the door or a pistol to be trained on him. But instead she slept.

He hadn't stopped thinking about her since he'd left, though increasingly, his thoughts took him to darker places where she was concerned. Espen sat down in the chair by the window at the foot of the bed and silently studied her untroubled face, half-hidden by locks of her loose brown hair. Even asleep, there was an aura about her. Her breathing rhythmically stirred the sheets. Her scent adorned the room. Did he love this woman or hate her? Was she simply using him or did she actually have feelings for him?

His gaze did not stray from Abrielle for a long time.

"What are you thinking?" she finally mumbled. She'd given no indication whatsoever that she was awake.

"How long have you known I was here?" he asked in English.

She turned without opening her eyes.

"Since I heard the key in the lock," she answered sleepily.

He groaned in annoyance.

"You should not fool people in such ways," Espen admonished.

She stretched and drew in a deep breath. Her brown eyes slowly drew open.

"It's what I do," Abrielle reminded him, with the faintest of smiles. "We're alone," she added by way of an invitation for him to either talk or climb into bed with her. Though both Christiansen and Jack seemed to suspect that something existed between her and Espen, both exercised the good sense not to say anything. A fact for which she was grateful as she herself did not know what to think of it.

Espen did not move, only turned his gaze out the window. Abrielle curled herself around the pillow she held and watched him. Neither spoke.

"I'm glad you're back," she said quietly after a time. The voice of the clock on the nightstand spoke into the void. She waited patiently. His demeanor was much different than when he'd left, then again, he'd now had many hours alone to ponder, where she had not.

Espen was angry with himself, furious with his father, conflicted about Abrielle, and scared of what would happen now that he was back. But there was really no choice. And so he'd returned to Salzburg.

"I did not see her," he finally declared.

Abrielle's expression became melancholy for a moment.

"Did anyone see you?"

He made no attempt to answer and was still unwilling to look at her.

"Espen?"

"What would you have me do?"

The sudden anger in his voice took her aback.

"Right now I just wish you'd talk to me," she answered honestly but attained little by way of response. "I never said this would be easy, any of it."

Her eyes searched him.

"You still don't trust me? Do you?"

"We might lead the enemy to them," Espen said defensively, skillfully evading her questions. With limited options, she decided to play along.

"Were you followed?" She waited before repeating the question.

"No, but …," he sighed in disgust, unable to bring himself to raise the paramount thought in his heart.

Abrielle donned a robe and sat on the end of the bed, crossing her feet. Espen still refused to look at her. Was he angry because he was still jealous of Jack's attentions towards her? Was he upset because she'd forbidden him to rescue Tara on his own? She reached out a hand, which he recoiled from. She'd have to try something else.

"Espen, all I want …"

He glimpsed at her for only an instant, his expression hard. She took a breath and continued.

"All I want is to rescue my niece. It's not that I don't trust you, but if you attempted to save her and something went wrong …"

"And is that all you want?" he challenged, finally meeting her gaze.

Her lips parted as each looked deeply into the other's eyes. The question smoldered between them. Was he asking her for a future together? How could she make him understand?

"Tara is my life, Espen," Abrielle whispered, "and until she's safe …"

She looked away as the words died upon her lips, uncertain how to conclude her thought. She'd been able to ignore the future, only rescuing Tara mattered. Confronted anew by the issue, however, she now realized how delicate such thoughts seemed. The future was a mystery, one her heart would not allow her to explore beyond the present. There was too much at stake to dream. Espen stood and walked several paces from her.

"And what would you have me do to save her?"

Abrielle swallowed.

"Just get me to the camp."

"You don't need me for that. You have Jack."

So that was it.

"Please don't start," she held her head and exhaled a heavy sigh. "Jack is back with his wife. And he doesn't know exactly where your clan is now, remember? I need you."

Espen refused to be pacified.

"No, but we both know if he found them before, he can do so again. If I was not here, you would not allow such a thing to stop you."

She was fed up.

"If you're not going to help, then just go home," she tersely suggested as she stood and left the room.

She was sick of this petty jealousy. He followed close on her heels.

"Why, so you can track me like you did before?" he demanded.

Abrielle did her best to suppress her rising frustrations as she rounded on him.

"I didn't even know who you really were then, and you lied about your name for days after I found you. Dammit, why are you acting like this?"

Espen continued unfazed.

"The whole trip I asked myself why. Why does she really need me? What advantage do I give her?"

Abrielle shook her head. The trip was initially Espen's idea, but it was also true that it served several of her own purposes as well. It kept Jack and him separate while she trained. She hoped Espen would be able to quickly find his people so they could do likewise when they left Salzburg, and most importantly, the trip had allowed Espen an opportunity to witness for himself his father's unforgivable sin against Abrielle's family. Before he left, despite all evidence to the contrary, some part of him had still refused to believe his father was capable of such a barbarous act.

"Oh, and you've figured it out, have you?" she shot sarcastically.

Espen glared at her, but his voice became very soft.

"What will you do to my father when you find him?"

The words beckoned forth the darkest recesses of her soul. At the mere mention of Jal, Abrielle's eyes burned with the rage and pain of seething hatred she worked so hard to contain.

"Kill him?" Espen prompted.

"He took everything from me," her icy voice trembled as she spoke, stalking towards him.

"And you would do the same to me?" Espen incredulously asked. "My sisters, my mother, my grandmother, all dead, and you would take my father from me as well? Even ask me to help you destroy him?"

Abrielle hesitated only a moment before responding. She would not be dissuaded now. She'd known only fear and suffering all these terrible months because of Jal.

"After what he's done, your father doesn't deserve to live!"

"And when you fell off that cliff in the Pyrenees, you did?" Espen asked quietly.

Abrielle froze, and suddenly she was hiding behind her glare. Time evaporated. When it resumed, she turned away in anguish, only to find herself reflected in the room's large wall mirror. Disgusted, she shrieked and without thought, hurtled a nearby candlestick at it. An arcing array of cracks appeared throughout the thick glass, testifying to the brute force of the impact. Her breaths were short; her pulse deafening.

"It's different," she affirmed at last, as she attempted to regain control.

"No, it's not," Espen countered. "Your mistakes are different, your crimes are different, but life and death are the same."

"And what do you know of life and death?" she contested.

Espen's head hung slightly as he answered.

"Only that I've known too little of one, and far too much of the other."

Abrielle ran a hand over her forehead and down her neck as she turned on her heel away from him. Espen quietly sat down behind her and waited as she crossed her arms and stood silently brooding in the shaft of sunlight that shone through the balcony doors. She did not speak.

"I can never forgive my father for what he's done or the pain that he's caused," Espen finally declared, "and I think we have a chance to restore your niece to you. But I will not allow you to kill him."

Abrielle laughed bitterly.

"Tara's life for your father's," she said without turning.

Espen nodded.

"It is balance," he observed darkly.

The silence stood between them for only a moment.

"I'm going to get dressed," she declared, without deigning to look back at him.

"We will have to hurry," Espen called after her, "he expects me back in a few days."

Abrielle halted.

"You spoke to him," she stated flatly. Her only request had been that he not reveal himself to the Wild Rose clan.

"I did."

The reverberations when she slammed the door to her room shut caused several of the nearby paintings to clatter nervously against the walls. After several minutes of thunderous silence, Espen leaned further back in his chair, exhausted after the fight and days of travel. Still he did not close his eyes, instead, they gazed intently at the impassive door. No, this was the last time he'd allow her to leave his sight until this was all over; one way or another.

*

It was well into the afternoon by the time Christiansen arrived in response to her summons.

"Afraid the unpacking is going slower than either of us would like," he commented as she poured him some tea. His eyes kept drifting involuntarily to the heavily damaged wall mirror and the stone-faced gypsy seated next to him.

"Ah, thank you."

Espen made no motion to acquire a cup, nor did Abrielle offer one, as they transparently avoided one another. Christiansen stirred the contents of his and listened to the rain drops against the windows, grateful for something to focus on other than the festering tension in the room. After blowing the steam off her own cup and taking a sip, Abrielle continued the conversation as if she didn't have a care in the world.

"What does your wife think of Salzburg?" she inquired casually of Christiansen.

"Actually, I'm not sure how it suits her," he shook his head as he took out a cigarette. "The past few days have been so …"

The door to the apartments suddenly swung open.

"Sorry I'm late," Jack declared loudly, shaking off rainwater as he walked in. "Hell of a day. Had a prowler last night and Stanza's … oh," his words vanished at the sight of Espen. Neither man offered the other any type of greeting.

"Have some tea, Jack," Abrielle suggested, indicating that he should sit in the vacant seat next to her, which visibly annoyed Espen.

Jack recovered immediately.

"Well then, don't mind if I do."

"You had a prowler?" Christiansen asked as Jack settled in.

"Apparently," Jack observed, studying the cup Abrielle gave him as if he'd never considered drinking tea before. "Whole study was wrecked, broken window, somebody was lookin' for somethin', I'll tell you that."

He abandoned the tea and reached for a biscuit.

"Well, did they take anything?" Christiansen pressed as Jack absently considered his first bite, before taking his second.

"Huh?" Jack exclaimed before nodding in the affirmative.

"What did they take?" Abrielle asked pointedly.

"I bet it was the Duke's men," Jack managed as he chewed.

"Why?" the older man asked.

"Well, they took that fake letter of yours."

"That was all?" Christiansen asked in puzzlement.

Jack shrugged as he scooped a handful of biscuits from the tray.

"Far as I can tell, place is a real mess and like I started to say, Stanza's not handlin' it all too well."

"How surprising," Christiansen observed wryly.

Jack grinned.

"Might be 'cause she's exhausted. We haven't been sleepin' too much," he winked at Christiansen before turning to Abrielle then Espen. "Or maybe 'cause she's nervous about leavin' for Vienna tomorrow as your replacement, or perhaps she's worried it was thievin' gypsies breakin' in, who knows."

"Has your house ever been broken into before?" Abrielle quickly asked before Espen could begin to protest. Jack's amusement suddenly vanished.

"Yeah, once. Last time Ern was here, in fact. The same night that giant hobgoblin made a grab for him during Stanza's performance."

No one spoke for a moment.

"What is hobgoblin?" Espen asked in confusion.

"Good Lord, do you think he's back?" Christiansen asked in alarm.

"I was just assumin' that the Duke was still sore about Stanza and the wager and the like," Jack said quietly as he reached habitually into his coat pocket for a cigar.

The Duke did indeed have excellent reasons to be perturbed. The loss of money he could ill-afford to part with was one thing. The blissful reunion of Jack and Costanza under his own roof was another. But, as if all this wasn't traumatic enough, when he called upon Christiansen the day after the competition, he learned that the man's niece had apparently suffered a total nervous collapse. This was an unfortunate result of her losing Jack, and, therefore, she'd been sent back to France to recover with her nearest relation, lest she embarrass the family further. Abrielle even scribed a brief, drama-laced note to help sell the fraud.

This forced the Duke, now desperate to fulfill his obligations in Vienna, to seek out the Clervals and beg for Costanza to perform in her rival's place. Abrielle's note was taken as proof of the Duke's sincere need. The entire experience was rife with humiliation and would undoubtedly some day incur retribution between the longstanding rivals.

Christiansen, whose wife had now joined him from Geneva, moved into his own apartments several blocks away. Since the performance, Abrielle ventured out only sparingly and dressed far differently than her operatic persona.

"Wouldn't the Duke be the only one who knew that he'd left the note with you?" Christiansen pointed out.

Jack nodded as he stuffed the cigar back in his pocket, in favor of his flask. He still couldn't break himself of the habit of not smoking when Abrielle was around.

"So he's probably responsible," Christiansen asserted.

"Just glad I left Stanza with my parents before I came. You don't think they're in danger, do ya?"

Abrielle shook her head.

"If the thief was that specific about what he took, I doubt it. Christiansen, perhaps you should consider setting up your temporary office in Vienna, not here," Abrielle suggested as she searched her memory for any other recent, unusual occurrences the others had mentioned. She could recall none. It was certainly possible that the Moon Shadows could have followed Christiansen's wife from Geneva, but why would they then take Abrielle's fake letter, and how would they know where to look for it? Ideally, she would have examined Jack's study before she left, but under the circumstances, she doubted she'd have time. The older man shook his head.

"I'm not certain my marriage would withstand another move, Abrielle. Besides, I'm in enough trouble already because of you three."

"Exaggeratin' a bit aren't we, Christiansen," Jack said smugly as he downed more of his flask's contents.

"Having to explain kidnappings, fictional nieces, fraud, and you people is no small matter. And neither is asking my wife to suddenly pick up and move hundreds of miles," Christiansen bristled.

Jack raised his hands in mock defense as he replaced the flask in his coat pocket, patted it, and smacked his lips together.

"So is this somethin' we've got to worry about or what?" he asked of the group.

"Since we're all leaving tomorrow, I'd say no," Abrielle answered, fervently wishing she felt more certain about her conclusion.

Christiansen rolled his eyes in frustration. Hadn't they heard a word he'd just said?

"Right," said Jack agreeably. "Where to now?"

"You're both going to Vienna," Abrielle instructed. "But Jack won't be staying."

"And where exactly will you be?" Christiansen asked.

"Traveling, with my husband," she replied frostily. Both men suddenly looked as if they'd drop dead from astonishment.

"Husband?" Jack stammered, following her eyes and locking his own onto the young gypsy seated across from him.

"It is the easiest way to get her into our camp," Espen explained, flashing a grin of superiority at Jack who immediately popped up from his chair.

"Of all the … you're not actually gonna marry that … that …"

"Jack!" Christiansen admonished.

" … person, are you?"

Abrielle refused to answer Jack until he resumed his seat. He did so grudgingly.

"No, but Espen's right; it's the easiest way to get me close to Tara."

Abrielle's tone sounded as if she were trying to convince herself of this fact, rather than the others.

"Hardly," challenged Jack. "You don't think that's gonna raise a whole host of questions like how'd he just luck into endin' up with you when he was supposed to be out rescuin' people?"

"I have already provided my father with an explanation," Espen stated calmly.

"Oh, this oughta be good. Mind cluin' us in then too?"

Espen nodded.

"I told him that during my failed mission to rescue the Moon Shadow captives and subsequent escape, I was grievously injured but was discovered by a Rom woman who revived my health and with whom I fell in love. We were married in a ceremony performed by her people, and so she comes to our clan as my wife."

A heavy tension smoldered between Espen and Abrielle, one that hadn't been present before, Jack and Christiansen privately noted, rekindled during the gypsy's explanation. Both glared at the other with resentment. For once, Jack decided not to enter the fray, mindful of all Abrielle had recently subjected herself to on his behalf.

"Okay, so let's assume that all works, then what?" Jack asked.

"We wait," Abrielle said harshly as she and Espen's eyes finally parted. "Wait for an opportunity for me to get Tara out of the camp safely."

Jack leaned back and crossed his leg, resting his foot on his knee as he stretched an arm out behind Abrielle and looked directly at Espen.

"I've got a few problems with this plan of yours, gypsy. Just how long are we supposed to wait for this rescue opportunity?"

Espen's gaze never wavered from Jack's.

"I can't be precise, but my father insisted that I return within a week's time. All he said was an hour of retribution was at hand, one I would be needed for."

"That doesn't sound very promising," Christiansen noted, raising his eyebrows. "Did he tell you about Tara? Did you actually see her there?"

Espen shook his head.

"I strayed across one of our patrols, and Father rode out to meet us. Everyone seemed to be greatly on edge. We spent most of our time discussing my failed mission. I mentioned my new wife, whom I had left behind while I sought out our clan. He bid my immediate return and we parted. I never ventured inside the camp."

"The point is that whatever is about to happen could either endanger Tara or give us a chance to free her," Abrielle explained. "Either way we need to hurry."

Jack scoffed.

"And if you can get to her, do you actually believe that dear old dad's not gonna wonder where his son's new wife and the baby he stole suddenly went. End up huntin' you down is what'll happen."

Abrielle's countenance grew dark.

"We'll deal with that," she promised, a ruthless menace in her voice.

Espen's eyes watched her closely.

"I don't see how," Christiansen commented soberly. "This sounds like an awful risk. Who knows what he'll do if you're caught. And it's not a simple matter to escape from an armed camp, then there's wilderness to endure."

Jack nodded in affirmation.

"We're leavin' an awful lot to chance here. Too many things could go wrong."

"I know," Abrielle said gravely as she momentarily gazed down to the scar on her right hand. Her fingers began to trace its length. "That's why you're coming too, Jack."

He blinked in surprise then smacked his knee and wagged a finger, punctuating the air.

"That's more like it. Now what am I playin'? The brother you couldn't leave behind?"

"A shadow," Espen answered, crossing his arms appraisingly, wondering if this swaggering loud-mouthed man could manage to do what would be required of him and remain hidden. Or would he be their downfall? To Espen, the man was nothing except a liability, but Abrielle was obstinate that he be included.

"The clan is in the Carpathians near Miskolc. Espen will make you a map. You'll take Costanza to Vienna tomorrow and meet us two days after we've arrived in Hungary. We should have more intelligence by then and can plan a safe means of escape," Abrielle said hopefully.

Jack's face was lined deeply with concern, but he only issued a determined nod.

"Long as you're keepin' me in the action this time, I'm with you. Not sure how Stanza's gonna handle me leavin' though."

"Well, find some credible explanation that doesn't lead me into another singing competition," Abrielle requested, as she took another sip of her tea.

"Why? Worked out all right this last time, Mademoiselle Christiansen," Jack asserted as he kissed the back of her free hand.

She shook her head and smiled. Espen, however, looked far from amused.

"Anything from Ern?" Jack asked ignoring the young gypsy and shifting the conversation as he turned to Christiansen whose eyes immediately fell, his heart suddenly heavy with emotion at the mention of his godson's name.

"Nothing," he replied dejectedly, "And my wife brought me all the recent posts from Geneva when she came."

Silence reigned as unspoken nightmares unfolded to each, as they pondered the fate of the missing; or were they now the dead? Finally, Jack cleared his throat.

"Guess we'll just have to go rescue him next then," he stated in a poor attempt at levity.

Abrielle's cup and saucer clattered to the table as she hastily stood, her manner betraying confusion as to her purpose for doing so.

"I'm going to pack," she declared distractedly and disappeared into her room.

"What'd I say now?"

"Learn when to shut up someday, Jack," Christiansen snapped as he stood.

Jack sheepishly lit his cigar and shifted in his seat as he reached into his coat pocket.

"Here," he declared as he laid a hefty sum of bound bank notes on the table.

"What's that for?" Christiansen sputtered.

"I know how particular you get about money, so there's what she borrowed from Ernie's safe with interest, courtesy of the Duke. Wanted to make sure I left that with you just in case none of us make it back," Jack explained through a haze of smoke, nodding for Christiansen to pick up the money, which he did.

"Thank you," he said grudgingly.

"Don't mention it," Jack replied as Christiansen left the room.

Alone now, Jack and Espen silently regarded each other. Jack exhaled a toxic burst of smoke.

"I don't like you," he stated simply pointing his cigar at the other man. "You're like a useless stray dog that can't take a hint when to get lost."

He replaced the smoldering roll in his mouth and waited.

"I don't like you either," Espen grinned. "You're simply a desperate lap dog who barks incessantly so people will notice him."

Jack smirked through a swirl of smoke. If they were going to be forced to work together, he preferred their open hatred to pleasant deceit. At least that was honest, and despite their differences, honesty was something that both men could respect.

"So you gonna get on with drawing me a map or are you planning on pullin' some lame gypsy hoax like trying to talk me into buying a magic horse that always knows the way home?"

*

Christiansen entered Abrielle's room unannounced to discover her pacing erratically. The veneer of calm she possessed when he first arrived was completely vanished now, the months of unyielding stress and fear telling upon her face. She was so frantic that she didn't even initially notice his presence. She offered no protests, gave no acknowledgement, as she remained lost in her frenzied state of mind.

"Abrielle?" Christiansen waited a moment for her to respond. Her random wanderings continued.

"Abrielle!"

She caught her breath and turned to face him as if she'd just been discovered committing a crime. Her eyes darted madly about for a moment before she stopped against a wall and slowly sank to the floor, holding the back of her head with her hands.

"It's too much. It's too much," she repeated, a vacant look upon her face.

Her heart and her mind were too deeply divided. There were too many factors she could not reconcile. Christiansen knelt beside her.

"You don't have to do this."

"I do," she said numbly, memories of her last attempt to infiltrate an encampment disguised as a Rom gypsy fresh in her mind. That mission had nearly resulted in her death and set Imperial Intelligence at her heels. What if she saved Tara only to fall back into their hands?

"We can find another way," Christiansen promised. "Jack and I have contacts in Geneva, men we'd trust with our lives, who could bring a strong force …"

"No, no. Jal will kill Tara if we try something like that. Ernest said so. He would have killed her that night if I hadn't …," she struggled to suppress the guilt. "Our only hope is surprise."

"Our only hope is rational thought," Christiansen passionately corrected. "You clearly have no faith in this plan, and if it results in getting you killed, what becomes of your niece then? You may be all she has left in this world. Have you even thought about that?"

Abrielle looked away with tears gleaming in her eyes. Christiansen continued.

"And we're doing all of this based solely on Espen's word. We know almost nothing about him. His motives for helping us are certainly questionable at best. And none of us really know if he's telling the truth about what happened while he was gone. It could all be a ruse. He could be planning to double cross you just as his father did to Ernest."

Abrielle's hands dropped to her lap as she took a deep breath.

"Ernest trusted me to do this," she said in a trembling voice. "Ailis, trusted me."

"They did," Christiansen agreed soberly, squeezing her hand. "And you've been amazing. But this may not be the only way."

"And what if it is?" Abrielle demanded, recoiling from him. "You think I should just sit here and wait for this 'hour of retribution' to happen?"

"That could mean anything, have no connection whatsoever to Tara," he asserted. "But it could be just what he needs to say to ensure that you'll walk willingly into a trap, like you did before."

She closed her eyes, her body and mind collectively recalling the horrific price she'd paid for Chloe's betrayal.

"That wasn't because of him."

"Are you sure? From what you've told me, there were several times that the woman you were supposedly working with could have talked to him without your knowledge."

Her brown eyes shone when the lids drew open.

"He could have died when we went over the falls," she said defensively.

"Perhaps he chose that," Christiansen suggested. "It sounds like he would have died as their prisoner. But above all people, you should know that when faced with extreme choices, people will do just about anything to survive. And you don't know the extent of his injuries. You were blind."

"Then why did he save me?" she challenged, her heart raging.

Christiansen was not about to back down.

"Say he's working with the Imperials now, that they've continued to shadow you all this time. Think about all he's learned since he met you that they couldn't. Who you're working with? What your strengths and weaknesses are? The scope of your resources? What you seek and how you plan to get it? Information that's useful for either them or his father's purposes."

Abrielle stood. Christiansen followed her lead.

"You sound like Jack," she darkly asserted as she crossed the room to the bed. Christiansen grabbed her by the arm and forced her to look at him. If she didn't settle this crisis of faith, her indecision and emotional turmoil could very well lead them all to disaster. She must be absolutely certain that her choice in this moment was the right one.

"Maybe I do, but never forget that Jack is willing to surrender his life to help you, as Ernest was, because they both believe in you. They both believe that you will bring Tara home. And you need to decide right now if the risks of this plan are worth their sacrifices because if you're wrong, you may all die."

They gazed intensely at one another. She shook him off, the hardness slowly returning to her eyes, as her resolve stiffened. If she failed to act, Tara would die. She believed that in her heart. *Aut viam inveniam aut faciam. Either I shall find a way or I will make one.* All that mattered was fulfilling her oath to her family, in this there was hope. If Espen was a traitor, then she must be ready to act.

"We leave before dawn," she commanded. "Be ready."

Christiansen held her eyes a moment longer before he made his way to the door.

"And if you're wrong," he asked.

Her thumb traced the scar on her right palm, as her chilling voice betrayed the scars within.

"If I'm wrong, if Tara dies … then I'll kill them all."

Chapter 21
Fractured Innocence

"Traitor," the dying woman mouthed soundlessly for a second time as her eyelids again drew closed.

This subsequent pronouncement elicited a new curiosity from Tasaria, whereas the first time the accusation was mouthed, fear and guilt motivated her response. Initially it caught her off guard, in part because Vochallet's moments of lucidity were increasingly brief. What if someone else saw the voiceless indictment?

Tasaria swung her face towards the doorway, but it remained sealed. Then a new thought assaulted her. Could Vochallet somehow know that Tasaria had disobeyed her Master, committing an unthinkable act of betrayal, one even she herself did not fully understand? The Master trusted her to relinquish her control over the Old One, actually commanded it. Why had she failed to do so? By now the Old One could be anywhere in the fortress. Would its actions expose her secret disloyalty?

Tasaria attempted to reassure herself. No, she was projecting her own fears. She'd said nothing while in the room that would have revealed anything regarding this matter to the wounded Wild Rose woman. She could always claim she'd simply forgotten to mitigate her control over the Old Ones, that the combinations of stress and alcohol, not deception, were to blame for her mistake. But this excuse too would be a lie, little more than an elaborate plea for the Master's mercy. Should she try to locate the Old One before Pias returned to tell her it was time for them to leave?

Reason trumped emotion. Given her circumstances, it was simply impractical to attempt to locate the Old One she sought. She would remain with Vochallet, though there was precious little she could actually do to aid the unfortunate woman.

"Traitor," the unfortunate prisoner mouthed uselessly again.

Tasaria's response this time was more thoughtful as Vochallet's consciousness abated again. She studied the pitiable woman's body as it fought dearly for each breath. It seemed a battle that could have but one result.

They'd never really known each other, but still they shared a past. Vochallet, unlike the other Wild Rose prisoners, was old enough to recall the vivid details of their lives before and the events leading into, the war. For her, the accusation was a literal truth. Tasaria could only be a traitor to the clan, not a leader and a prophet as she was to the Moon Shadows. Vochallet struggled for another breath.

"I'm sorry. I wish you could understand." Tasaria whispered to her unconscious enemy.

Tasaria never wanted the war, but still it had happened and brought untold miseries to them all. Of course, that was the price of pride. There could be no other outcome when all parties viewed their faith as incorruptible fact. Her guilt shifted as another notion emerged. Perhaps Vochallet was not even really seeing her. Could 'traitor' refer to her disturbed companions? She shuddered. What could have happened in this room?

Earlier, after leaving the dining chamber, Tasaria returned to her own room and fell asleep for a time. The shrouded figure of Isyll, Tasaria's spectral mother, and her beloved husband haunted her dreams until she suddenly awoke with a start. Her heart was pounding with the certainty that there was danger, her ears rang as if someone had been shouting, but the room remained silent.

When no imminent threat emerged, Tasaria attempted to banish her misgivings. She hadn't meant to sleep so long and hurried to Vochallet's chamber to watch over her as the Master had bidden. When she arrived, she discovered the prisoner's room was dark and bitterly cold, an unpleasant aura tainted it. She could hear faint noises from within, but no one answered her repeated summons. Unable to visually penetrate the gloom, she retrieved the guards from the bottom of the stairwell and sent word to the Master that something was wrong. Those remaining took up torches and entered the room. When Pias arrived with their Dark Lord, those within were still attempting to unravel the bizarre sights that greeted them.

All of the women were burnt, though not severely. Stone, wood, bedding, clothing, and flesh were also pitted and scorched; traces of wax littered every inch of the room. Could they have been trying to kill themselves?

Baseria and Etolie were huddled together on one of the beds, quaking uncontrollably, each nearly catatonic with fear as they clung fiercely to one another. Vochallet appeared to be even more fragile: her breathes barely audible, her face damp with sweat, her skin the color of fresh snow.

Neither Pias nor the Master entered the room, instead, an intense, hushed conference was hastily held in the entryway from which the ominous shadow vacated first.

"Bring them," Pias commanded the guards, indicating Etolie and Baseria.

"Pias, what …," Tasaria began.

He held up a hand, never bothering to look directly at her.

"If you still want that one to live, tend to her," he stated, pointing indifferently to Vochallet.

"What are you going to do with them?" she demanded, but Baseria began to shriek and sob hysterically the moment the guards tried to separate her from Etolie. Her frantic struggles ultimately proved useless, and she was hauled from the room with Pias following close behind.

Etolie's reaction, though, was far different and more disquieting. She'd risen slowly from the bed and allowed her hands to be bound by the remaining guards. As this was done, she turned her vacant gaze upon Vochallet, and a profound and haunted look of both guilt and remorse settled upon her face. She left the room without a word.

Uncertain of what she should do, Tasaria sat down and examined Vochallet. The burns on her arms and face looked painful, but the woman was mercifully unconscious. Tasaria wrestled with her emotions. Was her niece responsible for this?

She should be interrogating the Wild Rose women with the others. Her eyes roved endlessly across the room, eager to decipher clues. Food finally arrived for her, as well as word that she was to remain with Vochallet until summoned by the Master. Reluctantly, she had done so.

As the trying hours passed, she decided to attempt the employment of a basic healing technique her mother had taught her. It did not require an intense connection to the powers of the unseen world and might revive Vochallet to some degree. This could ultimately prove useful in the interrogation of the others, and if nothing else, it gave Tasaria something to do. Her consciousness stretched outward as she meditated and touched the Elemental Winds. The effect was not dramatic or even visible, but it did convey a subtle, but powerful notion to Vochallet's mind and body that deeper breathes could be taken without pain. In time, her breathing became more regular, thus inducing these brief moments of consciousness.

Tasaria was only dimly aware of it when she began the healing exercise, but touching the unseen powers confirmed it. The room was stained with violent, Elemental energy. Everything within the confines of the space was affected by it. The remnants of the energy itself seemed confused and unsettled, as if it were beautiful music that had been deliberately played off-key. The echo of tortured notes still pulsed disconcertingly around them. The implication was clear. One of these women must have received advanced training in the ancient arts from Tasaria's mother, which meant that Pias was correct. Tasaria was not the last Seer after all. But what was to be done now? Her heart searched in vain for an answer.

The door opened and a Moon Shadow guard entered.

"He sends for you."

Tasaria nodded serenely then rose.

"Who will tend her in my absence?" she inquired, nodding down towards Vochallet.

"Another," the guard replied directly. "That was all I was told," he hurriedly added.

The man stood to the side and motioned that they should proceed. Tasaria hesitated a moment, then reached down and drew the heavy blankets more tightly about the prone patient. She promised herself that she would continue her efforts to heal the woman when she returned; then the Moon Shadows passed from the bitterly cold room, leaving Vochallet alone.

*

She was dimly aware of voices. Were those her children? Her mind tried to focus, to locate them in the mists, but their voices were growing fainter. Vochallet felt as if her legs were rooted in a bog. She longed to move, but could not remember how. Soon they would be gone. She must call to them or they would not find her. She must find her children. Vochallet struggled to free herself, to utter a cry.

There was light now. There was pain. Her mind rebelled, bid her to return to the shadows, but her spirit would not relinquish its pursuit. She'd been hurt, she remembered now. Were the others injured as well? The question only increased her agony. She needed to see them, to know that they were safe. And then she opened her eyes.

The room was familiar. Her eyes searched for a remembered face, but the Moon Shadow leader was not beside her now. She wanted to cry out in pain, but found herself unable to do so. Was she already dead?

Her body felt weak, the blackness clung to the edges of her vision. What had happened to her? Why couldn't she breathe? Her nerves writhed in pain. Vochallet closed her eyes for a moment as she fought to remain conscious.

Then a sight greeted her which cast all her senses into doubt. Were her eyes open once more or was she dreaming? The demon bled through the wall. Its black form stalked threateningly towards her. Where were the others? She found herself unable to turn her head. She could not look away. She could not scream. He was coming. He was coming for her, but she could not move.

The sound of her body fighting for life was sickening. Each short, wheezing breath was the flicker of a dying flame. The creature loomed over her. Vochallet's pain-filled face was wet with tears as her silent screams cried out to the heavens. But her pleas were dry as dust, and heaven and earth remained deaf to them.

The creature sat upon the bed and caressed her cheek with the back of his hand as she struggled in vain to move.

"No," Vochallet's soundless voice screamed over and over as her tears moistened the abrasive, mummified skin of his hand as it settled upon her swollen neck. His fingers shifted. The unpleasant moment was upon them.

*

From the entry of the hidden passage through which the creature had emerged into the room, Ernest Frankenstein witnessed the woman's body seize then go still. The creature did not stir from her bedside. Ernest numbly willed himself to step forward.

The woman's eyes were open. Her lips were parted, a partially bandaged gash was torn across her throat, the angle of her head only slightly unnatural. Ernest's heart mourned as in her he beheld his own cherished dead and suffered in the anguish of their absence, as others would now do for this woman.

"What was her name?" he asked softly.

The cloaked killer was silent for a long time as it regarded the corpse.

"I often wonder if Father ever asked that question of his helpless victims," he pondered as he turned. "Perhaps it is asking that, which makes one human."

Blackened lips drew into a stoic expression.

"I see no humanity here anymore," Ernest observed as he leaned over and closed the deceased woman's eyelids and drew the blanket over her. He saw only Ailis as he did so.

"I have acted no differently than you, Uncle," the shadow countered as he stood. "Or was killing your friend at Trafalgar somehow nobler than my ending of her suffering tonight?"

Ernest's hands began to tremble.

"I didn't do it to be noble. There was no hope for Ives," he contended. "They would have drowned him alive."

"So you ended his suffering early. You interfered with the natural order of life for the sake of mercy. Tell me, in that moment, did you act as an instrument of God or became one—a master of life and death?" The fiend thundered down.

Ernest was silent.

"She died for nothing," he finally said.

"Death is always selfish," the creature asserted. "Therefore, life must be made so as well. Only then can humanity hope to transcend its infancy."

"And you will guide us to this future?" Ernest bitterly asked as he gazed down at the dead woman's form.

"Your future has already begun."

*

Tasaria sat alone in the gloomy dining chamber. The winds howled mournfully outside. She'd listened to their inhuman wail swell and dissipate for over an hour now. The isolation augmented her frail nerves.

"Good evening, Tasaria," the Master's voice suddenly intoned.

She caught her breath. When had he entered? She rose and bowed reverently to the blight framed before the light from the great fireplace. To her surprise, he strode away without commanding her to rise. Tasaria did not move; she had been patient; she could afford to be for a moment longer. Her lord seemed unusually preoccupied, even anxious.

"Have you completed your interrogations, Master?" she cautiously inquired.

"None were needed," he stiffly replied, pacing ceaselessly.

Tasaria's stunned disbelief surmounted her manners. She rose.

"What have you done with them?"

He turned to face her, clearly annoyed.

"One travels with Pias, as we agreed. The other remains."

The Moon Shadow prophet could feel the blood drain from her face. Tasaria was having a difficult time even speaking the words as the grim realization dawned upon her.

"Pias is gone?"

She was trapped. He stopped pacing and faced her.

"Yes. Your purpose here is not yet fulfilled," the Master explained shortly.

She tried to suppress her rising distress and bitter disappointment as pleasant thoughts of being reunited with family and home dimmed. There must be some mistake.

"But Master, Nicabar will need me. I was to be present when Baseria …"

"I have not sent your niece."

Tasaria could feel her mouth hanging open but did not care. Why hadn't he spoken to her of such possibilities earlier? He always confided in her before. Why was he doing this? She trusted him. He was endangering everything—Nicabar's fragile truce, Etolie, Frankenstein's infant. Fears for her husband's safety gripped her heart and erupted into anger.

"Then what can be gained?" she demanded in exasperation. "Jal will never offer the child in trade for Etolie, that is not our way. He'll only use this as an excuse to …"

"Enough!"

She'd never seen her Master so angry with her. He stalked towards her, and the Moon Shadow priestess genuflected in fear. He loomed over her like an angry storm.

"Each of these women has a destiny to embrace if the prophecy is to be fulfilled—as do you! Or have you suddenly forgotten your great purpose?"

Tasaria shook her head with downcast eyes.

"No, but Master, the girls have been trained. Vochallet's room burns with Elemental energy. If Etolie has that type of power and is returned to our enemies …"

"Soon no enemy will exist," he vowed darkly, cutting her off.

Tasaria could say nothing, only look up and stare into her Master's awful eyes.

"The reward for your faith is close at hand," he said softly as he motioned for her to rise. She took his hand for balance.

"I don't understand," she muttered in disbelief.

A hint of white teeth appeared from beneath the black lips surrounded by putrid flesh.

"All will be made clear to you soon," he promised soothingly. "In the meantime, I wish for you to begin to reconstruct the chronicles of the Seer, which Frankenstein destroyed."

She nodded slowly as the magnitude of his request registered.

"That will be most difficult."

In this she was not exaggerating. Tasaria could chronicle basic information and some advanced concepts, but the larger mysteries presented in the ancient scrolls were now but dust. There was no hope of retrieving the knowledge that had been consumed by the fire. It was lost forever. So what purpose could new chronicles serve? Did he intend that she tutor Baseria? The idea was revolting.

"But Master …"

"It is necessary," he asserted directly.

Tasaria's sense of unease grew deeper, though she could not fully explain why.

"It will require a great deal of time, and I have been attempting to heal Vochallet's injuries."

"Another will tend her now. Think no more of her," the other bid.

Tasaria managed an awkward smile, then bowed, and left the dining chamber. And for the first time since she'd known him, she realized that the Master was not telling her the truth.

*

They were being separated, and Baseria could not reach her, could not hold onto her. Their individually bound hands prevented it. But in an act of both panic and defiance, she managed to momentarily break free of her captors and thrust her arms desperately over her friend's head and shoulders. The motion knocked off Etolie's headscarf. She tried to press their bodies together for protection, but was rapidly torn away from her friend by the much stronger guards.

Baseria struggled intensely as they pushed her away and held her forcibly against a wall. The man they knew as Pias stood coldly behind Etolie, who serenely retrieved her headscarf from the ground, and walked, unmolested, to Baseria. They stared into each other's eyes. The younger gypsy woman stopped struggling and bit her lip. Her eyes stung with tears that would not come as the gravity of the moment came fully to her. This was the end.

Etolie leaned forward and softly kissed her on the cheek, pressing her headscarf into Baseria's hands as she did so.

"I love you, Ba."

The friends gazed upon each other one last time, then Etolie stepped backward, and was calmly lead away by Pias and his guards to meet her fate.

Baseria was taken in the opposite direction, so distraught over the loss of her friend that she initially failed to notice where she was being led. She felt confused and dizzy. Her legs became unsteady. Etolie was going to die. Her friend's beloved face swam before Baseria. Her stomach lurched, and she became sick upon the staircase. She gasped for breath when it was over. She was going to die.

They were forcing her to move again. The air they descended into was bitterly cold, and there was a familiar sound, dull and throbbing, which grew louder with each troubled step she managed. And then she realized where they were taking her. Baseria's eyes frantically began to search the stairwell. Would the phantom return?

Despite her fears, they reached the bottom without incident and then followed the familiar path to the unwelcome door. Still, she offered no resistance as it was opened, and she was shoved harshly inside.

Baseria hit the floor of the chapel, hard. The uncompromising stones flashed across the burns on her hands as she attempted to control her landing. Some of the wounds broke open and began to bleed as she managed to stand. She brushed black hair from her eyes as she sought him, but discovered the chapel was empty. Maybe he was dead, too. Baseria staggered to the benches, one of which contained a half-eaten meal. She knelt beside the bench, dropped Etolie's headscarf upon it, awkwardly clasped the partially frozen food in her still-bound hands, and ate, ignoring the burning in her throat.

She didn't want to think. She didn't want to feel anything. Her mind lost itself in the repetitious sound of waves marching against unseen rocks in the sea below as she devoured her food.

After a time, the rhythm of the waves calmed her, and she began to mutter the words from a song her mother sang to her as a child. Her voice brought little inflection to the words as she whispered them over and over to herself. Actually, the song had never made much sense, but she still found it oddly comforting. It always reminded her of those dear to her heart. Eventually, the words left her, and she stared vacantly at the floor. She shivered. All she wanted right now was her mother or Nasi. They would have known what to do.

The power within her was growing stronger again, taunting and tempting Baseria. Her eyes fixed upon the wall torches. Should she unleash it upon her captors? It might destroy them, yet set her free. Her right hand pressed against the tightness in her chest. Such thoughts repulsed her as she considered the drying blood on her hands, the memory of Vochallet's pain-filled face, their screams in the darkness. She'd almost killed them all. And now she was alone.

"Please," she pleaded to the empty chapel. "Please," her jaw quivered.

Only the dull echo of the waves answered her.

Her body shook with fatigue, cold, and fear. When would they come for her? What would be her fate? There was no escape. Having previously explored the chapel with Ernest she knew that there was but one way to access it. If only she could devise some means to reach the windows high above. She searched in vain for a means to free herself from her bonds before resigning herself to settle on a bench and reclaim the blanket left there. As she fumbled to wrap herself up, an object dropped from within it.

The journal landed on the floor with a sharp, hollow thud. Baseria paused only an instant before reaching down to retrieve it. The passages it held might provide insight into Ernest's fate.

Her eyes scanned the pages for a moment before she suddenly flung the journal back to the ground, recoiling from it in horror. Baseria regarded the object with revulsion and trepidation. She fearfully waited, but no specter materialized. Still, Baseria felt she must do something.

Finally, her curiosity insatiable, she seized the blanket, stooped down again for the damaged journal, hastily collected a candle from the altar, and then nestled herself with the assortment underneath it. Baseria felt safer in the confined space. Still her heart pounded as her shaky fingers reopened Ailis' journal. This might be her only opportunity to learn about the woman who haunted her.

At first her eyes vacillated between the journal and the chapel, nervous that the angry spirit might suddenly descend upon her. She flipped randomly to various passages, only to discover some destroyed by exposure to water, while there were others she could still read. However, her fears of Ailis' ghost slowly began to fade as the mysterious woman's life gained new dimension on the pages. As she read, Baseria found her to be intriguing, humorous, and above all kind.

from the journal of Ailis Tierney Frankenstein

(1807)
Tomorrow will alter me forever as I embrace my union to Ernest and cast aside my doubts and the loneliness I have known in life. But I must always bear in mind, if ever we fail to see the goodness, which brings such joy into our lives now, reflected between us—as one gives freely to the other—then I will know we are truly lost.

(1807)
The chickens got out again this morning and made an awful mess of the garden by the north stone wall. Ernest says he'll sell the lot to Dr. Martin tomorrow when he stops by. Sometimes I still can't tell when he's joking. I know this delights him to no end.

(1808)
In these still hours of another tranquil day I thank God for the tender patience love brings to one's life.

*

When she felt ready, Baseria reluctantly turned to the entries towards the end. Each was progressively shorter as Ailis struggled with her illness, the demanding pregnancy, and her husband's prolonged absence. In some passages she wrote to herself, in others to her unborn child; a miracle she feared she would never know.

from the journal of Ailis Tierney Frankenstein

(1809)
I think I have settled on a name. Abrielle rejected the other eight in her most recent letter.

*

Then a sister arrived and illuminated her dark world. The entries after their reunion contained, for a time, a new energy of hope, but underlying all of the passages was a profound sense of loss, pain, love, and sadness. Would she live long enough that her child could be born? Was her husband already dead? What would become of their baby? If she ever sensed Baseria, she never wrote of it. There was no anger, no blame. Baseria marveled at the tenderness, the compassion, the loneliness of the dead woman's voice.

from the journal of Ailis Tierney Frankenstein

(1809)
Can life exist without love? I fear I have lost him forever.

*

The distant noise made by the chapel door opening frightened Baseria, and she immediately extinguished the remains of the candle. She listened intently as lazy smoke swirled into her eyes. She only heard the echo of one person walking across the great stone floor. Her eyes momentarily flashed down to her bound hands. How could she hope to defend herself?

The footsteps halted. She held her breath. The intruder must be near the benches. There was a scraping sound. Someone was turning, searching for her. Baseria pressed herself back against the unyielding stone and drew the blanket over her head. Maybe her adversary wouldn't see her hidden in the shadows under the altar.

She waited, breathing hard now. The thick blanket was obscuring sounds. Should she risk lowering it? Who'd entered? Her aunt? An Old One? A Moon Shadow guard or their dark Master? Who would lead her to her destruction? There was a sound, very close, an instant before the blanket was pulled back.

Frozen, she stared blankly at Ernest Frankenstein. His beard and hair had grown, his face looked thin and hollow. The faint trace of a smile touched his lips, a gray light shown in his eyes.

"You're still alive," the words, spoken in relief, expressed the same astonished sentiment in her eyes.

She said nothing as he began to untie her bonds, only gazed at him, uncertain what she felt. He paused when he noticed the condition of her hands. Embarrassed, her eyes tracked to the object he'd set down, Etolie's headscarf, while his discovered his wife's journal.

The rope fell away from her wrists; she began to rub them. Baseria's face was wet again as Ernest withdrew from the confined space, taking Ailis' journal with him. Baseria picked up Etolie's headscarf, which she'd forgotten on the benches earlier. Then she crawled out from under the altar, accepting Ernest's offer of aid when she stood. He returned wordlessly to the benches where he sat and tenderly kissed his dead wife's journal as if it were some treasured holy relic.

Baseria retrieved the blanket and joined him. As Ernest put the journal away, she studied the scarf in her hands. Neither looked to the other.

"I thought …," he cleared his throat. "When I saw that on the bench, I thought they'd brought the other girl back."

Baseria's fingers stopped caressing the fabric of the scarf.

"The other girl?"

She finally looked to him in expectant puzzlement.

"Isyll," she whispered, when Ernest had completed his description. "You've seen Isyll?!"

"If that was her name, then yes," he nodded somberly.

"When?" she prompted hopefully.

Ernest shook his head.

"Several days ago, I guess. I don't truly know when they took her anymore."

Baseria's anguished eyes mournfully returned to Etolie's headscarf as Ernest's hands rubbed his tired face. Both struggled against utter despair.

"And … and you haven't seen her since?" Baseria barely managed.

"No," Ernest replied after a lengthy silence. "She wasn't here very long. She … she was so frightened. I couldn't really understand what she was saying. I honestly don't know what's become of her."

Baseria knew. Isyll was dead, just like Etolie was, just as she soon would be. Ernest hung his head. Baseria wanted to berate him, to blame him, to burden him with their deaths. But she didn't. He already had, and there was so little time left to them in this world.

Quietly she drew closer and covered them both with the blanket. They reluctantly clung to one another, desperate for warmth and companionship. A precious hour passed, and then another, but still no one came for either of them. Eventually each fell asleep, only to awaken and discover that nothing had changed. They remained, alone.

In this crucible of silence, forgotten by time, they finally began to talk. Much of their relationship rested on the connection forged by the healing union they'd experienced in Hungary; one that until now had long been absent.

"Your powers have returned, haven't they?"

Baseria closed her eyes in shame.

"You know they have," she whispered.

She'd fervently hoped that their union was permanently severed when she lost her powers. But the longer they were exposed to one another, the more evident it became that this was not so. This was the first time they'd been near each other since her powers had come back. Unlike before, however, no images, flashes of insight, or glimpses of the future accompanied their return, but the same disquieting intimacy of their joined levels of consciousness was definitely emerging again. Both could sense it. What would happen to them if she gave in to the temptation of her power? Would it bind them further or tear them apart? She feared this and longed for it, as she struggled to maintain her control.

A different type of intimacy was also beginning to grow between them as they conversed. Across the lonely hours, mutual fear and shared need were slowly forcing them to acknowledge one another for the first time as friends. And as that intimacy deepened, they began to speak freely of the darker chapters of their past. Months of loneliness, bleak uncertainty, and personal reflection compelled them now to speak of incidents and emotions long buried. Each was repulsed, yet drawn to the other.

"I deserve this," Baseria asserted softly. "For murdering my sister and my cousin. I deserve this fate."

Ernest looked away from her in sorrow.

"If that's true, then you deserve it no less than I," he said.

"No," Baseria shook her head as she lightly touched his arm. "No, you're not a killer, not like me."

Wretchedly, he turned to face her, at last ready to share a story he'd only told once before, to his beloved wife.

"Yes," he said quietly. "I am."

***

CHAPTER 22
THE SKY ACROSS THE WORLD

I wandered the Earth for nearly five years before I arrived in China. By that time, I'd already lost myself in awe to the wilds of the Serengeti, to the mysteries of Egypt, to the thrill of the hunt, to the tragedies of the African coast. I sailed far into the Pacific and landed in places of exquisite beauty and wondrous terror. I learned of cannibals firsthand, saw men die at the mercy of the sea, or be devoured by a Komodo dragon. I knew disease, violence, lust, greed, jealousy, and fear. Years spent in the company of desperate men, thieves, and fools left me coarse and hard. I no longer dreamt of anything better in this world, and I had no better world to return to.

I shackled myself to no oath, no hopes. Time lost all meaning as I struggled against the living nightmare within my soul, but nothing could purge that great emptiness. I allowed death to come to me as often as it wished, welcomed it, begged for it to annul my miserable existence. I lived for death. My family was destroyed, my love, Justine, butchered before my eyes. But cruelly, I alone remained. The most unworthy of the Frankensteins remained, while those I loved lay in ruin on the other side of the world.

My name was long lost to me as I became a shadow of my former self. I attempted to forge a future by embracing ever shifting identities, but with no success. I existed, without purpose, without an ardor for life. I was vain, disobedient, and cruel, adrift in sophistry. As such, imprisonment and punishment were familiar patterns to me, especially when I served aboard a ship. The authoritative structure of most commands required that I be whipped or starved for my insubordination, but one captain saw fit to keelhaul me. I was drug underneath the ship, the flesh on my back, arms, and legs, lacerated by the barnacles affixed to the keel. Before this near drowning, I made a last entry in my journal which simply professed that I had died. I did not write in its pages again until long after I married my wife, and then only at her behest.

After this incident, I abandoned the ship at our next port of call and served or stowed away on vessels until I arrived in Canton. This was the only region of China where the West was gaining a marginal foothold for trade. I made landfall with no intention of remaining, quite the opposite. After so many years of hearing fanciful tales of India, I'd resolved to travel there. However, before I could begin those adventures, I was set upon by thieves who robbed me of my meager means and left me a beggar. For a short time, I considered stowing away again, but the regional threat of piracy and the allure of the vast Empire I was already in began to assert itself. India could wait. I took to the Chinese countryside and began to drift across it as a ghost, a nomad.

I roamed for some time, content to live off the land or steal from it as I saw fit. As I wandered, the customs and culture became increasingly fascinating to me. Since fleeing from Geneva, I had beheld many unique societies and traditions, but it was in China, after years of vanishing, that I first began to regain a measure of self. I wanted to understand this place, interact with it, not consume or conquer it.

As I traveled the roads along expansive coasts, green mountains, and flowing rivers, I opened myself to this new existence and the pace of my life began to slow. I avoided cities, rarely stopped in villages, and seldom remained in any area for more than a day. I trudged endlessly through sun and storm, morning and night. I was an object of curiosity sometimes, others a mere whisper across the land, an evil spirit given form. Children silently regarded or jumped around me. Occasionally old women would stop and curse at me, and men regarded the passage of this foreign beggar with either casual or confrontational notice. Women often did not meet my gaze at all.

I was awakened near a beach one morning by the sensation of an animal licking my face. Startled, I sat up sharply and frightened the child who was going through my pockets. Her dog jumped and fled along with its young companion to a safe distance. The girl, perhaps eight, did not, however, continue to flee. Instead she stood a few feet away petting her dog and regarding me. She asked me several questions, but I could only shake my head as I could not understand her words. Still she remained. I got up slowly, stretched and began to head down towards the beach. The peasant girl followed me as obediently as the dog trailed her, apparently curious as to where I was going.

Brilliant sunlight assailed me as I strode out across the warm sand to the pulsing waters of the blue-emerald sea. My shadows moved down the stretch of beach but remained vigilant to my actions as I removed my boots and waded out a measure into the rolling waters. The girl did likewise. I knelt and splashed cool water on my face. The young child squealed when she did so. She sat down beside me on the sands as I resumed my boots, and for a short time, we gazed silently upon the shifting expanse of the South China Sea before us.

I did not particularly mind the companionship, but I didn't want her following me everywhere either. I felt her small hand upon me again as she reached unabashedly for the necklace I wore, a trinket I'd collected on some remote island in the Pacific.

"Do you like this?" I asked as I untied it, suddenly remembering William's fascination with Elizabeth's locket. She said nothing as I handed it to her, only studied it, then suddenly smiled in sheer delight at what she obviously considered a valuable treasure. When was the last time someone had genuinely smiled at me? The child's openness was touching.

"It's yours," I grinned, "Keep it."

My gift given I rose to leave, but she stood and shook her head, pointing in the opposite direction of the one I planned to head in. When it became obvious my protests would be ignored, I relented and followed her.

She led me to a modest house on the edge of what appeared to be a small fishing village. The child vanished inside yelling excitedly, her canine friend loyally trotting in behind her. Uncertain what type of greeting to expect, I waited listlessly, my only real hope for the encounter was that I might be provided with some food. A peasant woman appeared in the entryway and restrained her child who was eagerly attempting to run back out the door. I remained where I was.

"Jesuit," the child asserted to her parent as she pointed at me. "Jesuit."

I blinked wondering how she had reached the unexpected conclusion that I was a missionary priest. Perhaps it was because I'd spoken to her in French. I moved slightly closer to the house, willing to test a theory.

"Madame, I am not a Jesuit, only a simple traveler. If you have any food you could spare for my journey I would greatly appreciate it."

It was clear she understood me for her grip on the little girl relaxed a degree. After a moment's consideration, to my surprise, she gestured for me to remain and ordered her daughter to stay inside. The child hovered in the doorway until her mother reappeared and waved me closer. Together the family members set up a pair of crude benches and a table, and began to lay out a meal. Apparently I arrived just in time for their midday repast. They sat on one side of the table, while I sat on the other with the begging canine.

At first no one spoke as we ate and studied each other. The woman was probably almost fifty, guarded in her demeanor, but still possessed an approachable quality. As our meal progressed, her daughter began to ask her questions about me, only to receive short responses in return.

"What does she wish to know?" I finally muttered.

She did not answer me, however, her daughter persisted.

"You name?" the older woman finally managed in broken French.

I nodded.

"I'm called Swiss by most people," I explained, using the title I'd been christened with while traveling the seas. Only the nightmares of Ernest Frankenstein remained.

The curious girl's mother translated this to her child who repeated "Swiss" rapidly several times, pleased with the knowledge. She ended by banging the table, upsetting several dishes. Her mother reached over to clean up some spilled soup, and it was then that I first noticed her crippled right hand. It was badly mangled and seemed to be completely lame. Her expression was unreadable as I helped her clean up.

Not long after, it began to rain, and as I stood in the doorway, I realized that it was only marginally dryer inside the house. Their roof obviously needed serious work, though neither seemed to notice, a sign that it had likely been in this condition for some time.

I attempted to communicate my willingness to help but the peasant woman ignored me and tended to dirty dishes. Her daughter, however, took more of an interest in my offered intentions and showed me the best way to scale to the roof. After slipping several times, though, I decided it would be best to wait. It rained the rest of the day, and I ended up sleeping under an overhang near a pig sty.

When I arose the next morning, the woman seemed more willing to accept my offer to help. The rain had stopped, and I spent several hours mending the roof as best I could. I also got my first real look into the village, if it could be called that. It was situated between a series of fields, which lay before a low range of wooded hills and the seashore. The loose arrangement of structures all appeared to be decrepit or damaged. There were a series of deep rifts torn in the earth, and high watermarks were visible on several of the buildings.

I could have left that day, should have left. But instead I decided to remain. Perhaps I was simply tired of wandering or my reawakened sense of pity for others compelled me. Maybe my simple curiosity and need for purpose drove me to stay. Whatever the reason, I chose to remain with the Maas. I came to learn that the young girl was named Ai Qiu. She was the only child of Xiu Xue, whose husband had died seven years earlier. She was something of an outcast in the village, and my presence did little to change this, though it seemed to delight Ai to no end. A few in the village allowed me to work on their homes as well, and little by little, their world was revealed to me.

I never took up residence in the Maa house, except when it stormed for prolonged periods of time. They had one common room, and I always slept on the opposite side from the bed that mother and daughter were obligated to share. The longer I remained, the more I began to converse with those who had previously learned French. Many years prior, a devastating series of floods had annihilated lives, property, and ultimately their collective prosperity. Jesuit missionaries aided them for a brief time but left them years earlier, never to return. The land had forever been altered by the great floods, and now, such natural disasters were common.

Against the commandments of the Qianlong Emperor, they grew poppy crops in the fields beyond the village as a means of survival. These were used to produce opium, a substance which the British were beginning to illegally import and trade from India. The Emperor saw no value in trading for this drug, but his Empire was too vast and corrupt to effectively control its trade and use. Canton, far removed from the edicts issued by those in the Forbidden City, was becoming the epicenter for such illegal trade practices.

As if all this were not enough, Chinese pirates sporadically descended upon the village, raiding what little they had and stealing most of the crops. Piracy was steadily rising along the Chinese coast, and many villages were compelled to offer such extorted tributes lest the marauders turn more violent. All of this, coupled with their society's class structure, ensured that these peasants would remain so for as long as they lived.

One morning after Ai Qiu left for her daily teachings, I was working on repairing a length of fencing when Xiu Xue came to me. Our conversations were typically brief as each of us was still struggling to learn more of the other's language. Despite this, I began to learn more about their beliefs and traditions. It had rained most of the previous day compelling me to shelter indoors during the night. She handed me a cup of water, which was a welcome relief after working for several hours in the humid air. I could feel her gaze upon me, and my eyes inadvertently moved to her crippled hand.

"Bad dreams?" she asked as I drank.

I stopped and blinked away the sweat that ran into my eyes. The dream, which plagues me still, is always the same. Justine rises from mists, anxious to tell me something, as William screams, his gaze transfixed by something beyond me. But when I turn to see what he sees, the mists vanish and I realize that I am in a grave, buried alive. Apparently, my unrest and cries had awoken both her and Ai in the night. It was not the first time.

"Sorry," I nodded as I returned the empty cup to her, content to abandon the matter.

Xiu Xue, however, was not. She reached down and touched my shoulder with her crippled hand motioning me towards the house. It was sweltering inside, and the incense she burnt upon a small altar hung heavy in the stale air. The small table held a symbol-laden tablet, small portions of food, some coins and remains of burnt items, and several candles.

My benefactor knelt, tucked her legs underneath her body, and sat silently before the swirling incense on the altar.

"Why here, Swiss?" she finally asked as she turned to face me.

Nothing in her gaze or tone seemed to indicate that I had overstayed my welcome. It was a simple, direct question, but one I had great difficulty answering. For so many years, I remained remote from others as I struggled with my guilt, lived my nightmares. William's murder, Justine's betrayal and loss, Victor's madness, and the deaths of Elizabeth and my father made it all but impossible for me to feel close to anyone. I sought to outrun my past, not to confront it.

"I am a haunted man," I whispered at last as I sat beside her.

Our eyes broke.

"All men are," she observed. "Your ancestors are angry?"

I peered into the dancing smoke.

"I don't know."

Xiu Xue was silent for a moment before she continued.

"If you do not honor them, you break your connection, fail to serve their needs in the *yinjian*[21], they will not guide and protect you," she explained as she motioned to the altar. "Their *egui*[22] will return to punish the living, as I have been."

For a moment this unexpected confession startled me into silence. Again my gaze drifted to her hand.

"No, not this," she answered my unspoken question, "but it began with this. My hand was crushed during one of the first floods, long before the Jesuits came. Soon after, I lost my son, but did not honor him properly. Much sadness has followed."

I swallowed as my emotions overwhelmed me.

"I've lost everyone dearest to me," I admitted aloud for the first time in years, the next thought wrenching my heart as the image of that once-beloved face formed fully in my conscious mind. I could barely continue to speak. "The woman I loved was killed for taking my brother's life. For murdering …," I could not go on. "I dream of them."

For a long time neither of us spoke.

"And what of happiness?" Xiu Xue at last asked.

"There is no happiness in this world," I asserted bitterly.

Her eyes did not waver from mine.

"Not until you seek it or allow it to be."

She did not give me a chance to protest before she continued.

"Many years I suffered before I could accept Wei's loss." She pointed to symbols on the tablet, to her son's name. "But my husband and I honored him, and my ancestors, created gift of new life, Ai Qiu. She brought happiness."

Xiu Xue eyes held hope for me, but I could only shake my head. It seemed impossible that I could ever be happy again. And that night the phantoms of my past rose again.

*

---

21 *Chinese*. Underworld where the spirit exists after death.

22 *Chinese*. Starving spirit.

For the next several weeks we began to converse regularly about our lives, every discussion adding to our knowledge of each speaker's native language, culture, and philosophies. As our friendship grew, so did my sense of trust, a nearly forgotten attribute of my nature. Our relationship was never destined to be romantic. We were bound by mutual need for the other's understanding and had encountered each other at a point in our lives when we were at last ready to be more open with another after years spent in relative self-isolation. Many believed, as Xiu Xue herself did, that she and several others were responsible for the misfortunes of the village. They claimed her mangled limb was a bad omen and marked her as such. So she was routinely ostracized. I tried many times to convince her that this was mere superstition, but she refused to listen.

I began to wander the countryside again as my mind and my spirit considered new perspectives regarding my life. One question, above all others, tended my solitary hours—could I ever be happy again? My journeys started as modest trips of an hour or more, but over time began to extend into days. But always I returned to the Maa household. Gradually, I began to focus less on understanding why and more on how I might achieve some degree of peace in my life. I had come to realize that before I could embrace a future, I must be able to envision one.

As I descended from the mountains one night, I paused to refill my water bladder in a small stream. Tomorrow, I had been informed repeatedly by Ai Qiu before my most recent departure, was her birthday. To that end, I'd been working steadily on carving her a flower-shaped decoration. Hopefully when I returned to the village, I'd be able to locate a means to add color to it.

I was very close to the village and momentarily considered camping along the stream for the night, but the thought of rising early after so many days on the road was none too appealing, so I resumed my journey. It would be quite late, but at least I would arrive home tonight.

My dreams of late were more quiet, sleep more restful. During this trip, a new question transfixed my spirit, one which I had not dared to consider before now. Should I return to Geneva? Victor argued fiercely against my ever doing so, but what if he'd vanquished his own demons and returned? Might my brother still live? Could we now, after so many years of sadness, be reunited as family? I was eager to discuss such possibilities with Xiu Xue.

The trees began to thin as I finally neared the coast. As usual I opted to forego cutting through the poppy fields and soon came across the familiar, craggy road that led to the village proper. As I walked the air became perfumed with an odd scent, chased by a familiar one. Something was burning, but the shifting winds from the sea made it difficult to determine the origin of the scent. A stick snapped behind me, and suddenly, I was violently struck in the back of my head. Unprepared for the assault, I lost my footing and looked up to discover several men with pistols and swords held at the ready. One began to beat me savagely while the other kept his weapons trained on me. I could barely regain my feet when they were finished.

I was taken prisoner. Many of the buildings were ablaze when I entered the village. Its residents had been rounded up by the pirates who were loading both their prisoners and the opium crop onto ships. An old man was pleading and protesting vehemently to the pirate's leader on behalf of his people. The young man appeared unmoved as he surveyed those remaining on the beach. His men cast me roughly to the sand. Though I understood little of what was actually said, it was clear that they had begun to explain how they'd intercepted me to their leader.

**

Ai Qiu was terrified. The pirates had never been this malicious before. Why were they burning their homes? There was so much shouting when the attack began, even more when they drug people from them, but it was quiet now. Many were already aboard the ships. Her mother would say nothing to her about what was happening but she'd heard other women crying as they were taken to the ships.

"What are slaves, Mother?" Ai Qiu asked in response to their screams.

Her mother stroked her hair as her trembling voice answered.

"We are now."

Another pistol shot echoed in the night as the village elder, who'd been arguing with the pirate leader, fell to the ground dead. But Ai Qiu never saw his body. They looked only to the person who now knelt before the others. He'd come back to them! Would he be shot now, too?

"Swiss!" Ai Qiu cried as she frantically broke free of her mother's grasp. "Swiss, Swiss!!!" she shouted tearfully as she ran across the sand. For a moment Ai Qiu was in his arms, and then she was being hauled backward by the pirate leader as her mother ran to them crying her daughter's name. Xiu Xue slowed as she closed the distance, suddenly uncertain and fearful. She averted her eyes when the pirate looked to her and demanded.

"Was this her father?" he kicked at the body on the ground.

Xiu Xue shook her head, her eyes downcast. The pirate studied her. Why did she hide her right hand? Did she carry a weapon?

"You wish your child back, yes?"

Again she nodded, avoiding his gaze. The pirate leader motioned to one of his men who roughly grabbed her arm, exposing her deformed limb.

Xiu Xue and the pirate leader froze, each staring speechlessly into the other's face. He tore his eyes away to study the burning structures as if confirming something then retuned his attention to Xiu Xue's with a vile certainty as he drew a dagger from his belt.

"If only I'd known," he said, his voice rich with loathing.

"Please," Xiu Xue began.

"DON'T!" the pirate leader roared, pointing the blade at her as he shoved her to the ground and kicked her. "Don't. Where is he? WHERE! Where is the coward?"

"He's dead, many years now," she panted. "Please, she knows nothing. Please."

Xiu Xue's eyes pleaded for him to release his iron grip on her daughter. The pirate again struck her viciously as the prisoner the child ran to yelled and struggled against the men who restrained him.

"You plead for the life of your child from the one whom you abandoned!"

Xiu Xue coughed as she struggled to stand.

"What life could we have given you here? There was only disease and starvation after the floods. What we did, we did because we loved you. We never wanted to, none of us did. What choice did we have?"

The pirate's eyes smoldered with pain. Ai Qiu's were full of terror as the blade of the dagger came to rest against her throat. She stood stock still.

"So you abandoned your children …," he nodded down at the girl, "and replaced us as if we'd never existed."

Xiu's crippled hand attempted to wipe tears from her eyes. As she did, she smeared the blood hanging from the corner of her mouth. Then she tried in desperation to cling to her son's leg but abandoned the attempt when Ai Qiu gasped as the pressure from the dagger against her throat increased.

"Your father left you in a work camp, with food and shelter, a chance," she finally managed.

"A chance? You abandoned me, enslaved me. All I've known is savagery because of you, Mother," the pirate affirmed coldly.

Xiu Xue struggled to her knees, begging.

"Please, Wei, please. She's all I have left in this world. Take my life, not hers. Please. She's your sister."

**

What were they saying! They were speaking so rapidly that the only thing discernible was that they shared some past connection. One of my guards mercilessly struck my kidney again causing me to gasp for air. Xiu Xue and the pirate leader were talking so rapidly, I had no hope of keeping up. They yelled, pleaded, shed tears, as I continued to shout challenges and protests, but the man ignored these completely.

He bent low and whispered something to Ai Qiu who cried out to her mother seconds before they began to haul her away to the awaiting ships. Her mother's scream drowned out Ai Qiu's final desperate cries. They intended to take her and sell her as a slave.

In that black moment, all I wanted was vengeance. I tore my shoulder muscles as I twisted away from one of my guards who was accidentally shot by his companion. I dove for the dead man's sword and swung it upward. The blade removed my other guard's hand, and he crumbled to the ground. I was free to strike down the monster. The pirate leader abandoned his dagger and began to reach for his own sword. With all of my strength, I thrust the blade forward, intent on fatally stabbing my enemy. It never reached him.

Xiu Xue's eyes went wide as the metal plunged deeply through her chest. She was dead before I realized what had happened. Her lifeless form fell to the earth the moment I withdrew my blade from her body, my sword clattered uselessly to the sand. I sank to my knees, barely conscious of anything going on around me. All I remember is the pirate leader's sickening laughter as he loomed over us.

CHAPTER 23
PANDORA'S LOVER

Baseria wept for lives she'd never known. She wanted Ernest to stop, needed him to, but could not bring herself to ask it of him. Her eyes looked to nothing while she clung to him as he continued.

"They struck me unconscious and left me with the bodies as they stole into the night with their captives and cargo. I never saw any of them again. Much of what happened after that night is lost to me. I burned the dead in the darkness, and eventually, made my way to India, unable to understand any of it.

For a time I thought Xiu Xue suddenly stood and blocked my blade from killing the man who was abducting her child into a life of slavery. But why would she do that? It's my fault. I'm responsible. I brought them death, just as I did my family. I survived, they didn't.

I no longer saw any value in humanity or myself. I began to abuse opium as I tried to forget but something in me refused to die. I languished in that nightmare existence for months, but within a year's time found myself an unwilling participant at Trafalgar. And then I … and then I met Ailis."

Ernest's voice broke when he uttered the name of his beloved. At some point, Baseria's fingers had interlaced themselves among those on his left hand. She was painfully aware of his metal wedding band against her finger as she squeezed his reassuringly. Baseria's own thoughts turned to those revealed by Ailis in her journal. Her heart began to beat faster. His voice was soft.

"She was beautiful. Ailis was the only person who ever accepted me completely for who I am. And now she's gone too. She and Tara."

Baseria held him, and for a long time, neither was able to speak, their existence devoid of words, each consumed by loss.

"Why did she write in English?" Baseria questioned, trying to refocus his emotions.

"What?" he asked in surprise.

"Your wife, in her journal, why did she write it in English, not Gaelic?"

Ernest's short laugh to this unexpected question was a welcome release for them both.

"I asked her the same thing once, a few days before we were married."

He could see Ailis smiling at him on their wedding day, everything around them a dazzling array of white in the cold dawn.

"She told me that she'd learned English first and that writing in it was a habit left over from childhood."

Baseria sat up and awkwardly pushed a loose length of black hair behind her ear. She tried to summon her courage as she looked into his eyes, but it faltered when she spoke.

"I didn't mean what I said before … about her."

Her gaze dropped.

"Before you read her journal?"

His voice betrayed none of the emotion within. Baseria struggled to explain.

"I … it was an accident. I didn't know what they'd done to you, I was scared they'd … I couldn't understand all of it," she finished, her heart pounding.

"You could never understand what she was to me."

This time the pain in his words was unmistakable, as it was clear in Baseria's when she finally replied.

"You're right. I could never understand. I've never known love. No one's ever tried to accept me for who I am or allowed me to do the same for them," her voice shook.

As their eyes met, each recognized the terrible loneliness and fear within the other. Their fingers were still laced. but their hands felt light. They'd been defined by their suffering, and now shared the most intimate details of their miseries with the other. Their eyes closed as their heads unconsciously drifted closer together. It was impossible to say who began to kiss the other first.

*

The creature's heart smoldered as he watched. How could this be? He had done everything he could to ease his uncle's great burden. He reached out to him as family, as an equal, offered him a gift beyond all others. And this was the result? How could he so selfishly choose the girl over being reunited with his wife as the creature promised?

Victor's son leaned heavily against the small alcove's wall, unable to endure seeing anymore of what was going on in the chapel below. He'd heard the stories they shared, studied their reactions to one another, hoping to learn …

But now she would reject him in favor of Frankenstein, in favor of humanity. His eyes were wet with embarrassment, confusion, and anger. The image of Ernest and Baseria's embrace blazed in his mind. The solid mass of frigid rock that comprised a corner of the alcove shattered to dust as he grasped it in his palm. Jealousy, unrestrained, burned white-hot in his heart as he suffered the depth of their betrayal. He fled down the black tunnel in a towering rage.

*

Baseria's heart swelled with emotion, her body shuddered. She had never been kissed like this before. Her hands gripped his body. She'd been right. He loved her.

Someone needed her as much as she needed them. It was beautiful, frightening, and exciting. Their kisses were deep, passionate. Baseria gave herself completely to the moment. Being desired made her feel safe, alive. Her soul sang with gratitude and love.

They parted slightly, breathing heavily, their foreheads touching, their eyes closed. Baseria smiled. The warmth between them was intoxicating. Her eyes drew open.

"Ailis," Ernest's shaking voice whispered to her.

His eyes closed, he did not at first see the look of utter devastation that shock inflicted upon her precious face. She was too wounded to respond as his eyes slowly opened. Realization blessed them in that horrific moment as she turned from him in crushing anguish, waving away his outstretched hand. Dazed, Baseria staggered towards the altar and collapsed before it, too shattered even to weep. Ernest hung his head, his heart beset by guilt and shame, his voice lost to grief.

*

"Mother?"

The word died in a hollow echo. Tasaria looked down at her hands, still able to feel the sensation left by Nasi's grasp. But she was alone in her chamber. She blinked back tears. It was impossible. Her mother had looked so young, as she did when Tasaria and Mayte were children. Despite the numbing cold, her face was damp with sweat.

She must be sick. It was the stress. There was no other reasonable explanation, unless she was losing her mind. It was a terrifying thought. She extended a trembling hand to her temple. No, she was tired, that was all. This was not the first time she'd attempted to meditate when she was fatigued. Yes, communing with the unseen powers always had a disquieting effect when she was not fully prepared to interact with them. Tasaria knew this. She breathed deeply and tried to focus on recalling the rest of her vision. Her eyes, momentarily, closed in concentration.

"I can't," she sighed to the empty room.

"You must."

The Moon Shadow priestess leapt from the bed and grabbed a candle. She swung it wildly about as she spun and pivoted in search of the speaker only to find nothing unusual. She backed into a corner, every nerve alive with fear. But there was no one. Tasaria managed to set the candle down as she clasped her head between her hands.

"Stop it!" she pleaded, "Stop it!"

Her heart was racing. She was not going mad.

"Not real. You're not real," she repeated as her eyes probed the room." You're not real."

Tasaria reached down for the candle and drew it towards her.

"Not real," she whispered again to herself as she raised it. Her icy breath mingled with the smoke from the flame. The silent room stared back at her. After several minutes of this, she leaned back against the frigid wall. She turned her head to see what her left arm was brushing against as she did so.

"You must save her, Daughter."

Tasaria dropped the candle and screamed as the sight of her shrouded, wizened Mother greeted her eyes. She clawed maniacally at the ground, desperate to escape the phantom, as the toppled candle's flame flickered from existence. In blind terror, she flung open the door, but was arrested moments after setting foot in the corridor. Two of the Old Ones restrained her and wordlessly began to haul her away from her chamber and the specter it held.

*

She could sense him kneeling beside her, but she did not care. Baseria's mind turned inward to remembered sensations long lost to her. Visions of green grasses, fields lush with scents, warm breezes upon her bare skin, wrapping herself in her mother's favorite blanket, even the taste of Nasi's tea momentarily flooded her mind. Then the memories dimmed, and her breath caught when he began to speak.

"Your grandmother gave me something before I destroyed the writings. She called it a gift."

Baseria did not turn.

"She told me that I was to open it in an hour of darkness."

Was he asking her for permission? Her heart felt wretched.

"Please," she swallowed hard, "just go away," she begged. He'd left her nothing.

"Baseria," he implored.

"Go," she whispered, drawing her knees a little closer to her shivering body.

But Ernest did not leave her. His hand lightly touched her.

"I didn't open it when Ailis died," he confessed, "or when your father took …"

Baseria's breath echoed in the silence that followed.

"Tara," Ernest finally managed to speak his daughter's name.

His child. Her father had taken his child? Baseria felt dead inside. None of her thoughts made any sense. She waited, but he said no more. Awkwardly she finally struggled to her knees, uncertain of what she would say. As she turned to Ernest, terror gripped her heart.

Her eyes had never before beheld such a grotesque image. For a moment they met those hideous orbs that glared down at her. She began to scream as her overwrought mind propelled her body to crawl back towards the imagined sanctuary under the altar. Her cries alerted Ernest, whose back was turned to the silent demon, seconds before he viciously struck. The thing hurtled Ernest into one of the stone walls, then stalked relentlessly towards his prone form and drew a sword.

"NO!" Baseria cried, frantic to stop the unhooded beast before it killed him.

It sadistically drove the unsheathed blade into the back of Ernest's left hand. Baseria shrieked in agony as her own left hand's nerves exploded in unmitigated pain, as Ernest cried out in misery. The creature twisted the blade, widening the wound, and grinding the tempered metal against bone. Baseria wailed in distress as the weapon was finally withdrawn from Ernest's flesh. She was close to blacking out when the Moon Shadows' dark Master loomed over her.

"Do not dare beg for his life," he angrily commanded, pointing the blood tipped blade at her.

"You've taken too much from me already," Baseria labored to reply.

"I will suffer no rivals," the creature asserted as she lost consciousness.

A crimson pool was rapidly spreading out beneath Ernest, his face having been cut against the abrasive surface of the wall. The nerves in his wounded hand were all firing at once. It trembled uncontrollably causing blood to pour from it more freely. He should have been unconscious, but though he was in terrible agony, his senses remained.

His eyes turned to the unmoving form of Baseria.

"Don't touch her," he demanded through clenched teeth.

The other crossed the distance between them and began to crush Ernest's fingers beneath his heel. The room spun crazily as Ernest fought the churning nausea within.

The creature bent down and took Nasi's box from Ernest's pocket.

"You misplace your faith, Uncle. The dead mystic's trinket is nothing."

With great power, he hurtled it to the frozen stones of the floor, but it did not shatter or open. Without hesitation, the great being returned to Baseria, retrieved her from the floor, and carefully set her body on the benches, draping several blankets over her. The girl's face, what little Ernest could see of it, looked grossly strained, despite her unconscious state.

By now the freezing temperatures slowed Ernest's blood loss, and with shaking fingers, he tore sections from his shirt to further restrain its flow. The creature resumed his hood as he tenderly caressed the sides of Baseria's cheeks and whispered to her. Would he destroy her, end Baseria's life as he had her friend's?

A noise suddenly attracted the monster's attention as several of the Old Ones entered with Tasaria who fearfully surveyed the scene before her. The creature uttered a command to one of the Old Ones as he again stood. The smaller robed figure forced Ernest to his feet and marched him across the room to Tasaria's side. With unmitigated menace, the towering shadow approached. The yellow eyes were glowing slits beneath the concealing hood.

"It is time you were made to understand," the harsh voice said. Then he stalked from the chapel as his prisoners were forced to follow.

*

They traveled by a path unfamiliar to either Ernest or Tasaria. Instead of going up the turret and back to the courtyard, they traversed a hallway that ended in a modestly proportioned, dirty, poorly lit room that appeared lost to the ages. It had likely been a storage room of sorts at one time, for piles of junk and antiquity filled the space.

In a far corner, the Moon Shadows' Master ushered them into another hidden passage. This was relatively short and ended within a portion of a partially collapsed turret. The roar of the waves pulsed and echoed through the tower. The stairwell looked incapable of supporting their weight, and large gaps in them were illuminated by dull, dying sunlight. The mournful groan of the icy winds only added to their sense of foreboding as they proceeded downward.

The spiraling stairs were partially encased in ice, and out of necessity, Ernest began to help Tasaria descend them. They rested momentarily on one of the few safe landings, and both were involuntarily drawn to the dimming light without. By it they spied the masts of several ships, lain at anchor, a host of people climbing about them as they worked, their forms black against the snow. What were they doing? Was another departure imminent?

A command was uttered by their Master, and the Old Ones obediently pressed the prisoners to continue their descent. The world grew darker. At last they reached the murky depths. Waves now crashed dully above their heads. The silent shadow pointed a claw-like finger towards a gloomy, tortured path.

Awed by fear, the prisoners proceeded across the jagged and broken floor, only to discover they were alone. Water ran freely down the dark walls and frozen mist entwined with stone and breath. At points they were forced to crawl up piles of slick rocks. The jagged floor would suddenly sink, and the stone would be replaced with ice alone. Several times the awkward tunnel rose above the water and revealed the last faint traces of sunlight through the shattered ceilings of partially sunken towers, which illuminated the falling snow that danced and shimmered all about them.

Neither Ernest nor Tasaria spoke to the other as they proceeded. The tunnel began to grow narrower, and its black expanse descended deeper under the water. A lone torch flickered against the darkness. Ernest retrieved it and held it aloft before them. It revealed what could only have been the fortress's catacombs. Skeletal remains and crystallized dust adorned the slots hewn into the wall. Ice claimed large portions of some walls, and the empty eye sockets of grinning skulls glistened in the torch light. The tunnel grew so narrow they were forced to walk single file through the twisting realm of the dead.

Finally they reached a wide, short shaft, through which the dark, pulsing glow of torches could be seen. Their nerves were charged by the damp, frigid air and with unmitigated terror of what awaited them in the chamber below. Ernest gazed down the shaft, Tasaria to the blackness behind them. Then their eyes met fully for the first time. Each shared an unspoken understanding that their lives would never be the same after this moment. Did crossing the threshold make them enemies or victims? There were no answers one could provide the other, no solace in the face of the unknown.

Ernest's finger traced the scar on the palm of his right hand. Touching it gave him strength, as did the memory of she who had marked him with it. Hesitantly, he stepped to the edge of the shaft. Something was waiting. An undulating layer of mist clung to the unseen ground. He slid down the short length, tested his footing, and turned to aid Tasaria as she followed. It took several moments for their eyes to adjust to the light from torches burning along the walls, but as they did, both clung to each other as their senses lost themselves in the horrors of the vast chamber.

Their passage down the shaft dissipated a portion of the swirling mists, which retreated to reveal a sight neither was prepared to meet.

Tasaria covered her mouth in astonishment and fear. Ernest stood, rooted in place. Their heads swiveled as their minds strove to comprehend the unholy environment in which they now found themselves, for this could only be the world of the damned. At first they could only see the mutilated, frozen bodies, remnants of humanity, piled atop the ground of icy crimson.

Unlike the ancient dead above, these silent, mist-adorned corpses still bore evidence of who they had been in life and even how they had died. Gaps in the swirling vapors provided them glimpses of the woeful mass of dead bodies stretched out all about them, great piles of death reaching above the level of their knees. Though tempered by the frigid temperatures, the nauseating stench of the charnel was unmistakable.

Unable to endure the nightmare before his eyes, Ernest began to press Tasaria to move forward. She slipped and found her fingers buried in cold, bloody slush, incapable of tearing her eyes away from another's unseeing visage. Ernest reached down and freed her from its ghastly trance, and the two staggered towards the center of Death's cathedral.

Their progress was agonizingly slow as paths abruptly ended, forcing them to delve once more into the embrace of the macabre. It became increasingly difficult to avoid looking at the bodies, so bizarre was their state. Some appeared in peaceful repose, while others, more tortured forms lacked limbs, skin, torso, or even cranium. Many still were clothed in the tattered remnants of various uniforms of service from different nations, several of which Ernest recognized. Others were more simply dressed, and as they finally neared their freedom, Ernest paused before one of these bodies.

The woman's face was hidden, but her manner of dress seemed familiar to him somehow. Tasaria feigned an effort to stop him, but he knelt, and with some difficulty, turned the stiff corpse towards him. Looking upon her frozen face sickened him, and it took several moments before Ernest was again able to summon his voice. She was probably younger than Ailis had been.

"This girl … she was at the camp in Hungary," he sighed, unable to draw his eyes away from hers. What was the last sight they had seen? How long had she lain abandoned in this homage to sin? Could her missing companions be in eternal repose here as well?

Tasaria was silent. She did not recognize the girl but her clothing,

Ernest's remark, and the whispered dread of the other Wild Rose women left no doubt that this was Sebbi. Ernest scanned the area for Vochallet's body but failed to locate it. He tore a portion of his jacket and placed the cloth over Sebbi's open eyes then stood, emotion and cold made his hands shake. Strangely, his left hand felt fine. Perhaps it had simply grown numb from blood loss.

"What is that?"

Tasaria's voice quivered. Ernest looked to where she pointed.

Rising from the gloom was a stone platform, atop which rested a unique assortment of equipment. Wordlessly he indicated that Tasaria should remain where she was while he proceeded, alone, to the top. As he climbed a short series of steps a new, familiar noise attracted his attention.

The sound grew louder as he completed his ascent. Water poured in freely from the sea above, cascading down a wall, ringed by the flames of torches, which struggled to keep ice at bay. It was by no means a torrent, but it appeared that the aperture could be manipulated to increase the flow. Ernest's eyes now focused on the series of wheels below the artificial waterfall. They traced the wooden shafts that opened beneath a stone table, under which a series of tubes, within other tubes sat idle. He reached out to touch one of the outer cylinders and discovered that his ring magnetically clung to it.

The floor surrounding the table was a mosaic of stone and crimson stained ice. The top of the table was a cool, hammered, copper slab, with protruding nodes on all sides. A shroud of white lay folded at the end closest to him. His fingers' touch revealed the fabric was inlaid with some small, hard substances inside.

His gaze took in other tables nearby. Several were covered with chemistry equipment, others held specimen jars, still others medical tools. The stubs of candles bore testament to which locations were most frequently occupied. He sensed her presence a moment before she spoke.

"What is this place?" Tasaria whispered to herself as she too studied the surreal setting.

Suddenly Ernest seized her by the arm.

"Why did you come here?"

Tasaria struggled against his unexpected embrace, the wild emotion in his eye.

"To kill that girl, those people, your niece?"

The harsh clang from the metal cylinders tolled loudly through the dead, cavernous chamber when Tasaria's heel backed into it. Neither's gaze wavered.

"Is that why you came?" she shot back.

The charged air between them begged for violence, for release from their mutual horror and guilt. But before a crescendo could be reached, movement attracted their attention as a host of Old Ones appeared all around them. Ernest had never been near so many of them. Their unwelcome, disturbing presences seemed to have come from all directions at once. And now they stood as silent sentinels, only their frozen breath betrayed that they lived. There was no escape.

Several parted as their Master joined them, and in a language lost to the ages, uttered a single command. Without hesitation the Old Ones removed their hoods. Tasaria's scream echoed through the vast chamber, the copper slab vibrated in sympathy, as she and Ernest clung fearfully to one another. He was breathless with terror as he finally bore witness to the true visages of the Old Ones. Still his mind refused to accept this reality; his pulse was deafening as the sole hooded figure towered over them.

"Father's legacy has been difficult to fulfill."

Ernest did not truly hear these words. All he saw were the mutilated faces before him.

Each of the Old Ones was similar yet different. Some were hideously disfigured monstrosities barely recognizable as having ever been human. Others, though deeply scarred, still retained evidence of their former identities. But it was the absence of self in all of them that was irreconcilable—that repulsed every nerve in Ernest's being. Whoever they had been, there was no humanity left in them. Was this to be his and Tasaria's fate as well?

"You've come to destroy us!" Tasaria cried.

The Master grabbed her and forced her to look directly at the Old Ones.

"I know you recognize some of these faces. The faces of Moon Shadows, of friends long absent from your clan. Look upon them now. You see only the imperfections. You see only with your fear. You do not see the hope our faith has brought us."

Tasaria stared at the empty remnants of several Moon Shadows who'd departed with the Master years earlier.

"Look upon them. See the years of loneliness and doubt you have suffered in the absence of your child," his claw-like fingers withdrew from her chin. "Humanity and the Old Ones once existed together. We have always believed it, fought for it, died for it."

The Moon Shadow priestess' eyes slowly rose to meet her Lord's as his hand closed over hers.

"Our great purpose is almost complete. Your niece …"

"No, no," Tasaria shook her head, "she cannot be."

The creature released her hand and grabbed Ernest's injured one. Wordlessly, he held it out for Tasaria.

"She is the key. Or do you still doubt it is so?"

Ernest stared in disbelief. Where the gaping wound in his flesh had been, now only a rapidly healing gash remained. But there had been no ritual, not even physical contact between him and Baseria after he'd been stabbed. How could this be possible?

Ernest's eyes traced the corrupted, demonic visages all around him. Did the creature intend to somehow use Baseria to complete what he'd summoned from the netherworld?

"They were human," Ernest rasped.

The Master nodded.

"Slain in battle, by disease, accident, and now they are reborn to hope, destined to restore the natural order."

Ernest's thoughts came slowly.

"The prophecy?"

The other nodded in assent.

"Unlike Voltaire's God, my creation shall be perfected. These were merely a beginning. Angels, summoned to aid us in a just cause."

"Spirits you have damned! Puppets, slaves you have mutilated …"

The monster grabbed his adversary and flung him onto the unforgiving, frigid metal of the table. Ernest blinked against the blackness circling the edge of his vision, as the mummified hand again clasped his windpipe.

"They are not slaves! We will never be slaves as Father intended, as the perversions of humanity would have us be."

His mad eyes bore as brutally into Ernest's as the iron grip that constricted his breathing.

"But Master, they have no free will," Tasaria asserted quietly from behind. "I have seen this for myself." The pressure on Ernest's throat eased momentarily.

"And until now that has been my greatest failing," the creature acknowledged. Then his lips curled to reveal white teeth, which leered down at Ernest in the form of a sickening smile. "But at long last, Father has provided me with the answer, one that will make whole my creations."

"You're not a god," Ernest choked.

The merciless orbs bore down at him, their gaze a battle.

"Then let us meet one."

*

The Master again commanded his followers, who in unison resumed their hoods. Tasaria bent to retrieve the folded shroud as it was knocked off the end of the table while several of the Old Ones aided an unwilling Ernest back to his feet. She gasped in surprise as her eyes roved from the cut on her fingertips to the glittering mass below.

"Diamonds?" she breathed.

The underside of the white cloth glistened with the precious gems inlaid to the shroud.

An Old One helped her to her feet as several others reclaimed the cloth, folded it, and replaced it upon the table. Her eyes pleaded for answers from the Master.

"They focus energy," he stated by way of explanation as his minions completed their task.

Ernest ceased struggling and offered no resistance as the Old Ones escorted him down from the platform. His pallor was white, his eyes vacant. The Master paused only to relay orders to those who served him. All but three of the hooded figures vanished into the dark recesses of the chamber. Additional commands were given to those remaining and then he took Ernest roughly by the arm, leaving Tasaria with his repulsive companions.

They crossed the chamber to a narrow, dark tunnel, the floor of which was pure ice. Here the low level mist returned. From the impenetrable shadows, a sound reached them, marred by ice and rock, yet plaintive, pitiful.

"Please … don't do this," Ernest begged, his frozen voice shaking. Every nerve pulsed, alive with fear and anguish.

For an instant, the harsh eyes of the other softened a measure.

"Fate chose us for this; justice demands it."

Their souls aflame, the Angel of Destruction bid the misbegotten family members forth, from the gloom of the chamber, into the dark recesses of the tunnel. The treacherous footing and mind-numbing terror slowed Ernest's progress, but the other urged him ever forward. Something was waiting.

The flicker, cast by a lone torch, eventually illuminated a small circular room, the entry to which sloped downward. Ernest backed down the short ramp of ice. The impact of his boots made the frozen surface below him groan. But something else stirred in the shadow-laced chamber.

As he turned, Ernest's senses grew dull, his knees buckled as he beheld the corrupted sight before him. Disbelief in the naked face of the abomination banished reality to an endless eternity. It wept softly. The frozen breath of the hideous speaker reached Ernest before his words did.

"Did not Dante encase his Devil in ice, forever isolating him with his miseries, which he suffered for his own crimes? Only I have taken his wings."

Unwillingly Ernest rose and began to stagger backwards, away from the impossible perversion. The solid mass of the creature blocked his path. It withdrew its own hood. Watery, putrid yellow eyes hung suspended before him.

"I have fulfilled my promise to you, Uncle. Now stand in judgment of your great tormentor, of the Creator, of the monster who destroyed your family, of the demon that would be man."

Ernest felt as though he was drowning in blood. He could no longer deny the screams of the dead. The thing stirred. It wasn't real. None of this was real. The mummified face, the sunken eyes studied him. It wasn't real.

Hate filled Ernest's heart, and his body moved absent of thought. He struck the terrible thing before him over and over. It wasn't real. His soul burned as their cries surged and echoed. His fingers were hot and wet as was one cheek. The creature restrained one of his bloodied hands. Ernest looked down to it, sensed the blood upon his face. The eyes of the other narrowed.

"It is not death but life you fear," the fiend observed.

The thing below them erupted into a fit of coughing. Warm rivulets of blood now congealed on its fractured skin. Ernest shut his eyes, but the nightmare image followed him. It wasn't human. He struggled against the pressures within intent on stealing his senses.

Then it spoke. In a voice at once barely to be recognized and yet wholly familiar, the wheezing, legless, near mummified husk of what had once been a man spoke.

"Hello … brother."

CHAPTER 24
CHANGELINGS

Abrielle's lips sucked at the glistening stream of blood. She rubbed the offended area of her forefinger with her thumb. The needle hadn't gone very deep. Her head leaned back against the tree trunk and she sighed. Sewing did not require an abundant amount of concentration, but right now, it seemed to take more than she could summon. Abrielle had hoped repairing Tara's blanket would prove a useful distraction, instead, it seemed only to have unsettled her more.

Her senses filled the void of her mind. Were those sheep? She sat up straighter and listened. Far below a soft baying repeated itself, and as the minutes passed, a small chorus of bleats sang to the mountains, which seemed majestic, foreboding, and peaceful all at once.

Her eyes traced the dizzying path across the natural stone bridge that Espen had crossed nearly an hour ago. Thick woods concealed much of the trail on the far side where he'd vanished from sight. She hoped it didn't keep climbing. It felt like all she'd done for the past several days was climbing either up or down—endlessly.

This alone would have been tolerable were it not also for the emotional turmoil within, coupled with her persistent lack of sleep since leaving Salzburg. She drew a sip of water and shook the hollow bladder. If they didn't reach the camp today, they'd have to be sure to refill their supply the next opportunity they had.

A steady, cool breeze ushered an assortment of leaves and pine needles to the ground. Her gaze returned to the woods across the rock bridge. She closed her eyes. Maybe he would just leave her here. The recurring thought both alarmed her and comforted her. Maybe this time he wouldn't return. In many ways, it would be easier.

They must be extremely close by now. Abrielle felt certain she could reach the encampment on her own, then neither could blame the other when fate enforced its will upon them. Would they chase off a stranger or take her prisoner? Either outcome would prevent her from having to assume the role of Espen's wife, a task which had grown increasingly difficult to fathom.

While her own doubts regarding the plan would not diminish, it was clear that Espen now regretted his choice to bring her here. She didn't blame him. If Christiansen's fears about the young gypsy being a spy were unfounded, then Espen had knowingly placed himself in a no-win situation. For her part, Abrielle actively resented his doing so. It made her choices more difficult. Had he done this out of love, his own sense of morality, an innate sense of martyrdom, or to conceal a trap? Whatever the reason, Abrielle's heart refused to be swayed. It didn't matter. Too much depended on her making the right choices. The abduction of her niece by his father cried out for justice and if it resulted in Ernest's death too ….

Her spirit again shied away from the horrific thought and desperately foundered upon a new, albeit related one. If she escaped these mountains with Tara, where were they to go? Enemies seemed to relentlessly encircle her.

It appeared. A shadow, its symmetry bent on brutality, moved swiftly across the bridge, but her dull mind kept her body inert. It would be upon her in seconds, just as it had before. Still she could not escape the mesmerizing yellow eyes of the wolf as it pounced. She was helpless. Abrielle's body jerked as she awoke, her startled cry long since diminished by the time her senses began to return. One hand steadied her body as her breathing began to slow.

"Are you all right?" The concern in the voice was casual but genuine.

Abrielle hastened to rise.

"When did you get back?" she asked without further preamble.

"Does it matter?"

Abrielle gathered up her hair in her hands as she pushed it back and began to re-tie it.

"I fell asleep," she declared unnecessarily.

"I noticed."

"Were you planning to wake me?"

Espen paused.

"After I finished smoking this, yes. It looked like you could use the rest," he rubbed unconsciously at one of his eyes with the heel of his palm.

"I'm fine," Abrielle lied.

She was, in point of fact, exhausted, as was he. They faced the unknown, but they did so separately. Each was deeply suspicious and conflicted about the other, private doubts only added to the tensions. Neither allowed the other to stray from their sight for long, even when they were supposed to be sleeping. They would argue, remain silent for hours, and then argue more.

"What's on the other side?"

Espen shrugged, "More mountain." Then his eyes met hers. "We'll reach the camp in a matter of hours."

A shadow passed over Abrielle's face, but her pulse remained steady. They both knew what was coming.

"I need more," she insisted.

His expression became dour.

"So do I," he bit, "but we keep ending up at the same point, don't we."

Her tone mirrored his.

"I told you, until I can evaluate the layout of the camp and we find Jack, I can't be more specific about how I'll get her out. But if you don't tell me more about your customs, then this will be over before it begins."

His words mingled with the pipe smoke he hastily exhaled.

"You're my wife. All we need to know is how we met, the type of injuries you cured me of, and how long we've been married. You know Romani customs just fine." Espen prattled dismissively as he beat the spent pipe against his boot heel. "Keep a low profile, and everything else will take care of itself naturally."

She glared at him.

"I think you want me to get caught."

"Oh, please."

Their eyes broke, the moment given to a brooding silence that only the wind dared intrude. Espen suddenly laughed.

"This is ridiculous. You just made half of Salzburg believe you're an opera singer."

Abrielle shook her head as her eyes returned to his.

"This is different."

"Why? Because you actually have to depend on someone else for a change?" he asked.

"No," she responded quietly as a calm settled over her features, "because no one will ever believe that we're married."

Espen blinked as she drew closer.

"You told your father that you fell in love with me." Her hands reached for him, one began to delicately trace across his skin. The rhythmic pattern was soothing, her brown eyes filled with emotion. "Tell me you love me," she whispered in warm tones.

Abrielle's gaze was soft, her demeanor inviting. Espen's fingers unconsciously laced among hers.

"I love you."

Their lips met, teasing, pressing, retreating. Their embrace followed an identical pattern but all the while their actions, minds, and hearts remained at odds. Abrielle needed him to understand. At his most vulnerable now, she leaned in close and whispered in his ear.

"I'll do anything I have to do to get my niece back—anything." The threat was incongruous to the manner in which her fingers lightly played across the hair on the back of his head. She pulled back so again their eyes could meet. "Now, tell me that you love me."

Espen pushed her away and swore viciously as he turned from her and kicked at a nearby stump. He began to stalk away. Abrielle pursued him.

"You see our problem, don't you?" she demanded.

He spun back upon her.

"The only problem I see is you wasting our time with these games."

"This is no game. You don't see me as your wife. You see me as myself, and that makes you hesitate. If we break character, it creates doubt in others about us. And doubt endangers me, so it imperils Tara as well."

Espen shifted uncomfortably. Abrielle continued.

"Words and memorized feelings for a role are one thing, actually allowing yourself to embrace them is another. And you … you can't do that with me. Can you?"

It was his turn to glare.

"Not with someone who would kill my father. After everything …"

He turned from her impassive face; again she pursued him.

"Don't ask something of me I can't give," he barked over his shoulder.

"Then don't expect it from me either," she bit as she blocked his path. "Do you think I can just smile, passively meet his eye after all he's done?"

"Dammit, I'm not asking you to forgive him," Espen snapped.

"No, only to allow him to live."

Espen shook his head curtly as he clenched his jaw.

"Justice requires courage …"

"And will you forgive those who took your sister and the others?"

Abrielle's chest heaved in the silent moments that passed.

"Will you?" she challenged her suddenly bewildered companion. "Is that true justice?"

The instantly recognizable sound of unshod hooves striking against rock interceded as a rider and his mount clapped across the natural bridge. Espen shook his head to Abrielle's unspoken inquiry. Her hand released the hilt of the concealed knife, which she had instinctively reached for at the echoing report of the clattering hooves. By now the rider had spied them and waited along the edge of the path, which Abrielle and Espen diligently trod back towards.

"Thought that was you I saw," the man on the horse hailed to Espen who waved briefly in return.

"Just having a look at the terrain before we continued. She was tired."

The other studied Abrielle who'd assumed a polite, modest, noncommittal air of slow-witted innocence. A demeanor she maintained when the man attempted to speak directly to her. His effort unsuccessful, his focus returned to Espen.

"Heard you finally took a wife; doesn't she know our language?"

Espen smiled and placed his arms protectively around Abrielle as he kissed her cheek. She smiled as he did so.

"She's coming along, but the Germanic tongue or English are easier for her, unless you know Romani."

Espen returned his attentions to Abrielle.

"This is Hytr," he explained to her. "He'll guide us the rest of the way to my people's encampment."

"How much further?" she asked in a weary voice. Espen translated for the other gypsy who was apparently wholly unfamiliar with English.

Hytr released a short laugh as he dismounted his horse to allow Abrielle to ride. She tried not to think about riding the powerful animal across the rock bridge and the towering void it spanned.

"I'm surprised you made it this far up without being intercepted,"

Hytr stated. "Guess that's what happens when you take the scenic route, not so many of us guarding this approach. Your father expected you two days ago," he added.

"We were … busy two days ago," Espen explained, glancing briefly to his counterfeit wife.

Hytr looked to Abrielle, grinned, and slapped Espen on the back.

"Don't forget our things," Abrielle bid from atop the horse.

She pretended not to notice the additional crude comments Hytr openly made, believing her to be ignorant of his words, however, thanks to Espen she was actually becoming quite adept with their native tongue. True, during their time together they'd communicated primarily in English, but Abrielle quietly embraced any opportunities that exposed her to Espen's native Hungarian. Such knowledge and her natural abilities with language now afforded her an important advantage.

The men continued to bond and banter as they gathered the gear and renewed their assault on the heights of the Carpathians. She fought against the urge to close her eyes as they traversed the bridge; though her fingers mercilessly grasped Tara's blanket, which Espen had made a point to return to her. Despite the cool air of the mountains, her skin was damp with sweat by the time they reached the far side, as dark memories of the cliff in the Pyrenees assailed her.

At first she listened intently to the men's conversation, smiling occasionally or responding when Espen would take a moment to speak to her in English. However, Hytr turned out to be both dull and evasive, and soon Abrielle's mind began to wander as her eyes roved the eternally vertical landscape. According to Hytr, the mountain was well guarded, scouted, and fortified, should the Moon Shadows attempt more treachery. She alertly studied the terrain, but could detect no evidence of the Wild Rose clan's presence.

Privately, Abrielle's misgivings increased. If they were here, passing before her eyes, she did not have time to plan an effective route around their defenses, not if Jal's "hour of retribution" was near. And Hytr's remark that Espen was two days overdue seemed to validate that it was. He also implied that the route they now traveled was less direct than others Espen could have chosen. Why had he apparently taken her to the encampment the long way, especially knowing how critical time was? What had he been doing while she slept? Hytr's timing was certainly convenient. Might Espen have anticipated his father sending out scouts or could he have been in secret contact with Hytr before now? Her fears of betrayal grew. Paranoia began to cloud her judgment. Soon every time they reached a level area she almost expected to find Chloe and the others waiting for her.

"Do you need to rest, Orfilia?"

When had the horse stopped? Both men were staring up at her. It was clear from their expressions that the question had already been asked at least once before. Her eyes left theirs and frantically searched the area. Was this the ambush? She shook her head.

"Are you sure? You look … uncomfortable, dear."

Abrielle began to shake her head again, but instead, suddenly found herself scrambling down from the horse. She became sick behind a nearby tree seconds after reaching the ground. Hytr hovered awkwardly in the background as Espen knelt beside her, sympathetically rubbing her back. What was wrong with her? Abrielle pushed hair out of her eyes.

"Here."

Espen held out a full water bladder. Didn't she empty it earlier? When did he fill it? Was it Hytr's? Her thoughts turned to Berryer and his poisoning. If this was a trap, maybe he'd left something in his earlier to make her sick so she could now be taken without difficulty. Abrielle concentrated on her memories. The more Berryer drank the more rapidly his condition had deteriorated. She eyed the proffered bladder. Her throat was burning.

"Is it cold?" she tentatively asked.

His fingers pressed the sides of the pouch.

"Not bad," he asserted.

"Try it," she bid.

He hesitated before asking Hytr something. The other man nodded and exchanged water bladders with Espen.

"This is fresher," was the provided explanation.

Abrielle masked her discomfort as she drank a little, swished it around, and then spat it demurely upon the ground.

"We're very close," Espen assured her as he helped her to stand.

She said nothing as she repacked Tara's blanket, which had fallen to the ground, back among their scant possessions. She waited. Her enemies did not appear. Perhaps there was no need for them to do so.

"I'd like to walk," she finally requested.

*

Jal swore as his left boot slipped. The unanticipated motion caused his crossed arms to flail outward. One found a nearby tree, which he used to secure himself to a full halt. He cursed again as he bent to retrieve the pipe that fell when his balance waned and waited impatiently for the saddled form of Hytr to reach him. The intrusion had best be justified. The horse and rider drew even with him.

"What news, Hytr?" Jal demanded as he resumed his pipe and re-crossed his arms across his formidable bulk.

"Your son and his wife have returned," the younger man anxiously announced. "They approach."

"My son may approach," Jal corrected, gesturing with his pipe as he exhaled a cloud of smoke. "Take the woman back to the encampment. She has no place up here. Have someone watch over her."

Hytr nodded and galloped off to carry out his orders. Jal shook his head. Young people never took the time to think their decisions through, to marry so frivolously, outside of their people even, and then to insist that the girl be brought to the Carpathians at a time like this. His back was bothering him again. He was tempted to lean against the tree or to step inside the small tent while he waited, but decided neither was an appropriate choice. He was displeased with Espen and his demeanor should reflect that. His son still had provided no real answers regarding the loss of the men under his command. Such matters were not to be taken lightly. The minutes passed. His gaze lingered at the point where Hytr had descended. What was taking so long?

Without fully realizing that he was doing so, he began to pace again. There must be something he'd overlooked, though weeks of endless thought had not revealed this to him. Still, he must be absolutely sure, leave no possibility of a repetition of the last disastrous Moon Shadow attack. His people must be protected.

"Father?"

Jal offered no pause in his motions as he dropped his arms behind his back and firmly clasped his hands together.

"You're late."

Espen nodded

"I did not come by the direct route," he disclosed matter-of-factly.

Jal halted and turned to face him, awaiting an explanation.

"Forgive me; I know time is against us but …"

"What's wrong?" Jal immediately interjected.

"I'm," Espen cleared his throat, "I'm not sure how to tell you this, but it seems that my wife is ... um … expecting."

Jal withdrew the pipe from his mouth.

"When?"

"Not for awhile," Espen assured him hastily. "I just … ah … I just found out myself," he stammered, somewhat confused.

For a moment Jal's expression remained frozen in quizzical surprise. Then he began to laugh as he slapped his son approvingly on the back. Espen still looked ill at ease with the news, but Jal was elated. The Nalie line would continue.

"It was the samc for your mother and me," Jal smacked his hands together and thrust them outward. "Marriage, children."

He wrapped an arm tightly around his son's shoulders, laughing again, before becoming serious.

"Come, our time is short and we have much to discuss." Jal gestured for Espen to enter the modest sized tent.

"What is to happen here?" Espen wondered aloud.

Jal breathed heavily.

"My child, your sister is to be restored to us."

Espen turned to him in amazement.

"Baseria," he whispered.

His father nodded gravely as he placed a large hand on Espen's shoulder.

"We must ensure our children's survival—and our people's."

*

Abrielle opened her eyes as the image of Bellange faded from her mind. In the dream was her former master warning her or providing her counsel? Her mouth tasted terrible. After the last time she became sick, she'd fallen asleep. The tent they provided for her and Espen was comfortable, contained an assortment of packed belongings, and was well within the confines of the large encampment Hytr had led her to.

She stood and tried to work the stiffness from her muscles. Dehydration, days of travel, and emotional stress prevented her efforts from being more than moderately successful. Abrielle retrieved several empty water bladders, one of which she concealed, and then hovered near the doorway. Hytr was no where in sight.

A few faint rays of dying light echoed across the sky and through the stand of low twisted trees that seemed to pervade the encampment. To Abrielle they seemed horribly flawed. It appeared as if they'd once aspired to rise higher towards the light, but instead became fearful and now wallowed in these tortured shapes. Even most of their leaves were already cast aside. Their yellows and oranges rustled against the hem of her dress as she began to wander about the encampment.

But this activity, though casual, held a more definitive purpose. Her mind relentlessly sought details. Her senses devoured them. In these lay the key to her success. How many more opportunities to wander this freely would she be given? Her eyes seized upon a likely source of useful information.

In somewhat labored Hungarian, she called to a passing child, "Excuse me. Water?" Abrielle held up her empty water bladder.

The young girl, no more than six, followed the woman's gaze down to the heavy bucket she carried.

"Where? Can you show me?" Abrielle asked pointing to the water still sloshing against the sides of the bucket.

The child studied her. It was not the first time an adult had made such a request, however, she couldn't recall ever seeing this woman before. And why was her speech so bad? Though she was tired from her chores, the girl decided to take pity on the stranger. She motioned for Abrielle to wait then vanished among the tents, reappearing several minutes later with the newly-emptied bucket.

The two proceeded through the encampment and eventually arrived at a mountain stream. When Abrielle touched it, the water was so cold that it burned her hands as she filled the bladder. She cleansed her mouth fully, then refilled the bladder. The child, though patient for her age, quickly refilled her bucket and left her by the time Abrielle was finished. For the moment, she was alone. She filled the second bladder, scuffed it lightly against a rock, and then hid it from view. Now she had a reliable source of water.

As she did so, Abrielle's heart quivered with emotion, and a single thought pulsed through her being: Tara was here. She tried to focus. Waiting now when she was so close was infuriating, but there was little real choice. She reluctantly threw a measure of icy water onto her face, gasped slightly at the numbing sensation, and shook the drops away. Though unpleasant, it did refresh her to a degree.

Without patience, all hope was lost. Her mind attempted to continue its examination, but the gloom was making it difficult to survey the surrounding landscape. She was anxious to judge the accuracy of the map Espen had provided Jack with against the real thing.

Abrielle stood and innocently began to wander further up the stream. A low growl from the darkness arrested her steps. A man with a large dog emerged from the woods on the opposite side of the stream. Abrielle suppressed the urge to defend herself as they leapt over to her bank.

"Wandcring a bit far, aren't we?" he inquired.

She smiled and began to back away only to run directly into Hytr, the by-now resentful young girl at his side. He bristled with both relief and irritation.

"See, I told you she was down here. Can I go now?" The girl begged, her eyes fixed on the imposing canine.

"Yes, fine, go. Thank you," said the exasperated Hytr. He barely registered her immediate departure.

"What's your name?" the man with the dog demanded of Abrielle.

Hytr interceded.

"This is Espen's bride, Orfilia, and she doesn't speak our language. Do you?"

It was not difficult for Abrielle to look uncomfortable. Hytr uttered both the statement and question as if she were deaf.

"Really?" said the guard skeptically. "Could have sworn she was conversing in it a few minutes ago with Ebba's daughter."

Hytr shrugged.

"Well, she wasn't with Espen or me this afternoon." He began to lead Abrielle away. "Think he mentioned teaching her some though."

His companion looked unimpressed.

"Keep her in the camp," he commanded.

"Hey, I'm not married to her," Hytr scoffed.

Curious, Hytr momentarily tried again to speak to her in Hungarian, but Abrielle offered no response aside from another polite smile. They marched on in an uncomfortable silence back into the main encampment. Abrielle spotted the girl being lectured to by her mother; it would not be difficult to guess on what subject. Abrielle soon received one of her own.

"Now you stay put this time. Last thing I need is you wandering off causing more trouble. If you need something, I'll get it," Hytr promised when he again closed her in the tent.

Abrielle ignored his indignation as she began to rummage through her and Espen's belongings, searching for certain items of personal value. Locating some of them, she began to arrange each into a fixed, and by now, familiar pattern. She closed her eyes as she attempted to relax and recall the events and sights of the day.

Since leaving Salzburg, this had become her own private ritual—a recreation and expansion of the map Espen had created for Jack. To this end, she'd designated a given number of their effects to represent objects and unique landscape features. By arranging them and adding to the grouping, she could keep track of distances and memorize details associated with the geography of the area. Hopefully, if anyone walked in unexpectedly, it would merely appear as if she were unpacking. This was far less compromising than bringing a paper copy, but it must be kept up to date and accurate.

Her lower lip screwed in concentration as she adjusted the distance between certain items. Abrielle could only guess how far Hytr rode up the mountain to where Espen now met with his father. Still, there were clues. How fast had he been riding? How many minutes between when he vanished from sight and when he reappeared to bring her alone to the encampment?

She also needed something new to represent the approximate location of the unexpected guard. His presence added another unwelcome layer of complexity. How many more surrounded the camp? Did they have regular patrol stations? Were all of them accompanied by canines? The sentry seemed to be quite interested in what was going on inside the perimeter. Did they expect trouble to emanate from within the encampment as well?

As her mind considered these problems she inadvertently smacked her foot against one of the trunks in the tent. Perhaps one of them contained suitable objects she could use. None of the trunks were locked, so she began to search all of them, pulling out clothing, cookware, bedding, even jewelry.

She laid a brush down to approximate where Jal might be on the mountain. Her fingers lingered on it. Was Tara with him there or was she here in the encampment with her?

Abrielle closed her eyes for a moment and took a deep, measured breath, but when she reopened them and looked down, her fingers only clasped the brush more intently. The metal felt cool against her skin, against her scar. Reluctantly, she released it and returned her attentions to the other items she'd discovered. One bracelet she found, in particular, attracted her fancy. The style was one she recognized as French. She slipped it on.

"Put it back!" Espen barked.

Abrielle jumped both at the surprise of his sudden presence and the clear note of anger in his voice.

"Put it back," he forcefully repeated as he knelt beside her and began to shovel items back into the trunks.

"Wait, some of that is ours," she began reaching out a hand.

For an instant he paused.

"Dammit, then find ours," Espen harshly bid.

Confused, she diligently began to root out and separate their items as he abruptly stood and stalked across the tent. Abrielle felt guilty and ashamed as she finished reloading the items into the trunks. Her face was hot.

The final item—the bracelet—she stood, removed it from her wrist, crossed the tent and presented it to Espen from behind. He snatched it from her with disdain, and she retreated, seating herself on one of the closed trunks. Though his back remained to her, it was obvious that Espen was studying the bracelet. Whose items were these? Abrielle turned her eyes from him as he crossed the tent and returned it wordlessly to the remaining open trunk, the lid of which he closed as if it were a coffin, bound for the grave. He stood over it for a moment of quiet reflection.

Espen turned to her, but Abrielle would not meet his gaze. He looked away.

"Orfilia," he finally said.

Abrielle swallowed hard.

"Yes, my husband."

"My father would like to meet you."

*

Except for her senses, Abrielle's mind was blank. The fallen leaves swirled and bent beneath her; the evening air was crisp. By the dim light of muted fires inside tents, she saw faces; shadow forms rushed past; she heard laughter but felt none. Conversations rose and ebbed as Espen's hand guided her—though to what future she could not say. They stopped underneath one of the numerous twisted trees.

"Orfilia," the note of tenderness did not reach her. "Orfilia?"

Abrielle blinked. She felt the warmth of his hands as they gently cupped her cold cheeks.

"A friend once told me she would do anything for that which she treasures most."

Espen's expectant gaze bore heavily down on her.

"If she were here now, I would ask only that she forgive herself. In this there is strength."

Their kiss was brief but passionate. It spoke what they could not. They parted awkwardly, silent. Then she reached down and took his hand. It would be expected. She could not bring herself to look at Espen when she spoke.

"I hope he finds me adequate for his brave son."

Their fingers shifted among each others.

"Say little," Espen advised after a moment. They renewed their steps.

As they progressed, Abrielle realized that the encampment was becoming a labyrinth to her. One she might never escape. If she failed in the moment to come, then she would certainly be lost. But what if she already was? What if Jal had seen her in Ireland? If so, would he recognize her now? Could presenting herself before him deny Tara to her forever? Or had Espen already told him who she was, and all of this was but an elaborate ruse utilized to close the final trap? Her mentor would have relished such brutal efficiency and betrayal. Her breath grew shallow as they suddenly halted outside of a tent.

"Father?"

Espen squeezed her hand, and momentarily, Abrielle forgot herself as she released her grasp on his. Every instinct beseeched her to action. How often did she dream of the fiend who had stolen Tara, snatched her innocent niece from the cradle, the infant from her family? Of making him suffer. No. No, she was Espen's wife. She must be his wife. That was the reality of this moment. And this was nothing more than one of Bellange's deadly games. She again clasped her husband's hand as they stepped together into the tent.

It was empty. A small fire smoldered, which Espen bent and stirred, illuminating the space.

"Father?"

Abrielle studied her surroundings. The tent was much larger than the one she and Espen occupied. It bore curtains that could separate sections of tent if necessary. The warmth was a welcome change, and all of the fabrics held an aroma rich in tobacco smoke. Espen drew back one of the closed curtains only to discover it stacked with sundry items. He was about to draw back another when a large, black-bearded man erupted into the tent, laughing as he threw a dead animal carcass down beside the fire.

"Dinner is served," Jal announced, "Tyh promises me this is quite fresh," he chuckled, pausing to regard Abrielle. "So this is her?"

Espen nodded.

Unexpectedly Jal bent down and wrapped Abrielle into a powerful hug.

*

"Tell me more of your life, Orfilia"

He reeked of alcohol and pipe smoke, and would, undoubtedly, soon smell even more strongly of both now that dinner was over. In fact, he began to withdraw a pipe as he waited for Abrielle to respond. She looked momentarily to Espen before clearing her throat. How long did he intend to continue this cruelty?

"What else can I tell you of?" she asked politely in English. For two hours now she'd endured this humiliating torture. They had already engaged in lengthy discourse about her nonexistent family, of her and Espen's marriage, and about the similarities and differences between their peoples. He even joked about the scar on her palm.

As he lit his pipe in the fire, Abrielle wondered if Jal was always this inquisitive. From her perspective, the conversation kept degrading into a thinly veiled interrogation with questions and topics repeatedly raised, as if he were deliberately checking if her answers remained consistent. Was his continued drinking responsible for these supposed lapses, as he claimed, or was it an act to cover the true nature of their dialogue?

"You have much experience as a healer?" he asked leaning back against a pillow.

"In some matters, not all," she said modestly. "There is always more to learn, and I am happy to be of service whenever I can," she hastened to add withering momentarily under his questioning gaze, afraid her response would displease him. "I've seen much."

There was a noise from the back of the tent. Espen suddenly interceded, reaching down to help Abrielle stand.

"It grows late, Father, and there will be much to do in the morning."

For a moment, the older man hesitated then rose. A sound repeated itself from behind one of the unopened curtains.

"We should rest, Orfilia," Espen suggested, a trace of urgency in his tone.

"Jal?" a muffled voice inquired from behind the veiled drape.

"In a moment," he replied, smiling down at his false daughter-in-law.

Abrielle's heart began to beat faster. She was certain she heard …

Jal laid a hand upon her shoulder, returning her attention to him.

"Orfilia. Twice you have blessed my son, first restoring his life to him and now bearing him another. You come to us at a time of great reunion," he placed the other hand on Espen's shoulder, "of family. The generosity of your spirit honors us. May you find much happiness here among our people."

It was perverse. He again enfolded her in an embrace of warmth and acceptance, forcing her to do the same. But this time as he held her, the curtain parted to reveal another section of the tent, one with its own entrance. Framed there was a middle-aged woman holding a child.

Abrielle could feel her legs buckling as she fought back tears and the overwhelming stillness of her heart as she beheld the infant. It was Tara. The flash of short, blonde hair as the woman repositioned the fussing girl's wrapping would have been enough for Abrielle to recognize her, but there was more. Tara's face was that of her mother as it was the day she'd been taken by the monster that now held Abrielle.

Jal began to release Abrielle. She could kill him, shatter his spine in an instant.

"Why are you crying?" he asked his son's wife.

Abrielle's fingers smeared the silent tears across her cheeks as her eyes finally parted from Tara and turned to those of her niece's abductor.

"I didn't … I didn't know, if … if you'd like me," her voice broke.

Espen drew close to her before his father could respond. He lightly kissed the side of her cheek as he placed a covering over her shoulders.

"It's been a very long day, dear. Come."

"Yes, rest," Jal advised before turning his attentions to the woman. "And what is wrong with my little Chavi tonight that she complains so?"

Abrielle could feel Espen pulling on her arm, but she stood firm.

"Her teeth again," the other woman explained. "She's been worked up like this for …"

She paused.

"May I hold her?"

Jal turned, surprised to find Orfilia beside him, wearing a strange expression as she stared intently at the baby.

"What did she ask?"

"She'd like to hold the child," Espen solemnly translated.

The woman looked to Jal for instructions. He momentarily considered the request, then nodded in agreement.

As the woman stepped forward, Abrielle held out her arms. They felt awkward, slow to respond; but her nerves sensed the texture of the cloth, the warmth, and the weight of her niece. The other retreated, and at long last, Tara was in Abrielle's arms.

For an eternal moment of joy, all she could do was stare down in disbelief and wonder. Her niece was so delicate. Abrielle drew her closer. Her cheek tenderly rested against Tara's head. She closed her eyes as her fingers began to soothingly rub the distraught baby's back. Her body swayed gently as she began to quietly hum a familiar song, one she'd often sung to Ailis as her dying sister drifted into sleep after Abrielle had finished combing her hair.

She was barely aware of the others' departure into the back of the tent. Her soul was too entranced with relief and gratitude. Tara's cries began to abate. Abrielle could feel the girl's small heart beating against her breast. She would never lose her again, never.

The distinct sensation of a blade pressing firmly into her ribs renewed the nightmare, as did her husband's hushed words to her.

"Don't make the mistake of your life."

CHAPTER 25
CORRUPTIO OPTIMI PESSIMA

She was home. Her senses told her that much, though her eyes remained closed. Was she feeling grass beneath her? It was cool. Baseria slowly drew open her eyelids to behold a sky of clear blue far above, while dancing blades of rich-scented grass and wildflowers hovered invitingly within reach. She basked in their fragrance. Everything around her was alive.

Her bare toes rubbed against the earth as she sat up. Soft breezes enfolded Baseria. She began to smile, though the act itself felt like a distant memory. How long had it been since she'd last been able to do so? She let her hair out, relinquished it to the winds, as she momentarily re-closed her eyes, yielding fully to the passions of the sun. Her lungs drew lusty breaths of temperate air.

Nothing was dark here. She rose and small insects fluttered upward as she did so, vanishing. The high meadow spread its bounty in all directions around her. Baseria's fingers played among the tall, swaying grasses as she began to walk. Her feet leaving subtle impressions on the landscape she traversed. The sensation amused her.

She'd been a child when she left this place. What was she now? The question troubled her. Why was it so important that she be able to answer it? She knew. All else depended on it.

The shore of trees to her left, their boughs waving, yielded to the ocean of grasses she drifted in. There, near where the two met, stood a lone tent. Baseria considered its existence for a moment, then her spirit grew light as the breezes whistled past her sprinting form. She would be there, waiting. Someone who cared for her, someone she could trust.

"Nagyanya," she cried as her hand reached for the flap and swept it open. For an instant she saw her.

"Nagyanya."

Baseria's eyes were open. The world was dark, harsh, and cold. And she was alone, so abjectly wretched in her solitude. She tried to move. Her body ached as though she was feverish. A throbbing pain shot through her left hand the moment Baseria attempted to use it to turn.

Delicately, she withdrew it from beneath the blankets. The back of it now bore a bruised, angry scar, one mirrored on her palm. She fought to collect her thoughts as she studied the wound. She hadn't been stabbed …

A disturbing sequence of images returned to her consciousness: Ernest, the sword, their mutual agony as the blade mangled his flesh, of the thing that wielded it. As did the monster's chilling last words to her. Baseria's eyes cast fearfully about. Frigid air and stiff muscles made it quite difficult for her to rise, but she managed. She'd been sweating, and her clothing scratched against her raw skin. Her fingers trembled as an unsteady hand caressed her throbbing temple.

A wooden box lay near the frozen pool of blood on the floor, the one Ernest claimed that Nasi had given him. Baseria retrieved the object and carefully regarded it. She'd never seen anything quite like it. Why had her grandmother given this to Frankenstein?

A frenzied hope seized her. Could its contents possibly provide the key to her freedom? Might it grant her wisdom about how to control the raw, deadly power surging through her? Baseria's injured, though clearly healing, hand made a complete examination of the box difficult. Still, the cursory one she gave it afforded her no insight into how it opened.

She set it down on the bench and, for a moment, only the sound of the waves echoed beneath the chapel. Then she attacked the final gift her grandmother had given to anyone.

Baseria shrieked as she forcibly threw the box at the stone altar, pursuing the bouncing form seconds after it harmlessly struck. She ignored the pain in her hand as she used it to grip the offending object. Over and over she drove it down, first into the floor of stone, then into a nearby basin, part of the floor that was full of ice, fragments of which erupted as she mercilessly hammered the box against it. Nothing worked.

"I don't want to die! I don't want to die! I don't want to die!"

The box clattered uselessly to the floor as she reached out and embraced her grandmother.

"I'm sorry. Oh, God, I'm sorry."

Nasi held her, Baseria held nothing. What else could she do? She was going mad. Still her thoughts asked the question.

"What more can I give?"

She was desperate, frantic. Everything she did only brought pain, death. But there was no answer. Her grandmother was dead. Baseria closed her eyes in anguish.

"Doubt, Sunflower."

They were together in Nasi's tent before the fire. Baseria's head on her lap, the old woman's fingers calmly, reassuringly stroking her granddaughter's hair.

"Change is elemental. Our choices reveal our true hearts or provide us lessons that will. Without doubt you abandon yourself to fate, to the absence of spirit. You are strong, child. Your choices must be yours."

Was this a memory or a ghost? Baseria didn't care, though she feared to speak again lest the moment end. Her hand touched the old woman's, and then Baseria rolled upward from the cold floor. She was alone. There was no trace of the former Seer.

Mournfully, her grandchild again began to reach out to retrieve the wooden box, but she paused in disbelief. Where her fingers had touched Nasi's the skin looked grey, shriveled, and dead. However, the back of her palm now was completely healed, though perplexingly, the palm itself bore an even wider wound.

There was no sensation of physical pain but this made the moment no less excruciating. Perhaps she was too cold to feel it, or the shock of what she was seeing too great. Baseria's eyes cast downward. She must have somehow frozen it on the ice in the floor basin or …

Had she actually been touching her grandmother? Could doing so have brought about this corruption of her flesh? Or might this new degradation also be linked to Frankenstein, just as the original wound from the blade had been? Was her mind collapsing? Was this real? Did this mean he was dead? The tears this time were silent as she finished picking up the wooden box and shuffled stiffly back to the benches.

Baseria lay numbly upon them and again lost herself to the sound of the crashing waves below. She could conceive of but one way to purge her flesh, to again attempt to use the wild and seductive powers within her to heal. Powers she did not fully comprehend. Ones that effortlessly consumed her spirit, which frightened her as they ceaselessly beckoned to the very essence of her being. She was a prisoner to them, no differently than she was to the Moon Shadows, their dark master, or the abysmal fortress they controlled.

But this had not always been so. Her frozen breath hovered above her chapped lips as the new thought formed. Yes, once touching Elemental energy had been a transitory experience. At times she was able to exercise her will upon it, others it did so to her. The contact, however, was never of a possessive nature. Then the visions had come, the healing union, and finally her grandmother's death. The energy changed. Her thumb traced one of the dead areas of her hand. There was still so much she did not know about her power. What enabled her to sense it, use it? She'd asked Nasi this question several times and been told only that it was a gift given long ago. Baseria never pressed the matter, always assuming they would speak of it more when both were ready. But that conversation never took place.

Baseria rose as if she were suddenly immersed in ice water. It hadn't taken place with her, but what if it had with another? Her aunt and her mother, they were once trained together. They must have asked Nasi about the nature of such power and their unique ability to connect with it. She pursed her lips. Their loss still saddened and angered her. She and Ernest managed to avoid directly discussing the subject for endless weeks, as each offered only perfunctory or seemingly rehearsed comments. He maintained that their destruction, at the behest of her grandmother, was somehow meant to protect her, while Baseria mocked the suggestion. How could their immolation possibly aid her?

Until this moment, she'd always interpreted the scrolls' annihilation as her grandmother's final judgment of her. Baseria was unfit to continue the traditions of the Seer. But if she had, in fact, just spoken with her grandmother's spirit, then it called that understanding into question.

Perhaps Nasi foresaw her own death and took steps to ensure that Tasaria never regained access to the scrolls. If so, then was this because the information itself was inherently dangerous or her aunt's potential use of it was? The memory of Vochallet covered in blood returned to her. Elemental energy was unquestionably perilous, but it also had healed Baseria and Ernest of their wounds. If she'd been able to harness the power in the past, why was she unable to control it for that purpose now?

Vochallet!

Baseria's heart carried her almost to the door before her steps faltered. Could she hope to escape? What awaited her beyond the door? Baseria looked woefully around. Nothing could be gained by remaining here. She did, however, return momentarily to the benches. Maybe Tasaria could reveal some clue as to the significance of the box.

As she retraced her path, her eyes locked on the crimson marks upon the floor of stone. They grew fainter as she approached the door, as if Ernest ceased to exist outside of the chapel. An all but imperceptible tremor permeated her uninjured hand as her fingers gingerly tested the handle before gripping it firmly. It was unlocked. Outside, all was masked by the murky cloak of shadow and night. Would the demon claim her there?

With only her fears to guide her, Baseria became one with the darkness.

***

Geneva,1787

Ernest's fingertips sang across the sparkling water. Sometimes they bounced unevenly atop the restless surface. Other times they erupted through the small waves the lake erratically lobbed at the sides of the sailboat. The pattern was mesmerizing.

"I thought you wanted to learn about sailing?" Victor called out to him over the wind.

"I do," Ernest asserted.

"Then why am I the one doing all the work?" Victor countered.

"Don't you do all the work when you take Elizabeth out?" his younger sibling playfully inquired.

Victor withdrew Ernest's arm from the water and fixed him with a gaze.

"Yes, but you're not Elizabeth," the elder brother stated with a wry smile as he handed his younger sibling a measure of rope. Ernest rolled his eyes.

"Four knots, like I showed you, about this far apart."

"Right, start them here?" Ernest asked as Victor stood to rework some of the rigging.

"What? Yes," he replied distractedly. Ernest looped the rope as he'd been shown, affixing a portion of it into a tight knot and smiled proudly at his quick work.

"How's that?"

Victor stooped back down to glance at the results of his brother's effort.

"No, no, no. Start it lower down than that or we won't have any slack to work with." He shoved the rope back at Ernest and returned his attentions to his previous task. Ernest studied Victor. He seemed possessed by a singular energy.

"Wait, what am I tying this for anyway?"

"To help keep the sail under tight control so we can catch more of this wind."

His suspicions roused, Ernest bit his tongue. This trip better not be part of some experiment again. Victor was perpetually fumbling with small tests involving some combination of various chemicals, philosophies, physics, or mathematics. Ernest often found these a distraction as Victor rarely informed anyone of his intentions to conduct his field work prior to their commencement. Suddenly, Ernest fervently wished his father had taken him sailing. He glanced down at the knots he was tying. Distracted, he hadn't fully paid attention to their creation.

"Are you done?" Victor asked.

Ernest shrugged.

"I guess."

"Good, tie it off, and I'll get the sail ready."

Ernest completed his task seconds before the sail billowed full. The boat shifted, and he let out a whoop of excitement as their speed increased. He loved to sail, but Father was often too busy to take him, and worse, was unwilling to allow him to take anything other than the row boat out on the lake by himself until he spent more time under his brother's less impulsive tutelage. This forced Ernest to rely on Victor and his whims.

But life was changing. He looked up to his brother's smiling face. Soon Victor would be gone to university, and despite their differences, Ernest would genuinely miss his company, even his guidance. Still, undoubtedly, he'd come back often to see their parents, his brothers, and of course, Elizabeth. They were inseparable.

As he looked out across the lake bathed in shadow and sunlight, Ernest dreamt, as he often did, of the day he might really go to sea and the adventures that awaited him there. He turned.

"Do you think that …?"

The sail struck harshly against the side of his head. The motion of the sail was internalized as his body pitched to starboard. His arms flailed, desperate to regain control. Ernest's hands swung in opposing directions, one of them coming to rest upon a re-enforcing strip of metal. Both his hand and body retracted instantly.

"Are you all right?" Victor asked.

Ernest probed the knot on his head and peered questioningly at his brother. His eyes felt as though they were still shaking from the force of the impact.

"What was that for?"

"One of your knots must have slipped when I tried to trim the sail," Victor explained, holding up a measure of rope from the deck.

Ernest glanced down at the remains of his work as he flexed the fingers that had come into contact with the metal strip. They felt as if they'd been singed.

"What happened? Did you cut your hand?"

"No, shocked," Ernest responded, studying the affected skin.

Victor glanced at the metal strip then up at the sky.

"Yeah, atmosphere's right on a day like this, probably the water's humidity and all the static in your hair from the wind. It would be interesting to know how much of a charge you received. Here let me see that." Victor leaned closer to study the knot on his younger brother's head.

"I'm fine," Ernest protested. This certainly wasn't the first time such an accident had befallen him, as they both well knew.

"Too bad we're not hiking by any glaciers. That's really swelling," Victor noted. "Maybe we should head back in."

"What, over this?"

Victor's fingers rapped the mast as he momentarily looked away before fixing his eyes squarely on Ernest.

"I'm a little worried about Elizabeth," Victor confessed. "She didn't seem to be in good health at all this morning."

"Well, if she's sick, you know Mother and Justine will take good care of her."

"I'm a little worried about that, too," Victor noted as he tapped Ernest and pointed to the ominous clouds rapidly amassing behind them. For a long moment, they both gazed wordlessly at the darkening sky.

"I don't think we'll be able to outrun that," Ernest finally declared.

Victor was already in motion.

"We're going to try," he asserted. "Hurry up and re-tie those knots."

The boat slowly shifted as Victor maneuvered them against wind and tide for home.

***

"Hello … brother."

The devastating words drew Ernest to the earth, the ice, his abused heart a bitter mixture of egregious anguish and fearful hope. His soul was drowning in fury and loathing. There was no mercy in the hollow eyes before him, only wretchedness.

"Are you my brother?" Ernest choked in a mixture of misery and disbelief. "Are you … Victor?"

It recoiled from the name. A mummified hand, lacking several fingers, rose upward and covered those decaying eyes.

"Kill me," it pathetically wept. "Kill me."

His soul was a tempest. Ernest's eyes seized upon the dark, towering nightmare behind him.

"You may grant him whatever compassion you wish, Uncle, though I have done so already."

Ernest sprang up and grabbed the creature's cloak as his voice and emotions surged.

"What have you done to him?!" he demanded as the other apprehended his hands. "What have you done?!" Neither relented their forceful grip.

"I've given him the chance to become human," the creature sneered.

"You've destroyed him, butchered my brother!"

The fiend flung Ernest away, though he remained upright.

"I've destroyed an enslaver and brought a false god to his knees by making him a kindred spirit. Before, always before, Father could not understand his offspring's plight, would not, idly allowing others to suffer for his crimes while he broke his promises. His very soul bereft of compassion for his child, his wife, his family, for you."

"You're not his son!"

The words echoed momentarily through the chamber.

"You're not," Ernest insisted, shaking his head.

The massive shadow withdrew his hood and peered pitifully into Ernest's eyes. "Victor Frankenstein created me, gave me life. We are family, as you and I are, Uncle. He and I are kindreds in physical death and by guilt. But we are kindred as innocents, in suffering."

"Innocent?" The word elicited another brief coughing fit from Victor. "You slaughter our brother, murder my best friend, my wife ..."

"My only birthright was hatred. I was a failed experiment to be forgotten, destroyed, left uneducated, alone, without guidance, denied family, love, friendship," the creature thundered. "Even after you knew I'd survived, you marked me as an enemy, refusing to fulfill the only compassionate promise you ever made. They died by your hands, Father, there is no difference."

Ernest could not navigate the furious maelstrom of insanity. He was powerless to stop it, uncertain if he should, as his sanity was vulgarly infected by his stark, unprotected soul.

"He abandoned you, as he did me," the ghoulish being vehemently asserted.

"He annihilated our family; our loved ones. Elizabeth. I had to stop him!"

"Your sympathies were never with your family, otherwise, you would have told them the truth. But you were always far too selfish for that. Better to allow the innocent to suffer in your place."

"How could I have known you'd survived? Those months were lost to me," Victor cried.

"You could have saved the innocent girl during the trial, Father. Where was your vaulted compassion, your humanity? Why did you not speak the truth then?"

The crushing horror of the moment banished Ernest's rage as his mind became a prisoner of the past. All he could see was the face of the woman he'd loved, silently pleading for understanding from atop the grim scaffolding; her fate certain, his guilt eternal. Ernest's face was wet with mingled kisses of blood and tears.

The corrupted mask of Victor continued to struggle to answer the question. His mouth moving dully, void of sound, then nothing.

"Who created you?" the creature finally asked as he resumed his hood.

"You did," Victor responded without hesitation, his voice empty of thought.

"Then tell me of Elizabeth," the other commanded as he leaned close.

The words died. The moment lengthened. Then madness, Ernest had only witnessed once before, in Victor's old professor, seized the pathetic remains of his brother. His face was charged with rapidly shifting emotions. Breaths were resisted then craved. He drew blood from his lips, as his repulsive form convulsed violently.

"Tell me," the creature persisted. "Tell me of Elizabeth."

"She is death! SHE IS DEATH!" The words were horribly distorted as Victor's agony involuntarily wrenched forth. "ELIZABETH!" he cried out with a passionate, insane fervor as if she would appear. The torment continued.

"You love her."

"Yes! Yes! Yes."

"Then save her from oblivion, Father. Tell me."

Victor began to laugh, the sound was rasping, mirthless, and deranged.

"She is free … they are all free. I set them free."

The creature moved his bulk.

"No. Your brother is not free."

"My brother?" Victor struggled now as he peered in perplexity at Ernest.

"No … no, all dead. They're all dead. All dead! All dead!"

The other grabbed him violently.

"Look Father, look! Your brother lives. He is here with us. I've restored him to you as promised, kept my word. The same can be done for her. I swear it … I swear it."

Victor slowly drew his eyes away from Ernest to his unholy creation.

"You've done this," he whispered in disbelief

"Tell me," the monster commanded.

The mutilated figure of Victor shuddered violently before a series of equations erupted spastically from him: mathematical and chemical. Interspersed within were words from philosophy, musical notation, and phrases from a variety of dialects. To Ernest these sequences meant little, though he recognized them as code similar to that which had appeared in Victor's journals.

The creature would, at points, interrupt, responding in kind, eliciting either the censure or acknowledgement of his creator. At last, the great being drew the bizarre exchange to a close by uttering words wholly foreign to Ernest, but ones which promptly rendered Victor unconscious.

Ernest knelt beside him.

"He sleeps?"

At length the creature answered.

"Such habituation has become necessary."

"Because of your torture?" Ernest charged.

The other did not reply as he again lost himself to black thoughts.

"Answer me!" Ernest demanded. His companion sighed deeply.

"He followed me in pervasive madness, stalked me to the frozen excesses of the earth and there he perished, smote not by my hand but by Nature's dominant one."

His vile eyes set upon Ernest's.

"But I have learned my progenitor's secrets. Father lives, Uncle."

Ernest regarded the ruined man before him.

"You call this living?"

"He suffers no more than you and I already have. I watched you. I know how your brother's deceit, his betrayal, destroyed your life, your family. He abandoned you as he once did me, of the pain and misery he inflicted when he drove you to flee the Continent alone in search of answers you could never find. I know your heart. And while you blame me for his condition, a part of you is rejoicing that I have restored him to you. But you fear it as well."

The unwavering gaze from the demon's eyes seemed to pervade Ernest's very soul.

"I know it is more than justice that you seek. Why have you done this?" Ernest asked breathlessly.

"He left me incomplete and aging at an unnatural rate," the creature bitterly asserted. "I needed guidance. My work had progressed, but there was knowledge I lacked. Father's unwillingness to aid me in life has been balanced in death. And what he has shared with me, I will now use to heal us."

"What do you …?"

"Your wife, Frankenstein," the creature fervently said. "With the techniques I have perfected and the knowledge I have gained …"

"NO!" Ernest propelled himself backwards, away from the loathsome fiend. But as he looked up, he realized escape was hopeless. An

Old One now blocked the entry.

"Hear me, Uncle. Father both is and is not the man you knew. Exposure destroyed his limbs before his death, and I have been restoring them, but his mind I could not save from madness. But what we need is there, and I now possess the power to open it fully—because of you."

Ernest was only aware of his thundering pulse.

"The Seer is the key. She trusts you, as does Father," the grim specter continued.

"And you would have me betray that trust?"

The cloaked figure's dark shadow seemed to lengthen over the frozen ice.

"Once humanity and the Old Ones existed together. We shall again, and the Seer will ensure the dawn of our future. Or have you forgotten the prophecy?"

"How do you know of it?" Ernest challenged reflexively.

The hooded figure sneered.

"I have many to credit for my enlightenment, including the girl's aunt. Much of her early life was dedicated to the study of the scrolls, which you foolishly destroyed. A chronicle I have already set her to recreate. I have the power to resurrect the flesh." A mummified hand seized Ernest's previously wounded one. "As we know, the girl can heal it, and once her aunt has properly taught her how, she will be able to summon spirits of our choosing. Think of it! Your wife alive, reunited with you and her child, free of disease, immortal. All of this is within our grasp!"

Was any of this possible? His essence felt stained by the thoughts in his mind, but Ernest's heart could not dismiss the offer. Could he deny his child her mother, Abrielle her sister, abandon Ailis to the grave when before him was a chance to rescue her from such an unjust fate?

The creature released his hand, and Ernest looked down to both: one scarred by Abrielle's blade, one made whole by Baseria's mysterious power. Which fate should he chose? Always before, he'd been helpless as loved ones were torn from his life. What would happen if he refused? The ice beneath him was so cold.

"What do you ask of me?"

The devil rose in triumph and extended his hand down to Ernest.

"Often Father has cried out for you. Make him see your pain as I do. Convince him that helping to end your suffering will mercifully end his misery as well. "

"And Baseria," Ernest's voice cracked.

"She, too, must be shown her true purpose. Tasaria must help her fulfill her destiny and ours. You must not interfere."

"Use them?" Just as the creature had used all those who now lay dead in the outer chamber. Ernest hung his head. The dark figure placed a decaying hand on Ernest's shoulder.

"There is always a price, Uncle. But think of the world we will create. Draw strength from the knowledge that we will re-establish the true natural order and finally allow humanity to surpass its limitations."

Releasing him, the fiend moved to the Old One and issued instructions using the same language he'd used to render Victor senseless. The vile offspring turned.

"Father will awaken soon. The Old One will wait in the outer chamber and guide you back when you wish to return to the surface."

Ernest turned from thc hatcful eyes and considered Victor's unconscious, disfigured form. They were insane—creator and creation—completely, unreservedly mad. But was it a madness which Ernest now shared?

He could not banish Ailis' lovely face from his mind. The odious speaker behind him issued one final vow before departing.

"A great moment, prophesied by Creation draws near Uncle, but I must warn you. If you attempt to betray me, my mate and I will raise your child as our own, and you will never see your daughter again."

*

The hiss erupted into a brilliant shower of sparks that cast harmlessly off the stone and then from existence. Tasaria stirred. She'd forgotten about the fire as her mind drifted numbly among the flames and their pulsing dance for so long that her senses simply ceased to register it.

A sudden awareness of a hollow, lonely, unearthly moan caused her to turn in alarm. Her eyes momentarily probed the dark recesses of the reading room beyond the fireplace before fixing upon the hastily-patched window on the far side of the chamber. She listened to the plaintive cries of the frigid night winds as they pervaded the barrier. She shuddered. It felt as though Nature itself berated her. Or were those the voices of the dead crying out to her in anguish. Tasaria turned and stared to where her mother's spirit had first appeared. Did the winds carry her voice?

The scene began to dissolve into darkness. Another involuntary tremor coursed through her body. The fire was dying again. After all Tasaria had witnessed in the Master's hidden chambers, she found it impossible to feel warm. For a brief time, she attempted to convince herself that her pilgrimage to the reading room was solely to indulge in the sin of heat. Then again, where was she to go?

She could not return to her room, not with the spirit that haunted her there. Nor could Tasaria bring herself to follow the Master's instructions and continue her work of resurrecting the scrolls of the Seer from memory. With all she'd seen, how could she? The bodies bereft of souls.

Angrily her hands began to seize books from the nearby shelves, which she flung vehemently into the withering flames. They were to blame. The rapidly growing mound smoldered and smoked momentarily before igniting. As the room brightened, Tasaria stopped herself from condemning more bound pages to the fireplace. It was enough for now.

She considered the objects in her hands. Her fingers, then her palm, traced the texture of the covers. They had provided these texts to the Master years earlier, at the beginning, and added to the collection over time—works of science, language, art, philosophy, history, mathematics. How had these conspired to give life to the nightmares she'd helped to create? But if the Master was correct about her niece …

Slowly she lowered the books. They were close. However dark and repugnant it all was, they were at long-last close. Her heart measured the sense of joy and fear the thought held. Tasaria imagined embracing her daughter once more. How often had the Master impressed upon her that there would need to be difficult sacrifices before they could achieve their ultimate triumph? He kept his word, as he always did; rewarded her faith. How could she even consider betrayal? She must obey.

Tasaria replaced the unburnt books on the shelves and then tended the fire, adding oil and peat. Behind her there was a sudden muffled cry, one not caused by the winds. The Moon Shadow priestess' hand seized an iron poker.

"Show yourself," she commanded in a voice that sounded stronger than her spirit felt.

An Old One separated from the shadows, restraining Tasaria's frightened and helpless niece. Questions tumbled rapidly through her mind. When she'd come to the room, Tasaria felt certain, she was alone. How long had she been observed? Were there others concealed in the room? The mere sight of the hooded figure made her ill. What remnant of humanity lay beneath the obscuring cloak? Did it bear the remains of a face once known to her?

Baseria's breast rose and fell rapidly. Her gaze held fear and a plea to be heard. The Old One restrained her tightly, restricting her motions, voice, and air as she wheezed for a deep breath.

"Release her," Tasaria ordered before considering the uselessness of such a command. The Old Ones belonged to the Master, only he held dominion over them. The events of the day had made that quite clear. To her great astonishment, however, the shrouded figure obeyed, folded its arms beneath the concealing cloak, and stood, waiting.

They silently regarded one another.

Why did it comply? There was no reason for it to do so. No, twice it had followed Tasaria's commands—when it first revealed itself and now. Her puzzlement conjured a latent solution. Could this be the same Old One whom she'd been given temporary control of when the Master urgently spirited away the other Wild Rose clan girl? Could it have been shadowing her ever since?

For now her speculations must wait. Baseria shrank to the stone floor, coughing and breathing hard.

"You risk much by spying on me," Tasaria dispassionately remarked to her sister's child as she circled around her to stand beside the Old One.

"I was," a fit of coughing interrupted Baseria as she massaged her throat. "I was not spying on you, my aunt."

"You've always been rather good at it," Tasaria continued unabated. "You spied on your sister's training sessions readily enough. I wonder if that's where your jealousy of her began."

"I must speak with you," Baseria declared as she regained her feet.

"When I'm ready for you," Tasaria affirmed dismissively. "Return her to the chapel and keep her there," she ordered the Old One who immediately seized Baseria.

"NO!" Her niece's cry was stifled, but another followed as she was drug from the reading chamber.

"Nagyanya! Nagyanya! Help me. Nagyanya. Help me!"

"Wait!" Tasaria bellowed. The Old One ceased its movement towards the entryway. For a moment only the low moans of the wind and the cracking of flames could be heard. The Moon Shadow priestess crossed the room to the others. The light was dim, the gloom beyond them deep.

"That name, why do you…you will not speak that name." She raised the poker threateningly. "You will not speak that name!"

Baseria slowly began to smile.

"I will," she said defiantly. "I will speak it. Until I no longer draw breath, I will speak it. You murderous …"

Tasaria struck her. Baseria could feel the blood from her broken lip cascading off her chin. Any physical protest she offered was quickly quelled by the superior strength of the Old One. The hatred in her aunt's eyes burned with more fury than the flames of the nearby fire.

"You think you know pain, that you can stand in judgment of me?" her aunt raged. "I can kill you this instant."

At Tasaria's command, the Old One withdrew a blade and forced Baseria's head back, exposing her neck.

"What have you ever done other than kill my child and your sister? The Master has deceived himself," the older woman's voice was rich with contempt.

The dagger hovered, poised to strike. Tasaria did not see her niece, only Jucika and Patia's killer. The primal rage and palpable bloodlust within dismissed all other considerations from her mind. Baseria was helpless. The next word her aunt spoke would bring the girl's immediate death. Her niece spoke first.

"I'm not a monster … and neither are you," Baseria's strained voice implored.

Tasaria hesitated an instant, briefly suppressing the last word her sister's child would ever hear. Then her mind regained its focus. Her heart its hatred. She once more drew air into her lungs.

"Daughter!"

All of the air and color drained simultaneously from the Moon Shadow priestess. The fireplace poker pinged off the stones as it dropped from Tasaria's horror-stricken grip. She spun away from her niece and the sound of her mother's voice.

"Get out! Release her and get out!" Tasaria frantically wailed as she huddled near the fire, covering her ears and closing her eyes. The Old One sheathed its weapon and departed.

Baseria's eyes probed the darkness all around her but could find no trace of the supernatural speaker. Her aunt, so full of anger and cruelty moments earlier, now trembled uncontrollably before the fire—sobbing. Uncertainty coursed through Baseria. Should she leave, confront her aunt, or destroy her?

The metal poker was solid and felt cool against her skin as she lifted it from the floor. She considered the object, used as a weapon only moments earlier. It had not been here before when Baseria and the other Wild Rose clan captives used this room for retreat, isolation, and protection. This place was all they'd had. Now only Baseria remained.

She rubbed the blood across her chin as she approached her aunt. The older woman took no notice of her, too lost in her own terror and guilt. The rich, iron-scent of blood filled Baseria's nostrils. It would be easy to strike her enemy dead. If not for her grandmother's interference, Tasaria would have killed her already. Her thoughts returned home. How many had Baseria seen suffer, die needlessly, for this woman's cause? She gripped the weapon more forcefully.

"Tell me, where is Vochallet?" Baseria's voice trembled with raw emotion. "Where are Isyll and Sebbi? And Etolie. What have you done with them? What have you done?!"

Tasaria seemed to wither under the weight of the names. Baseria dropped the poker, fell to her knees, and clutched the shoulders of her aunt who finally became aware again of her surroundings. Baseria involuntarily recoiled as the older woman raised her head and met the younger's eyes. She could not recall ever before having witnessed her aunt's current expression of relief at seeing her niece.

"Of course, of course; I've been blind. Truly. How could I have been so blind?"

Tasaria's icy fingers reached out and touched her niece's warm face. Uncertainty kept Baseria still, as did the Moon Shadow priestess' inexplicable look of tenderness towards her.

"You've already begun to … you loved my mother … and now you've brought her back. You've brought her spirit back, even healed Frankenstein's flesh with your sacrifice," Tasaria momentarily studied Baseria's damaged hand.

"No."

"But there's more. We walk the same path," the older woman passionately decided.

"No," Baseria's strained voice whispered.

Tasaria pulled back her hair, exposing an array of marks similar to the corrupted skin of Baseria's hand, as if the imprint of supernatural fingertips had clasped her.

"Mother has marked us both, spoken to us, given us the power to fulfill our destiny. You saved her once, brought her back. You can again."

Baseria's soul rebelled. Her aunt couldn't be right. This was never what Nasi intended.

"Nagyanya, NO!" she cried bitterly. "No, no …"

"You are the Second Light, the power that will aid the First Light until balance is restored."

For the first time since she was a young child, Tasaria lovingly drew her youngest niece to her as Baseria wept, too overwrought to overcome the profane embrace. The girl was hope. She was the future.

"Your grandmother was taken from you as unjustly as my child was taken from me. We shall restore them. That is balance."

Chapter 26
The Choice

It was all collapsing in upon itself, and there was nothing he could do to stop it. Perhaps this was how the end was always intended to be. Maybe she would grant him a measure of mercy and kill him tonight. He'd been expecting her to do so for weeks now. Why should this dark hour change that? The only other option was that he strike her down first, the woman who had quite literally saved his life.

Espen blinked as he reaffirmed his command over his fatigue. She was a threat. He should never have returned to Salzburg. It would have been better to have left the whole affair. But he couldn't, anymore than he could kill her now. What hadn't his family taken from her? And what if she did, in fact, carry his child?

Neither had spoken since leaving Jal Nalie's tent hours earlier. There was nothing to say. Espen's lie had been affirmed by her only thanks to the concealed point of the knife he'd jammed into her back. Even so she'd barely relented in time for him to salvage the situation. The woman finally relinquished her niece back into the arms of her abductor, agreeing numbly with her husband that she was tired, and that the loss of her niece in a flood some months ago was to blame for her impassioned state. Then they left Jal's tent. She was senseless, silent, never once attempting to speak or meet his gaze.

Abrielle's body remained motionless through the depths of night, he could not tell if she was awake or asleep. Her back was to him. He could end it now: have her arrested, bear his father's wrath, attempt to free Abrielle and Tara later. No, no there was no later. Nicabar and the Moon Shadows were to arrive any day now, and Tara was the price they demanded for Baseria's return. If only there was more time. Jal would hear nothing of his son's protests. Honor demanded the abduction, honor required he now keep his promise to trade Tara for his daughter, otherwise, his actions would be unforgivable.

To Abrielle, they already were. Espen could not save them all—Abrielle, his father, Tara, his sister, possibly an unborn child. Who did he sacrifice? Who did he save? What if it was already too late for him to decide?

The first rays of light were beginning to assault the interminable dark. He crawled to the entry and crouched there, both worshiping and fearing twilight's end. Wisps of smoldering campfire smoke from outside made him cough softly. She did not stir. He closed the flap seconds before his mind seized upon a faint hope. It would be difficult for him to manage without Abrielle's knowledge, but it might be the only way. Espen reached for his coat.

"After I murdered Paul," Abrielle's soft voice broke off hoarsely.

"Abrielle, please."

Her voice was stronger the second time.

"After I murdered Paul, I wrote Ailis for the first time."

She was silent for a moment before continuing.

"She was my last chance, unmarred by my crimes. She was my family. I never considered I could feel worse than I already did until I heard nothing back from her. I hated myself. It was then I knew that there was nothing good in me, and eventually, I decided it was better that she not know me. I had rejected her when I rejected my father. I hated him too. He abandoned me. There was nothing worth saving in me, until my sister made me realize that there was. She forgave me by reaching out. She saved me when no one else could. I loved her … and I have failed her in every way possible."

Abrielle finally turned. Her eyes were bloodshot, her face swollen and bore a stoic mask of unspeakable pain.

"Never ask me to forgive myself. It honors your father. And my sins deserve no absolution."

Without further utterance, Abrielle turned and resumed her silent, consuming penance. Espen lowered his head and left her without a word.

*

"Jack."

"Merciful Christ!"

Jack half turned, half ducked as he attempted to retrieve his pistol.

"Oh, it's you. Get your damn hand off my mouth and stop sssshhin' me."

"Then shut up for once unless you want the whole encampment down on our heads," Espen warned.

"Look at that … and these were good boots," Jack lamented.

"They'll dry. Come on and keep low."

They moved in relative quiet farther away from the Wild Rose camp until Espen felt satisfied they were safe from the patrols. They crouched low.

"A simple good mornin' would have worked fine, ya know," Jack noted as he swatted his boots.

"I ought to send you home now," Espen sternly said.

Jack paused.

"For what?"

"Stupid risks for your petty indulgences. It worries me that no one found you before I did," Espen admonished whacking at the flask in Jack's pocket.

"Hey."

"It's like a torch when the light hits it," the gypsy charged.

Jack wasn't backing down.

"Now look, gypsy, I've given up smokin', bathin', eatin' decent food, Stanza, all the creature comforts so I can play hide-and-seek with your friends out there for Lord knows how long."

"Well, hide better so you don't give them need to seek. You'll live a day longer if you keep that flask hidden in your coat. Better yet, stop using it at all, and stop peeing on rocks."

"Oh, is that what gave me away? Nothing ever pees in the woods here?" Jack smirked, shaking his head, and muttering under his breath.

"Most of the animals don't hum waltzes while they do, Jack."

Actually Jack was quite well hidden, despite these factors, but Espen needed to do everything in his power to ensure the man remained so. Besides, it was gratifying to have the upper hand for a change.

"Right enough, you found me, so talk already. Where's Abrielle?"

"Orfilia," Espen pointedly corrected, "is … you'll have to deal with me. There's no way she's going to be able to slip out of the encampment without being detected."

"You did," Jack pointed out.

"Only because they know me and trust me," Espen forcefully asserted. "If I'm to have any chance of saving anyone, you must do exactly as I say."

Jack didn't know Espen very well, but even he could tell the young man was unusually stressed.

"What do you need me to do?"

Espen gave a tight but appreciative smile that Jack would not argue the point with him.

"The Moon Shadows have secured a truce. They want Tara in trade for my sister, and my father is prepared to do so. They will be here any time, if they aren't already."

Jack remained silent.

"I thought you'd be safe here, but this is too exposed. They'll be probing our defenses, and that only increases the chances of someone finding you, especially with their wolves. You've got to move farther out. There's a ravine to the east. The bottom of it drops out eventually, but there are several downed trees that can be used to cross it. The rock outcroppings and trees that surround it will give you better cover. Set yourself across from the clearing about halfway down the ravine and move around only near twilight and dawn. I'll make contact when I can."

"Anythin' else?" Jack inquired as Espen moved to leave.

"Pray."

The men nodded solemnly to each other; then the younger one disappeared. Jack waited several minutes before he removed his flask from his jacket.

"Never thought I'd die sober," he reflected to himself as he carefully poured the container's contents upon the sodden earth before replacing the object in his pocket. Espen was right. He needed to be as clear and alert as possible.

**

It wasn't moving, did not even acknowledge as Ernest entered the room. The dining chamber's nearby fire's dance bathed parts of the nightmare visage beneath the hood in a shifting battle between light and shadow. The vile, yellow orbs were veiled. Even the rattling breaths were muted. The head was tipped back against the back of the high chair. The exposed neck pulsed regularly beneath the thin layer of mummified skin. It slept. Ernest studied the thing.

How could Victor have ever hoped for good to spring forth from one such as this?

Ernest should destroy it now, while it rested.

Without warning the figure sprung to life and drove a dagger into the wooden table top. For a moment the inhuman gaze burned into Ernest as the dull vibrations from the metal withered and perished. The eyes became slits before closing again completely. It uttered a sigh.

"Speak, Uncle," the hateful voice said quietly.

Ernest remained still and silent, his companion likewise. Ernest's eyes fixed upon the glint of the blade. It was well within reach of either of them. There must be another weapon available to him. His brief search proved fruitless. Only the dagger or his bare hands were valid options.

The creature was fast, powerful, ruthlessly efficient. It could kill Ernest anytime it wished. Instead, it rested, almost with a sense of disdain for his enemy, as a predator certain of victory over its prey.

Ernest crossed behind the other's chair and walked to the narrow sun-filled slits that served as windows. The vantage offered a meager view of the world outside his prison, but through the hazy light he could see ships being loaded. At least one appeared to have been retrofitted in an unusual fashion. The mast configuration was radically altered, and the tallest appeared to be encased in hammered metal. The vessel's stern seemed very low in the water. Too much of it remained hidden from view to afford him any genuine insight into the purpose of such modifications. Where was it to sail? Ernest's thoughts returned momentarily to the distant shores of home.

"Have you any word of my daughter?" Ernest asked without turning his eyes back into the gloomy chamber.

There was a long pause.

"I expect Nicabar has her by now and is on his way to us."

Could it be true?

"And yet you load your ships for a voyage," Ernest tersely replied as he slowly returned his attentions to the seemingly halcyon figure in the chair.

The creature's voice sounded weary.

"He will send word at least several days before his arrival. I will leave when he does. I have work which must be completed."

"At sea?'

"Yes."

"What type of work? Stealing another ship and slaughtering its crew as well, for your fantasies?" Ernest challenged.

Silence.

"Victor may have created you from the ruins of humanity, but you …"

"I transcend humanity!" the ghastly form asserted.

A brief, harsh laugh escaped Ernest.

"Nothing as soulless as you could ever transcend us."

The diseased yellow eyes hung in the darkness beneath the hood as the great being rose.

"I go to sea to test new procedures, ones that would not exist without Father's cooperation. If they are successful, then I will fulfill my vow to reunite you with your wife more rapidly. I also go to meet Nicabar so we may safely conduct my cousin to you more swiftly. "

Ernest returned his gaze to the radiant light. It was already too late to save any of them, he bitterly realized. If Tara was brought here, they would never escape. The fiend could use the promise of Ailis' resurrection or threats towards his daughter or Victor against him forever.

He had succeeded, twisting Ernest's personal struggles with guilt, hope, grief, and love, of the demons of his past, all to blind Ernest to his true intentions and to foster an unholy bond between them. What had become of Abrielle? Did the weight of her soul now rest upon his, too?

"How long do you intend for all this to continue?" The tone of his words was so flat, so unnatural to Ernest's ears that he scarce believed he'd spoken them.

The response was not immediate.

"Do you still dream, Uncle?"

The creature's voice was soft. His gaze set upon the hearth's fire, his back to Ernest, who crossed the chamber to the table.

"All I have left are nightmares. What does one such as you dream?"

The shadow seemed to ponder the question before it turned to him.

"We live them," he said plainly, gesturing to their surroundings. "We exist within my dreams, as well as my nightmares. Perhaps I am soulless for I cannot dream as humanity does. A gift from Father, to keep me forever separated from your kind. Early in my life, I was unaware of this for my body is capable of rest, but there was nothing beyond respite to comfort me, to guide me, only the fathomless depths of an infinite void."

Ernest tried to reconcile these words.

"Perhaps, my brother did not know …"

"Of course he did not know!" The creature snarled, the force of his fist causing the table to jump. "I was conceived by a selfish and soulless creator who cared nothing of my great suffering until I was forced to make him endure a similar existence, one forever beset by sorrow and loss. Isn't that how a soul is earned? I admit my crimes against you freely, Uncle. Did your true oppressor ever possess the grace to do so? I was blinded by hate, my sole purpose, destruction. My victims were innocents, and I must serve penance for those crimes as long as I exist."

Ernest stared, transfixed by this abomination. The aridness of his parched throat almost prevented the words from escaping.

"What were you before … before my brother gave you life?"

The other drew his cloak closer, as if Ernest's gaze threatened to expose his tormentor.

"Was I expelled from Heaven or outcast from Hell? Or does life emanate from beyond either realm? Which do you believe, Uncle? Now that my efforts have given you insight into the deformities of your brother's soul, where does his reside? Perhaps we have merely transposed our existences and neither of us truly dead or alive."

"End this."

The other's eyes were bereft of either mercy or judgment of Ernest's plaintive plea.

"End this!"

The room around Ernest faded for an instant into a brilliant white, a form moved towards him, and then the chamber returned. The creature continued speaking, unaware of any interruption.

"… many enemies. Pias understands, or believes he does, but his treachery is limitless, his eventual betrayal certain. You are different. You do not worship me. You seek no power. You are family and I have learned much from you during our time together. When my true purpose in guiding humanity from this dark age has been fully realized, you will understand the necessity of my vision and the reasons for your presence here."

"Pias? Your vision?" Ernest asked in confusion. Had he imagined the burst of light or nearly lost consciousness?

The shadow seemed perplexed.

"What I have just spoken of … Tasaria?" he said for clarification.

"Yes … yes, you said," Ernest closed his eyes in concentration. "Your visions started before you met her, but she taught you how to gain clarity from them."

"You need rest, Uncle," the creature declared after studying him for a moment.

"Yes," Ernest agreed, suddenly dizzy and exhausted.

Victor's offspring summoned one of his kind to him.

"Conduct him back to the chapel; wait until he is ready to return to the lab."

The Old One bowed slightly in acknowledgement.

*

It was just a room, Tasaria thought. The notion again brought her little comfort. She crossed her arms. Her head followed the path her sunken eyes sought, as they gazed downward. She closed them tightly. The vision of the suffering form of Vochallet was there but still absent when she looked upon the empty chamber. The sight of the grim death masks of the Old Ones from the Master's lab returned to her mind, the endless fields of mutilated and frozen dead. She never should have come back to this room, but Baseria's words echoed in her heart. Tasaria fingers formed a steeple beneath her nose as she cupped them over her mouth and chin.

"I can make this right," she muttered to herself. "I can. Make it right."

She closed the door. There was truly nothing more for her to do here. Tasaria retraced the steps that led back to her room. There she'd resume the impossible task of recreating a chronicle of Seer knowledge. If ever she needed her mother's guidance, it was now.

*

Baseria rubbed her eyes. How much longer could she manage to do this? Was it even possible she could? Her aunt believed so. However, after all these hours, Baseria still had nothing to show for her efforts but a mind, body, and spirit plagued by fatigue.

Meals arrived without any regularity. The sun, raging storms, and ageless nights played out their existence but robbed her of any sense of time. The pervasive cold both lulled her to sleep and prevented it. These discomforts paled when matched against the turmoil within.

What had she done to make Nasi appear to her in the chapel? After all these days, were it not for the condition of her hand, she'd have thought it all a dream. But the corruption of her flesh, where her grandmother touched her, remained. Something had clearly happened, but so far she remained largely ignorant about how to even pursue answers to her myriad of questions.

Her aunt, whom she hoped would at long last provide enlightenment, remained distant, with few visits these past days—or was it longer? She blinked. What should she attempt next? More meditation, wait for her aunt who promised to join her soon, try again to harness the seductive powers of the Elements? But to what end?

Her back was stiff. She crossed her arms as she stood. Sleep might be her best alternative she decided. Several hours earlier, she'd nearly fainted while meditating, the world momentarily becoming awash in a brilliant white light. In her memory of the moment, a figure was walking towards her, yet, when the world lost its blinding opulence, there'd been no one here, except for an Old One who stood watch by the entrance. Baseria shivered as she pulled her outer garment closer to her body and coughed. When did she last tend the fire?

Turning, she gasped upon discovering the Moon Shadows' dark master near the fireplace. The demon seemed to be able to manifest near her at will. He busied himself with one of the nearby books on the shelves.

"You have not been too lonely, I trust," he muttered as he ceased to peruse his selected tome.

Baseria's eyes looked away from his. There was an intimacy in the gaze she dreaded.

"No."

Silence followed.

"Have you read any of these books during your time here?"

She shook her head. A lie. He'd often overheard her telling the others about her past. How aside from a horse her father had once allowed her to raise, a love of Greek mythology was one of the few passions they shared.

After learning this, he'd rearranged the books making those which discussed Ancient Greece more prominent. How would she react if she knew he'd done this for her? The creature had watched her read these, heard her discuss them, and knew she possessed a rudimentary understanding of the Greek language thanks in part to her grandmother. A language he too studied.

"Look at me," the powerful voice commanded.

Baseria closed her eyes and drew a deep breath as she obeyed.

"Where is Ernest?" she asked as she opened them.

"Unharmed," the other evenly declared after a brief hesitation.

"I'd like to see him," the girl requested.

The shadow gestured to a nearby chair.

"Sit … please," he added, seeing her momentary resolve betrayed by fear.

The compulsory invitation brought them into closer proximity as the creature took up position in a chair opposite hers. Again she cast her eyes downward.

"Frankenstein sleeps now," he stated. She tried not to wither under his penetrating gaze.

"May I go to him?"

The creature wordlessly regarded her. Ever since Ernest's departure to the chapel, he'd been watching her, pondering how to approach the girl, revealing his presence only now. Baseria's breath seized in her throat as he enclosed his hand over hers. The softness of her skin, the warmth of her hand was intoxicating to him.

"These past days have been … difficult for my uncle, as I know they have been for you." He paused before continuing, "You must come to know me. I am not ignorant of your suffering, Baseria."

The neutral expression she'd forced her visage into shattered as her pain-filled eyes met his. She fell to her knees and clutched at his decayed hand.

"Please," her trembling voice whispered, "please let me go. Please. Please, the Moon Shadows see you as a god, and a god knows mercy. None of this is necessary. It's not right. I'm not a threat. I never wanted … oh please take me home. Please."

The creature leaned back and inhaled a tight breath. Her soft sobs weighing on him. But the hollow, empty years echoed within. He suppressed his heart. There would be time for mercy.

"I … cannot release you."

As he reached out to caress her face, Baseria's tears of anguish and despair baptized his mummified, waxen fingers.

"Please," she entreated again.

"Do not ask it of me," the other said, trying to control his emotional turmoil.

"Please!"

"No." He withdrew his hand. "Man once worshiped the sun as a god. Do not make me the sun. I cannot change what must be."

"Then kill me like you did the others. If you feel my suffering then end it," she begged as he stood.

The creature was silent a moment as an internal battle struggled to resolve itself. Baseria's heart did the same when he again spoke.

"Soon you will …"

"Master? Master, are you in there?" a voice interrupted.

They both looked up as the pulsing sound of frantic knocking intruded from the other side of the door.

"Master we must speak with you! Master, you must come!" the voice urgently called.

The creature stole one last fleeting look with Baseria before answering.

"Enter!" he commanded.

The Old One guarding the door immediately resolved the lock, admitting several panicked Moon Shadow gypsies. Having gained entry somewhat unexpectedly, the men appeared uncertain if they should kneel as Baseria did or issue their report with dispatch. They hurriedly knelt in trepidation.

"Speak," the creature irritably ordered.

"My Lord, Frankenstein has been attacked."

*

The dead greeted him in his dreams. They rose slowly from their wretched mounds of ruin in the dark abyss below the frigid sea. A ghastly frozen array, looking at him, some lacking eyes, limbs, worse—all silently demanding, waiting. He could not speak nor turn away.

"Arise," a voice said as he peered into the endless mass.

Ernest's eyes opened to discover the sight of an Old One stalking toward him, knife drawn. Surely it did not speak to him. His senses returned. As Ernest sat up and spun to meet the threat, the hooded figure suddenly grabbed Ernest's wrist. Their momentary struggle for control of the weapon flung them harshly against a nearby wall.

The Old One was strong. Ernest acted instinctively upon prying the weapon from the wretch's hand. An unholy wail from the thing was prematurely cut off as Ernest tore the blade across its throat. It crumbled as more of its kind abruptly appeared, weapons drawn. Ernest looked to the weapon in his bloody hand. Should he strike them down or would they fall upon him if he attempted to wield the blade?

He could not hope to overpower them all. Though they tracked his movements, none of the new arrivals reacted aggressively toward him. Ernest did not dare to voluntarily surrender the blade to them.

"This one attacked me," he finally said. "Do you understand?"

He waited. They remained guarded, unresponsive, except for following his motions. With measured steps Ernest backed to the chapel's open door. The Old Ones moved as a pack, neither approaching closer nor retreating. Would they pursue him if he ran?

The metallic click from the hallway drew Ernest to a halt.

"Place the knife on the floor, then take three steps back away from it or I'll bury this shot in your chest," the man's voice behind him vowed. Ernest obeyed and raised his hands as several more weapons were primed.

"Good. Now go back inside, slowly," the man instructed.

"I was attacked."

The impact of the pistol's barrel against his skull brought stars to Ernest's vision.

"No talking. You, move! Get the Master while I hold him here," the Moon Shadow ordered his companion.

All of the Old Ones sheathed their weapons. They parted—a rolling black wave as Ernest and the Moon Shadows re-entered the chapel. Ernest sat back down on the bench and gingerly probed the damp, rising bump on the back of his head with his fingers. The Moon Shadow's eyes kept shifting from his prisoner, to the collapsed, robed figure on the red-stained floor, to the silent chorus of Old Ones.

"Is he dead?" the gypsy finally asked Ernest, who, after a moment, began to laugh at the absurdity of the question, much to the other man's consternation.

"We'll see," Ernest finally managed. "Won't we?"

A monstrous shadow bellowed through the doorway, the sight of which sent the gypsy down on one knee.

"My Lord."

"Leave us," the Master's expansive command included the Old Ones who followed the Moon Shadow gypsy from the chapel. The creature sealed the chamber door before venturing to inspect the robed corpse. Ernest finally stirred.

"Your gypsy was concerned that I couldn't answer his question."

"Which was?"

"If the Old One is dead," Ernest said without turning. "Is he?"

"Why have you done this?"

The question rang with anger—or was it fear?

"Why? Why did you set him upon me?" Ernest challenged.

"I?"

Ernest turned to face his tormentor.

"They're yours. You control them, right? Give them purpose. Then why did I awaken to find this one ready to stab me as I slept?"

Fleetingly, the putrid yellow eyes became lost in reflection. Ernest waited, but nothing else was forthcoming from Victor's hateful offspring.

"Maybe your control is not as absolute as you believe it to be," he observed.

The challenge returned the creature's attention fully to Ernest.

"Or perhaps this is your attempt to create chaos here, Uncle, a misguided effort if so."

Ernest rose.

"You doubt I was attacked?"

"Desperation is the most simplistic of motivators," the other sneered. "Were it possible, you had no compunction about attacking me several hours ago. Unable to overpower me, maybe you believed the slaughter of one of my creations would grant you solace or unnerve me. It will not succeed."

The creature turned away but halted with Ernest's next words.

"And what if this has nothing to do with me? What if this is simply human nature asserting itself? This Old One—rebelling against the unjust conditioning forced upon it by you. Or perhaps you're incapable of understanding the human spirit."

Suddenly the fierce yellow orbs blazed before Ernest's eyes. His words tore into the other.

"I have seen the human spirit take many forms, but one has always eluded me. Soon, however, I will finally come to know it fully and when I do, all of this misery, this darkness will be justified. You speak to me in a passion, as if you understand the mystery of your kind's collective spirit when there is but one truth to understand. Humanity is desperation. It is your existence. It is life. Your presence here alone proves it is so. Desperation for your child, for answers. A need for family, for justice, all of these brought you to me, as they brought Tasaria before you. Your brother's life came to ruin because of desperation borne out of the mutual fear of death and a need to control life. Your wife's choice to conceal the severity of her illness from you was a desperate act of love. The Moon Shadow's draw faith from desperation, and I will, at long last, know love as you have because of it. Fate demands it, destiny wills it, and I shall not be denied because of you."

In a tempest of black robes, the demonic presence swirled away.

"Guards!"

Three Moon Shadows entered immediately.

"The Old Ones are banished from this chapel. Frankenstein is confined to it. Treachery from either is death. Guard without until I return."

Alone, again banished to his prison, Ernest crossed to the corpse of the Old One, knelt, and drew back the hood. He was silent for a long time.

"What have you seen?"

*

"Master?"

A curt wave of his hand was the only indication Tasaria received that she was to follow him. She drew her coverings closer and unconsciously gritted her teeth. She hadn't been out on the docks since her arrival. It was dusk. Storm clouds laden with snow marched on commanding winds across the dark sea. Or was this a weak dawn, struggling for life in this unyielding wilderness? She was so absorbed in her task of trying to recreate the records of the Seer from memory that time had long since eluded her. The unexpected summons for this audience had come after several long cycles of both manic work and blessed sleep.

Somewhat to her surprise, they did not pause near any of the ships which rang with the clamor of a host of activities. They alone proceeded to the isolated edge of the pier and stood. For an eternity, they remained there as the icy winds whipped her clothing and stole Tasaria's breath. The Master appeared indifferent to the cold as his cloak billowed outward, creating the illusion of great dark wings. Why did they linger here?

He still had not turned to face her. She could physically tolerate this no longer.

"Master? Master?" she called out over the winds as snow began to whirl around them.

At last he stirred.

"I have always been able to trust in Tasaria," he stated without preamble as he turned to her. "I must be able to trust you now."

She nodded in agreement, too cold to speak properly.

"Our enemies have discovered new ways to attack us. They have learned to turn our own against us. You have been isolated by your tasks, but tell me, have you heard of any unusual occurrences related to the behavior of the Old Ones?"

Her guilty thoughts turned back to the Old One she still secretly controlled. She'd left it to watch over Baseria. Had it turned on her?

"No, Master," she cautiously asserted. "This was not another vision?"

He shook his head.

"There have been two attacks by Old Ones in less than a day: one against Frankenstein, who lives; the other a Moon Shadow who was alone in a corridor. He is dead, and his attacker is again concealed among the ranks of the Old Ones. I've ordered all of them to relinquish their weapons for now."

"But … but surely the Wild Rose clan," Tasaria sputtered.

"Is not responsible, at least not directly," the creature bluntly stated.

"I don't understand."

The creature leaned in closer to her.

"We have many enemies who would destroy us, both here and at home. But this I believe to be the work of one of two foes—Frankenstein or Pias."

Tasaria huddled even closer to the ghastly speaker, the brutal cold pressing in on her, uncertain if she'd heard him correctly.

"Might we go inside to discuss this or on to one of the ships, anywhere but here," she urgently requested.

"No," his eyes fleetingly shifted, "this blasted gale conceals us. It is difficult to say how many of the Old Ones have been co-opted; neither the fortress nor the ships are secure. I am sorry for your discomfort, Tasaria, but we must speak here."

"But my Lord," shuddered Tasaria, "how could Frankenstein gain control of them?"

"I'm not sure," he conceded. "A trick your mother taught him, something Pias told him. I was more willing to believe him guilty until the second attack occurred. Unless this was something he arranged before I banished him to the chapel, it is doubtful."

"Very well, then, what of Pias? Why turn on us now?"

The creature momentarily brooded.

"Master?"

"The Moon Shadows took in Pias after his escape from prison because of his skills in training your attack wolves, yes?"

She forcefully nodded in agreement, willing her protesting muscles to move.

"He was detestable even then, but his wolves have kept us safe."

The yellow eyes narrowed and pulsed with unspoken fury.

"Over time I have come to believe that his true loyalties lie … elsewhere."

Normally when her Master became vague Tasaria was willing to wait until he was ready to divulge more but not now. The cold was too persistent an inducement against lingering.

"Elsewhere? Please, Master. This wind is unbearable."

"Do you recall the female spy you discovered at your encampment?"

"Yes. She poisoned a man to keep those Roms close to us."

"There may be others. Pias has given me repeated indications of mixed loyalties. I believe he will eventually betray us. These attacks may be proof that he already has. The methods of control for both the wolves and the Old Ones are not so dissimilar. He could have circumvented my safeguards and tasked them to spy or sow discord here."

"For what purpose? Why now? Does that spy have something to do with this? If Pias is planning to betray us ...," she paused. "Oh God, Nicabar!"

The creature's massive hands came to rest on her shoulders.

"I will handle Pias. Your husband will be protected," her Master vowed. "Tasaria?"

She returned to the moment, temporarily setting aside her fears for both her husband's and her people's safety.

"I must know if Frankenstein is responsible for these attacks, and you are the only one here I can entrust with such a vital task."

He seemed tired when he said this, the words as much a plea as a command. A great weight seemed to press down upon him.

"I must know," he could say no more, only plunge his gaze into the shifting, black Arctic waters. Tasaria persisted.

"What of my work with Baseria? What about the Seer writings?"

He looked up but not at her.

"For now you may continue your work. I will post a Moon Shadow guard outside your door. I must apply myself to work in my lab and oversee the final preparations of these ships. At dawn you will return to the lab with Frankenstein, take your writings with you. See if any of their secrets were revealed to him. He destroyed the Seer chronicles, it is only fitting that he should aid your restorations of them."

"Must we return to the lab to do this," the numbness within Tasaria had little to do with the cold. The Master drew his own robes closer.

"He must."

**

Espen strode hurriedly across the encampment, casually nodding or waving to those who called his name. Despite his haste, he did not wish to alarm anyone, however, every time he walked this path, he expected disaster to greet him at the end. Abrielle would have killed whomever he left to keep an eye over her. She'd be missing. He'd spot Abrielle running away with Tara. She'd have killed herself. No. Her rage prevented that. She would rather see them all destroyed before she renounced her own life. He was certain of this, though to all outward appearances this woman had never been happier in her entire life.

In the days since last seeing her niece, Abrielle had completely immersed herself into her role as Orfilia. She cooked for him, sewed, slept close to him at night, never once speaking of Tara or Espen's father. Ever since returning from his initial meeting with Jack, it was as if the incident with her niece had never happened. This above all alarmed Espen. Well, this and the fact that she still refused to confirm if she was in fact pregnant with his child.

She was polite to everyone, wandered the encampment and interacted freely with the other women—bartering for goods, washing clothing, sewing an assortment of clothing and blankets, dumping what little rubbish they generated in the compost mound, engaging as best she could in gossip and storytelling, playing with children. She even managed to help reset a girl's broken limb after she fell. To the best of his knowledge, she had not once attempted to leave the camp or probe the boundaries or defenses as she did the first day.

The few times Espen mentioned Jack, she merely smiled as if he was discussing some mutual, casual acquaintance and that was all. No questions, no requests to try and see him, no concerns expressed in the slightest. The transformation was disquieting to say the least, but there was little he could really do about it and still worse possibilities if he did.

As he approached, he discovered Abrielle seated outside the tent. She paused her sewing efforts to hover over the nearby cooking fire, stirring onions into the pot perched above the flames. His stomach turned.

"Orfilia."

"Husband," she rose and kissed him. "Try this," she promptly intoned as she stooped back down and ladled out a measure of her mixture from the pot.

Espen's sense of urgency wavered momentarily as she held the concoction up for him to try. The scent from it was overpowering.

"How many onions did you put in there?" he asked, blinking the stinging sensation from his eyes.

"Try it before you complain," she suggested a moment before dumping the hot liquid toward his lips. He danced backwards, fanning his mouth and coughing.

"Good?"

As he recovered, Espen became aware that people living in the nearby tents were interested in and amused by the newlyweds' culinary drama. He wiped a sleeve across his lips. If they were actually married, he'd have banished her from his tent by now. How many times did he have to tell her to cease putting onions in everything? But if this petty vengeance kept her in character, then he'd just have to live with it.

"A bit hot, that's all," he commented as he leaned down, ladled out more soup, gingerly blew over it, and forced it down while making a pleasant expression.

Abrielle smiled.

"I'll get a clean bowl for you then," she declared cheerily.

"Actually, I forgot to tell you that several of the women in camp have asked for your recipes."

He followed her into the tent.

"They're here," he announced directly as soon as the flap was closed.

She did not even pause as she picked up the bowl and turned back toward both Espen and the exit, trying to force herself past one and through the other. He grabbed her wrists, and the bowl clattered to the ground.

"The Moon Shadows. My sister. They're here, Abrielle," he said more forcefully.

He had not spoken her true name in days. Abrielle did not meet his eyes nor did she speak. He released her. She bent down to retrieve the bowl.

"Father wants us both up at the top for the exchange," Espen added.

She paused.

"Why?" Abrielle asked as she finally met his eyes.

Espen steeled himself as he cleared his throat.

"Because he says that…that this issue involves family, Orfilia."

She pushed a length of hair that had escaped her headscarf back underneath it, then held up her hand. Espen helped her to rise, their expressions mutually impassive.

"I'll get my shawl."

*

The wooded path to the top of the mountain was surrounded on either side by armed members of the Wild Rose clan. Their dogs whined as

Abrielle and Espen passed. Almost unconsciously she continued to count her steps and observe the landscape. As they ascended the last rise, Jal came into view, waiting impatiently just outside the tent where the formal truce discussion was to take place. He seemed less than pleased to see his son's wife.

"Espen, I told you, this matter concerns only us right now," he gruffly asserted.

Abrielle fleetingly touched the young gypsy's hand. Their glances met for an instant.

"She is family," Espen stated before pulling his father aside and drawing him into a hushed but intense conversation.

Several times Jal looked uncertainly at Abrielle before aggressively returning his attentions to his son. Their whispered exchange quickly threatened to erupt into a full argument, but there was no time. The Moon Shadows awaited inside the tent. The men returned to her.

"Explain," Jal finally commanded Espen with a single thrust of his large hand towards Abrielle.

Espen obeyed.

"I have told you of my youngest sister and how she was unjustly taken from us?" he asked in English, as he took her hand into his. She meekly nodded.

"Our enemy now seeks to return her to us. I told my father your knowledge of medicine and healing might be of help to us if she has been mistreated."

Abrielle blinked.

"You can't ask this of her," Jal said. "This girl has no idea what's at stake."

"I understand," Abrielle stated in Hungarian, before quietly adding in English. "I had a sister once."

Espen held her for a moment.

"Inside," Jal tersely commanded his son. "You will obey me, and you will say nothing. Understood?"

"Yes, Father," Espen asserted as he separated himself from Abrielle.

"Wait outside," he told her, seconds before disappearing into the tent.

Abrielle pulled the shawl more tightly about her hunched shoulders and watched as the sun was consumed by the endless wilderness of the Carpathians.

*

Nicabar's fingers absentmindedly manipulated the small matchbox as he focused on the sound created by the rattling contents inside. For some reason, it soothed him, laid into momentary abeyance his deep concerns about his wife's well being, his people's safety, and the outcome of these negotiations. The heel of his boot tapped dully against one of the legs of the small table he was seated at as his eyes tracked round the interior of the modest tent yet again. They came to rest on the silent man standing a measure behind him.

"How long, Pell?"

Pell shifted the burning cigarette between his fingers as he addressed the question to his pocket watch.

"Over an hour now since he left, sir," he declared, snapping the casing shut.

Nicabar passed a hand over his balding head. What the devil was Jal up to? Each minute of his absence only increased the odds that a Wild Rose clan attack was imminent. A vengeful type of man, Jal could simply be using this agreed-to truce as an opportunity to slaughter his enemies. The only consultation Nicabar might take from having known his former brother-in-law all these years was that, despite his ire, Jal did value personal honor. The thought was scant comfort. Every instinct in Nicabar cried out for him to abandon this mission, too many omens of misfortune already surrounded it, and the Master's sudden unwillingness to divulge pertinent information to him only strengthened those feelings.

"I don't suppose the delay could in any way be related to Pias' mysterious whereabouts, could it?"

Pell took a long drag from his cigarette.

"I relayed the Master's wishes to you. I told you I don't know what his orders to Pias were, only that he and most of the men we returned with separated from my group shortly after we landed."

"Yes, you told me," Nicabar darkly remarked. There were too many unknowns, too many shifting parts.

"We have what they want," his underling persisted.

"Be silent, Pell! And remain silent."

Nicabar stood and began to pace in the confined space. Instead of negotiating from a position of strength, fate conspired to make him rely solely on guile. Pias' disappearance weakened the Moon Shadow force, and Pell's explanations for this disastrous change in plans offered Nicabar almost nothing to work with. Worse, it compromised his honor.

Still he must find a way to achieve his goals, otherwise, it could be years before he was reunited with his wife, and still longer before the Master's vision was realized. Yes, guile was the only path left to him, and fortunately, Nicabar was blessed with cunning and quick thinking. However, he felt, in this situation, his iron resolve was the trait that would best suit him in this moment of crisis. It must. Jal was too gifted an antagonist.

Suddenly he heard them as a host of voices ebbed between fits of intensity and near silence just outside the tent. He resumed his seat. The lit table lamp flickered in response. It did so again as Jal and Espen Nalie at last entered.

*

The men were silent as they entered. Jal's eyes tracked between the seated form of Nicabar and the armed man behind him who was grinding a smoldering cigarette into the ground.

"Do you hold intentions other than truce?" Jal asked, gesturing to the man's gun belt.

Nicabar smiled as he leaned forward in his chair.

"No. Blame it on habit and a mind dulled by too long of a wait."

The younger Moon Shadow grinned in agreement, but neither Jal nor Espen stirred until Nicabar uttered his command to Pell.

"*Retirez*[23]."

Pell unbuckled the belt before stepping to the Moon Shadow's entryway for the tent. He set the weapon outside before returning to his position behind Nicabar.

"Satisfied?" the Moon Shadow leader inquired.

Jal reluctantly stepped forward and reached slowly into his coat pocket. He withdrew a clutch of various bird feathers, laced together by decorative lengths of fabric.

"My bond," he said simply before sitting down.

---

23 *French* - Remove.

Nicabar reached into his own coat and produced a similar collection of feathers and set them beside those already lain by Jal.

"We are at truce," Jal declared as Espen took up position behind his father.

For a time only the wind outside spoke until the Wild Rose clan leader broached the question.

"Where is my child?"

"Where is Frankenstein's infant?" Nicabar rejoined.

The two men silently evaluated each other before the conversation continued.

"She will be presented to you when Baseria is returned to me. That was our agreement and the only thing I am interested in from you, Nicabar."

"I'm afraid my Master is interested in a bit more from you."

Jal's eyes flashed.

"More I will not give."

Nicabar shifted in his chair.

"You would walk away so easily, after all these years? I am here to negotiate in good faith with you, Jal."

"Then return *my* daughter and be gone."

"Your ...!"

For a moment an ancient, unspoken grudge smoldered between the men. Finally Nicabar backed down.

"Out of respect for family, I will say no more than this—you will be reunited with Baseria. I promise you. Provided you agree to one concession."

"No, only as we have agreed," Jal insisted.

Espen said nothing but placed a hand on his father's shoulder. He'd suffered too much to allow this to end so quickly. They all had. Nicabar met his nephew's eyes evenly.

"A smart boy. My apologies, Espen, for your treatment in our camp. Your aunt and I are most pleased you survived your ordeal, if only it could have been the same for the others."

"Enough!" Jal roared. "Speak, Nicabar. What is your condition?"

Nicabar held his gaze with Espen several heartbeats longer before returning his attention to Jal.

"A simple, yet, essential one. We need to confirm the identity of the child before Baseria is released."

"What?" Espen asked, breaking his silence. Jal held up his index finger, bidding his son to remain quiet.

"Continue. What would this confirmation entail?"

"Merely your presence, Jal," Nicabar stated with a degree of self-satisfaction. "We already have the child's father, and you claim to have his daughter. If you are telling the truth, then reuniting Frankenstein with his daughter will enable you to once again be with yours. All you need do is accompany us, alone."

Jal's eyes narrowed.

"If I refuse?"

"That would not be wise," Pell smugly intoned.

Nicabar turned and faced his subordinate.

"Neither is your disobedience, Pell. Go outside and stand ready," Nicabar ordered. Pell nodded in deference before stepping out of the tent, disappearing through the entry leading to the Moon Shadow's side.

Jal stood as the man departed.

"Is this your answer then?" Nicabar asked returning his attention to his former brother-in-law.

"You have broken your word to me. My child is not present here, therefore, there is no further business between us," Jal asserted as he picked up the clan's symbol of truce from the table. He turned to leave.

"Surely you do not think I've come empty-handed, Jal?" Nicabar said.

Espen paused beside his father at their entryway to the tent as Nicabar opened the table lamp's vent to increase the illumination of their surroundings.

"Will you permit me to show you?" he asked as he stood.

Espen's heart thundered in his ears. This was it. Yet, his father did not stir; he even appeared reluctant to do so, seeming suddenly weary. Finally Jal turned and faced his old adversary. He nodded solemnly. Nicabar turned, but only for an instant.

"I would ask," began Jal loudly, until the other's gaze again met his, "one small favor of you, Nicabar."

Nicabar crossed his arms across his chest.

"Which is?"

"My son's wife is waiting outside. I ask she be allowed to join us now."

"His wife? What business could she have here?"

"What is your answer?" Jal asked sternly.

The Moon Shadow leader shook his head.

"Very well," he agreed.

Jal motioned to Espen.

*

The muted echo of sunlight that remained in the sky was rapidly retreating under the relentless onslaught of night, one that resonated with sound and motion. Abrielle's senses engaged in a silent communion with both. What they witnessed alarmed her, drove her heart to embrace wishful fantasies. If only she could transform, fly safely away from this dreadful mountain with Tara. She swore she would never ask for one thing more in life.

But the dream could only be supplanted by a harsh reality. She was alone, surrounded by enemies, and there was no escape. This mountain was a living fortress, populated by the Wild Rose and Moon Shadow clans. From her vantage point she could occasionally glimpse flickers of torches passing among the trees as patrols sought out any signs of incursion from the enemy. There were whispers, much closer to her, the speakers of which remained largely concealed in the deepening dusk. The real menace, Abrielle realized, was the subtle beauty of the mountain that embraced one's senses and obscured the fact that the forces here need but a single catalyst to unleash destruction upon the other. The only doubt was when it would come.

In spite of this turbid environment, Abrielle knew there were peaceful families, children, back down the path she'd walked. Just as she now knew with unrelenting certainty that the Moon Shadow guards on the other side of the tent had brought their wolves. Upon hearing their growls, she closed her eyes in a bid to retreat from her senses, but terrors well-remembered from her last encounter with the wolves forced them back open.

Her soul was adrift in fears. How many wolves did they Moon Shadows control? What if Tara was being brought to the tent right now? Had she regained her sight only to be forced to watch Jal trade her niece's life for his own daughter's? What if she was already inside? What if the

Moon Shadows recognized her in spite of her altered disguise? A single error on her part now would prove fatal. How could they hope to escape? Where could they run? And then truth came.

"We'll die here," she muttered softly to herself.

A sudden flash of light forced her eyes to instinctively close for an instant.

"Orfilia."

She felt Espen's fingers entwining with hers as she blinked against the light spilling out from the tent's entryway. She couldn't see his face, not really. What had happened? Were they leaving? No. He was guiding her inside.

*

Abrielle's vision cleared. Jal was glaring at the bald man who stood opposite him on the far side of the table set in the middle of the tent. She was not surprised to discover the tent's other entrance behind him. There was no sign of Tara. Had she already been taken through to the Moon Shadow controlled side of the mountain?

Her breaths were short. She kept expecting to feel Espen's blade digging into her back again. It would happen any second now. Yes, expose her here, trade Abrielle to them as well as Tara. It would be madness not to solve these two conjoined problems so efficiently.

The man across the table, whom she could only assume was part of the Moon Shadow leadership, studied her. She tried to remain aloof, summoning thoughts that the woman she was supposed to be would have, trying hard to suppress the mounting fear he recognized her. He seemed to brace himself slightly before he spoke.

"*Lui apporter*," he commanded, somewhat loudly.

Unconsciously she took a step forward. Abrielle was shocked when the order did not result in her being taken, rather, that another woman was brought into the tent. The prisoner never looked up, only down at her bound hands. This must be Espen's sister, Abrielle reasoned. Her eyes were drawn instantly to obvious signs of physical abuse the poor girl had suffered.

Her back to him, a short, muted gasp was the only warning Abrielle received before Espen attempted to force his way past her, followed within seconds by his father's cry, and instant attempt to hold back his son. Together, she and Jal managed to restrain him.

"Etolie! Father, its Etolie!" Espen pleaded. "Release me! Etolie!"

The battered prisoner gave no response, but tears parted the dirt on her bruised face. Nicabar waited until he felt Espen was secured.

"You see, Jal. I have not come empty-handed. If you give yourself to us, we will trade this girl back to you."

Espen passionately continued his struggles.

"Heartless knave," he spat at Nicabar, "Father, you must …"

"Outside Espen, NOW!"

The older man forced his son to the entryway. The younger gypsy stood his ground, his stance and expression made of stone.

"NO! Free her. NOW!"

Animosity swelled between the men. Uncertain what exactly was going on, Abrielle decided there was only one option to avoid a disastrous confrontation between father and son. She turned and fixed her eye upon the Moon Shadow leader.

"Is this woman such a threat to you that you must keep her bound?"

An abrupt stillness in the tent greeted her words.

"You speak excellent French," Nicabar observed in kind. "What is your name?"

"Orfilia," Abrielle bluntly stated.

"Nicabar, I ask forgiveness for my son's outburst," Jal stated as Espen removed himself from the tent. "He is young. I will speak with him."

"By all means," Nicabar agreed, eyes still locked with Abrielle's.

"Orfilia was a healer among her people."

"Really. Ah. Is that how a French-speaking Rom came to be here?" Nicabar wondered suspiciously.

Jal ignored the question, but brusquely posed one of his own.

"May she be allowed to tend Etolie's injuries while I speak privately with Espen?"

Nicabar considered Jal a moment before returning his attention to Abrielle.

"If she stays, she must understand that I will kill her at the first sign of treachery."

Jal nodded before addressing Abrielle in English.

"Orfilia, treat Etolie's injuries, nothing more. I will return shortly."

He fled the tent without another word.

*

Espen fought to regain control of his rapidly shifting emotions. Etolie was alive, but where was Baseria, and where were the other women taken by the Moon Shadows?

His friend was alive having survived unspoken torments. The others must be suffering as Etolie clearly did. His anger towards the Moon Shadows rose drastically before being quelled by a new thought. He could now only add to her miseries. How could he tell her about her husband's death? His face turned hot with guilt and shame.

Upon exiting the tent, Jal wasted no words on his son, rather, he drove his massive forearm into Espen's throat and pinned him harshly against a tree.

"You give our enemies every advantage with your insolent disobedience. Desire makes you weak." Jal allowed his son a moment to recover.

"Does sacrificing Etolie make you strong?" Espen asked.

Jal shook his head.

"Being a leader means you must always weigh love and sacrifice, sometimes they are the same thing."

"Is that what happened with Mother?"

Jal stepped back, releasing Espen, each breathing heavily.

"Your mother's fate was …, "Jal shook his head. "What of the others, Espen? Have you even thought about them? Not just those who were taken, not about your sister, but all of the souls in our camp? Have you thought about them? There is more at stake here than Etolie's life, much more."

Espen turned and walked a few steps away.

"What do you intend to do?" he finally asked.

*

Etolie's head lulled dully away from the touch of the damp fabric against her face. She closed her eyes. She knew this Rom woman was only trying to help her, but she didn't care. Fingers delicately probed the bruises on her face and sought out traces of the others on her body. Etolie sharply drew in a breath when the woman's examination discovered her cracked ribs.

"*Désolé*," the Rom woman said, realizing she'd unintentionally caused Etolie pain.

Etolie concentrated on breathing slowly.

"*Pouvez-vous parier*?"

She ignored the stranger's question and drew her bound hands over her face.

*

"May I loosen her bonds?" Abrielle asked.

"She seems to be able to function with them on," Nicabar observed as the false-Rom woman looked up at him.

"Hasn't she suffered enough?" Abrielle asked.

"That was not my doing," Nicabar replied stiffly. It was clear that he too found Etolie's condition troubling.

"If you truly disapprove such brutality, then help her now," Abrielle begged.

Nicabar stared down at Etolie. Damn Pias. Not only was such abuse unnecessary, but it was needlessly cruel. It endangered the truce and Nicabar's mission. Part of him was glad that Baseria hadn't been brought by Pias as originally planned. At least she had not suffered this fate. With a silent curse, he vowed that the Master would learn the full extent of Pias's brutal indulgences.

"We are at war," he explained simply, "however …"

He nodded ruefully to Orfilia.

"Thank you," Abrielle said, managing a faint, broken smile. "She needs water as well."

Nicabar sighed.

"Give me your water, Pell," he ordered. Pell frowned but complied by laying the water bladder down next to the women. He knew when all this was over, Nicabar would continue to demand answers from him about events at the fortress and Pias' role regarding the Wild Rose woman's current condition. It was a conversation Pell was resolved to keep short.

Orfilia's fingers fumbled with the knots of Etolie's bonds. She didn't dare try to force them. The ropes had already rubbed the poor woman's wrists raw.

"I need you to lower your arms so I can untie these knots," she explained to the prisoner. Abrielle knew the woman was weeping behind her hands.

"Etolie," she said softly.

Abrielle waited until the gypsy woman lowered her hands a measure. For the first time, she made eye contact with Abrielle. Hidden behind the bruises were eyes alive with a deep sense of shame and anguish.

"Please, let me untie these," Abrielle pleaded.

Unconsciously, Etolie's gaze flashed fearfully to the Moon Shadows before retuning to Abrielle.

"It's all right," Abrielle said as reassuringly as possible. "They said it's all right to loosen your bonds."

Etolie looked once more to the Moon Shadows before cautiously lowering her arms. Abrielle set to work on the blood-encrusted ropes, but was interrupted almost immediately by the return of Jal and Espen.

"Well?" Nicabar demanded of the Wild Rose clan leaders.

"You know such decisions cannot be made lightly or in haste, especially when the true whereabouts of my own child remain in doubt," Jal stringently asserted.

"Your son seems to feel differently," Nicabar noted.

"I speak for the Wild Rose clan, Nicabar. Not he."

"Then speak Jal. What is it you want?"

"We are at truce. I ask for two days to consider your offer and to make any necessary arrangements."

Nicabar smiled.

"You're stalling, Jal. One day."

"Thirty six hours," Jal countered.

Nicabar took out his pocket watch and pointedly studied it.

"It is roughly a quarter past the hour. As of this moment, you have thirty hours. No more."

"Agreed," said Jal. Espen also nodded in assent.

"Be warned, any attempts to break our truce will be met with all deliberate force."

"Save your threats, Nicabar. The truce will not be violated by us, provided it is honored on your side as well. Before we leave here tonight, I would like to ask you several questions."

Nicabar resumed his seat.

"Please."

Jal ignored the invitation for him to resume his chair, instead, he remained standing, crossing his arms over his formidable bulk.

"If I go with you, how long should my people expect me to remain absent?"

"Several months, I should think," Nicabar replied.

"And will this truce between our peoples remain during that time?"

"Let us see how well it works for the next thirty hours. If it does, I'm sure we can negotiate the matter before our departure."

"I see," said Jal. "And if I refuse your offer?"

Nicabar leaned forward and folded his hands upon the table.

"Then I'm afraid there is very little I can do to alter the fate of your people, including Baseria's or hers," he said, inclining his head towards Etolie.

Jal was not so easily dissuaded. Nicabar would not be requesting that Jal accompany the Moon Shadows unless he believed it gave them a tactical advantage. Why take Jal now? He probed further.

"But you offer me no proof that the women you took are still alive."

"I've brought one," Nicabar graciously offered.

"One so traumatized, she can't even speak," Espen bitterly observed. "You show her to us now, then lock her away so we can't even talk to her. That's your plan, isn't it?"

Nicabar stood slowly, his countenance severe.

"She is our prisoner and will remain so until you decide otherwise, Jal. That is the way of things."

"I'd like to stay."

The men all seemed to have forgotten that Orfilia was still present. They looked upon her with a mixture of emotions: surprise, approval, worry, hope and suspicion.

"I have not finished examining her injuries," Abrielle explained as she stood, "or treating those I've already discovered."

"No," Espen began to protest.

Jal reached out and touched his son gently to silence him.

"At the very least, her ribs need to be bound to lessen the pain she is in," Abrielle stated matter-of-factly.

"What say you, Nicabar?" Jal asked.

The Moon Shadow leader appeared less than pleased, however, he also realized this could work to his advantage.

"She may remain for an hour, under guard. After that, we return to our camp with the prisoner, regardless of her medical status."

Jal looked briefly to Orfilia.

"Agreed. Espen will remain outside to escort her back to our encampment when the hour is reached."

"That is acceptable," Nicabar agreed, inclining his head a measure.

Espen crossed to his wife to exchange a short embrace.

"What can I do," he muttered in her ear.

"Bring me something that reminds her of home," Abrielle answered.

They parted. Jal stepped forward and touched her shoulder, approvingly. Then both Wild Rose clan men left.

**

As she lay down upon the meager bed, Tasaria rubbed her eyes, and for a moment, she gave into her body's urgent craving for rest. Immersed in her work once again, obsession with the task had replaced time. Still her mind raced furiously as she fought to extricate knowledge of the Seer arts from her own memories of the past.

Far too often now, her assignment forced her to recall images, feelings, and realities best left undisturbed: Nasi's training sessions with her and Mayte; the first time she met Nicabar; her infant daughter crawling around the tent; joking with friends who were now dead. Woven among this jumble of memories was the information she sought.

The key was remembering when she'd read about, learned, or applied specific skills as a Seer. The work was proving to be emotionally draining as she literally painted words onto blank pages, using thought as her sole resource. Hour after hour, she meditated, recalling pieces of information which would lead to a question or a series of questions—some pertaining to her task, others more personal, and some purely existential, all of which had to be organized and related to the greater realities of the Seer arts. To her sorrow, Tasaria began to realize just how much of her life she'd buried beneath her pain, secreted away all these long years.

One moment the work would seem simple, then, however, if it was supplanted by doubt, her progress slowed until reassurance again made something fact. Another source of constant irritation was the basic difficulty of keeping the inkwell from freezing. Several times now, she'd nearly burned her hand while holding the bottle over one of the chamber's candles. Invariably the stress took its toll. Her muscles were stiff from lack of rest and from unconsciously holding her body in positions for far too long.

Tasaria's mind also posed other challenges than just those relegated to her past. What was happening at home with her people? Was Nicabar safe? Could Pias pose a legitimate threat? Why had the spy been hidden among those Rom gypsies? What was behind the Old Ones' sudden attacks? How did Frankenstein figure into all of this? Was the Master being honest with her? Who did she trust? What of Baseria?

She was asleep. Tasaria knew it, but instead of dreaming, she found herself massaging the tension from her neck, touching the corrupted mark left by Nasi's phantom touch. Why was it there? What significance could it possibly possess? How might it link her to the corruption of Baseria's hand? Yes, there was a connection there.

Tasaria's eyes flashed open. She must speak with her niece.

"It is time for us to go to the chapel for Frankenstein," a Moon Shadow guard declared from the now open doorway. "Take what you'll need."

Tasaria blinked against the brighter light emanating from the hallway behind him. When had he entered? She coughed as she sat up.

"I must see my niece first."

"No. Master said she's not to be disturbed, and I'm to ensure you arrive at the chapel before the top of the hour. We don't have time."

"But …"

The man raised his gun suggestively.

"Shall we go?"

*

The creature knelt beside her, transfixed. He dare not touch Baseria, disturb her slumber with his still-bloody hands. Her breathing was rhythmic, soothing. After all his great crimes, all his sins, this last, should have been simple, yet, his heart could only weep at the repugnant thought.

"You alone," he whispered. "If only you could understand. All this I have done for you alone."

She stirred peacefully. In despair, he bowed his head.

*

Her crimes were magnified here. Since leaving the unholy lab, it was easy for Tasaria to rationalize the atrocities this pit of death held. Confronted with it once more, however, she grew faint again. Why did the Master insist she subject herself to this odious place once more? In fact she'd been doing everything in her power to avoid returning here.

She and Ernest hadn't spoken a word to each other since their reunion in the chapel. For over an hour now, he'd surveyed the grim chamber. It was evident that bodies were missing from the pile, including Sebbi's. Some of the equipment bore obvious signs of recent use, while other pieces seemed to have vanished. And there were fresh pools of frozen blood everywhere.

"He's preparing for something," Ernest finally declared, as much to himself as to Tasaria. "He wants us to see he's ready, show us that we can't stop him. But …" He stopped short as his eyes met Tasaria's. "Why send you?"

She cleared her throat, trying to ignore the queasiness she felt.

"You know the Old Ones have been compromised, so I …"

"He could have sent a guard down here with me," Ernest challenged. "No, no, he has a purpose. What does he want?"

His eyes momentarily lingered on the pages she clutched absently in her hand.

"What does he want you to understand? Somehow you're the key to him getting what he wants."

Tasaria took an involuntary step backwards, suddenly all too aware of her vulnerability. Ernest lunged at her, snatching the pages from her hand. He paused to consider them as she fled a number of steps away.

For a long time, the only motion he offered came from the clouds of mist produced by each of his frozen breaths. The writings were in a host of languages, but one word leapt from the page repeatedly: Seer. He quickly strode to one of the burning torches alight on the walls and set the pages ablaze. In a matter of seconds they were ash.

"Where did you get those? Where?!" he demanded.

Tasaria's resolve stiffened.

"You understand nothing."

Wordlessly, she strode to where the ruined work smoldered and took the torch down from the wall. Uttering words, she released a plea, one which was answered. What the fire had destroyed, Elemental Fire rejoined; the pages were once again whole. Ernest stood still in astonishment.

"My niece is not the only one who can summon the forces of the unseen world," Tasaria haughtily declared.

Ernest remained silent.

"You wish to know why we have returned to this accursed place. Because you are responsible for the destruction of our ancient heritage, you are to help me retrieve it," Tasaria asserted, pointing the torch toward him with one hand and brandishing the reunified pages in the other.

"How?" he asked. "I destroyed your mother's writings months ago, very far from here." Ernest looked significantly at the pages in her hand.

She smiled.

"At first I thought Pias was responsible for their loss when he killed…," she looked away and steeled herself for a moment before continuing. Was that fear he saw in her expression? "Form and energy are constants. So the knowledge can be retrieved and channeled through a conduit … unless …" Her pallor grew even more pale, stricken, as a long-forgotten memory awoke, one which could endanger everything. Tasaria closed her eyes.

"Cold fire," she whispered, the words escaping as a sigh.

A shadow stirred.

"Look out!" Ernest intercepted the Old One's blade seconds before it would have struck down Tasaria, but the demon possessed both greater strength and more solid footing than the ice Ernest stood upon. He shifted and strained against the indomitable will, but knew he was losing. It wanted her dead.

The torch in Tasaria's hand clattered against the ice as she maneuvered away. From the darkness, another robed figure appeared and dispatched the would-be attacker with a single, lethal thrust. Then it stood in silent repose over the corpse.

Ernest pulled Tasaria closer to him, but the Old One did not stir.

"I thought we were safe down here," she gasped.

"This fortress has a maze of secret tunnels," Ernest explained. "Looks like they missed checking a few," he added.

"They were all supposed to be disarmed …," she lamented, considering the remains of her attacker. But there was something even more troubling to her.

Before Ernest could stop her, Tasaria reached up and pulled back the surviving Old One's hood. She stared in disbelief.

"But I ordered you to remain in Vochallet's chamber," she said in puzzlement. Why did it continue to return to her, unbidden? Was it choosing to do so or was it all part of the Master's mental conditioning for the Old Ones, a habit they were unable to renounce?

Her arm was seized by Ernest, whose eyes still probed the laboratory for signs of any other assassins.

"You can control them? You know how to communicate with them?" he demanded. "If you're giving them orders …"

"NO! No, I have no power over them," her voice shook as she averted her eyes from his.

The Old One suddenly stooped and retrieved the knife from its victim. Ernest slowly released his grip on Tasaria, took a step back, and allowed his arms to rest calmly by his sides. The Old One's stance relaxed in kind.

"Power or not, this fellow seems quite taken with you," Ernest wryly observed.

Neither voiced the questions which were mutually paramount in their minds. Why would any of the Old Ones try to attack her? Who was responsible? Tasaria's heart pounded. Baseria had seen her control the Old One. What if she'd told the Master?

"We should go," Tasaria advised brushing past him. The Old One followed. She was almost lost to the darkness before he bent down and retrieved the torch she'd abandoned there.

"Wait," Ernest bid, calling after her. She halted. "Wait," he said more quietly as he approached.

"What?" she tersely implored.

She was frightened, and Ernest realized that her fear might hold the last chance for any of their salvations. He held out his hand.

"We haven't finished."

"There is nothing left for us to learn here," she said breathing heavily.

With a mournful gaze, his eyes tracked through the gloom and located a well-remembered low, dark tunnel. His soul grew faint. How great the sin it contained, but it also seemed to be his last hope to reach Tasaria's heart in time.

"No," his voice broke. "There is one thing more."

*

Where was he taking her? Her knees and palms kept slipping on the glass-like ice beneath her. The dark, frigid, confining tunnel was shrouded in mist. Only a faint, flickering light ahead offered hope that there was something beyond. Ernest kept urging her forward. What could he possibly want to show her? The Old One remained at the entry to the tunnel. She was again defenseless should Frankenstein chose to exact some measure of revenge against her. Perhaps he'd arranged the attack in the first place. The Master believed he was capable of such acts. But if that were so why would he have fought to protect her against the Old One's attack in the lab?

"We're almost through," he promised.

She halted again, rubbing her frozen hands against her dress for warmth.

"And what is it you wish me to see?" she demanded.

He grabbed her arm and hauled her across the ice.

"Truth," he bitterly responded.

The tunnel ended in a small circular chamber. Tasaria blinked as her eyes adjusted to the stronger light offered by several torches alight upon the walls. Her vision cleared. Ernest's hand covered her mouth before the scream escaped her mouth. Her nerves coursed with terror, but Ernest denied her frantic struggle to retreat back into the tunnel.

"No. Look at him," he implored in anguish. "Look at him!"

Victor did not stir. Ernest's revulsion grew more pronounced as he realized one of his brother's arms was now partially, deliberately severed from the decrepit remains of his body. And there was only one being vile enough to make it so.

"His own son has done this to him," Ernest declared as Tasaria's efforts to escape eroded momentarily to exhaustion. She fell back against Ernest who persisted.

"Your mother told me that I'm the Second Light. He is the First, the father, the one who summoned your Master, his creator. Look at what he has done."

Aside from shallow breaths, there was little to betray signs of life in Victor's tortured frame. Tasaria ceased her struggles and stared helplessly at the wretch before her.

"They've hidden their sins from us, your Master and my brother, driven each other mad. They have been the architects of their own miseries and created untold suffering for all of us. Is this what you seek for your people, for Baseria, for us?"

"Please," Tasaria cried, "no more. No more."

"This is why he sent us down here," Ernest continued. "To force me to show you the truth, to share my family's sin openly with you," he said.

"Why?" she gasped, overcome with emotion.

Ernest released his grip on her. Tasaria sought refuge against the nearby wall.

"I don't know," he finally admitted. "All I know is that he needs us, just as he needs information from my brother to complete his plans. Maybe he hopes that forcing me to acknowledging my brother's sin to another will justify his actions or strengthen his connection to your prophecy, forge a stronger bond among us, I really don't know. He's mad."

Ernest knelt and visually examined his brother's arm, which appeared to be in the process of being surgically removed.

"Maybe he thinks you and Baseria can heal Victor so he can butcher him further. Or maybe he's just tired of concealing all of these crimes."

He did not see Tasaria's expression turn to one of disgust. This man knew nothing. Perhaps he was in league with Pias, and all of this was some type of deception, a final test of her loyalties.

"You're mad," Tasaria said, regaining a degree of composure. "The Master came to us in fulfillment of prophecy."

Ernest laughed mirthlessly.

"A prophecy even its originators can't agree upon. If you could, your war would not exist, none of this would." He massaged his temples, "I wish someone had destroyed those Seer scrolls long before I did."

"With cold fire?"

"What?"

"Did you summon cold fire from the earth?" the Moon Shadow priestess demanded.

"Yes," he said quickly before shaking his head. "No. I don't remember."

He paused before continuing.

"Your mother gave me some decorative box and then, asked me to destroy the scrolls. The next thing I remember is watching the last of them burn and looking down at my brother's journals in my hand. But I have no memory of leaving her tent or climbing up to that cliff where they burned."

Tasaria's eyes narrowed.

"What box?"

He briefly clasped his hands to the back of his head.

"It was small, decorated with carvings of some type. It's missing," he admitted.

"When did it go missing?" she pressed.

"It vanished after I was first brought down here with you into the lab," Ernest recalled.

"You brought it to this fortress?"

Ernest nodded.

As she paused to consider his words, Victor's mummified and mutilated form stirred, the veiled, diseased orbs drew open.

"Elizabeth? Elizabeth?" he asked frantically before calming a degree. "She was here," he affirmed as if in need to convince himself. "She was here."

"Victor?"

The eyes flashed to Ernest.

"Victor, do you remember me? I'm your brother, Ernest."

The corrupted form struggled before responding.

"No. No. Never. Ernest is safe, beyond your reach," Victor said triumphantly, not recognizing to whom he spoke. "I saved him from you."

Ernest reached out and touched his brother gently.

"You're right," he agreed, his eyes filled with tears. "He's safe, and Elizabeth is safe as well."

"Elizabeth," Victor breathed. "She was here."

"I know, Brother," Ernest agreed. "I know."

He braced himself.

"Why does your creation take your arm?"

"Arm? Arm?"

"Why does it take your arm, Victor?"

Victor's eyes darted back and forth as he considered the question before his mind again was, involuntarily, locked away behind the creature's conditioning. Ernest watched as the remains of his brother fought to speak. The words, when they finally came, escaped in short bursts.

"Punishment, demands, always more and more answers. Sorrow-burnt unity. Possible if ever I told of the ship." His head struck the stone behind him. "The power to make them whole. Too many, too many. The key to all. The key …"

Ernest stared in bewilderment as Victor grew agitated.

"NO! Must not unlock the wild and lonely expanses of existence. Death of humanity. Pain. Pain. Everlasting darkness will damn us all." These words rushed from him rapidly. He turned and looked directly at Ernest, then past him to the stone wall, his rasping voice, suddenly mild. "She is beautiful, so beautiful."

What did his brother see, Ernest wondered. Did he imagine he saw Elizabeth there? Perhaps, trapped so close between life and death, he did see her. Ernest turned to plead once more with Tasaria, only to discover that she had vanished back through the tunnel at some point. Her heart would not be swayed. Ernest covered his face with his hands. She'd been his last hope. As he withdrew his hands, his eyes lingered on the scar left by Abrielle.

"Ernest." It was Victor's voice this time, as it had been in life. Slowly Ernest met his brother's eyes. They were focused, strong. He knew his brother was with him.

"You must end this. He cannot live."

"Victor," Ernest cried his brother's name in a profane blend of relief and anguish. He sank against his brother's good shoulder, and there they remained, embracing a bond forged in another lifetime.

"Why, Victor?" Ernest asked after an eternity.

For a long time, Victor was silent.

"There is no answer. Is there?" Ernest said at last to his older sibling.

"I wanted to create life … end suffering. But, I am become Death," Victor said softly. He paused. "I am sorry, Ernest. I was not strong enough. Promise me, brother, promise me he will not live. He cannot be allowed to destroy any more lives."

Ernest took his brother's decayed hand into his.

"I promise," he said, moments before another fit of madness consumed Victor's tormented being. Sometime later, the creature and his guards forcibly removed Ernest back to the chapel.

*

The only emotion she was clearly aware of was rage. Frankenstein was wrong! It was a trick, a test. All that she'd done was right. It served a higher purpose than vengeance and murder. The Master was right; in conquering death, there were bound to be mistakes. Ultimately these would be overcome. Her niece was key to achieving that, and when they did, Baseria would restore Tasaria's daughter to her, the child she'd murdered. That was balance.

Her frenzied search of the chapel failed to discover the box Ernest had described. She paused in the turret stairwell. If it even existed, where would the box be? Could the Master have it? Perhaps it never made it as far as the fortress. Maybe Frankenstein lost it during the sea battle with the Norwegians, his claim to the contrary serving as nothing but a distraction. No. She could not passively accept that. It was here and she must find it. She resumed her steps, dimly aware that the Old One still followed her.

What might the box contain? The use of cold fire was so complex, an ancient-Seer art that Tasaria had nearly forgotten about its existence. In all the years spent training her daughters, Nasi had mentioned it only once or twice in passing. Were it not for Tasaria's in-depth study of the Seer scrolls during her youth, the use of it would never have even occurred to her, but it could change everything.

She crossed the snow-laden expanse of the open commons before entering the great hall, followed by more steps, into the maze of hallways. Could Frankenstein be correct about the fortress being honeycombed with hidden passageways? If so, her next actions might prove fatal should another attack befall her; then again, attempting to conceal her blatant disobedience might save her life. She paused at the foot of a familiar set of stairs and turned to her ever-present shadow. Without knowing exactly why, she reached out and touched its robe covered arm.

"Listen to me. You must remain in Vochallet's room until I return or you endanger us both."

The Old One offered no reaction.

"Go now," she commanded before beginning to walk away, but she stopped suddenly and turned back to the hooded figure.

"Thank you for saving my life."

As she watched the misbegotten being ascend the stone staircase, she could not help but wonder if it had inclined its head towards her, ever so slightly, before it began to walk.

*

Baseria put down the by now, all-too-familiar pages her aunt had left her. She sighed. It was no longer a matter of knowing what words to say or how a ritual was supposed to work. It was having the courage to try.

She looked down, yet again, to her corrupted hand, which appeared, burnt, dead-looking. Healing it would require not only applying the information her aunt shared but opening herself, once more, to the all-consuming power within. The last time she attempted to do so, it nearly killed both her and Etolie.

The thought of her friend's death, as well as those of the other Wild Rose women who'd suffered with her here, filled Baseria with agony. She'd been helpless to change their fates or her own. The power she possessed simply overwhelmed her. But her aunt had revealed an axiom she had not considered.

Due to the secretive nature of her training with Nasi, Baseria's instruction was a rushed and incomplete affair. Limited by time, her grandmother's delicate health, and fears of Jal learning of his daughter's efforts, Nasi focused on introducing Baseria to means of accessing Elemental energies for only short periods of time, showing her how to apply her powers to various situations. She omitted much of what she'd taught her own daughters, including many of the deeper mysteries of their power. Baseria was only now beginning to understand how vast, intricate, and terrifying the power she accessed truly was.

Now as she entered the next phase of her training, Baseria was awed by the simple truth Tasaria had revealed to her. It lay in the principle philosophy her people had always lived by. All life is balance. As such, calling upon the awesome power of one form of Elemental energy quickly proved overwhelming, but when balanced against another Elemental source of power, the user gained greater control.

When she'd healed her grandmother, Baseria was still young. Her connection to the powers of the unseen world was tenuous, instinct more than skill had guided her actions. Throughout her secret training with Nasi, her grandmother was available to help guide Baseria's connection to the Elemental energies, a fact Baseria had been largely ignorant of. It wasn't until her near death experience with Frankenstein that she'd summoned Elemental energy unconsciously to aid her healing, however, by then, Baseria's connection with them was already greatly strengthened by her visions of Ernest, and later, his dying wife.

She understood now that thcy used her just as she used them. With this in mind, Baseria was reminded of another simple truth her mother once taught her—take only what nature is willing to share and always appreciate such gifts. Such thoughts now changed how Baseria approached opening herself to the power all around her, for she was just as much a part of the energy as everything else in existence, which made her both master and servant to it. Time dictated which.

Baseria knelt and touched her palm to the stone floor. Such a physical connection was probably not necessary, but she liked the notion of having something solid to touch as she opened herself up to the ethereal. She closed her eyes and began to embrace a more meditative state.

The power was there as she knew it would be. She waited as one did when quietly inviting another into conversation. Unlike her earlier attempts, this time when she made her request, she did not aggressively immerse herself into one form of Elemental energy. She relaxed, secure in the knowledge that she could end the contact when she wished, knowing instinctively which of the shifting Elemental energies to balance and when.

Everything dissipated when her concentration broke. Her aunt was looming over her, a questioning look etched upon her features. Baseria felt a little drained, but to her joy, discovered that all was as it should be in the room. Her contact with the unseen world did not appear to have resulted in disaster as it had previously. She allowed herself a brief smile.

"You have been practicing what we discussed?"

Baseria nodded as she rose. Her aunt gasped and stood back from Baseria who looked down at the source of her aunt's amazement.

For Baseria, shock quickly turned to elation as she noticed the partial change to her corrupted hand. As she stood, what appeared to be ash began to separate from her hand like a trailing mist. Brushing at the substance on her hand revealed that there was now new healthy skin beneath it. The healing process was incomplete, but still nothing short of miraculous.

"It worked," she whispered to herself in disbelief.

Tasaria reached down and felt her niece's hand.

"It did," she said absently before continuing. "The powers have granted you a gift. Soon you will no longer be marked by cold fire."

Baseria paused, considering her hand as her memory turned the words over, searching for a reference.

"Cold fire?"

"Yes, your grandmother's lessons must have mentioned it at some point," she stated casually as she gratefully stood closer to the reading room's fireplace.

Baseria frowned.

"No. Or if she did I have forgotten it. What is cold fire?"

Tasaria did not turn to face her niece.

"A complex application of Seer arts, an ancient magic, seldom practiced by our order. It consists of blending all four Elemental energies at once. The result is a flame of unique properties that creates as it destroys. Tell me, Baseria, how exactly were the Seer scrolls destroyed?"

Her niece hesitated before answering.

"Frankenstein burned them."

"Ostensibly at my mother's request?" Tasaria requested.

Baseria paused again.

"Yes," the utterance was tinged with uncertainty.

"You witnessed their destruction?"

"You believe they were destroyed using this cold fire?" her niece concluded.

Tasaria turned.

"Of course, but more than that, I believe your grandmother used it on herself as well."

Baseria's gaze drifted a moment.

"No. She would never destroy herself."

Tasaria drew closer.

"No. Listen, child. Cold fire may change the physicality of something, but the essence continues to exist. Look at your hand again, Baseria."

She did.

"Now."

The corruption to their flesh did appear to be identical she noted as Tasaria's fingers traced the side of her own neck.

"She touched me here, when I saw her in my chambers. Mother marked me here. Your hand is the same."

"I don't understand," Baseria said quietly after a moment. "How could her spirit have touched us? What does this have to do with the scrolls being burned?"

"Everything," her aunt passionately declared. "This is the key to everything. Frankenstein says Mother gave him a box."

Baseria's heart leapt.

"You've seen him? Is he all right?" Her questions flowed rapidly. By her aunt's expression, she knew something was terribly wrong. In fact the questions seemed to elicit confusion, even fear in her. She attempted to mask her distress by avoiding her niece's eyes for a moment.

"What's happened? Is he hurt?"

"Baseria. We don't have much time." Her aunt looked away.

The young woman lightly touched the older woman's hand.

"What happened to him?" Baseria demanded seeing tears in her aunt's eyes.

It took her several moments before Tasaria could bring herself to answer.

"Something … from which … I fear he will never recover." Her voice was quivering.

Baseria's pervasive gaze demanded more. How could Tasaria hope to explain? Her nervous hand played unconsciously across her lips and chin.

"I … the Master, he …," Tasaria's expression collapsed into one of bewilderment before she turned her gaze to her niece. "Why did you kill them, Baseria?"

The girl recoiled from the unanticipated question. She knew all to well to whom her aunt now referred. Baseria's lips moved to deny she was responsible for her cousin's and sister's deaths. Instead, she uttered different words.

"I'm sorry."

Tasaria's stance became more aggressive.

"Was it jealousy?"

Baseria backed away, but her aunt seized her.

"All these years, you claim ignorance for your crimes when it should have been you. It should have been you! Do you hear me? It should have been you who died. Not them … not Jucika, not my precious child."

She shoved Baseria to the ground and prowled around her.

"You've always taken everything from me, haven't you?"

Baseria raised her arm defensively.

"Please, please my aunt."

"Do not beg for mercy now when you showed them none then. What was it? Did you learn the truth that day about your filthy whore of a mother?"

Tasaria seized Baseria's hair.

"Answer me! Is that why you killed them?"

Each was breathing hard, wordlessly begging for answers from the other. Tasaria discovered hers first. She began to laugh in disbelief.

"My God, they never even told you, did they?"

"Told me what?" Baseria desperately entreated as her aunt's increasingly morose laughter continued. "Told me what?"

The other woman collected herself before answering.

"Jal Nalie is not your father. My husband is."

Baseria was too stunned to speak. They were silent for an endless measure of heartbeats until Baseria finally stirred as if awakening from a dream.

"Before you deny it outright, hear me," Tasaria implored touching the girl's arm. When her niece said nothing in response, she continued. "This is known by only a very few. I know, all too well, the pain of a sibling's betrayal. They kept it hidden from Jal and me for a long time. Mayte's affair with Nicabar was intermittent, so we could never be sure, but upon your birth, Jal refused to claim you as his own. It was only after your grandmother intervened that he agreed to raise you as his child."

The turmoil within rendered Baseria still. She was too wounded to speak. Could it be true? Her aunt knelt and awkwardly held her. Baseria offered no protest. She did not want to think of anything that had just been said. All she could see was her family, recall only their best qualities—her dear deceased mother's warm, knowing smile, Jal's proud heart, Espen's steadfast belief in her.

"You could have been my daughter," Tasaria said after a time. "Then all of this might have been different."

Her niece started.

"Well, it isn't," Baseria said bitterly.

Tasaria straightened, releasing her.

"You're right. This is the reality we chose. Now, where is the box?"

Baseria turned to face her aunt.

"Don't speak to me of your box. I refuse to help you or your Master."

"Why?"

Her gaze faltered slightly.

"Because you both enjoy killing the innocent," Baseria cried. "I won't help."

Tasaria regarded the girl.

"I have seen the First Light … here, in this place. Frankenstein's brother … or what still exists of him. Before I came to you, the brother admitted unfathomable crimes against the innocent to Ernest. He suffers terribly for those sins, as I have, as you have, Baseria. But we can end all of this, honor your grandmother's wish that we be brought together now to summon forth a new world. She has marked us for that purpose so that we may regain our Seer heritage, which has been transformed by the cold fire, locked safely away within the Elemental energies, waiting. The box is a conduit. It must be, one capable of uniting us once more with the ancient knowledge of the Seer by helping us to accurately balance the Elemental energies that now contain it."

"And then what?" Baseria challenged. "You use it? Use me to help you destroy life as you did my friends, as you did my grandmother?"

"No," Tasaria said softly. "You will restore it. Create it anew. That is our great purpose. It has always been. Your grandmother knew this, even if she lacked the clairvoyance to fully understand how we would ultimately achieve it. I tried to explain it to her, begged, her, but she would not listen. Still she has not allowed the crucial Seer knowledge to be destroyed. She has saved it for us."

"At the cost of her own life," Baseria moaned.

"So do we now fail to honor that sacrifice? She was never meant to die in that attack, never. Have you ever considered that she chose death? There must have been some reason, some purpose as to why the night of that attack she ordered Frankenstein to transform the scrolls. That she gave him the box …"

"Stop!" cried Baseria, holding her hands over her ears. Tasaria was not to be dissuaded.

"She has marked us because her wraith knows you can restore her using the Seer knowledge. Why else would she have appeared to us both, bringing us together? It is clear what you must do."

"I can't," insisted Baseria.

"Where is the box?" her aunt harshly demanded before she began rummaging through Baseria's meager belongings. She discovered it wedged down behind the blankets Baseria had been using as a pillow.

Her fingers delicately probed the carved surface in vain.

"How does it open?"

Tasaria felt the disturbance in time. Without thought, she summoned Elemental Wind and extinguished the nearby fire. She grabbed her niece.

"Do not dare attempt to use the powers against me," she warned. "Now, how does this open."

"I don't know," Baseria said, massaging the wrist her aunt had twisted. "When I first came to you, I brought it with me hoping you would know."

The older woman considered the box.

"You said it was a conduit," Baseria reminded her. "Perhaps it does not need to be opened."

Tasaria regarded the box a moment longer.

"Come here," she ordered her niece.

Warily Baseria approached and sat upon the ground as her aunt did, the box between them.

"Very well, we will test your theory," Tasaria asserted, drawing her niece's hands into her own as she closed her eyes. "Or shall I tell the Master of your refusal?"

Baseria was silent for a long moment before protesting.

"But I don't …"

"Ssshhh," the older woman scolded. "It is the same, always the same. Relax. Meditate. Allow the energies to enfold you, then we shall make our request of them. They should be able to guide us to the Seer knowledge."

This was far more advanced than anything Baseria had previously attempted. Conflicted, she found it difficult to truly feel at ease, to be receptive to the powers of the unseen world. Still she could sense her aunt's strong, clear, purpose probing the currents of Elemental energy which remained discordant. Without conscious thought, Baseria guided her imperfectly healed hand, as well as her aunt's, to rest upon the modest box between them.

When she drew open her eyes, she realized that they were simultaneously together and apart, existing as one, but separate, still touching physically but drifting among the tides of time and space. They sought knowledge here, restoration, truths. Larger powers understood this. They answered.

Where was she? Baseria was dimly aware of the mountains, the snow. But this was not the Arctic wastes. He was here, Espen, surrounded by Moon Shadows. The woman with him wore a disguise, Baseria was certain. She saw her aunt at the edge of her vision with the cruel man who'd taken Etolie. He was accompanied by a host of wolves.

"She's a spy," another cried, pointing to the woman in disguise with Espen.

Wolves beat a murderous path towards Espen and the woman, both of whom fled. Baseria could feel herself yelling 'no,' bidding the wolves to stop but knowing they would not—shots, confusion, more gunfire, the edge of a great cliff. Baseria's heart seized as she watched in horror, her brother and the woman tumble over the edge into oblivion.

Her aunt was there. Their eyes met. This was truth. It has already occurred. Her brother was dead.

"No. They escaped. We found no bodies."

The older woman had not spoken, but Baseria knew this thought emanated from her.

"The woman?" Baseria's mind was fixed upon the memory.

"I don't know. A spy who took your brother from us."

There was no time for Baseria to process this thought.

It was not over. Tasaria must know. She had to know.

Baseria tried to hide in the shifting energies. No. She could not bear to relive that moment. Tasaria beckoned. Her aunt would not be denied. The energies demanded it, as did her soul. The knowledge they sought to retrieve was close, but this must take precedent.

It happened. Baseria was watching events from afar, while simultaneously reliving them. She could feel the kitten playing with her fingers as she looked out over the chasm to the grandeur of the Carpathians. Some part of her never failed to marvel how the light played among the rocks, the groves of trees, the mists from the nearby waterfall.

Then she heard the voices.

"NO!"

The faces of those whose deaths haunted her life appeared before her: Jucika and Patia. The argument would begin and then … how could she possibly relive a moment so long suppressed by her own mind? Baseria's revulsion, her crippling guilt, mounted as half-remembered scenes began to play out through her. Inwardly, she struggled for escape, any means of escape from this loathsome moment.

Tasaria could sense the girl fighting, knew that as powerful as Baseria was, this might be her sole chance to know the truth, one long denied her. Why had Baseria killed Tasaria's daughter and her own sister? What forces conspired on this day to irrevocably change all of their lives forever? Tasaria watched as events played out, a series of arguments and counterarguments ensued among the girls.

As their fight escalated into the physical, the event became muddled. Baseria was succeeding in drawing away from her bond with Tasaria. She must not be allowed to escape, now when the answers were so close at hand. With all of her remaining strength, her aunt fought against Baseria's efforts to withdraw.

The memories became more confused, increasingly sporadic as each of them attempted to assert dominance over their Elemental bond. The images, sounds, and emotions of those awful moments saturated Tasaria. And then, at long last, the full truth lay bare before her, just as their connection broke.

They were back in the reading room. Both women were coated in sweat. Their hands parted. As she looked upon her niece, Tasaria's trembling hands attempted to hide the repressed scream of anguish. In pain, she fled from the chamber, leaving Baseria alone, weeping for all of the misery she'd brought into this world. She could recall little of what had been forced from her memories, but her aunt's reaction now confirmed the worst. She could no longer deny it. Baseria was a killer.

**

Jal studied his boots as he mindlessly blew rings of smoke at them, but the swirls always seemed to dissipate before they encompassed the toe. He was dimly aware of his son continuing to pace behind him. The boy only paused when he was glaring at his father. Jal paid him no mind.

"We will discuss these matters in the morning," he declared at last.

"No, we'll talk now," Espen asserted.

"Quiet, Espen, the baby is sleeping," Jal reminded him as he set down his pipe and rubbed his eyes.

"We have time and such decisions should not be taken lightly."

"I take none of this lightly," Espen stated, biting at each word in a harsh whisper. "That is why we must act."

"We are," Jal noted as he stood and crossed the tent. "Your brave wife is hopefully gathering information for us as we speak. Her findings may prove invaluable to my decision. You married well. She is quite a woman."

He leaned down and splashed a measure of cool water from a bucket onto his face, which he began to gently dab. He sighed. Espen's incredulity was beginning to wear on him.

"Baseria is missing, Etolie suffers, and you just sit here. What decision is to be made? If we catch them by surprise as we did in Hungary …"

"And risk losing others as we did your grandmother? No," Jal said flatly. "No. We strike only if they do so first. There is too much at stake."

Espen was not to be dissuaded.

"What is it? I've seen you make choices like this in an instant? Why can't you now?"

Jal looked away a moment before drawing closer to his only son.

"Because I realize now that you are not ready to lead. You may never be. You are too rash, Espen. You endanger yourself and get others killed. Good men. I cannot simply entrust this encampment to you and hope for the best. I must consider the needs of all of our people, their survival. Not just the lives of a select few."

The words hurt Espen as he nodded fervently.

"Entrust me? Are you an expert in trust, Father? Did Frankenstein entrust you with his daughter? That's what all this is about, right? Were you concerned with our people's needs then or just your own?"

"That is my affair," Jal's voice rose menacingly. "And it remains so."

"Even if her presence endangers all of our people's safety? Is that wise leadership, not to be counseled?"

"I succeeded where you failed, nothing more. You claim to want Baseria back, yet, you obstruct my efforts to do so."

"Because there are better ways," the younger man began.

"Different, not better, Espen, different. Now your wife's hour is all but up. Be gone from my sight until daybreak. I must think."

*

Abrielle continued to rub warm water over Etolie's wounds, but she was all out of ideas. Over the past hour, she'd made several requests designed to not only garner materials to help her treat Etolie, but also to allow her a moment alone with the woman, however, each of these efforts had been steadfastly thwarted, always one guard remained close at hand, observing her every word and movement. Consequently she'd been able to help Etolie physically, but accomplished little else.

Where had she been? Why had they beaten and abused her so? Were the other women alive? What might she have potentially overheard that could be useful? Probably not much. As Abrielle held the poor suffering woman's hand, she realized that the prisoner had retreated into herself. What choice did she really have? She was a pawn, and she knew it. A reality Abrielle knew only too well.

Espen stepped into the tent just as one of the guards abruptly reached down and began to pull them apart.

"Time's up," he said gruffly.

"Don't!"

The man's grip slackened as he was spun around by the force of Espen seizing him. Instead of focusing on the men, Abrielle's attention returned to Etolie, whose eyes sought hers. Abrielle leaned closer.

"Don't let them trade me for Frankenstein's child," Etolie's pained voice pleaded in French.

"He's alive?" Abrielle asked breathlessly.

"Yes."

Abrielle was hauled callously to her feet by two guards. Nicabar gripped her hair tightly.

"What's it to be, Espen? I told you treachery would not be tolerated."

Her false husband instantly released the guard he was grappling with and put up his hands.

"He was mistreating my wife."

"No, he was enforcing our agreement of one hour's access to the prisoner. Were it not for our truce, neither of you would still be standing here alive," Nicabar assured him.

He shoved Abrielle roughly towards Espen.

"Get out," he ordered.

Espen retrieved a hairbrush from his jacket and laid it down on the table in front of Nicabar. His eyes lingered on Etolie for a moment, while Abrielle's focused on the hairbrush. She recognized it from the possessions stored in her and Espen's tent.

"It's hers," he said simply, before he ushered Abrielle from the tent.

They walked on in silence until they were well within the confines of the Wild Rose camp, both of their souls aflame with torment and ecstasy.

"I hope that diversion worked," Espen muttered as he rubbed at the tenderness in his jaw.

Abrielle offered no response, her eyes remained fixed forward. A deepening certainty was growing within her. If she could discover the proper means to exploit it ...

"Did she tell you anything?" he finally asked.

Abrielle turned to face him.

"No," she said evenly. "She never had the chance."

**

CHAPTER 27
SOUL'S ECHO

"Baseria! Baseria!"

"Is she dead?" the Moon Shadow guard asked.

Tasaria felt her niece's pulse. It was slow and steady, but the girl remained unresponsive.

"No."

"What's wrong with her?" The man's stance betrayed at once curiosity and caution.

Tasaria's eyes were drawn to the modest wooden box, which now lay on its side on the chamber's floor. Could it be responsible for this? Baseria was clutching it tightly when they entered.

"She needs to be tended to," Tasaria noted quietly as she attempted to exam Baseria's pupils. They'd rolled back into her head.

Growing disinterested the guard turned to leave.

"Carry her," Tasaria commanded as she suddenly stood.

"What? To where?" the man demanded.

"To the chapel."

"Why? That's mad. That's on the other side of the damn fortress. The Master ordered …"

"I'm ordering you, and unless you wish me to inform the Master that you've disrupted his plans, you will obey me."

The gypsy hesitated, his mind and body clearly at odds.

"I'll need help," he finally begrudgingly said.

"Then get it," Tasaria commanded as she crossed her arms.

*

"What happened to her?"

Ernest knelt beside the unconscious Baseria as she was laid on the chapel's benches.

"Leave us," Tasaria harshly ordered the Moon Shadow guards. They reluctantly obeyed. The older woman did not stir until they completely vacated the chapel.

"What did my mother tell you this was?" Tasaria immediately demanded without preamble as she held out the wooden box to Ernest.

"Where did you find that?"

"Answer me!"

The words reverberated off the bare stones. There were tears in the woman's wild eyes.

"Something she claimed would be useful to me in an hour of darkness," Ernest said evenly as he studied Tasaria.

To his surprise the older woman handed him the box, then began to walk away.

She paused after several paces and turned. Her voice shook.

"If my niece awakes, tell her … tell her …"

Overcome with emotion, the words died before they were born, leaving only an expression of solemn self-reproach on the Moon Shadow priestess' face. Ernest silently watched her retreating back until she vanished through the chapel's entry, which was quickly locked behind her.

All of his efforts to revive Baseria proved useless. With little else he could do, Ernest covered her thoroughly, and by the dim light of the torches, he pondered Nasi's gift.

**

The cold rain was miserable. Espen pulled his hood closer and fervently hoped it stopped soon. This day, his life, cried out for light. As he approached his destination, he wondered again what he could say to convince his father to save Etolie. And if he did, would Baseria die? Could she even still be alive? If only Abrielle had succeeded in learning something from her.

"Hytr? What's going on?" Espen asked the troubled gypsy who suddenly emerged from Jal's tent.

The young man frowned, shook his head, and patted his friend's shoulder as he passed. The words would have to wait.

"He's expecting you," was the best Hytr could manage before walking away.

"Father," Espen stated by way of greeting as he entered.

"Come in, Espen, come in," a hoarse voice replied before breaking into a fit of both coughing and nose blowing.

"It's good to know that the world still has a sense of humor, eh?"

Jal's laughter was smothered by more coughing.

"When did this start?" Espen asked in surprise.

"I don't know," Jal smiled as he wiped a tear from his eye. "A few hours ago. Chavi would not sleep last night, neither could I. So much for one heart to weigh. You and Patia, you were both very fussy babies, always keeping your mother and me awake, cry, cry, cry. It made for years of very long nights. But Baseria she slept, unless she was sick, the girl she … she slept."

His eyes grew distant as memories of a life long-faded from reality returned.

"Do you remember the tea your mother would make for us when we were sick?"

Espen smiled at the memory.

"Yes. I think Patia always preferred Nasi's tea."

"Nasi's tea, Nasi's tea," Jal waved a hand dismissively. "Your mother's tea, now that was special. She put an ingredient in it I could never figure out, very strong but sweet; worked every time."

"I remember." A part of Espen could not help but reflect that, with the exception of perhaps Baseria, every one of the family members they'd mentioned were now gone forever. All that remained were he and his father. Jal seemed to be lost in a similar fit of reverie.

"What happened in France, Espen?"

The question caught Jal's son off guard.

"What would you have me to tell you?" Espen asked quietly.

"The truth," his father implored. "What happened to your men?"

It took Espen a moment to gather his thoughts.

"I made a mistake. We were ambushed—more wolves. Kelv and I survived it, but …"

"How did you escape the Moon Shadows?"

There was something in the question that conveyed subtle mistrust. Did his father believe that Espen had somehow bartered a deal to save himself?

"I told you. It was foggy. I was being chased. I went over a cliff."

"By accident?"

"Yes," Espen curtly stated.

"But you saw Kelv die before this?"

"They drugged us. For a time, I wasn't sure what I saw."

"Fortunate that you came to your senses when the guard was careless with your bindings then,"Jal paused a moment before continuing. "Is there anything you could have done that would have changed the outcome for you or the others?"

In Espen's mind, there were endless choices he could have made differently, some that he should have.

"Yes," Espen answered softly.

"We are at war. There are losses in war, son. Failures in war. God knows I've had them. You learn to not repeat them. We were harsh with each other last night because of the lives at stake. Lives we care about, so much so that such feelings can blind us from making rational choices. But choices must be made nonetheless."

Jal tempered his renewed coughing fit with a sip of water.

"You haven't slept in days, and you're sick," Espen began.

"And I am the leader of this clan. I've made plenty of choices with little rest, and this is far from the first time I've been sick," Jal reminded his son.

"We should ask for more time to allow you to get better. How far do you think you could travel like this? God knows where they'd take you?" Espen shook his head.

"North. That Moon Shadow boy who died in Hungary said the Old One awaited Frankenstein in the north. I'll manage the journey. I just need rest."

A violent coughing fit descended upon him.

"Go now. I will call you when you are needed," Jal promised.

Espen rose.

"Is someone watching over you?"

"I'll be fine," Jal said. "Tend to others for now."

"Get some rest," Espen bid as he left.

For several minutes, the tent was silent. The boy was hiding something. Jal felt more certain of it than ever. He closed his eyes, opening them only when he heard the tent's rear entry being drawn open.

"Is he gone?"

"Yes," replied Hytr.

Jal stood and stretched his back. All traces of his illness vanished as he lit a pipe and took a deep draw.

"Conceal that look. I know you do not like it, Hytr, but this is one time when it is best to keep my son ignorant. Our plan is sound, and I have full faith in you and those we've chosen. Brief your men. Leave in an hour. I'll not turn myself over to Nicabar until the time of our negotiated truce is all but exhausted. That should give you plenty of time to get into position. Go with my blessings and bring us victory."

*

Try as he might, Hytr could not successfully evade Espen before escaping from the encampment. He'd sent his men on ahead, quietly, one or two at a time to avoid notice. They were all out there waiting for him.

"Hytr, Hytr," Espen called running to catch up to the horse and its rider.

"Sorry, Espen," his friend began. "I was lost in thought. Too many extra patrols with the Moon Shadows here, you know."

"Yes, well, I know Father's been keeping everyone busy. Where are you off to now?"

"Just another patrol, why?" Hytr casually inquired.

"You seem to have a lot of extra gear and provisions for a regular patrol. Is something up?"

"Not that I know of," Hytr shrugged. "We're stretched pretty thin, so Jal's kept some poor men at the more remote outposts for days. Just dropping some supplies off to them."

"I see. Mind if I ride along?"

Hytr shifted in his saddle.

"I don't, but your father probably wants you close by in case something happens."

Espen held his friend's gaze for a moment before responding.

"Sure, you're probably right, better to stick close for now."

"I'm sure he wouldn't mind your help on one of the shorter patrols," Hytr volunteered.

"Good idea. You should stop by later for supper. Orfilia's really coming into her own with cooking."

"If I'm back in time. Sure. Would love to. Look, I'll see you later," Espen's friend said in haste.

"Good luck."

Hytr whistled to his mount, and the two quickly disappeared over a small rise.

*

"I can't believe he's just going to surrender to them."

"He's not. That's where we come in. It's all a trick to give them a false sense of security. They'll have our leader and be expecting the attack to come from our side of the mountain, not theirs, not down at the base. That's when it will be the most devastating, right when they feel they're finally safe," Hytr explained.

"But what if they take this route?" one of the Wild Rose clan fighters asked pointing at the map.

"Well … Jype, what is it now?"

For the third time, Jype was standing, sword drawn, wandering away from the group of Wild Rose clan fighters being debriefed.

"I'm telling you, I keep hearing someone moving around."

Some groaned while others began to visually scour the woods and the rocks.

"We're about as remote as we can get from the back of our encampment, and we've done two complete sweeps on top of the one you all conducted before I got here," Hytr pointed out. "There's no one out there. It's just some animal."

"Wish we'd brought the dogs," another fighter stated to no one in particular.

"Too risky, too much noise," Hytr reminded him. "Jype, get back over here so we can finish this."

Jype continued staring off into the wilderness.

"If you're a part of this ambush team, I need you here now, Jype, otherwise, go back to regular duty. Jal asked for you specifically on this one, though."

Jype trusted his senses, but knew the others were eager to resume reviewing their plan. He sheathed his sword and returned to the group.

"I'm with you," he declared.

"Good. Now they can't go down this route, the terrain won't permit it. We scouted it thoroughly before the Moon Shadows arrived. No. This is where our ambush will be," Hytr explained.

"What's our goal?"

"Capturing Nicabar is our chief concern. The other is trying to rescue Jal, Etolie, if she's still a prisoner, and if possible, the infant Jal will have with him."

The men stirred uneasily. With the wolves the Moon Shadows controlled, taking Nicabar alive would be difficult enough, but rescuing prisoners while doing so seemed impossible. They would likely be executed the moment the attack began. And they were not a large force. Skill would be needed, but guile and luck were more crucial to this particular plan.

"Any questions?" Hytr asked.

"Are we getting any more help or is it just us?" one of the gypsies asked Hytr.

"We'll take the rear trail down from our side and pick up men from our outposts there as we go, then we traverse the valley to get to the Moon Shadows' trail."

"We're leaving our rear trail unguarded?"

"Practically," Hytr conceded. "Jal believes as soon as he's turned himself over, the Moon Shadows will want to begin pulling back."

"I would," one of the men commented, eliciting appreciative laughter from the others.

"We leave the bulk of our forces at the top to guard the encampment," Hytr continued. "Some though will follow the Moon Shadows down at a discreet distance and aid us when our attack begins."

A low murmur passed among the men.

"Too risky," Jype declared. Many nodded in agreement. If the attack started too early and too high on the mountain, then all of this would be for nothing.

"They'll have our weapon with them, and they'll have the high ground," Hytr reassured them. "Remember Greek fire worked for the Byzantines."

"Let's just hope it works for us."

Others muttered in agreement.

"Will Espen be riding in with the others?" one of the men asked.

Hytr began to fold the map.

"We'll only know if we get there in time. We've got a lot of ground to cover. Secure anything that could make noise and let's get moving."

*

As the onset of dusk approached, the persistent rain of the day was finally dissipating. Abrielle casually smiled to those she passed, still pretending to be ignorant of their conversations. The air itself reverberated with anticipation. Whispers conveyed that Jal Nalie was going to surrender himself to the Moon Shadows. This rumor was met and filtered through a host of emotions among the Wild Rose clan.

Abrielle sat down outside of her tent and retrieved the book she'd left underneath the moss-covered log which served as her seat. She feigned interest while she covertly observed those around her. All of them appeared too absorbed in the varied machinations of their own daily lives to take much note of a quiet woman peaceably reading her book in the last-lingering remnants of a misting rain. Casually she retrieved a piece of parchment from her pocket and set it on the ground near the cooking fire and waited. After a time, she put down the book and stirred the contents of a pot.

She bent down and studied the parchment as if consulting a recipe. The heat from the fire revealed a single word: Ready. She nudged the paper towards the hot coals as she dug at the fire with a stick. The paper emitted an instantaneous flash of ignition before being consumed seconds later. To the random passerby, this appeared as nothing more than the fire being rekindled. Abrielle stirred the contents of her cooking pot before entering her tent.

Espen was there, as she knew he would be, his attention riveted to the object in his hands.

"I took your father some soup earlier. You should eat something," Abrielle advised.

"I'm not hungry."

Abrielle abandoned her pretense and knelt beside him.

"Do you want her back?"

For the first time in several hours, Espen looked at her directly. By now Abrielle was sure to have surmised that many of the objects in this tent, including the bracelet in Espen's hand, belonged to Etolie. A guilty part of him wondered if she'd also rationalized the bracelet was something he'd once given to Etolie.

"How?"

"I've been in contact with Jack for sometime."

She waited a moment before continuing.

"He's ready to create a diversion for you to rescue her. I've given him some of your clothes."

He looked at her questioningly.

"The rubbish dump," she said by way of explanation.

Espen shook his head. Of course, all those voluntary trips to the encampment's rubbish dump, all the knitting of new clothes, blankets, all of it a cover for whatever she was scheming. It was a clever tactic. The rubbish dump was the only place near the camp left virtually unguarded, and its smell was more than sufficient to mask Jack's scent from the dogs when he snuck in to collect whatever she left for him.

"He could be killed," Espen asserted.

"Tara, Etolie, and your father could be killed if his plan succeeds."

"What do you mean?"

"Jal set Hytr out on an ambush, to take place at the bottom of the mountain. He wants to capture Nicabar even if it kills him and the others," Abrielle explained.

Espen's mind relived events from earlier in the day. Hytr's gear, his and Jal's behavior, the allusion that Hytr would not return from patrol tonight.

"Don't you see, he's leaving you out of this," Abrielle said.

"What time is it?" Espen asked, snapping back to the present.

"Close to eight, why?"

"What's your plan?"

A shadow of a smile crossed her lips.

"You meet Jack, and he'll show you how to get close to the Moon Shadow camp. He creates a diversion, you rescue Etolie."

"What if he's caught?" Espen questioned after a moment's thought.

"Then he pretends he's a mute and waits for us to come up with a new plan," Abrielle answered.

"I don't think Jack can handle playing silent for too long," Espen said, prompting a wry smile from Abrielle.

"It'll be a first," she agreed.

Espen stood, a new energy of purpose behind his movements.

"Where do I find him?"

"I made a map," said Abrielle turning her back to retrieve it from the bottom of a chest. “He’s expecting you.”

Her fingers prized it.

“I only see one problem with this plan,” Espen said as he suddenly clutched Abrielle from behind and held a chloroform soaked bandana firmly to her face.

“I’m not leaving you free to murder my father,” he whispered to her as the former spy lost consciousness.

He lowered her gently to the ground and kissed her.

“I’m sorry, Abrielle. You’re just going to have to trust me.”

He tried to wring out the extra liquid from the bandana with the chemical and wrapped a clean one around it before tying both to cover her mouth. Never having used the solution before, he hoped it did not endanger her. The apothecary in Salzburg had warned him that prolonged exposure could prove fatal. Espen made sure that she was able to get clean air through her nose, then moved her to a concealed area in the back of the tent, bound her hands and feet, and then looked one last time upon Abrielle serene face.

“I hope you understand someday, but I don’t have a choice. I have to save them all,” he muttered to himself before covering her, wondering if they’d ever see each other again in this life.

**

Tasaria wept. She mourned the loss of her daughter. She grieved for the suffering she’d caused her family and countless others, for shame, guilt, her mother’s murder. For all this, she wept and still more.

She was the epitome of anguish for all of this was her fault. At long last she could not deny it. There was no one else left to blame. She’d done everything right, only to learn now how misguided she’d been, all of it for hatred.

Now the emptiness of Vochallet’s former chamber consumed her.

“You were right, you were right. I am a traitor! To all I have ever known, a traitor!” She howled, for Vochallet’s children would have no mother now to raise them; she’d been taken from them as unjustly as Jucika had been taken from Tasaria and Nicabar.

Enraged she pounded the bed, striking out at whatever nearby objects her anger could abuse. Tasaria’s heart pounded as she tore the room apart. A looming shadow cast upon the wall arrested both her rampage and the beating in her chest. Her senses recalled, she fearfully turned to confront her dark Master, only to find the Old One she controlled standing by the room's sole source of light.

She staggered to the ground and began to laugh, first in relief, then in bitterness.

"I made you. I murdered you. Just as sure as he did," she explained. "I did it for her. The war, I did it for her, for what her cousin did. But she didn't. She didn't, not that one, not …"

The image that would now haunt Tasaria until the end of her days, the one she'd forced from Baseria while they'd held the decorative box, returned to her mind, played out silently behind her eyes. She knew it to be true.

This was not a wish, not some twisted memory. She watched helplessly as Baseria confronted the others. Patia Nalie savagely-struck, intent on murdering her sister by casting her over the side of the cliff. Horrified and confused, Jucika had intervened. The soil near the edge was loose; Patia reckless, incensed beyond all reason. Both Baseria and Patia reached for their cousin at the same time: one to save her and one for balance. Tasaria witnessed the final seconds, their look of mutual surprise an instant before the terror, the screams forever locked in Baseria's mind as they vanished from sight.

So potent was the pain of reliving the memory of that moment, it stole Tasaria' breath from her body. She coughed violently as her lungs fought for air.

"So much death," she muttered numbly. "I've caused so much death. There was a purpose I understood. Once, once …"

The word touched her lips as barely a whisper. Her eyes were drawn to light reflected off a piece of broken glass on the floor. Tasaria hovered in existence. It would take only a few minutes to free herself from this pain. The long shadow of the silent Old One still fell across the floor. Her eyes danced between the shattered glass and the shadow. Each breath measured the realities before her. She covered her face with her hands.

"Forgive me."

*

The Moon Shadow guard knelt.

"Yours to command," he pronounced.

The Master, somewhat impatiently, bid him to rise.

"Why were you not at your assigned post when I sent for you, Ghul?"

The man's initial response was nothing but a puzzled look.

"Well?" the grim shadow demanded.

Reflexively the gypsy bent his knee again.

"Apologies, my Master. Tasaria relieved me of my escorting duties several hours ago. I have been with my family ever since that time. I have seen little of them these past few days."

A sharp knock was heard before a gypsy servant opened the door to admit another man for an audience.

"Yes, Captain Ayt?"

The man bowed.

"My Master, if the weather permits, I believe both vessels will be fully loaded and ready to sail with the morning tide."

Again a crisp knock on the dining chamber's door announced the arrival of still another. This time it was Tasaria arriving to his summons.

"Very good, Captain. I believe several teams of the Old Ones have been rather isolated on the ships and the docks these past weeks, yes?"

"I've worked closely with several of them for a prolonged time during the retrofitting, yes," the man admitted.

"Fortunate. I want three of them on each ship, Ayt."

For several seconds, the captain clearly considered offering a protest to this idea.

"You have reservations?" the creature asked.

"If what I've heard is true, then yes," Ayt honestly replied.

Undoubtedly, he was aware that several of the Old Ones in the fortress had engaged in unprovoked attacks. Aside from destroying them outright, the creature was still attempting to reason the most effective means to nullify any threat they might pose. The sabotage would, unquestionably, slow his progress.

The Master did his best to placate his subordinate.

"There are risks to this mission, but I assure you, Captain, that your Old Ones will, as they have in the past, prove invaluable to our efforts. Ghul, you will be in command of the fortress while we are away. Tasaria,

I understand you have moved your niece to the chapel."

"Yes, Master. She is not well and needed observation."

"Leave us," he commanded the others, "Ghul, I will summon you shortly to make final preparations."

The men bowed in unison then departed.

"Speak, Tasaria, what is wrong with the girl?"

Tasaria lost herself in the penetrating, yellow eyes.

"Tasaria," he repeated.

Her words fell out in a rushed jumble.

"What you have asked is most difficult, and I have pushed her to exhaustion. We have made great progress, but she will need time to rest."

"She may have it aboard ship then," the creature declared.

"No. Frankenstein could …"

"Frankenstein will remain here and your niece with us," the other stated forcibly.

Tasaria looked away a moment before continuing. What motivated his anger with her on this issue? It seemed to be more than simple annoyance over one of his directives being questioned. There was a momentary flash of deep emotion in his eyes. Was it jealousy? Tasaria shifted her concern.

"Have your received any word from my husband?"

The creature seemed more at ease with the subject.

"We are entering the season," he said smoothly. "Storms to the south are likely delaying our supply ship. I'm sure we will have word of him by the time we return, if not before."

She nodded.

"Is that all Master?"

He inclined his head slightly.

"Thank you for your efforts. Try to get some sleep yourself before we depart, Tasaria. The seas are bound to be rough."

She smiled awkwardly as she began for the chamber's large doors.

"Have Ghul sent back in," the dark shadow bid her.

"Yes, Master."

"We sail at dawn," he called out as she vanished through the doors.

With a moment's peace, the creature tried to gather his thoughts. There were any number of factors that might determine the answer, but it was difficult to dismiss Tasaria's question regarding Nicabar for the creature too had expected some type of report by now. Could he be in trouble? Had he secured Frankenstein's child?

As soon as these tests were completed, he resolved to discover the answer. He briefly reflected on how much he owed both Nicabar and Tasaria. Without their faith, courage, and sacrifices, both he and his aspirations would be nothing. He could not help but note that the separation from her husband seemed to be weighing more heavily on Tasaria each day. Or was it what she'd finally seen down in his lab that was upsetting her?

As his own thoughts returned to the occupants of the chapel, a volatile mixture of emotions welled within him as he considered each of them. Suddenly, there was a loud knock at the door, undoubtedly Ghul returning. The creature attempted to focus. There was still much to be done before he left, but he knew that as soon as time permitted, he would return to his perch above the chapel to spy on those within. His heart allowed him no alternative.

**

"What in the name of blazes does that crackbrained gypsy think he's doing?" Jack muttered to himself.

He had a bad feeling, and Jack hated those, almost as much as the ill-fitting gypsy garb he now wore. True, Abrielle could have altered their hastily-outlined plan, but there were too many inconsistencies. Espen was completely ignoring the map as to his rendezvous point with Jack. It was only happenstance that Jack was a little late slipping into position, which allowed him to spy Espen vacating the Wild Rose clan camp and heading very much in the wrong direction. If he knew where Jack was, why travel away from him?

Maybe there was something he saw, which Jack couldn't view from his vantage, that would have endangered them both. But Espen did not seem to be moving as a man trying to avoid detection. As he struggled to catch up and remain hidden, Jack reviewed the plan as it was supposed to work.

He meets me. We finalize plans. We sneak up on the camp more or less together. He gets caught. I set off the distraction. If I get caught (God forbid), I play the mute, he escapes with the girl, and I get back across the gorge and wait for Abrielle. Simple, easy, why isn't that happening?

Jack lunged to the ground as a random patrol of Wild Rose clan fighters passed nearby. Fortunately he heard only one dog with the men, and the wind was in Jack's favor, carrying his scent away from the mongrel. Despite this, he cautiously elected to remain still for several minutes.

When he finally felt it was safe to continue, it took him an uncomfortably long period of time to locate Espen. He was steadily progressing towards the Moon Shadows' frontier.

Wolves, you idiot, you're gonna walk right into them, Jack thought.

He made a half-hearted, brief attempt to howl like a wolf before he realized the extreme danger such an act placed him in. Espen's pace might have slowed a measure, but only for an instant.

Damn, gypsy is trying to get himself killed. And me!

He should turn back. The voice in Jack's head repeated the thought. The last thing he should want was to encounter the roving packs of trained killers the Moon Shadows held at their disposal. Maybe if he traveled further uphill, he could stay out of their patrol range.

Jack began to put more distance between himself and Espen. For a time, Jack was forced to divide his time between trying to track Espen and minding the difficult terrain. Then he lost sight of him completely.

Uncertain if he should proceed, Jack crouched down and waited. When he finally reappeared, Espen was bound and escorted by a host of Moon Shadows and wolves. He'd voluntarily given himself up, apparently with no plan to escape. Jack sat back as Espen again vanished from view.

"Shit."

*

Each tiny movement brought her one step closer to losing consciousness again, but it was the only way to end this nausea-inducing torment. Abrielle's fingers fumbled drunkenly with the bonds that held her. Concentrating on the ropes was about the only thing keeping her mentally together. She was intolerably dizzy and drenched in sweat from the effort. Twisting her head she managed to loosen the bandana.

Abrielle voraciously gulped in the welcome relief of fresh air down into her burning throat. The suffocating blanket was now off as well. For a moment, Abrielle focused on nothing but breathing. The key was always in the breathing.

After a time, her senses began to return, and she renewed her struggle to free herself. She'd discovered Espen's vial of chloroform even before leaving Salzburg. Though she'd attempted to mitigate its potency by diluting the vial's contents, it still worked more effectively than she'd anticipated.

The knot she was fighting finally slipped. Her feet, now somewhat free from the bonds that still held her hands, she crawled to her bedroll and retrieved a knife she'd hidden. The blade severed the remaining lines in short order. Abrielle greedily consumed the contents of every water bladder she could find inside the tent. She couldn't help but think that if she'd been trying to incapacitate Espen, she wouldn't have forgotten to drug the contents of at least one of the bladders for insurance. As it was, though, she felt nothing but relief and gratitude that he hadn't; she even splashed some of the cool water on her face to aide her revival.

As she wiped it away from her eyes, they caught sight of the scar on her right hand, the symbol of her promise. Her fingers offered it the briefest touch before she sent all of them coursing through the brown hair atop her head as she closed her eyes and drew in a long, slow steady breath. Her fingers traced down the back of her neck and joined back together steepled before her lips and remained in this repose for a host of silent minutes until at last she spoke.

"Be with us, Ailis."

With this simple supplication, Abrielle stood and removed her clothes, which by now were damp and reeked of chloroform and sweat. She dressed modestly and retrieved several of the knives and the pistol she'd secretly procured and hidden. She placed several items, food, a small pillow, a pouch of tobacco to offer Jal, and Tara's blanket inside a basket large enough to conceal her niece in if need be. She wrapped a cloak about her shoulders, but left the hood down.

Abrielle allowed herself one final gaze around the tent before turning to face the entry. Jal's tent, her infant niece, and her destiny lay three hundred and eighty seven paces away. She began to silently count each of her steps as she'd been taught to do in another life. This time, however, long before she reached her destination, it was not numbers she was hearing, only the deafening thunder of her heart.

**

How could any of them ever have loved her if this is what she truly was? The question invaded the silence of Baseria's numb mind. For most of her life, Baseria had been treated with scorn and contempt for an act she could not confirm or deny she'd committed, much less understand it. Despite this, some people always found the courage to love her: Nasi, her mother, Espen, Etolie, even her father, in his own way.

Her eyes again sought the small, decorative wooden box on the chamber's floor. Was she a killer? Unable to face the truth her aunt sought within her, she'd retreated from their bond in shame and guilt. In doing so, she'd betrayed the love and faith those in her life had shown her. Baseria pushed hair away from her bloodshot eyes and took a deep, shuddering breath. This was her life. It was senseless to attempt to shield herself from the truth any longer when her aunt knew what Baseria's heart and mind were too wounded to remember.

She fell to her knees before the box. Her fingers trembled. Did she seek salvation or damnation? It didn't matter anymore. Baseria had to know or her life would remain incomplete. With both hands she clasped the box which also instantaneously seized her.

There were no words, in any language in existence, to describe the experience, sensation and knowledge without end—a gaining of control and awareness over senses beyond the physical, ones long suspected, but too vague and chaotic to understand. For the first time Baseria touched the full, vast extent of the Elemental powers without fear, encountering types and levels she could never have fathomed. The infinite mysteries of the unseen world were unfolding before her, unifying through thought, time, and space. She knew all the ancient knowledge of the Seer. It was a part of her, as it was all of existence.

*

Ernest prayed before the chapel's altar. There was precious little else he could do. It was simply too late for him to save any of them. For too long he'd given himself to the creature's promise that he could be reunited with Ailis and Tara. He stood, his hands outstretched against the rough stone, his head bowed. Quietly, Baseria rose from the benches behind him. She retrieved the wooden box he'd left there and walked serenely towards him. Lost in the knowledge of their fates, he did not perceive her presence until she was beside him.

They looked to one another as he straightened his stance. Tears were forming in his eyes as he beheld her. There was so much he wanted to say to her, so much he wished he could explain, but in the end, he could not find the words. They both knew they were already dead. Was this how Ailis had felt? Why she'd concealed the true severity of her illness from him?

Baseria looked away for a moment, and then she drew closer to him, her purpose never more clear. She took his hand and placed it with hers atop the wooden box.

"What are you doing?"

"Be quiet," she said softly as she opened herself freely to all the knowledge and power within her. If her life was to have any meaning, then perhaps, this moment was it.

Ernest could feel something passing between them, similar to the healing bond they shared, but much more powerful and intense. Baseria heard it clearly now, a voice, a familiar energy she'd encountered before, longing to speak, begging her to hear. No, begging for Ernest to listen. Baseria answered the summons.

The confines of the chapel slowly vanished as everything around them blended into a brilliant light. Ernest closed his eyes, unable to discern anything, only opening them again when the dazzling light faded somewhat. The reality that greeted him negated his senses completely. Justine Moritz stood before him.

Words and thought were lost to Ernest Frankenstein. For an eternity, all he could do was stare at her in awestruck wonder. His mind attempted to rationalize what he was seeing, to explain the warm hands he was holding, to realize that he was not dreaming. She was not a phantom, she was real. His friend was as real as she'd been all those countless years ago.

"Hello, my love," she whispered as she enfolded herself to him.

A host of emotions coursed through him simultaneously, and he wept, holding her longingly. Ernest had no concept how long they remained embracing one another.

"Justine, dear God, Justine, I'm sorry, I'm so sorry," he said when he was finally able to again summon words.

Justine smiled. Whatever evils had passed between them no longer mattered, only the love and gratitude each felt for the other. That survived, and because of it, so did forgiveness. His heart grew in opulence. He felt light, comforted. Her pain at their parting in life diminished. He knew, at long last, he knew. Now her journey could begin.

Their lips met. Ernest held her more tightly as the overpowering light shone once more. When it again grew tolerable, he opened his eyes and discovered Baseria in his arms, kissing him back passionately.

"Baseria," he whispered as her senses slowly returned. She felt extremely drained, but knew strength as she never had.

Neither spoke as they gazed into each others eyes, adrift in the bond that connected them.

It was still very bright in the chapel, too bright, in fact. They became aware of a dull sound, like thunder, and then they turned their heads towards the chapel's altar. The entire wall beyond it was now missing or in ruin before them as brilliant sunlight poured through a gaping wound in the fortress. The sound repeated more raucously. The floor violently shook beneath them.

"What is it?" Baseria asked in trepidation.

"Somebody found us. The fortress is under attack," Ernest said.

**

CHAPTER 28
CHAOTIC MANDALA

Jack carefully extinguished the flame from existence nearly as fast as the match strike gave it birth. In the gloom, the brief light afforded him the only means to check his watch, and he couldn't risk drawing the Moon Shadows' attention.

"Dammit," he grumbled to himself.

His time was running out. Espen had all but doomed himself by not coordinating anything with Jack before being captured. Jack now had no idea when to initiate a distraction so Espen could escape. If he attempted to get much closer, he risked detection, imprisonment, or worse. Several times he heard or saw the prowling shadows of wolves and their gypsy handlers below. Worse he needed to be in place to aid Abrielle's escape attempt, which was set to begin in less than ten minutes, and he was quite some distance from their escape route.

His fingers clutched the bags of gunpowder he'd brought. The simplest and most sensible thing to do was to abandon Espen to his fate. If Jack acted now, he could endanger all of them, including Tara. Still the thought of just leaving Espen behind bothered Jack. He'd never trusted Espen fully, but leaving someone to most likely be tortured and killed was shamefully inhuman.

Jack shook his head. No, he was being melodramatic. Espen could be acting on orders from his father as part of the truce Abrielle claimed existed between the clans at present. Perhaps that was why he'd given himself up to them so easily, so he could finish bartering Tara away in private. Why else would he simply walk into the enemy's hands? Inwardly, he sighed. There were a lot of possibilities, but Jack didn't have any of the answers.

A noise from below froze his thoughts. Nothing happened, but he was certain he'd heard something. Jack gingerly leaned forward and saw a distinct set of yellow eyes below, then another, then another. The Moon Shadow wolves had found him.

His mind raced. For the moment he was relatively safe. They could not climb directly up to him, but given time, they could circle around and reach him. That fact would matter less though when the wolves' heavily armed masters came to see what attracted their guardians' attention. The wolves would be eager to stalk him as soon as he fled to reach his position to aid Abrielle. He certainly couldn't go to help her with a pack of wolves on his heels.

So we live or die playing a poker hand, eh?

This particular hand was rigged and his cards were terrible, but Jack never walked away from a game. At heart he was a gambler. Of course, any betting man worth his salt always held a few tricks in reserve for special situations.

Jack reached into his pocket and withdrew the bags of gunpowder and some fuses he'd fashioned, after losing those he'd brought with him, from lengths of tree bark. After weeks of slinking around waiting for the true game to begin, it was time to show his hand, grab his winnings, while hopefully making a memorable exit.

The bluff, he smiled to himself before leaning over the cliff and yelling to the wolves, "Come up here and get me, ya uglified bark bags."

The wolves snarled and yelped. If the upheaval didn't catch the Moon Shadows' attention, nothing would. Jack continued taunting the animals as he packed the bags of gun powder just below the lip of the outcropping. It took him several moments to decide that lacing the fuse through a hole on the top would be safer than running it over the edge.

His bet placed, Jack sat down. Now all he need do was wait for them to call. He reached into his coat pocket and retrieved the lone cigar he'd brought with him. Jack ran it beneath his nose inhaling deeply and sighing in satisfaction. He lit it and held the smoke in, savoring the moment.

"This fresh air has been killin' me," he said to the cigar as he studied the terrain, deciding where he would take shelter.

He heard the voices of men approaching below, shouting to each other over the commotion the wolves were causing. He waited a moment before exhaling a deep breath.

"Okay, steady Jack, remember, you're crazy," he muttered to himself before standing just long enough to see how many men were below and allowing them a chance to see him. He barely got back down before shots began to sail over his head.

Jack touched the tip of the lit cigar to the bark strip fuses, then ran for cover. The fuses hissed as they burned. Over the clamor of the wolves, he could hear the sounds of men as they climbed the rock face. He waited as the endless seconds passed, but nothing happened. Jack peered around the rock he was using for cover. The fuses must have burned out without igniting the gunpowder bags. He heard voices just below the edge of the outcropping.

There was one chance. As he always did, Jack threw his lit cigar away, aiming for the gap in the rocks where the inert gunpowder sat. Hot sparks shot from the tip as it bounced across the unforgiving ground and rolled into the hole. Nothing happened. Jack grabbed his pistol and checked his knife. He'd lost his last bet, and now the wolves and the Moon Shadows would collect on his final debt.

Sorry, Ern. Think I blew it this time.

A hand reached over the edge. Jack crouched and took aim. Should he try to flee or make his stand here?

Unexpectedly, the earth violently heaved. Jack fell and was quickly coated by dust and an array of flying debris. The ringing in his ears was deafening, but nothing compared to the thunderous sound of the rock face as sections of it crumbled and rolled down the mountain. In disbelief, he staggered to his feet, ignoring for the moment the blood running into his left eye. Jack allowed himself only enough time to ascertain that no one would be immediately following him. Choking on dust, he lurched away into the gathering gloom.

*

Nicabar passed his hand over his bald head.

"We should attack them now while we have the chance. It must be a trick," Pell advised.

"Dammit, Pell. Give me a minute to think!"

Both his tone and gaze held enough steel to silence Pell momentarily. His nephew's unexpected appearance was indeed most unwelcome. All Espen would volunteer was that he'd turned himself over of his own accord and not at the behest of his father who was purportedly ignorant of his son's actions. Nicabar was inclined to agree with his underling's basic assessment, but what was the goal of such a trick? Was it a simple diversion to buy Jal time? Was an attack imminent? Did the Wild Rose clan intend to flee? Could Espen be trying to ensure a fight broke out?

Why else should he take such an absurd action so close to the end of the negotiated truce?

"We must know what we're dealing with."

"I'll pry the truth from him," Pell vowed.

"There's no time, I've got to go meet Jal, and we can't afford to torture Espen. We're too deep in enemy territory for such risks," Nicabar decided.

Pell frowned.

"The girl then," Nicabar said reluctantly.

"What?"

"We torture her while he is forced to watch. How much she suffers will be up to him." Even as he spoke the words, Nicabar was inwardly revolted by them. But there was too much at stake and not enough time. This situation was Espen's fault, not his. Perhaps if he could be made to see reason, no action would need to be taken against their prisoner.

"Bring them," Nicabar ordered.

Just as Pell turned to leave, the ground beneath their feet trembled. The men stared at each other in momentary confusion before a tremendous clap of sound roared all around them.

"Get the men to their horses," Nicabar yelled after it passed.

Pell ran off to issue orders. As he did, the ground began to shake again as a low rumble began to build in volume.

"Landslide!"

It was impossible to see very far in the gathering dusk. Without thought, Nicabar scrambled behind a tree for cover. A host of rocks, from pebbles to boulders, tumbled across portions of the Moon Shadow encampment, blasting into tents and trees, injuring both people and animals alike. One of the larger rocks shot past the tree Nicabar was using for cover, gouging the timber and dealing an intense, glancing blow to the gypsy's forearm.

The stone deluge was brief but destructive. Everyone was hesitant to move very far from their places of cover. Toppled trees, rocks, crushed tents, and the wounded lay strewn about the ground. Nicabar cradled his wounded arm as he surveyed the damage and studied the wooded slope waiting for either more boulders or an attack from his enemies.

"It's too bad, really, that the boulder didn't crush you, Nicabar," a familiar voice said from behind him. "Now I will have to deal with you."

Nicabar turned and beheld a man, but not the man he'd expected. Both the rider and the mount were black, imposing, confident, and barely discernible in the twilight. The rider wore fine boots and a type of armor made of both black metal and leather. And then there was the face, at once familiar, but totally different.

"Pias?" The Moon Shadow leader asked in disbelief.

Not even the man's voice was the same when he replied, "No. You will address me by my proper honorific, Boier Amăgitor."

"Boier Amăgitor, the Lord Deceiver?" Nicabar stammered in fear and disbelief. "But you're dead."

"Yes," the man agreed quietly. The blade sliced into Nicabar so fast he was only aware of it as it was being withdrawn from his body. "And as you have been useful to me, I grant you a quick death."

Nicabar fell to the earth and did not move.

Pias slowly turned his horse back so he could face the silent troops he'd brought with him.

"Obliterate both camps and their clans. Bring me Pell alive. Începe[24]," he commanded raising his sword. His men and wolves began to fan out to encircle the camps. Once they were in place, no one would live. Pias twisted his ring impatiently.

**

"Don't shoot!" Tasaria pleaded to Ghul as she and the Old One rounded a corner.

He hesitated a moment before lowering his weapon.

"Is anyone else with you?"

She shook her head breathlessly.

"No. All we've seen are bodies. What's happening?"

"A navy has discovered us. They'll probably land troops. Get to the ships," he ordered as he raised his gun toward the Old One.

Tasaria grabbed the barrel and forced it away.

"Don't," she said emphatically, a threatening tone in her voice.

It made little difference to Ghul if she died from the attack or from the Old One. Actually, unleashing the Old Ones on the invaders might

---

24 *Romanian.* Begin.

slow their incursion. There was certainly no need to protect them. He grinned mockingly and allowed Tasaria and her despicable companion to pass as rock and dust shook loose from above them.

The sunlit courtyard was chaos as Moon Shadow families and fighters dodged fallen debris and the exploding shells now sailing over the fortress walls. Tasaria tried not to look as she ran past the injured. There was no time, she told herself, over and over, no time. She had but one duty, one destination in mind—the chapel. She must reach Baseria. Tasaria slipped and fell near a dying woman.

"Help me, help me," the woman pleaded as she awkwardly tried to hold the wound in her chest closed.

Horror-stricken, Tasaria could not move. The Old One grabbed her and hauled her back to her feet. Numbly the Moon Shadow priestess kept running.

The end of the murderous gauntlet was in sight. She entered the turret that led down to the chapel, but suddenly her momentum was arrested. Tasaria felt her weight shifting backward, propelling her uncontrollably back into the courtyard. She hit the frozen ground hard, snow billowed up around her. Stunned, it took her a moment to recover. She blinked in disbelief.

The turret lay in ruin, collapsed in on itself. Baseria and Frankenstein were now buried under tons of rock. Tasaria stood and engaged in the futile act of shifting some of the rocks, attempting to discover some means to still reach them. Instead she found only the broken body of the Old One, her protector until the very end. Why had it risked its life to save hers?

Tasaria turned her head and peered back into the courtyard. The woman lay where she had abandoned her, clearly dead. Tasaria hung her head in remorse. All the pain and loss she'd inflicted on others had been for nothing, and the destiny she'd sought to lead them to lay in perverse ruin. Eventually someone came and guided her to the ship.

*

Ernest barely possessed the presence of mind to tuck the wooden box into his coat pocket, next to Ailis' journal, as they fled towards the wall closest to the cliff face.

"Look out," Ernest shouted as he pressed both Baseria and himself against the wall.

Huge sections of the ceiling soared downward, breaking apart large sections of the floor. The chapel was disintegrating, tumbling into the sea. Baseria screamed as the heavy door, under great stress, collapsed inward. Billowing clouds of dust erupted into the remains of the chapel. Ernest tried to blink the particles away.

"I think the turret's been destroyed."

He grabbed Baseria's hand and pulled her toward the entryway. They clambered through a hole in the debris and discovered their Moon Shadow guards, dead. Ernest knelt and retrieved a sword for himself and handed her a pistol.

"Where do we go?" Baseria asked breathlessly.

With the turret obliterated, Ernest could only conceive of one means of escape.

"Come on."

"Where are we going?"

"Down," he said without hesitation.

**

A beautiful silence filled Abrielle's head as she walked. Her right hand never left the hilt of the knife she bore under the blanket in the basket she carried. She paused beside a tree as a horse laden with a family's belongings passed. Without realizing it, her eyes were drawn to the brood following it. But even as she fixed her attention to the passing strangers, she did not really see them. Abrielle's mind overlay a false, parallel vision atop that which she was actually witnessing.

Ailis smiled to Ernest as he motioned for their children to keep up, but one of the daughters did not move away from Abrielle nor did she speak. Her stance was expectant. Who was the little girl waiting for?

The unspoken question reciprocated another, one she kept attempting to escape. Abrielle's hand released the knife handle and moved to her mid-section seeking any sign of a life there.

"Come here this instant."

At these words, reality fully reasserted itself. Abrielle started and looked down to see an amused young girl being taken by her stern-faced mother. Abrielle noticed that the woman's look of reproach did not appear to be meant exclusively for her child as she glanced over her shoulder once before they departed.

"How many times do I have to tell you not to stare?"

But the damage was done, her fears reawakened. Abrielle knew some of the symptoms of pregnancy but not all. Some of what she'd been experiencing these past weeks—changes in her cycle, nausea, fatigue, and headaches—might just as well be the result of stress. Still what if her lie to Espen was an unintentional truth?

She returned her hand to the concealed knife's hilt and began forward again. No. This was no time for such considerations. Or perhaps it was because of her intentions that the notion was taking on a new dynamic now. Though a persistent concern, with so many other immediate problems, she'd kept this one buried, but what if it was true and she and Espen had created a life, one now growing within her. Would she one day have to explain what had become of the child's father, his family? What would she say? If she rescued Tara, would she be forced to raise the progeny of the one responsible for kidnapping her?

Abrielle gripped the knife more firmly. She'd arrived at Jal's tent. It appeared to be unguarded. For an instant, her fears overwhelmed her. What if Tara was not there? What if Jal or Espen had already taken her to the Moon Shadows?

No, this type of thinking could only work against her. She needed facts not supposition. Deciding it was safe to do so, she consulted the watch she'd packed. The chloroform had slowed her. She would be late in meeting Jack, and according to Espen's timetable, Jal's meeting with the Moon Shadow leader was due to start shortly. Undoubtedly, if he was still inside and did not make an appearance soon, someone would come to check on him. She'd prepared for that.

Kneeling before the entrance, she bent down as if checking the contents of her basket. The cloak concealed both her checking that her pistol was loaded and muffled the sound as she locked the hammer back into firing position. She stuck the weapon in the pocket of her dress, took a deep breath, stood, and bowed her head slightly as she entered the tent.

The light inside was dim, the occupants all but silent. She entered by way of the tent's rear entrance. For a moment Abrielle did not move as she surveyed the situation. No one stirred.

Treading lightly, she first checked the woman who seemed to be serving as Tara's perfunctory nanny. She was asleep in a chair near Tara's bed, an empty bowl overturned by her feet. Abrielle grinned to herself. Much as she would have loved to have poisoned the woman and Jal, she could not afford to have their bodies be discovered before she fled. Jal's sudden illness provided her with the perfect cover. Several hours earlier, in the guise of a concerned daughter-in-law, she'd delivered them some of her soup for dinner, drugged, of course. Their lethargy would simply be blamed on the illness.

Jal lay resting near the fire in the main part of the tent. He too remained quiescent. A bowl lay beside his bed as well, but it remained upright. He was much larger than the nanny, the drug might not be affecting his body in the same way. It appeared he'd dozed off rather than passed out.

If she wanted to, Abrielle could escape without violence. Quietly, carefully, she stepped back toward Tara's humble nursery. Her niece was asleep on her stomach, tranquil, oblivious to the dangers surrounding them. Abrielle reached out and gingerly touched the infant. Tara made the faintest of sounds before descending back into slumber. This was one part of her plan Abrielle could not control. When she attempted to move Tara to the basket, would she awaken and her cries betray them both? She didn't dare attempt to use any of the sleeping drug she'd concocted. It could kill her fragile niece. There was only one way to eliminate that threat.

The bloodlust in her heart rose as Abrielle drew her knife and stalked towards Jal. The light cast by the cooking fire danced across her weapon's blade. As she looked down upon him, all of the rage and hatred she'd been suppressing welled-up.

This man deserved to die. She could not allow him to live. If she did, she would always live in fear that one day he would return and destroy them. He must not live. His cries must be muted. She poised the knife over his throat. Abrielle's entire body was shaking as the echoing seconds marched by, her blade remained poised to strike, but internal contractions arrested her actions as she stared down at Espen's vulnerable father.

Suddenly there were screams outside the tent, followed by shouts. Alarmed Abrielle turned momentarily to see if the nanny had reacted or if the perceived danger outside was about to descend upon her.

"Orfilia?"

Abrielle's heart seized as she looked down into Jal's open eyes, ones still dull with sleep but able to discern the hatred and confusion burning in hers. As she heaved back to strike him with the blade she wielded, Jal's groggy mind recognized the danger and he began to move. The motion was antithetical to her aim, but she still managed to plunge the entire blade deeply through a portion of his chest just below his collar bone.

Their cries of pain became one.

She viciously twisted the knife, but before she could withdraw it for the deathblow, Jal's left fist struck her so hard that Abrielle was knocked off her feet. The knife remained buried in his right shoulder. The impact of the blow rang in her ears and stole the air from her lungs. She tasted blood; heard Tara crying. Tara!

As Jal fought to pry the blade from his flesh, Abrielle reached for the smaller blade she carried. She slashed at a mass of nearby ropes, collapsing Jal's part of the tent. By now Tara's gypsy nanny was awake from her stupor though clearly not fully cognizant. Abrielle rolled and stabbed the woman's foot before striking her windpipe. She fell, gasping for air. Abandoning any hope for subtlety, Abrielle grabbed Ailis' blanket, hastily wrapped her distraught niece in it, and bolted from the collapsed tent.

Outside, she abandoned one nightmarish scenario for another as she was immediately almost run down by a horse and rider. All around her pandemonium reigned. Everything was in motion. Fires burned, people fled or charged to defenses as the sounds of pitched battle coursed through the darkness. The encampment was clearly under a large scale assault, one the people of the Wild Rose clan were banding together to repel. Abrielle could not manage to untie the knot of her cloak one handed, but she could retrieve the pistol from her pocket

The encampment overrun, danger came from all sides. Moon Shadow wolves fought the dogs of the Wild Rose clan. Horsemen, some in black uniforms, flew out of the night slashing and hacking at those on the ground as well as engaging the Rose clan mounted fighters. Some of these riders were immobilized by ropes of thorns the gypsies strung across their paths. Others were suddenly consumed in flame as the clan used some type of explosive weapon that burned on impact. Several times as she ran, enemy fighters or wolves pursued her, but each time, a member of the Wild Rose clan engaged them. Abrielle did not pause to witness the outcomes of these small battles. She ducked, hid briefly behind trees, sought cover near burning tents, but she kept moving, the cries of her niece urging her onward. Holding Tara, Abrielle was nearly defenseless. The pistol she held had but one shot. They had to get away. Abrielle must get them to safety even if she died trying.

**

Their flight was one of mad desperation as they descended deeper into hell. Though partially sunk from some earlier cataclysm, this part of the fortress was still experiencing structural stress as naval guns continued to relentlessly pound the Moon Shadow stronghold. The attackers seemed intent on eradicating all of it. All Ernest and Baseria wanted to do was survive its welcome downfall.

As they fled through the fragmented tunnel beneath the sea, sections of the ceiling buckled, releasing heavy stones or torrents of icy spray. He was forced to abandon his purloined sword. They kept losing their footing on the slick rock piles or had parts of the icy-choked floor begin to break up beneath them. The few places where the tunnel did rise above the water offered no escape. Though they could see sunlight, the sunken turret windows were too high and narrow. There was no choice but to continue deeper into the murderous maze.

Baseria halted as they reached the beginning of the catacombs where a lone torch still burned. She hated narrow spaces.

"We've got to keep going," Ernest urged.

"Where does this come out?" Baseria frantically asked.

There was a loud host of cracking as the ice around them began to bow and shatter. Water began rising around their feet.

"Run!" Ernest commanded.

They covered the remainder of the tunnel and slid down the shaft into the lab. Baseria clung to Ernest as they fell into the frozen mass of corpses, horrified. Water followed them down the shaft. Ernest drug her to her feet knowing they would permanently join the macabre surroundings if they stopped.

"Don't think, just move," he told her, and they began to clamber over the dead as fast as they possibly could.

When they were free of the grim obstructions, Ernest paused. If only he knew where the hidden tunnels the Old Ones used were. They might lead them back above the sea. There was the main tunnel back to the fortress that the guards had brought him and Tasaria through recently. But it didn't seem very promising. It only ran back to the main fortress, which was full of enemies and possibly invading forces. Still they couldn't stay here, it could collapse or flood any moment.

"Come on," said Baseria pulling Ernest.

"Where?"

"I think there's a light coming from that low tunnel, maybe we can get out through there," she breathlessly asserted.

He ran several more paces before drawing them to a halt. The tunnel led to Victor. What would he do if they went in there, try to save what remained of his brother or kill him? The chamber wasn't terribly high, but he didn't recall it having a window.

"We have to get out," Baseria insisted as she knelt down.

"I know," Ernest said. "But we have to be certain …"

"I can see sunlight!"

"What?" Ernest asked in surprise.

"Sunlight!" Baseria repeated.

Ernest got down on his knees and peered down the foreboding passage. She was right. The brilliant light, which flooded the chamber on the far side of the tunnel, could not be the product of torches. They could escape.

She spontaneously hugged him and smiled.

"Ernest, we can get out, we can get out," Baseria cried in elation.

"Yes," Ernest said evenly. "Baseria, there's something I have to tell you."

A huge chunk of the lab's ceiling moaned moments before it began to give way. There was no time to think. They ran the remaining length of the lab, dropped to their hands and knees, and began to crawl toward the shining light. The impact from the falling debris collapsed a portion of the tunnel behind them. It didn't matter. They would be out in a matter of seconds.

"Stop," Ernest cried as they reached the chamber.

The roof here had also collapsed, smashing through the ice, while the rest of the chamber, including the low wall at the base, remained intact.

The frozen ramp now spilled directly down into the Arctic Ocean.

"Vile wretch!"

It was difficult to say if the blow to the back of Ernest's head or the impact of his chest hitting the ice beneath him stunned him more. He dimly heard Baseria shriek.

"Go, Baseria," Ernest bid, desperate that she escape.

He was struck again. Ernest fought to remain conscious as he was pulled from the tunnel and gripped firmly by the leg. He felt his body being set against the wall as his boot was thrown off and an iron bond locked around his leg. His head was drawn violently back forcing him to look directly into the creature's putrid yellow eyes.

"You think I am blind. I offer you family, understanding, compassion, the miracle of your wife's resurrection, even your child's life, and still you will deny me my dream, my happiness just as Father did."

Ernest was having trouble concentrating through the pounding in his head.

"I don't understand ..."

He began before strong fingers choked off his words.

"I saw you, with her! And you," the creature said turning his attention to Baseria who clung frightfully to the wall on the other side of the tunnel's entry, "you find me nothing more than an odious thing, but I am more, much more."

Ernest's head wasn't clearing. A sound beyond the demon attracted his attention. The fragmented remains of Victor Frankenstein were now linked to his brother by the chain they shared; the one attached to Ernest's leg and his brother's mutilated, partially severed arm. The siblings looked toward one another as Victor's son gazed one last time upon his father's reanimated body before kicking the chain into the sea.

"Goodbye Father, now you can be at peace."

The weight of the chain was too much of a counterbalance for Victor's abused form to overcome. He slipped into the water. The chain pulled relentlessly on Ernest now.

"Since you have no love for the living, Uncle, I consign you to the depths of the dead."

Positioned as he was near the top of the ramp, there was nothing to hold onto but ice. Ernest followed his brother into the depths. The creature turned to Baseria only to find her aiming a pistol at him. He lunged at her, but not before she fired. The ball tore into his flesh. As she tried to escape, he grabbed her. Their weight off balance, they too plunged into the mercilessly frigid water below.

*

As she opened her eyes, Baseria could faintly make out Ernest as he grew more and more distant in the watery depths. They were caught in a current, and with Victor's dead weight, both he and his brother were sinking fast.

The freezing water seized her muscles as the pain of it simultaneously shocked and tortured her nervous system. Powerful fingers wrapped around her arms. The great being's hideous spectral face of death gazed at her with mournful but determined eyes. She could not move.

They hung suspended together in a shifting mosaic of sunlight and shadow, the air rapidly fading in her lungs. Her mind and spirit cried out for this to stop, for him to stop. Nothing responded to her silent pleas, not even the Elemental energies. A sense of unmitigated terror pulsed through her. She was dying.

*

The creature did not want this. His heart was filled with revulsion for his sadistic actions as Baseria grew weaker. If only there could be some other way. But he knew there wasn't. This must be.

*

Her vision dimmed as she felt water cascading into her lungs. The horrific yellow eyes ceased burning into her soul. She could feel her body closing down. Everything she truly was expanded beyond the darkness as her form in life grew limp and lifeless. Awed by her beauty the creature gazed reverently upon Baseria for a moment before he gently closed her eyes.

*

Somewhere between life and death, Victor's tortured mind sought to complete one final act. This was not one of redemption, but a final gift of love. His fingers pulled and tore at the stitching that held his arm, chained him to Ernest. The pain was liberating, for after knowing so much death, the sacrifice would give life to another. He was only faintly aware when it gave way, but he saw Ernest's body begin to rise up toward the light as he vanished into the impenetrable depths forever.

*

"Ernest."

Where was the voice coming from?

"Ernest."

He opened his eyes and looked up. There above him up on the shore was the silhouette of a woman, but the distortion from the water made it impossible for him to decipher her identity.

The shape grew closer as she knelt. She plunged her outstretched hand down into the water, the tips of her fingers reaching for him. Ernest began to strain upward trying to reach them, but they remained just beyond his grasp. He was very tired, but a calm, silent sense of reassurance from the woman above him kept his legs kicking, propelling him closer until their hands met and firmly clasped one another. A wonderful warmth consumed him as she pulled him up to the surface, and for an instant, he saw her face.

Ernest gasped for air as he crawled alone from the freezing water onto the ice encrusted rocks. Water ran from his lungs as he lay there coughing and shaking in shock. After a time, he tenuously heard voices approaching.

*

"Hold on, don't shoot, looks like another one of their prisoners," a voice said in English.

"Is he alive?"

"Barely, man's half frozen," the voice declared.

"This chain's stuck right good on something."

"Don't worry about it; we'll unlock him, then throw the whole lot in the water."

"Report" the voice of an older man ordered.

"Captain," one of the men answered in reply, "We've found another prisoner, sir."

"Well, get a blanket on him, Sparling," the captain demanded.

"Yes, sir. Sorry, sir. I'm just a little surprised to see you. I thought you'd be gone pursuing those two enemy ships."

"I tasked the Saville with that," the captain declared as he leaned down. "We'll join them soon enough, but I want to see for myself what these devils have been up to ... my God."

Robert Walton stared in disbelief. What was Ernest Frankenstein doing here?

**

They were coming. Why weren't his legs moving faster? If his lifestyle choices of liberally smoking and imbibing got him killed tonight, he'd be very unhappy. A new fear arose. What if he was on the wrong path?

Jack turned and glanced fearfully over his shoulder. At least with a human enemy he might be able to hide then get his bearings, not so with the foe that now pursued him.

Wish I'd been built for speed not looks, he thought panting as he ran.

The melancholy howls grew louder.

He assaulted the hill he came to, propelling himself downward faster by using the trunks of small trees for support. Jack landed hard at the bottom, but he was too frightened even to curse. His eyes flashed wildly about as they frantically searched the landscape. It had to be here.

"Where's the log? Where's the God …?"

He didn't waste breath upon spotting it, instead, pulling himself up and running to it as fast as possible. His deadly pursuers renewed their cries. Jack shimmied awkwardly across the log, trying not to worry if the rotting wood could hold him. At least he wouldn't be torn to shreds if he fell into the rift below.

Jumping down safely on the other side, he paused to look back on the other side. The wolves were coming down the hillside. Unwilling to risk learning if the gypsies had trained their canine killers how to cross logs,

Jack began to shove with all his might against the one he'd used. It gave very little as the wolves drew ever closer.

"Come on, come on, COME ON, COME ON!" Jack cried as he madly shifted positions, trying everything he could to make the heavy log move.

His leg muscles burned with fatigue, as did his face with strain, but he kept fighting against the steadfast log. Jack was unprepared when it finally, unexpectedly, gave way and almost tumbled into the crevice with it. Two wolves tried unsuccessfully to launch themselves across; the rest paced, barked, growled, and howled while they sought a means. Realizing he was momentarily protected, Jack lay on the ground and caught his breath turning over the host of problems he faced.

Even if he'd the time, Jack didn't have enough ammunition to handle all the wolves. More troubling, his path of flight had forced him very far from his rendezvous with Abrielle by now. Jack needed to keep moving, but the moment he did, his friends on the other side would undoubtedly continue to track him. If that happened, he might lead the wolves right to her and Tara.

"If only I still had that gunpowder," he lamented before an idea struck.

He reached into his pocket. They were still there. Jack grinned as he began to make piles of leaves and dry sticks. When he finished, Jack withdrew his matches and began to use them to set the piles alight. The modest fires began to smoke. He waited and added to the piles as needed. The smoke grew denser. The wolves retreated a measure.

Jack quietly withdrew directly back away from the breach. He'd have to stay out of their line of sight, but the smoke should, at least, mask his scent for a time. Jack just hoped it would be for long enough.

*

They could escape. Somehow deliverance was still possible. All Abrielle needed to do was make it across the crevice. Jack would be there, and they'd be safe. Then she could rest, comfort her poor niece, and tell Jack how grateful she was that they'd all survived.

Abrielle tore across the dark, uneven terrain as best she could. They were beyond the encampments, but she knew at least one wolf followed.

It was still at some distance. If she stopped to kill it, she'd use her sole round of ammunition. Abrielle's haste to flee Jal's tent forced her to abandon most of her resources. What would she do if more wolves came before she crossed to the other side?

Her chest was heaving, but she continued to mutter reassuringly to Tara.

"Not far, baby, not far, not far. We're gonna make it. We'll … hold on, hold on. Ssshhhh. It's okay Tara, It's …"

A low growl and yellow eyes appeared ahead of them. Abrielle did not hesitate. She immediately began to run in another direction. But there, too, she bore witness to the same sight. Again she tried to evade them only to discover more wolves. They were surrounding her.

She did not even attempt to control the shaking of her hand as she shifted Tara to retrieve the pistol. Turning endlessly around she took aim, but which did she shoot?

More eyes appeared, the pack closing in on them growing denser. They were so numerous that killing one would have no effect; the rest would fall upon her. For an instant, she thought of the image of Jal holding the gun to Tara's head when he kidnapped her.

"NO!"

Her mind screamed against the odium of such a horrific thought. But the alternative death stalking toward them was no less abhorrent. If only she'd spared Jal, they could have escaped in time. She had to do something. Abrielle raised the pistol and fired.

The shot rang out in the night as the flash momentarily illuminated their surroundings. Maybe the sound of the weapon being fired so close would make some of them scatter. The only sight Abrielle beheld was that of wolves all around them pressing ever closer.

Abrielle dropped to her knees and shielded Tara as best she could. Her niece would die in her arms. A final prayer filled Abrielle's trembling heart as the primal growls drew nearer. They were coming.

**

"Oh."

Tasaria's heart swelled with grief and anguish as she beheld the body of her niece. In her sorrows, she lovingly embraced the corpse.

*

"Agreed, Captain," the Moon Shadows' dark Lord stated as he closed down the spyglass he held. They'd shaken two in the ice, and the sole enemy ship still pursuing them was neither losing ground nor for the moment gaining.

"Keep the Enforcer between us and them at all times. Alert me only if the situation radically changes, Ayt."

"Yes, Master. What heading shall I set?"

The creature paused before answering.

"Southeast, but keep us north of the British Isles."

"You realized that with all the extra equipment you've installed, our drag in the water is greater."

"Of course."

"That ship carries more sail than us. If they gain a favorable wind, they will catch us. Why even take such a risk?" Ayt asked.

"See to it they don't," the nightmarish being harshly commanded.

"What about those we left behind?"

The creature narrowed his eyes.

"I am not insensitive to our losses, captain but we are running for our lives. Concern yourself with that fact alone."

The grim shadow descended from the bridge. He knew Ayt did not understand the situation anymore than he could comprehend the modification the creature had made to his vessel. They'd defeated enemies far greater than those who now followed, but at the moment, they were a secondary concern as were those of his subordinates. He could not risk damage to the ship in an attack. The moment was fading fast. Time was against him. Above all else, he must embrace his father's legacy to ensure his love's salvation. It was their destiny and would serve as his final triumph over Victor Frankenstein.

He halted his progression below decks only long enough to collect two Moon Shadow guards and present them with instructions.

*

Tasaria sat alone in the small cabin, a single candle burning in the wall lamp. All she could do was stare at the shrouded form that lay silently across from her. The door behind her opened. She did not move.

"Come Tasaria, you are overwrought by the grief we both share," her Master said.

"Am I?" she numbly countered.

Neither spoke for a moment.

"It has been many hours since you've rested. Come, these men will see to your needs."

She slowly turned and fixed herself to her Master's eyes.

"Tell me how she died."

The other's gaze did not waiver.

"I told you, Frankenstein led her to her death as well as his own."

"But how?" she passionately demanded. "Or did you not witness it?"

This time there was something, a subtle change, very brief, in those eyes she'd known for so long. Tasaria looked away in despair, the pain inside all but consumed her words.

"Don't do this," she said quietly. "Not to her, not to my niece."

He signaled the guards who entered and took Tasaria by either arm. She offered no resistance. The shadow towered over her.

"Father's new techniques will erase mistakes I've made in the past. She was more powerful, but you are not without the skills and strengths I will need. We have no choice now."

Tasaria shook her head, tears flowing freely from her eyes.

"I have done all you have ever asked of me. I ask of you but one thing now, leave her in peace. Please, Master, leave my niece to her natural fate."

He looked to Baseria's shrouded form before returning his attentions to Tasaria.

"The choices you've made fixed her fate long ago."

He addressed the guards.

"Take her to the lower deck so she can prepare."

Not a single utterance did Tasaria offer as she was led away. The creature sat and held his side where the ball from Baseria's shot had passed clean through. When all this was over, he would need time to heal. For now the best he could do was to clean and stitch the wound.

He leaned forward and pulled back the sheet. If the attack on the fortress hadn't come, there would have been time to make another choice. In time, he could have learned enough to honestly win her affections and fulfill all of his promises to his uncle. His actions toward Ernest left him deeply conflicted.

The creature brooded. Pias must be behind the attack. If so, then the whole of Europe might not be safe. Where should he make their new home? Or should he concern himself more with vengeance against his erstwhile companion? No, his first duty must be to her.

"Soon, my love," he whispered, "very soon."

*

As they journeyed farther below decks, Tasaria began to notice tubes and metallic cylinders of various sizes linked throughout the ship. When she entered the modest hold on the second level up from the bottom, near the stern, she was struck by two familiar sights: a series of large wheels that could be deployed out the sides of the ship and three silent hooded figures.

"You can't let this happen," she pleaded to one of the guards.

He hesitated.

"I'm sorry," he said remorsefully before shutting and locking the door.

**

It was not until the third day of her captivity that the same guard re-entered the storage hold. He set a plate of food before her. She did not acknowledge him, focusing instead on the patterns woven by nature into the wooden deck.

"Do you need anything else, Tasaria?" he asked, waiting patiently for a reply.

"Have you seen the Master?" she finally asked.

"No," he admitted. "He's shut himself completely away. He'll only speak to the captain, no one else, and even those conferences are conducted from behind a locked door."

"And the other ship, does it still follow us?"

"They've been steadily gaining over the past few days," he said tersely.

She stopped pretending to be disinterested and rose fully before speaking.

"The Master no longer cares for his people. He has betrayed us all, and I intend to take this ship."

Suddenly the guard was grabbed from behind, his mouth immediately covered as he was thrust against the outer bulkhead by one of the Old Ones.

"We are taking this ship with or without you. I will give you one chance. Make your choice."

She nodded to the Old One who relaxed its grip over the man's mouth.

"This is impossible. You can't control them, only the Master can," he said in disbelief.

"It is enough that I do. If you doubt it, cry out, it will kill you. Your name is Tyben, right? Tell me when did you last look upon your home, your true home?"

The frightened man hesitated before answering.

"Too long, over three years," he finally said. "My boy is twelve by now. I've missed seeing him grow up because I chose to serve here. There's a lot of angry folk on this ship, but many more who still feel our path with the Master is right."

She nodded.

"And how do you feel Tyben?" Tasaria probed.

The guard was silent a moment.

"I believed once. We all did. I can't blame them, but the Master's changed—abandoning all those people at the fortress, keeping our lives here on the ships in danger for his own selfish reasons, even his treatment of you, of us, is different."

He looked downward momentarily.

"How many would join us in a revolt?" Tasaria inquired.

"It's hard to say," Tyben admitted. "A lot of people talk, but often few are willing to back up their words with action. If we ask too many, word could still get back to the Master about us."

"It's a risk," she agreed. "What about Captain Ayt?"

Tyben shook his head.

"I don't know. He's pretty unhappy, but I don't think he's ready to support a full scale mutiny, and if you try starting one below decks, it will never succeed. They'll lock you down here and either flood you out or shoot you."

Tasaria considered the matter.

"Then we strike only when we're on the main deck. I believe our moment will present itself soon. Can you make some discreet inquires among the crew?"

"I can think of at least five who will join, maybe a sixth," Tyben said thoughtfully.

"Good," the Moon Shadow priestess praised. "Say nothing to anyone about the Old Ones. They too must be brought on deck when we are to act."

"That could be difficult. I heard the captain didn't want them here in the first place."

She smirked.

"I doubt he'll worry about keeping them locked up if that enemy ship catches us. He'll probably put them on the frontline of defense."

Tyben nodded.

"He's always treated them as disposable."

Tasaria put her hand on the Old One's shoulder.

"They're not."

*

The sudden knocking intruded upon his thoughts. The creature opened his eyes. It was the sixth day since his odious task's commencement. He did not dream, nor need he do so. Risen from the ashes of ruin, his creation was all but assembled. But he still required some measure of rest, of which he'd had little. Why was the captain so early for his report?

"What, Ayt?" he demanded of the summons at the door.

"My Lord, we've encountered a storm front that works to the enemy's advantage. They're full sail and gaining on us rapidly," the captain urgently reported.

The demon considered this news.

"Where are we?"

"Off the northern Irish coast, I suggest we attempt to find a safe harbor, wait out the storm, and avoid the enemy."

The creature ran a bloody hand over his face as he turned and considered the shrouded form on the table. Was she ready? There would be no second chance, not if his mate was to be constructed of the women he'd chosen: Sebbi, Vochallet, and Baseria. He could not preserve their flesh here as he could have at the fortress. Theirs was the physical, but it was Baseria's resurrection of spirit he sought from Tasaria. In failing to act now, could he lose her forever?

While he did have faith in some of Tasaria's powers, he was far from certain she alone could achieve the miracle he sought. Ideally, this was to have been something they tested with Baseria, but in acting rashly because of his own anger, fear, and jealousy the creature negated such considerations. It might already be too late. If so, then his modifications to Victor's methods would have to suffice. They had at least partially revived his father, recalling some of him back from oblivion. He'd learned much more since then from the unwilling Victor Frankenstein, knowledge he now applied.

The key for conquering the physical realms of life and death was energy, magnetism. The storm-whipped seas offered an abundance of kinetic energy. In tandem with the equipment installed onboard ship, he should be able to create a much greater charge than previously possible, the force of which could be harnessed and directed into the body by the diamonds in the shroud. The charge and chemical balance must be harmonious. There was a pattern, a rhythm, music to life's delicate gift.

He opened the door. The captain stepped back in terror and revulsion at the sickening sights and smells of the ghastly chamber.

"Turn us into the storm," the creature ordered.

"Sir," Ayt gasped in disbelief, "the currents here are too strong and the winds ..."

The cloaked figure paid him no mind.

"After we've entered it, bring the table and its contents from this room to the main deck when all is ready, Tasaria will join us there."

"Sir, that storm and these currents could destroy us, at least allow the Enforcer to seek shelter."

The Master seized Ayt, ready to throttle the life out of him. There was no time.

"Carry out my orders."

The command given, he released Ayt who scurried away to comply. He would wait no longer.

*

Lightning arched and raced across the black sky as wind heralded the waves' fury. The gypsy vessels plowed as best they could through the angry swelling seas. Billowing winds carried thick sheets of cold rain which battered the ships. Out there, somewhere, the enemy vessel still sought them, but the danger it represented paled greatly when compared to the ferocious power nature was displaying.

Tasaria and the rest of the crew found it hard to maintain their balance as the ship heaved and pitched among the dark, shifting waves and gale force winds. The equipment installed astern weighed them down further into the water, adding additional instability to the storm tossed ship as the devices drove the metallic cylinders.

They were forced to throw nearly all of their metal objects overboard lest the magnetism the creature was channeling through the cylinders be disrupted by magnctically attracted debris. Most of the crew, including the Old Ones, now tasked to perform the more dangerous ship duties in the storm, stood unevenly on the decks to bear witness to the creature's promises of immortality.

A copper table bearing a lone shrouded figure stood angled against the mast. A series of metal wires affixed to the table joined with others woven around the mast. The atmosphere crackled with building, pulsing energy.

"More sail, more sail!" the Moon Shadows' Master insisted as he released more of the cylinders' rapidly accruing energy into the conductors. Blue white currents coursed in vibrant patterns over the table and shroud, which both began to shake violently.

"Now!" he cried to Tasaria, the signal that she was to use the powers of the unseen world to summon her niece's spirit. Instead, she used the signal for her own purposes.

"NOW!" Tasaria shouted throwing her arms up as a visual signal to her followers.

Within a host of seconds, the decks erupted in chaos as civil strife was given both voice and action.

It was in this moment, as the Moon Shadow rebels rose, that lightning struck the ship's mast. The energy coursed down the metallic wiring igniting flames and sparks, which set alight the sails, mast, and parts of the deck. The charge the creature received in his desperate bid to save the shrouded form from the metallic table, knocked it over, and blasted him across the deck. The driving rains helped to mitigate the fires while winds spread the flames.

The form beneath the smoldering shroud struggled to rise from the deck, and as the veil fell away the new life expelled her first breath in a chilling scream of such raw, abject torment even the heavens wept and trembled.

Story concludes in
Frankenstein Book 3 of
The Resurrection Trinity

www.ingramcontent.com/pod-product-compliance
Lightning Source LLC
Chambersburg PA
CBHW060546310726
48982CB00009B/1390/J

* 9 7 8 0 9 8 5 0 9 8 2 4 7 *